hothouse flower

KRISTA & BECCA RITCHIE

ADDICTED SERIES
Recommended Reading Order

Addicted to You (Addicted #1)

Ricochet (Addicted #1.5)

Addicted for Now (Addicted #2)

Kiss the Sky (Spin-Off: Calloway Sisters #1)

Hothouse Flower (Calloway Sisters #2)

Thrive (Addicted #2.5)

Addicted After All (Addicted #3)

Fuel the Fire (Calloway Sisters #3)

Long Way Down (Calloway Sisters #4)

Some Kind of Perfect (Epilogue Novel)

A NOTE FROM THE AUTHORS

Hothouse Flower is a spin-off of the Addicted series. It follows Ryke and Daisy, secondary characters in the Addicted series, who meet in **Ricochet (Addicted #1.5)**. It is recommended, but not necessary, to read the Addicted books beforehand. However, it is necessary to read the first Addicted series spin-off book—**Kiss the Sky** —before reading **Hothouse Flower**.

A NOTE FROM THE AUTHORS: PART DEUX

To all of our kind-hearted, easily lovable fans:

From this point on, this book is yours. It's a fat one, containing more than just a romance. It wouldn't be fair to give you anything less than what our books are—a series about family, brothers and sisters, friends and real forces trying to break everything apart. Hothouse Flower started as just a romance, but these people wouldn't feel real to you or to us if you didn't know all of them. Every relationship. Every strain. Every struggle. And love. We wanted to give it all to you and not cheat you out of anything. So as you reach that last page, we hope you can understand why there's so much and why we refused to give you anything less.

So here it is. This is yours and all yours. Happy reading!

xoxo Krista & Becca

A NOTE FROM RYKE

My life is full of unconventionalities, abnormalities and awkward fucking situations.

If you're easily offended by crude language and inappropriate talks, you've taken a wrong fucking turn somewhere. You won't understand me if you can't handle me, and I'm not going to try to explain myself.

I'm raw.

I'm hard.

I'm the thing you shy away from.

So I'm warning you now. Back away.

Because once you enter my life, I won't ever let you leave.

‹ Prologue ›

Ryke Meadows

Every Monday was fucking identical to the last. No matter if I was ten or twelve. Fifteen or seventeen. A driver named Anderson came to my house in a suburb of Philly at noon. He dropped me off at a country club ten minutes later, and my father sat in that same fucking table in the back corner, by that same fucking window that overlooked two red and green tennis courts. He ordered the same fucking food (filet mignon with hundred-year-old scotch) and he asked the same fucking questions.

"How has school been treating you?"

"Fine," I said. I had a 4.0 GPA. I was only seventeen, and college recruiters were scouting me for track and field. I rock climbed with any spare time I had, and I juggled both sports. I built this plan in my head since high school. I'd go to college to run. I wouldn't touch a dime of his fucking money. I'd let my trust fund rot. I'd get as far away from my father and my mother as I possibly could. I'd finally find peace and forget about all the lies that clung to me.

My dad sipped his scotch. "Your mom isn't going to tell me how you are, and you won't open your goddamn mouth to say more than monosyllabic words. So what am I going to have to do? Call strangers to ask about you? Your teacher? They're going to think I'm a terrible fucking parent."

I glared at the table, not touching my chicken sandwich. I accepted the food when I was ten. I always ate the burgers when I was eleven. But when I was fifteen, I woke up, and I finally accepted that I was eating with a fucking monster. "I have nothing to say," I told him.

"Are you suddenly deaf now? How was your *week?* What'd you fucking do? It's not that hard of a question." He downed his scotch. "Ridiculous," he muttered and pointed at me, a finger extending off his glass. "You're supposed to be the intelligent son." Then he motioned to a waiter for another round.

My muscles flexed at the mention of Loren, unresolved hate flooding me and heating my whole body.

I had no control over this anger. It just consumed me like a fucking forest fire.

"Can we cut this short?" I asked. "I have fucking places to be."

The waiter arrived, filling my father's glass a quarter. He urged him to continue, and he poured more, three-quarters full. "He'll take one," my dad said.

Jonathan Hale was swimming in billions of dollars from Hale Co., a baby supply company. He paid the country club staff to stay quiet about the underage drinking. It was fucking normal by now.

My stomach clenched at the sight of the alcohol. I decided only four days ago to stop drinking for good. I knew every Monday I'd be tested by my father. And I wouldn't tell him that I quit. I didn't want to talk about it. I would just avoid the fucking drink. I'd ignore it.

The waiter poured me a glass and corked the crystal bottle.

He left us without another word.

"Drink," my dad insisted.

"I don't like scotch."

My father cocked his head. "Since when?"

"Since it became your favorite fucking drink."

He shook his head. "You and your brother love to rebel like little punks."

I glared. "I'm *nothing* like that prick."

"And how would you know?" he retorted easily. "You've never met him."

"I just fucking know." I gripped my knee that started to bounce. I wanted to get out of there. I couldn't stand talking about Loren. I always knew I had a half-brother. It wasn't fucking hard to deduce that the kid of Jonathan Hale would also be related to me. We shared a fucking father. But my dad and mom never said it outright until I was fifteen. After my mom bitched about that "bastard" kid, I asked my dad to elaborate. He finally gave me three facts that cleared up a picture I'd already started to construct.

One: Jonathan cheated on Sara, my mom, with some other woman when I was a few months old.

Two: The "other" woman got pregnant. Loren was born a year after me, and she left her son with Jonathan. Bolted. No longer in the picture.

Three: I lived with Sara. My half-brother lived with our dad. And the whole fucking world believed Sara's kid was Loren Hale. Not me. I was Meadows. I shared the last name with my mom's deadbeat family in New Jersey, all of which wanted nothing to do with her.

My mom was Sara Hale.

My dad was Jonathan Hale.

I was no one's son.

After the truth became painfully clear, my father *always* brought up Loren. He *always* asked the same fucking question, and I didn't want to hear it today.

He swished his glass. "What's made you into such a pussy?"

My nose flared. I couldn't believe I thought he was fucking cool when I was nine years old. He had acted like we were bonding, letting me drink his whiskey. Father and son. Like he loved me enough to let me break some fucking rules. But I wondered if it was all just some ploy to make me as miserable as him.

"I got into a car accident," I suddenly said.

He choked on his scotch and cleared his throat. "What?" He glowered. "Why am I just now hearing about this?"

I shrugged. "Ask Mom."

"That bitch—"

"*Hey*," I cut him off, fire in my eyes. I was fucking sick of hearing him degrade her. I was fucking tired of listening to my mom denigrate him. I just wanted them both to *stop*. They'd been divorced since I was a kid, not even a year old. When was the fighting supposed to end?

He rolled his eyes, but he looked serious again, more concerned. If there was a heart in Jonathan Hale's chest, it was fucking submerged beneath an ocean of booze. "What happened?"

"I drove into the neighbor's mailbox." I have no recollection of how I arrived home. I apparently ran four red lights. I fucking knocked over a fence. I basically passed out at the wheel, and I woke up when I crashed.

I wasn't driving home from a fucking party.

I had been drinking alone on the soccer fields of Loren's prep school. I fucking hated Dalton Academy. I was forced to go to Maybelwood Preparatory, an hour from where I lived because my mom didn't want me to see Loren's face every fucking day. And because no one could know that I was her son.

So Loren had gone to the closer school, where *I* should have been, while I was banished and cast out.

And I fucking hated him. I fucking *loathed* him to the core of my fucking body. My mom helped stir this sickening wrath. She constantly said, "Your brother is full of himself, swimming in *our* money. You

want to be surrounded by Jonathan Hale's brat, then you'll be headed
nowhere good."

I'd nod and think, *Yeah, that fucker.*

And then days would pass, and I'd begin to question everything.

Maybe I should meet him.

Maybe I should talk to him.

But he's a spoiled rich kid.

Like me.

Not like you.

He doesn't care about anything but himself.

Like me.

Not like you.

He's a drunk loser.

Like me.

Yesterday, I thought about going to my mom and saying something.
I thought about telling her to just get over this moronic feud, to stop
ranting about Jonathan Hale's infidelity and to quit being consumed by
the life of his bastard kid.

"Loren Hale got suspended for missing too much class, did you
hear that?" she'd ask me with a sick gleam in her eye. His failure was
Jonathan's failure. And to her, that equaled fucking success.

But I couldn't say anything. Who was I to tell a woman to forget
something like that? She had been cheated on. She deserved to be mad,
but I had to watch that hate eat at her for almost two decades. There
was no justice in her pain. There was just loneliness.

But deep in the pit of my fucking heart, I just wished she would let
go, so I could too.

So yeah. My father, he fucking ruined my mom. And maybe if she
was stronger, she could have moved on. Maybe if I was a better son, I
could have helped her.

I'd driven past Dalton, and I was ambushed with this hot rage.
Because nobody knew the *real* me at Maybelwood. They saw Ryke

fucking Meadows, an all-American track star, an honor student, a kid who got detention for cursing almost every other day.

Loren had both my parents on paper.

He had the last name.

He had the billion-dollar legacy.

I didn't even know how much they told him—whether he knew about me or not. I didn't fixate on that. I couldn't get over the fact that all this time, he stole them from me. I had *nothing* but the yelling and screaming of a complicated divorce. I was the *real* fucking child of Jonathan and Sara Hale.

So why the fuck did I have to pretend to be the bastard? Why was Loren given the life that I was meant to live?

On the field, I had *chugged* a bottle of whiskey. I was numb to the burn. I had broken the bottle over the goal post, hoping Loren was a soccer player, hoping it'd cut up his fucking feet, and every time he felt pain, it'd be my doing.

And then the next morning, I woke up after nearly killing myself and anyone in the wake of my swerving car, drinking too fucking much. I was cold inside. Just fucking dead. I didn't want to be like that. I made a promise to myself. My father wasn't going to destroy me, and neither was my half-brother. Or my mother. I was going to get my shit together.

I'd run.

I'd go to college.

And I'd find my peace.

Fuck. Them. All.

My dad relaxed. "A mailbox isn't a big deal. Your brother has done worse things." He shook his head at the mental images. And then his eyes flickered up to me, and I knew *the* question was about to come. "Do you want to meet him?"

I opened my mouth, but he cut me off.

"Before you say no, hear me out. He's had it much different than you—"

"I'm fucking over it." I didn't want to waste my energy on Loren anymore. I was done.

"It's not easy growing up with the Hale name. Our money comes from *baby* products. He endures a lot of teasing—"

"I don't *give* a shit," I sneered. We were both living a lie, but mine was worse. "I was never allowed to tell people who *you* were. Did he have to do that? Mom used to say that people would treat me differently if they knew my dad was a billion-dollar CEO, but really, you both were trying to fucking *hide* me." I leaned back in my chair and crossed my arms. For fuck's sake, she had to keep *Hale* as her surname, a stipulation in the divorce settlement, while I remained a Meadows.

"Not exactly," he said. "We were trying to cover the fact that Loren wasn't Sara's child. She was only pregnant once. We couldn't justify both of you without ruining my reputation."

That was why my mom had to keep her mouth shut about the cheating, to protect Jonathan. And every day she had to help this soulless prick, it fucking ate her up again. But she did it for the money. I didn't think any amount of cash was worth the fucking pain of these lies.

Everything was to save face.

"Why choose him?" I asked. "Why isn't Loren the one being hidden?" *You love him more.*

His face remained blank, all the hard edges not revealing anything to me. He wore a dapper suit that made him look as expensive as he was. "It's just how things worked out. It was easier for you to take your mother's maiden name. Loren only had one option. And that was me."

I ground my teeth. "You know, I just tell all my friends that my dad died. Sometimes, I even find clever ways to kill you off. *Oh yeah, my dad, he drowned on a fucking boat accident; perished in his golden fucking yacht while he was shitting on the toilet.*"

He became a ghost or demon I'd meet on Mondays. Nothing more.

He licked his lips and swished his scotch, not meeting my gaze. He almost laughed. He found that fucking funny. "Listen, Jonathan," he said.

"It's *Ryke*," I shot back. "How many fucking times do I have to tell you that?" I didn't want his name any more than I wanted his genes. I planned to use my middle name forever.

He rolled his eyes again and then sighed. "Loren isn't like you. He's not good at sports. I don't think he's ever aced a test in his life. He's wasting his potential by going to parties. If you'd meet him, you could help—"

"*No*," I forced. I put my forearms on the table and leaned close. "I don't want *anything* to do with your son. So stop fucking asking."

He took out his wallet and passed me a picture, one he'd shown me a couple times before. Loren was sitting on the stairs of our father's mansion, where he grew up. I always looked for similarities in our features and felt sickened by them.

We had the same eye color, only his were more amber than my brown. My face was harder cut, but our builds were more alike, lean not bulky. He wore a navy blue tie and a white button-down, the Dalton Academy uniform. He wasn't staring at the camera, but his jaw was so sharp, unlike anything I'd seen before. He looked like a fucking douchebag, like he'd much rather be popping open beers with his buddies than sitting there.

"He's your brother—"

I slid the picture back to him. "He's *no one* to me."

Jonathan downed the second glass of scotch, pocketing the photo. And he grumbled under his breath about my "bitch" of a mother. She never wanted me to meet Loren, just the same way that she refused to come into contact with him. As far as I knew, Loren thought Sara was his mom like the rest of the world. Or maybe someone finally told him the truth. That *he's* the fucking bastard.

I wouldn't know.

And frankly, I didn't fucking care.

What difference would it have made anyway?

❋⤙ 𝟾 ⤚❋

NINE YEARS LATER

< 1 >

Ryke Meadows

I run. Not away from anything. I have a fucking destination: the end of a long suburban street lined with four colonial houses and acres of dewy grass. It's as secluded as it can be. Six in the morning. The sky is barely light enough to see my feet pound the asphalt.

I fucking love early mornings.

I love watching the sun rise more than watching it set.

I keep running. My breathing steadies in a trained pattern. Thanks to a collegiate track scholarship, and thanks to climbing rocks—a sport that I sincerely fucking crave—I don't have to *think* about inhaling and exhaling. I just *do*. I just focus on the end of the street, and I go after it. I don't fucking slow down. I don't stop. I see what I have to do, and I fucking make it happen.

I hear my brother's shoes hit the cement behind me, his legs pumping as quickly as mine. He tries to keep up with my pace. He's not running towards shit. My brother—he's always running away. I listen to the heaviness of his soles, and I want to fucking grab his wrist and pull him ahead of me. I want him to be unburdened and light, to feel that runner's high.

But he's weighed down by too much to reach anything good. I don't slow to let him catch me. I want him to push himself as far as he can go. I know he can get here.

He just has to fucking try.

One minute later, we reach the end of the street that we were shooting for, next to an oak tree. Lo breathes heavily, not in exhaustion, more like anger. His nose flares, and his cheekbones cut brutally sharp. I remember meeting him for the very first time.

It was about three years ago.

And he looked at me with those same pissed off amber-colored eyes, and that same, *I fucking hate the world* expression. He was twenty-one back then. Our relationship balances somewhere between rocky and stable, but it was never meant to be perfect.

"You can't go easy on me just once?" Lo asks, pushing the longer strands of his light brown hair off his forehead. The sides are trimmed short.

"If I slowed down, we would have been *walking*."

Lo rolls his eyes and scowls. He's been in a bad place for a few months, and this run was supposed to release some of the tension. But it's not helping.

I see the tightness in his chest, the way he can still barely fucking breathe.

He squats and rubs his eyes.

"What do you need?" I ask him seriously.

"A fucking glass of whiskey. One ice cube. Think you can do that for me, big *bro?*"

I glare. I hate the way he calls me *bro*. It's with fucking scorn. I can count on my hand the amount of times he's called me "brother" with affection or admiration. But he usually acts like I don't deserve the title yet.

Maybe I don't.

I knew about Loren Hale for practically all my life, and I didn't even say *hi*. I think back often to when I was fifteen, sixteen, seventeen and my father asked every fucking week: "Do you want to meet your brother?"

I rejected the offer every single time.

When I was in college, I came to terms with the fact that I would never know him. I thought I was at peace. I stopped hating Loren Hale for just existing. I stopped listening to my mother condemn a kid that had no say in being born. I slowly stopped talking to my father, losing contact because I didn't need him.

The trust fund, I use. I figure it's payment for all the lies I had to keep for that fucking asshole.

One day. That's all it took to change my idealistic, head-in-the-fucking-sand, life. Outside at a college Halloween party, a fight started. I watched four guys on the track team—the one *I* was the captain of at Penn—go up against a lean-built guy. I recognized him from all those photos my father showed me.

He wasn't how I'd imagined. He wasn't surrounded by frat guys, crushing beers over their heads.

He was alone.

His girlfriend came into the fight later, to defend him, but it was too late. She missed the part where my teammate accused him of drinking expensive booze in a locked cabinet. She missed the part where Lo egged him on, just so the guy would swing.

He hit my brother. I stood and watched Lo get decked in the face.

It was in that fucking moment that I realized how wrong I had been. I didn't see a prick with a hundred friends and cash up to his chin. Not a jock, not an athlete like me. I saw a guy *wanting* to be punched, asking to feel that pain. I saw someone so fucking hurt and broken and sick.

Four against one.

All that time, I wanted to live the life he had. I hated playing the bastard outcast when I was really the legitimate son. But if our roles were reversed, if I had lived with my alcoholic father, I would have been there.

That would have been me: tormented, drunk, weak and alone.

My father was trying to tell me that Lo wasn't the popular kid I'd dreamed up. He was just as much of an outsider as I was. The difference: I had the strength to defend myself. I wasn't beaten down by our father like Lo had been. I didn't even contemplate the fucking horror of living with Jonathan twenty-four-seven, hearing the *why are you such a pussy?* comment every day. I had blinders on. I could only see what was wrong with *me*. I couldn't fathom Loren getting a shitty bargain too.

That night at the Halloween party, I left the false peace I'd built for myself. It wasn't a gut reaction. I stood there and watched Lo get beat on before I made a decision to intervene. And once I fucking made it, I never turned back.

"You want a glass of whiskey?" I give him a look. "Why don't I just push you in front of a fucking freight train? It's about the same."

He stands up and lets out an agitated laugh. "Do you even know what this feels like?" He extends his arms, his eyes bloodshot. "I *feel* like I'm going out of my goddamn mind, Ryke. Tell me what I should do? Huh? Nothing takes this pain away, not running, not fucking the girl I love, not *anything*."

I haven't been where he is, not to this extent.

"You relapsed a few times," I say. "But you can get back to where you were."

He shakes his head.

"So what?" I narrow my eyes. "You're going to drink a beer? You're going to chug a bottle of whiskey? Then what? You'll ruin your relationship with Lily. You'll feel like *shit* in the morning. You'll wish you were fucking dead—"

"What do you think I'm wishing now?!" he shouts, his face reddens in pain. And my lungs constrict. "I hate myself for breaking my sobriety. I *hate* that I'm at this place in my life again."

"You were under a lot of scrutiny," I back-peddle, realizing he doesn't need me to be a hardass, something I revert to on instinct. I push people too much sometimes.

"You're under the same scrutiny, and I didn't see you breaking your sobriety."

"It's different." I haven't had a drink in nine years. "The media was saying some pretty awful shit, Lo. You coped the first way you knew how. No one blames you. We just want to fucking help you." We're all public spectacles, under constant gaze of cameras, because of the Calloway girls, the daughters of a soda mogul.

By proximity to the Calloways, we've been roped into the spotlight. It's not fucking fun. I wear a baseball cap just to try to disguise myself, but thankfully cameramen have better things to do than film us this early in the morning.

But they'll be out trying to get a picture of us at noon.

"You don't believe them, do you?" Lo suddenly asks, his voice still edged.

"Who?" I ask.

"The news, all those reporters…you don't think our dad actually did those things to me?"

I try to hold back a cringe. Someone told the press that Jonathan physically abuses Lo. The rumors just kept escalating after that. I don't know if our dad could hit him…or molest him. I don't want to believe it, but there's a fucking sliver of doubt that says *maybe. Maybe it could have happened.*

"It's not fucking true!" Lo shouts at me.

"Okay, okay." I raise my hands to get him to calm down.

He's been like this since the accusations, pissed and angry and looking for a way to fix things. Booze was his solution unfortunately.

Our father filed a defamation lawsuit, but no matter the outcome of the court case, it won't change the way people look at both of them. Vilifying our father, pitying Loren. There's no going back.

"You just have to move fucking forward," I tell him. "Don't worry about what people think."

Loren inhales deeply and stares at the sky like he wants to murder a flock of birds. "You say shit, Ryke, like it's the easiest thing in the world. Do you know how annoying that is?" He looks back down at me, his features all sharp, like a blade.

"I'll keep saying it then, just to irritate the fuck out of you." *What else are big brothers for?*

He sighs heavily.

I rub the back of his head playfully and then guide him towards his house. I drop my hand off his shoulder, and he stops in the middle of the road, his brows scrunching.

"About your trip to California…" He trails off. "I know I haven't asked about it in months. I've been too self-absorbed—"

"Don't worry about it." I motion with my head to the white colonial house. "Let's go make some breakfast for the girls."

"Wait," he says, holding out his hand. "I have to say this."

But I don't want to hear it. I've made up my mind already. I'm not going to California. Not when he's in a bad place with his recovery. I'm his sponsor. I have to be here.

"I need you to go," he says. I open my mouth and he cuts me off. "I can already hear your stupid fucking rebuttal. And I'm telling you to *go.* Climb your mountains. Do whatever you need to do. You've had this planned for a long time, and I'm not going to ruin it for you."

"I can always reschedule. Those mountains aren't fucking moving, Lo." I've wanted to free-solo climb three rock formations, back-to-back, in Yosemite since I turned eighteen. I've been working up to the challenge for years. I can wait a little longer.

"I will feel like *shit* if you don't go," he says. "And I'll drink. I can promise you that."

I glare.

"I don't need you," he says with malice. "I don't fucking need *you* to hold my hand. I need you to be goddamn selfish like me for once in your life so I don't feel like utter shit compared to you, alright?"

I internally cringe. I was selfish for so many fucking years. I didn't give a fuck about him. I don't want to be that guy again.

But I hear him begging me. I hear *please fucking go. I'm losing my mind.*

"Okay," I say on instinct. "I'll go."

His shoulders instantly relax, and he lets out another deep breath. He nods to himself. I wonder how long he's been carrying that weight on his chest.

I can't explain why I love him so much. Maybe because he's the only person who understands what it's like to be manipulated by Jonathan for his gain. Or maybe because I know deep down there's a soul that needs love more than anyone else, and I can't help but reciprocate to the fullest degree.

I put my arm around his shoulder again and say, "Maybe one day you'll be able to outrun me."

He lets out a dry, bitter laugh. "Maybe if I break both your legs."

I grin. "Would you even be fucking fast enough to do that?"

"Give me a lacrosse stick and we'll see."

"Not fucking happening, little brother."

I don't say it with scorn.

I never do. And I never will.

‹ 2 ›

Daisy Calloway

I have this theory.

Friends aren't forever. They're not even *for a while*. They come into your life and they leave when something or someone changes. Nothing grounds them to you. Not blood or loyalty. They're just…fleeting.

I'm usually not this cynical, but I popped up Facebook this morning, my laptop resting on my bent legs. I should have deleted my account a couple years ago, around the same time my family was thrust into the public eye—when my older sister's sex addiction went public.

But alas, I had a different theory about friends back then.

Butterflies, rainbows, hearts holding hands—it was literally a PBS special in my brain whenever I thought about my friendships.

And now Cleo Marks posted this on her wall:

During Daisy Calloway's sweet sixteen party, she couldn't shut up about sex. It's all she cared about. You know she's a closeted sex addict like her sister. All the Calloway girls are skanks.

Those are the beautiful words of my former best friend. And it doesn't even matter that she brought up an incident from two and a half years ago. Resurfacing it is enough to elicit *457* comments, mostly all in agreement.

Four months have passed since I graduated prep school and I'm still being haunted by my former friends. Like the Ghosts of Hell's Past.

A hand reaches out and smacks my computer closed. "Stop wasting your fucking emotions on them."

A tall six-foot-three guy is in my bed. Beside me. In only a pair of drawstring pants. And I'm sitting against the headboard, wearing white cotton shorts and a cropped red and blue top that says: *Wild America.*

On the outside, we probably look like a couple, gently rising from the morning sunlight that peeks through my curtains.

On the inside, there's no touching. No kissing. Nothing beyond friendship status.

Reality is a whole lot more complicated.

"When did you wake up?" I wonder, avoiding any discussions that center on my old friends.

He doesn't sit yet. He stays beneath my green comforter and sheet, running his hands through his disheveled dark brown hair. Attractive doesn't even begin to describe his "I-don't-give-a-shit-about-it" hair. It never looks neater during the day, but he knows that.

"The better fucking question is when did you go to sleep?" He stares at me with narrowed, accusatory eyes.

Never. But he knows this too. "Good news, I finished packing in the wee hours of the night."

He rises and nears me a little. I tense at his closeness, reminded that he's a man, his body easily dwarfing mine. It's not a bad tense. More like the kind of tense that stops my breath for a second. That makes my head float and my heart do a weird little dance. I like it.

The danger of it all.

"Bad news, I don't give a fuck about your packing," he says roughly. "I just give a fuck about you." He reaches across my chest to grab a pill bottle off my nightstand. His muscles constrict as he accidentally brushes against my boobs. Neither of us announces the brief touch, but the tension has turned a corner, down onto Don't Go There Lane.

To relieve this new tension, I stand up on the bed and kick a decorative pillow off. "You *do* care about my packing. You thought I'd never get it done."

"Because you're fucking ADD and a lot of other things." He watches me from below, his eyes traveling up the length of my long bare legs. "Sit down for a second, Calloway." Instead of acting like he's into me and all that, he just reads the back of the pill bottle, his brows tightening in concern.

You know that theory I have about friends not being forever...or even for a while?

Well, every theory has an exception.

Ryke is mine.

As I watched each friend call me a sex-addict-in-training and a media whore, stabbing me routinely in the heart, Ryke was the one who pulled out the blades. He even shielded me from them. He's like my wolf—dangerous, alluring and protective—but I can never get close enough or else he'll bite me.

He's my last real friend. But I know that's not entirely true. He's the only real one I've ever had.

"What other things am I?" I ask with a smile, standing by his ankles at the foot of the bed.

"Hyperactive, fearless, crazy, and probably the happiest unhappy girl I've ever met."

I bounce a little, about to jostle the mattress, but he side-swipes my calves quickly. I fall on my back, smiling big as I turn on my side towards him. It fades the moment he tosses the pill bottle at my face. It hits me square in the forehead and thuds to the comforter.

He's also an asshole.

"You lowered your dosage," he says.

"The doctor did it. He was worried how fast I was going through Ambien."

"Did you tell him that you can't fucking sleep without it?"

"No," I admit. "I was too busy explaining how I don't want to be addicted to anything like my sister or your brother. And he said it was a good idea to start lowering the dosage." I tuck a strand of my dyed blonde hair behind my ear. It's waist-length and has a habit of being everywhere all the time. Like right now. I am pretty much swaddled in it.

I empathize greatly with Rapunzel. She had it rough.

Ryke glares. "Not sleeping isn't the fucking solution, Daisy."

"What's a better one?" I ask seriously. I am tired, and I realize today, like most days, will be fueled by energy drinks and endorphin boosts in the form of diet pills. Yippee.

He lets out a deep breath. "I don't know. Right now, I'm really disturbed by the fact that I knew you didn't sleep because you didn't scream or kick me. If you don't wake me in the middle of the night, it means you were up the whole fucking time." He shakes his head as he continues to think. "When you're in Paris, are you sharing a room with another model?

"No," I say. "No, I wouldn't." Because she'd hear me scream, and I'd have to explain why I have these intense nightmares. And no one knows but Ryke. Not my sisters: Lily and Rose. Not Rose's husband. Not Lily's fiancé (who happens to be Ryke's brother).

Just him. It's a secret he's kept for half a year. When I graduated from prep school about four months ago, I moved out of my parent's house and into a Philly apartment. Things got a little worse, so he spends the night.

At first he just crashed on the couch.

But I couldn't sleep, and his proximity helped keep my anxiety at bay.

Anxiety—such a weird word. I've never been anxious about anything before. Not really. Not until the media surrounded my family.

For the first time in my life, I'm truly scared.

And it's not even of sharks or alligators or heights and daredevil stunts.

I am scared of people. Of things that people can do to me. Of things they've done.

Ryke knows my fears pretty well because I never lie to him. Two years ago, when I was sixteen, he held out my motorcycle helmet, about to teach me how to ride a Ducati. He said, "For us to have any kind of friendship, you can't pretend with me. I've been involved in lies most of my fucking life, and it's not something I'm particularly fond of. So you can cut the *I don't know what you're talking about, I'm little and naïve* bullshit. I don't play that game. I never will."

It took me a full minute to process the gravity of his words. But I understood them. In order to be his friend, I couldn't save face. I had to be me. It wasn't a lot to ask. But back then, I'm not even sure I knew who I was. "Okay," I accepted. So far, I've kept my word. No lies. And in turn, I've opened up more to Ryke than I have to anyone else. Plus, he's been the only one here long enough to listen.

"Are you worried about going to Paris alone?" he asks me. "You haven't slept by yourself in four months."

"I can't keep you forever, can I? Like a miniature Ryke Meadows carry-on or pocket-sized version?" I try hard not to smile at this.

"I'm not a fucking teddy bear."

I gasp. "Really? I thought you were."

He chucks a pillow at my face.

I smile so hard.

He loves throwing things.

"If you're scared, maybe you shouldn't go to Fashion Week without your mom."

"No," I say. "I need to do this on my own." I've wanted this for so long—before the shit storm blew in from the press and paparazzi. I dreamed about sight-seeing, and my mother won't let me do that if she's attached to my side. She'll only steer me towards fashion designers, schmoozing everyone for the chance to be the face of their clothing line.

"Well, you have my number," he says. "Don't be afraid to fucking call me, okay?"

I nod, and he climbs off my bed and goes to my dresser, searching through the bottom drawer for some of his clothes that he keeps here. I trace his features quickly. He's unshaven, so he looks a little older than twenty-five, his actual age. And his brows do this thing where they furrow hard, like he's in a bad mood. But really, he's just brooding.

It's his normal expression, one that's insanely attractive in this possessive—*I will protect you even if it fucking kills me*—quality that I didn't think I would like until I met him.

And it drew me in like this magnetic pull or a moth to a flame. All those cheesy things people say about attraction.

But below the physical connection (which I'm sure isn't too hard for any girl to possess with a guy like Ryke Meadows) there's something more strong and pure. A friendship built from three years of non-fucking. Of talking and laughing and yes, maybe a little bit of flirting.

And below that. There is only need.

I didn't realize it was there—that *need*—until the nightmares of my dreams became the nightmares of my life. And he's the kind of guy who wants to slay all those monsters for me. Too bad he can't get to the ones in my head.

Even if he tries.

As he grabs a clean shirt and jeans, he straightens up and meets my gaze. I shouldn't stare anymore, but I end up eyeing his muscles, the ones that are so supremely cut. Most people would be able to tell that he's an athlete by looking—and not some muscular bodybuilder type. He's light enough that he can ascend a mountain quickly, but strong enough that he can carry his weight on a single finger.

A black tattoo with reds, oranges and yellows engulfs his right shoulder, right chest and ribs. It's an intricate design of a phoenix bound at the ankles, the inked chain extending along his side. A gray anchor is on his waist, a portion disappearing beneath his drawstring pants.

He looks kinda like someone you'd dream about waking up next to but never really think you would.

Despite this darkness that often swirls in his eyes, there's a hardness along his jaw that's dangerous, unapproachable, something that instantly hypnotizes me.

I can't look away.

Even though I should.

His eyes narrow with each ticking second. "Don't look at me like that, Daisy."

"I'm not looking at you like anything."

"I can tell when someone's attracted to me," he says without missing a beat.

"How?" I want that power that he has. I want to know if he finds me desirable. But maybe he never will.

His gaze falls to my shirt that reveals a little bit of my stomach. He inhales deeply, and something switches in his eyes, a look that says *you're fucking beautiful. I want to touch you.* He's never stared at me like that before—and if he has, he's kept it from me.

I wish it didn't affect me, but I can feel the back of my neck grow hot. I try to keep my composure, not wanting to be another silly girl that crumbles in his wake. He just barely licks his bottom lip as his gaze rakes me over.

And then his eyes return to mine again, and they're hard once more. "That's the look you were giving me, sweetheart."

Oh. *He called me sweetheart.* I linger on that for a second, not hearing anything else really.

"Daisy?" He glares.

I smile. "You called me sweetheart."

He rolls his eyes and repeats, "That's the *look* you were giving me."

"Oops," I say with a noncommittal shrug. I was just *staring*. I wasn't planning on jumping his bones. I wasn't even fantasizing about his cock inside of me. Chaste. My thoughts were so chaste. Maybe not now, but they *were*.

"Fucking understatement."

I stand up on the bed again so I have the height advantage. "I can freak out if you want me to." I touch my chest theatrically. "Oh Ryke, I fucked up big time. Kill me *now*." I hold out my hand towards him and bounce on the mattress again. "Apothecary, the poison."

His lips twitch into an almost-smile. And almost-smiles from Ryke are practically grins. I'll take 'em. "Cute," he says. "Just remember—"

"We're friends," I finish. "Platonic, non-fucking friends. I remember. And I agree, in case *you* forgot."

"I didn't forget." He tilts his head towards my bathroom door. "I'm going to take a fucking shower and then head out. I'll see you tonight at your sisters' place. They're still throwing that going away party for you?"

"Yep." In four days, I'll be modeling at Paris Fashion Week. One week will be for work. Three weeks in France will be for me. I nearly beam at the thought. I've never been allowed to tour France, and as a model, I go to all of these beautiful countries and cities, but I rarely ever see them. It's the first time my mom isn't chaperoning me. I know Rose convinced her to give me some space. For that, I hugged my older sister until she had to pry me off.

I plop down on the bed and hang my legs off the edge, closer to Ryke than before.

He glances at my computer on my pillow. "Have you talked to Rose about Cleo?"

I frown. "How do you know Cleo was the one on Facebook?"

"I could see the fucking screen."

I shake my head. "I'm afraid if I tell Rose, she'll confront Cleo and make this a bigger deal than it has to be."

"It is a big fucking deal. This goes beyond a Facebook comment, and you know it."

My throat closes up for a second.

Ryke glares, the silence sinking to my stomach. He waits for me to unleash more off my chest, and when he sees that I can't produce words, he ends the conversation for me. "Just stay off social media."

Before he takes a step towards the bathroom, my doorknob jiggles, trying to turn. "Daisy," a prickly, feminine voice calls through the wood.

It's unmistakable.

It's routine.

And it's my mother.

The only question left: Where should I hide Ryke Meadows today?

< 3 >

Daisy Calloway

My mom knocks loudly. "Why do you always have to lock your door?" *Because I know you have a key to my apartment and like to stop by unannounced.*

Ryke stiffens and glares at the ceiling before he points to the bathroom. *I'll be in here,* he mouths.

What? I mouth back and gape in mock confusion.

He flips me off and then messes my hair with his hand. It's an innocent, playful gesture. But with my mother on one side of the door saying, "You should be awake by now. Maybe this apartment wasn't such a good idea." He catches himself and our bodies sort of…tense in unison.

My arm accidentally makes contact with his abs like his did earlier with my boobs. But he's not wearing a shirt like me. So his warm skin heats my cheeks, and I feel his muscles constrict. I look up and he stares down. One of us has to step back first, but we both stay rooted.

He ends up putting on the shirt that's in his hand, but he stands so close to me while he dresses. I watch his muscles stretch as he fits his head through the collar and arms through the holes. When the cotton falls to his waist, hiding his abs, he meets my gaze once more, as though testing to see whether that helped eliminate any unburied tension.

Nope.

In fact, I only think it heightened the pull that says to *connect* with his body and elevated the strain that says *don't draw away.*

He fixes my hair that he just messed, combing the strands with his fingers so it doesn't look like I had sex or something.

"Daisy, are you in there?!" my mom shouts, worry lacing her voice.

Go, I mouth to Ryke.

He tucks a piece of hair behind my ear and then takes a moment to unlock the bathroom door. He slips inside and gently closes it behind him.

"Sorry!" I call to my mom. I rush to unlock my bedroom door. "I told you, I just like my privacy."

I hear her snort. "From who? You live alone." She pauses. "Are you sure you don't want to come back to the family house in Villanova? You'll have more company." She's lonely without me. That's what I've deduced from her impromptu visits at any hour during the morning, day and night. I'm her youngest child of four daughters, the last to fly the coop.

So far, Ryke and I have been pretty lucky with her barging in like this. I've always been too afraid to leave the door unlocked, so she's never entered the bedroom before Ryke could escape. And I don't have the heart to tell her to stop coming around. It'd be like saying, *hey, Mom, I'm eighteen—so I don't care about you or your opinions anymore. Thanks.* That's shit, right? I already moved out pretty quickly as it is. And I love her enough that I want her to be a part of my life. I just don't want her to be so…consuming.

When I finally open the door, she beelines inside, wearing a navy blue dress and a strand of pearls around her neck. She's a thin woman with a bun perfectly rounded on the back of her head. She has the same brunette hair as my sisters—and me, if my modeling agency allowed me to dye my hair back to my natural color, that is.

Her eyes ping around my messy room. Tank tops, jean shorts and shirts splay over my chair, my desk, some even on the end of my bed. I have a habit of tossing things and forgetting about them. Even when Ryke is around, I don't clean up much. His apartment looks worse than mine, which would just give my mom another reason to hate him.

He's too messy for you, Daisy, she'd tell me. Add that to: *He has no job. He's living off his trust fund. All he does is climb mountains and ride his motorcycle. He looks mad all the time. He's related to that witch Sara Hale. He doesn't even talk to his father.* (My mom is Team Jonathan Hale in the Hale feud, mostly because he's my father's bff.) *Ryke's related to Sara bitchy Hale.* (That's her main selling point.) *Oh and he's too old for you.*

The "too old" bit will come later because even though Ryke is seven years older than me, it's not an end-all for her. She's actually tried to pair me with a thirty-year-old before. He was loaded from holding the copyrights to some popular song. A month after I turned eighteen, I almost went on a date with him, per my mother's arrangement. My father was the one who put his foot down.

He cares about age difference.

"I called Hilda to come here last week to clean," she says with an upturned nose. "Did she not make it?"

"I turned her away," I announce. "I'm trying to be more independent." And that means *not* hiring a cleaning lady to fold my clothes. "Lily and Loren didn't have Hilda stopping by their apartment." Now they both live in Princeton, New Jersey with Rose and her husband. Not too far away to visit.

My mom scoffs. "They could clean up after themselves." *True.* Her gaze drops to my stomach, and she pinches my waist. "You're not gaining weight before Fashion Week, are you?" she criticizes.

Have I?

Before I look, she appraises me and says, "Never mind. You should be okay." She fixes my hair that must still be tangled, running her fingers through it like it's precious gold. "Are you sure you don't want me in Paris with you? I can keep you company while you're getting your makeup done."

"I just want to see what it's like on my own," I say, trying not to hurt her feelings.

She gives me a weak smile, pretending to be happy for me. "I love you," she tells me, and then she kisses my cheek. "Let's go shopping tomorrow. Noon. I'll have Nola pick you up."

"Okay."

And just when I think all is clear, as she travels back towards the door, the shower turns on.

He knows she hasn't left yet.

My mom frowns, and her neck elongates like a prairie dog. She zeroes in on the bathroom door. "Did someone spend the night with you?"

I'm not embarrassed or mad. I almost want to laugh at the situation. God, what kind of life do I live? "It's Lily," I lie. "Do you want to talk to her?"

I know she'll say no. Lily's sex addiction is what put my father's soda company, Fizzle, in a state of distress. The negative press affected our family in so many different ways, and most of them, my mom disapproved of. I don't hate Lily for it, not after seeing how guilty and ashamed she was. But my mom can't really see past the negative. She hasn't forgiven my sister yet.

"I won't bother her," she says. "Keep your phone on. And don't lock your door anymore." She always tells me that before she leaves. After she heads out of my bedroom, I listen for the shut of my apartment door. When it comes, I enter the bathroom.

Steam coats the mirrors and fogs the air. I can't see beyond my daisy-floral shower curtain that sticks out from the tub. I hear the splash of the water on the porcelain and spot his drawstring pants on my shaggy green rug. He's naked in there. *Well, no duh, Daisy.*

"My mom almost caught you," I tell him.

"Good," he says. "Then she can call me a 'disrespectful degenerate' to my face." Yeah, she said that the last time she was here. Ryke was hiding in the bathroom then too, and he heard every insult.

"Hey, I stuck up for you then and before that, and before that."

"No offense," he says, "but your mom really doesn't fucking care about your opinions on anything."

I can't really take offense to his words. I know it's true. Only two times have I ever confronted my mother with the truth. That I'd rather be doing something—anything—other than modeling. And she told me that I was being childish and ungrateful, so I shut up on the spot. If I bailed on a photo shoot at the last minute, her face would morph with an expression like *that's my daughter? That rude little snob?*

Disappointing my mother is like stabbing her in the womb—the very place I used to be. There's a metaphor in there, I think.

Ryke suddenly shuts off the shower and yanks the yellow towel from a hook. I've been around too many half-dressed, nearly-naked male models to be that alarmed. But it's different when you know the person. It's different when you have a crush on a guy beyond just his body, when you like *all* of him.

And I like all of Ryke Meadows.

The shower curtain whips to the side, and Ryke steps out with the towel tied low around his waist, beads of water still dripping down his toned chest and abs. I'm about to leave, to give him privacy, but he says, "Come here."

He's by the sink. And I watch as he opens his toothpaste and squirts a line on his toothbrush and then a line on mine. He holds out my green Oral B. I take it gratefully, and we both brush our teeth at the same time, pretending not to look at each other through the mirror, even when we do.

It's like we're a couple.

But we're not. And we never can be.

Some things are too complicated to ever come to pass. I know this is one of those things.

< 4 >

Ryke Meadows

I'm so fucking sick of taking cold showers, which is why I said *fuck that* yesterday. I need to start going to my apartment where I have the freedom to jerk off.

Every morning is about the same. Wake up in Daisy's bed. Try to suppress a horrible fucking boner. Take a shower. Run with my brother. Take another shower. Try my absolute fucking best to stroke my cock without thinking of her long legs and that gorgeous fucking smile.

Usually I succeed. Sometimes I don't.

I'm only fucking human.

I enter a gated street and slow my Ducati down as I pass each fucking mammoth colonial house. Four sedans trail my ass. They've been following me since I left my apartment in Philly. Two cross the double yellow lines to ride beside me, their windows rolled down, cameras snapping and flashing.

I should be used to this shit by now, but I'm not. I don't think I can ever be, not after I watched a fearless girl go from being completely fucking fine to scared of the dark to traumatized. It's not just the cameras and invasive media. It's everything that comes with it—her fucked up old prep school friends being one of those.

I flip off an entire sedan. At least my helmet is tinted and they can't capture a picture of my face. I speed up and weave in front of them. The four cars attempt to block me in, wedging me between their vehicles. I rev the throttle, switch gears, and fucking take off.

I lose sight of them as I approach a gated house, hedges concealing most of it. I punch in the code, and the iron grinds open.

Daisy probably had a harder fucking time getting to her sisters' place than me. I should have left with her. She lives two floors below me in the same apartment complex. I could have distracted the paparazzi while she rode off in another direction, but I didn't. I left late because I was researching about Ambien, cognitive fucking therapy, other sleeping medication—anything to solve Daisy's problem.

And I'm still at a loss of how to help her sleep without medication.

I park my Ducati on its kickstand and look up at the white house with black shutters, a wraparound porch, rocking chairs, a flag pole on a newly mowed lawn. It's cute—all of them living together. My brother, his girlfriend, Rose and her husband. I've shared a house with them before, and it's not something I'd repeat. For however much I love my brother, I fucking need space from him sometimes. He likes to test my tolerance. I have a ton, but I worry that if I lived with him for a long time, he'd break me down and I'd rip him apart.

I never want to hit Lo.

It's a line that I fear crossing on a weekly basis.

I open the front door with my key. A yellow banner hangs low and crooked over the archway that connects the living room to the kitchen. It reads:

BON VOYAGE, DAISY

The messy scrawl looks like Lily's handwriting. I have to duck underneath it to enter the kitchen.

My brother stands by the oven, cracking eggs into a large bowl. Connor watches him, cupping a glass of water. Normally he'd have red wine, but since Lo relapsed, he won't drink alcohol in front of him.

"Hey, Betty Crocker," I say, setting my helmet on the breakfast table. "Where's your apron?"

Lo flashes a dry smile. "Wherever your watch is." His eyes flicker back to the eggs. "You're an hour late."

"Yeah, I know," I say. "Everyone left me nasty fucking text messages."

I highly doubt you have the capability to read a clock, but you're verging on forty-six minutes late. And here, I was going to reward you with a treat. — Connor

If you disappoint my little sister, I will personally snip off your balls and feed them to Connor's cat. — Rose

Can you be here on time? Please?? — Lily

The girls are getting pissed. And I'm not too happy with you either. — Lo

"My text was the best, wasn't it?" Connor asks as he smiles into his sip of water.

I restrain the urge to roll my fucking eyes. "Your wife's was better."

"Impossible."

"She said she was going to feed my balls to Sadie." I come up beside Lo and inspect the bacon frying in a pan and a tray of biscuits.

"She's overused that threat," Connor tells us.

I peek underneath a towel, a spinach quiche steaming. "I may not own a fucking watch," I say, "but I do know it's nighttime and I'm pretty sure none of us are nursing a fucking hangover. So what's with the..." I tilt a bowl towards me. "Grits?"

"Daisy wanted breakfast for dinner," Lo explains. "So we're cooking."

I look around the kitchen, the living room just as quiet. "Yeah? Where are the fucking girls anyway?"

"Daisy's in the garage. Rose and Lily are in the bathroom," Connor says casually.

"Why the fuck are they in the bathroom together?"

Lo shakes his head at me. "I tried to ask and Rose rebutted with *female menstruation.* And then she slammed the door in my face."

Connor says, "I was smart enough not to question it." He leans against the cupboards, wearing black slacks and a white button-down. He looks like how much he's worth—over a billion fucking dollars from inheriting his mother's Fortune 500 Company.

"You too much of a princess to help Lo?" I ask, stealing a slice of apple from a fruit tray.

"I offered to break the eggs, but Lo said I should beat them into submission," Connor tells me.

Now I do roll my eyes.

"Might as well put your best skill to use," Lo says, passing the bowl of eggs and whisk to Connor.

I go to the fridge and grab a jug of orange juice, and when I turn back, I catch Lo whispering quietly to Connor. They shut up when they see me watching.

"What?" I ask, unscrewing the cap to the juice. It's not the first time they've gossiped like fucking girls. We all selectively choose who to share information with.

"We were talking," Lo says, motioning from his chest to Connor.

Connor innocently beats the eggs.

"You were talking?" I repeat, staring between them. "Well fuck me then. I didn't know either of you could talk."

Lo ignores my sarcasm and cocks his head. "We just think it's weird."

I glare. "You're going to have to be a little more specific, Lo. I can't grasp what you're saying with two words."

"Sorry," Lo says dryly. "I forgot you aren't Connor."

Connor smiles.

"Why compliment his intelligence?" I ask my brother. "Isn't it enough that everyone has to stare at his framed Mensa certificate in the living room?" It's also next to his wife's. Both of them are annoyingly intelligent.

Connor interjects, "I don't need validation that I'm smarter than all of you. I know it's true."

"Then why hang the certificate?" I ask.

He shrugs. "It matched the walls."

I shake my head. "It's a fucking miracle that I haven't punched you yet, Cobalt."

"Back to the situation," Lo says, eyes locked on me.

I grab a glass from the cabinet. *Fuck, he can't know, can he?* My heart starts pounding. *How would he find out that I'm sleeping in Daisy's bed?* He wouldn't. I'm being fucking paranoid. This is information that I *never* want to share with him. "What is it?" I pour orange juice and listen.

"We think it's weird that you haven't brought a girl around in a long time."

I frown. *That's what this is about?* "So?"

Lo shifts his weight, confusion blanketing him. "So...you used to date someone new every week."

"You know," I tell my brother, "there are reasons why I don't fucking live with all of you anymore." I hold up a finger. "*One*, I like my privacy, and that means not showing off the *couple* of women I date every month." I raise another finger. "*Two*, you *all* like to blow shit out of proportion. And *three*..." I lower my first two fingers and hold up my middle one.

And then I turn my back to them and cap the orange juice slowly.

I'm lying to my brother right now.

It feels like I'm walking over burning coals. I hate lying to him, and I've done it before. Each time never gets easier. I can see the thick fog I've created, the one that clouds my relationship with Lo. But I'm not my father, hurting his sons to protect his own reputation.

I lie to protect Daisy.

To protect Lo.

I lie because it's going to hurt less than the truth. And when the truth does come out, I want to make sure that Lo is strong enough to bear it. Right now, he's not even fucking close.

So I can't say, *Yeah, man, I've stopped dating for four fucking months because I've been busy taking care of your girlfriend's little sister, spending nights at her place, even sleeping in her bed just so she can stop being so fucking scared. And I don't miss those other girls, but I do miss being laid.*

I'm not used to jerking off every fucking day.

"Ryke," Connor says, and I spin around to meet a face that studies mine with too much fucking knowledge and suspicion. "It's just odd. You're what I would call a serial dater, as is Daisy, and since she graduated and moved into *your* apartment complex, no one has seen either of you with someone else."

"What is this?" I say, looking between Connor and Lo. "Watson and Holmes? I hate to break it to both of you, but there's no fucking mystery to be solved."

"Cut the shit," Lo says. "It's weird, and you know—"

"I'm *not* with her," I interject. "I'm not fucking Daisy. I'm not touching her. I told you, Lo, I wouldn't." We've been through this for over two years. And he still looks at me like I'm one second from betraying him, like I'm going to choose a girl over him, like I'm going to cross a big fucking line that will destroy the relationships that matter to me.

I wouldn't. I fucking won't. Because at the end of the day, if Daisy and I got together, if something happened and we broke up, I'd lose my brother. She's like his little sister. He grew up with the Calloway girls. Daisy has known him her whole fucking life. I've known Lo for three years. For fuck's sake, I am the thing that can be tossed aside. Everything's confusing. Nothing makes complete sense. My dick says one thing. My head says another. I have morals. I have Lo's constant warnings. I have five kinds of wrong and no kinds of right.

What the fuck am I supposed to do?

"Okay," Lo says, watching me closely, seeing the anger pulse in my eyes.

I'm so fucking screwed. If he ever finds out that I sleep in Daisy's bed, that I'm practically her fucking roommate, he's going to kill me. Really, *murder* could be a fucking option in Loren Hale's twisted mind, and I think I'd let him do it.

"Look," I tell Lo and Connor, "I date girls for a week, sometimes a couple of fucking days if they don't pan out. I'm not going to bring one of them to Princeton so you guys can meet her. It's never serious. The strings that I tie down are the ones that mean something to me." My eyes flicker to each of them. "I haven't found a girl that I want to tie myself to, and I don't know if I ever will."

"You will," Lo says certainly, nodding like he's trying to convince himself of it.

"It's okay if I don't." I'm surrounded by people I care about. That can be enough for me.

Lo's sharp gaze meets mine. "You're not going to be alone forever."

He says it like a declaration. I think he wants the best for me, but I also think that side battles with his selfish feelings. The ones that say: *I need one-hundred percent of you or else I'm going to drown.*

"So what if I am?" I say. "Lo, I didn't grow up with a Lily Calloway. I didn't have a best friend turned girlfriend." Lily was literally the girl next door, a family friend that he trusted with *everything*. Now they're engaged. I'm not envious of their co-dependent relationship that has thankfully grown a little healthier throughout the years.

I just recognize that he's different from me, even if we are alike in some ways.

"I'm fucking used to relying on myself," I add.

Lo just shakes his head like I'm an idiot—to be satisfied with something less. But maybe I don't deserve something more. Maybe the point of my fucking life is to help my brother get on his feet.

Connor passes Lo the bowl of whisked eggs, and my brother hesitates to pour them in the pan. "Let's wait for the girls to come out."

"How's Lily doing?" I ask him.

He sets the bowl on the counter. "Better than me." He rubs the back of his neck. "She tries to bring up my dad and alcohol, but honestly, it's just fucking hard sometimes." His amber eyes meet mine. "His lawyers said they can't reach you for questioning. I told them that you don't want to go on record."

"Thanks," I say.

Lo shrugs. "Yeah, whatever."

I run my hand through my hair, feeling Connor watching us like a psychiatrist fucking would. There's a lot there, okay? I don't want to see our dad, and Lo is complying with that for now.

"I'm going to go check on Daisy in the garage," I tell them, avoiding any plans they have to convince me to see Jonathan Hale. And plus, I want to know what she's fucking doing alone in there.

"Tell her the food is almost ready," Lo says.

I nod, heading to the back door.

We each have our roles, and I know mine is to keep an eye on this girl and that guy.

I just don't ever want to be faced with the decision of having to choose between them.

If that day comes, then fuck me.

< 5 >

Ryke Meadows

I shut the door behind me, finding Daisy almost immediately. She sits backwards on her parked Ducati, the same brand as mine, only red to my black. She leans back against the gas can near the handles and props a map on her legs, a Sharpie cap between her teeth.

Her carefree nature *always* fucking draws me to her—even when I wish I could stay fifteen feet away. It doesn't help that her legs are spread apart. I'm so fucking thankful she's single right now. I *hate* her ex-boyfriends, and I hate how men look at her and all they see is a girl they believe they can mount. They can't. She's out of their fucking league, and yet, she entertains them, too nice not to.

It pisses me off.

"There's a party inside, you know," I tell her roughly, "and it's for *you*." I walk across the concrete floor to reach her side.

"I know," she mumbles and then spits the cap out. "Rose and Lily shut the door on me when I tried to go to the bathroom with them. And Connor and Lo looked like they wanted to talk about something private too, so I figured I'd let them discuss what they needed to."

I frown. "Why would your sisters do that?"

"Lily is five years older than me and Rose is seven," she says with a shrug. "I'm used to being left out. It's the younger child syndrome." She sits up and hands me the map.

I scan it quickly.

"It's for your road trip to California," she explains. "I marked some places that are supposed to be cool."

"You also drew a fucking smiley face over North Dakota."

"That's because North Dakota is the happiest state. Everyone knows that." She grins, brightness in her eyes that I haven't seen in a while. It's gorgeous beyond fucking words. But at night, that light starts to slowly wane. It's like Daisy Calloway is powered by the sun.

"Says who?" I ask, folding the map and tucking it into my back pocket.

"I read it somewhere," she says. "I've forgotten the source, but I'm sure it was credible."

"Yeah, says the girl who reads her horoscope every day."

She mock gasps. "How did you know that? Have you been reading my diary?"

"No, I've just been sleeping in your bed."

"I thought that was some other guy," she says.

I scrutinize her position on the bike, her legs on either side of the seat, clutched tightly, still backwards. I've ridden on the same motorcycle with her before. She does this thing where she rests her hands on my thighs instead of wrapping them around my chest. I always have to grab her wrist when she purposefully nears my cock.

She likes to tease, to see how far she can push me, and I've never had a girl play with me like that, with confidence that radiates. It drives me fucking nuts, and I find myself wanting to be around her even more, seeking those give-and-take moments and her fucking joy.

But there's a silent understanding between us. We both know we can't cross a certain line.

"You've let other guys in your bed?" I question with the rise of my brows. Anger burns my muscles as I imagine the losers she's been with, all fucking her, all older. *Don't think about it.*

"Not lately." Her oversized sweater snags on the handle behind her, almost flashing me. "Oops."

My body heats, and the only thing that stops any kind of arousal is the idea of another strange guy getting hard at the sight of her. I don't want to be one of them.

She adjusts her shirt, and I read the words stitched on her chest: *Ooh la la.*

I think it's been about a year since she started choosing clothes with sayings—kind of like her way of talking back to the paparazzi without speaking. It's cute.

"Have you ridden like this before?" she asks with a playful smile.

"Backwards?"

She nods.

"No. I didn't want to kill myself the billions of times it's crossed my mind," I say dryly.

"I think I could do it," she says, ignoring my sarcasm. "But you'd have to be on the bike too, steering." Her green eyes grow big. "Can we try?"

I don't dismiss her wild fantasies. Last week, we took the wheels off a skateboard and tried to balance on a sideways trashcan. It was more fun than it fucking sounds. But this—me on a motorcycle with her facing me—it's an image that's too fucking intimate. I don't even know if she realizes this.

"My head will knock into yours," I tell her. "It's impossible for me to reach the throttle and the brake."

"You can wrap your arms around me to grab onto the handlebars," she says. "I can prove that it'll work." She scoots up towards the gas can, giving me plenty of room on the seat. "Unless you're scared."

My eyes narrow. "You can call me a fucking coward all you want, sweetheart. I'm not falling for it." *And neither is my dick.*

"Then I'll just try to ride backwards *without* you present. How's that?" She's about to turn her fucking key in the ignition. I have no doubt she'll try.

She's done wilder things in her free time, learning how to whitewater raft and how to fly a plane. I've watched her fall off the back of this fucking motorcycle. I've seen her crash into a tree on a black diamond ski slope. And with every daring event, I've been there, by her side, carrying her almost every time she's fallen.

"Fine," I tell her easily. I near her Ducati, and she stops fiddling with the keys. I swing my leg over and straddle the fucking seat like I normally would, facing the handlebars. She's the one who's all turned around.

Our knees knock together, and I'm satisfied with the fact that I can't near the handlebars. But she's not ready to give up. She lifts her legs on top of mine and scoots down towards me. *Fuck.*

She's straddling me, her back against the gas can, lying on the motorcycle. I touch the fucking throttle and brake easily, extending my arms over her, and her chest rises and falls in a shallow rhythm, acting like I'm about to push into her. Like this is about to go somewhere it is definitely fucking *not.*

"You're a wicked girl, Calloway," I tell her. My cock is pleading with me to thrust forward, and in this moment, I visualize the one thing that keeps me down. My brother beating the shit out of me. And if that doesn't work, I imagine Lily's whiny voice in my ear. She's admitted to thinking about me to stop her sexual cravings, so I don't feel fucking bad about it.

It works. I don't move. And my face remains dark, never letting on anything past *pissed*—and I kind of am. This doesn't feel fucking good. And yet, I always end up back at this place with her because I love her company so fucking much.

"You're right. It's kind of uncomfortable in this position," she teases. "We don't fit well at all." Her lips lift in a mischievous grin again. "I know how we could fit better—"

Fuck me. "Don't," I say, sitting up before her head nears mine and subsequently her lips. We've never kissed. I don't plan to start now. Her feet are hiked on the back of the bike, her legs still split open to allow us room.

I fucking swear if she rocks her hips against mine one more time, I'm going to throw her off the bike. And it won't be nice.

She smiles even wider at the risk that's clear in my eyes. "I was just going to suggest taking off my boots. What were you thinking?"

My tongue in your mouth. My cock so far inside of you.

My gaze darkens, and I try to ignore her silly smile and roaming hands that grip the bike seat and then drift to her thighs. Some part of her is always moving.

I say, "Something that's too fucking dirty for your virginal ears."

She sits up like me, and her chest is only an inch or so from mine. I set my hand on her knee to keep her from scooting any closer.

She says in a more serious voice, "I lost my virginity when I was fifteen."

"I meant that you haven't popped your cherry on a motorcycle. I know you aren't a virgin." She asked her sister for sex advice on her sweet sixteen trip, and I was there to help Lily chaperone. I was filling in for my brother who was in rehab, and Daisy pretty much said that she already had sex. I just wish her first time wasn't so fucking awful.

And I kind of wish she stopped at the first guy and waited for someone better. Like…no one. I don't think anyone is good enough for her. Yeah, it's fucking selfish. I don't care.

I add, "I'm not surprised that you lost it that young either."

She nods. "Because my older sister is a sex addict." As if that fucking makes her one?

"No, because you try a lot of stuff, and I'm sure you felt like you were missing out on something."

Her lips rise a little. "When did you lose it?"

"I was fifteen too," I say. "I was with an eighteen-year-old girl." My first time was on a fucking golf course at three in the morning.

Daisy digests this. "So you like older women then?"

"I like all women, sweetheart."

She wears a crooked smile. "You like me?"

Fuck me. "Daisy—"

She holds up her hands, her palms touching my chest because there's no fucking room. I go rigid beneath them. "I know, sorry, I shouldn't have said anything." She drops her hands quickly, her breath heavy.

I try not to look at her as anything more than she can be. But she's gorgeous, not because she has this natural fucking beauty—no makeup and bold green eyes, smooth skin and a delicate face.

She's beautiful because she can make the saddest person in the world grin. And she can make the loneliest guy feel something more. She's youthful and wild. Primal and really fucking innocent. She's all these things that scream *big fucking risk.*

"You know, I've only had sex with six guys in my entire life," she announces.

I stiffen. "Yeah?" I don't really want these details, even though a part of me masochistically craves them. "For some, six guys would be a lot at eighteen."

She shrugs. "I was testing out the waters."

"And how were those fucking waters?" I snap. I shouldn't have asked. But I do. And I'm not going to take it back.

I wait for her to answer because I know she will.

< 6 >

Daisy Calloway

I should really rethink hashing out my sexual history to my sister's boyfriend's older brother. (Yeah, it's a tongue-twister.) But you know, I started so now I have to finish. I try not to half-ass things. *Go full force, Daisy. No hitting the brakes*. Yeah, I can do this.

I stare at his eyes that are hard and harsh, never softening for me. Our close proximity doesn't really alleviate anything between us, but I like his closeness too much to jump off the motorcycle. And hey, he's not moving either. Good signs, I think.

"The first guy sucked," I tell him. "We did it once. It lasted like thirty seconds." I should probably blush, but that time feels ancient. I just remember sitting up in his bed and being like *that's it? That's sex? What the hell is so awesome about it?*

Ryke keeps his face unreadable, just dark and brooding. Okay. I can continue without crumbling under his intense silence. *Go, go, go.*

I lick my lips and say, "And the second guy, we did it a couple times. He lasted maybe three minutes."

"How old were these guys?" he asks.

"Only a few years older than me. I mean, I've dated guys in their late twenties, but we couldn't have sex. I wasn't eighteen yet." And I wasn't about to break the law and have a guy thrown in jail for sleeping with me.

"I've met most of the older guys you've dated," he reminds me. "They were complete fucking morons by the way."

"They weren't that bad."

"Julian?" he says. "You think he was better than a fucking rat?"

"Connor called him an ape."

"Connor gave him too much fucking credit."

"Connor also called you a dog," I say with a crinkled nose. "Do you think I'm the cat to your dog or am I like a squirrel?"

"How'd we get to this place?" he asks like this is the stupidest 'fucking' conversation.

"I'm a hamster, aren't I?" I stick out my bottom lip.

"You're not a fucking hamster." He rolls his eyes and runs his hand through his hair. I don't think he realizes how hot he is when he does that. "You're a bird."

"A bird."

"Yeah a fucking bird that won't stop flying or squawking."

"Like an eagle?"

"You're prettier than an eagle." He rolls his eyes again. "Fuck."

"You called me pretty." I poke his chest, my smile overtaking my face.

He stares at me hard. "Julian," he finds the beginning of our conversation. "You still like him? Because if you do, we need to have a heavy fucking talk."

I shake my head quickly. "No, I don't like him."

Julian actually really scared me. He went on a trip to the Alps with all of us. I didn't realize how in over my head I was until I tried to break up with him, and he wouldn't listen to me, as if I was too young to really understand. Maybe I was. I don't know anymore. All I know is that I don't want to be afraid of the person I'm with. That isn't a danger I like.

"And just so you know," I say, "I haven't been ecstatic by some of the girls you've chosen. One of them called Lily a slut." And behind Ryke's back, she literally pulled my hair. *Hard.*

"I broke up with her the second she said that," he reminds me. "You were with that idiot for months."

"I tried breaking up with him," I retort. "I even wrote him a letter. It went something like: *Julian, I think we're better as friends. Xoxo Daisy.*"

Ryke groans, but his hand unconsciously rises from my knee to my thigh. The affection speeds my heart.

"The hugs and kisses were too much, weren't they?"

"Who breaks up with someone in a fucking note?"

"Someone who's scared." I'm not as fearless as my sisters would like to believe.

"You're not a fucking coward. You're just with the wrong guys." He glances at his hand and takes it off me. Then his brown eyes flit from the small space between our bodies to my gaze again. "Did any of them last longer than five minutes?"

I try to think back. "I think six minutes was the highest."

"Were you seriously timing them?"

"I was waiting for it to end."

He grimaces.

I pretty much dislike everything about sex. The before. The during. The after. No moment is fun.

I've kept trying to see if it gets better.

It doesn't.

It's just a load of uncomfortable and awkward. Nothing about sex gives me that fulfillment that other girls talk about. What is an orgasm? Nerve-spindling? Head-spinning? I've had that skydiving and racing my motorcycle down a steep hill alongside Ryke. That's as orgasmic as I've ever been.

"Sex is stupid," I tell him.

"It is when you're with guys who can't satisfy you."

I flush at his words. "Rose just told me to try it with more guys and see what happens."

Ryke looks ready to spring off the bike and go track down my sister. "Are you fucking kidding me?"

"I thought it was nice. She's a proponent of experimenting."

"Says the fucking *virgin*."

"She's not a virgin anymore," I point out.

Ryke glares. "So she's slept with one guy her whole life, and she's telling you to fuck around to find someone. *She* didn't fuck around, Daisy. Do you see what I'm getting at?"

"She has no experience with experimenting, got it," I nod. "I've tried to talk to Lily about it, but she's uncomfortable discussing sex with me." I shrug. "Sometimes she'll open up though. It's just hard finding a day where she feels good enough to do it."

Ryke relaxes a bit at the mention of Lily's sex addiction and her shame towards the whole subject.

"Maybe I'm doing something wrong," I say. "Is it normal for guys to last so short?"

Ryke runs his hand through his thick hair. He's never held back with me before, so I don't expect him to now. "They're probably really fucking attracted to you, and when they get you in bed, they just come early. It's not a fucking reflection on you but them."

"So I need to find a guy who's not attracted to me?" That doesn't make sense.

Ryke shakes his head. "No, Dais. You need to like the guy you're with as much as they like you. That way, you'll fucking come too."

"But what happens when the guy I like isn't *emotionally* available?"

"Stay single," he suggests.

"Forever?"

Ryke's whole body tenses. I don't know if that's a *no* or a *yes*. Inside I'm screaming, *give me something! Blink once for yes, twice for no!*

And then the garage door opens. "Hey," Lo calls, "dinner is…" His voice dies when he catches us on the motorcycle together.

Uh-oh.

Ryke slowly climbs off the bike, acting like he did nothing wrong. I mimic his guiltless expression, and I follow him, swinging my legs over the seat and standing up.

Lo's eyes flash murderously at his brother. "Did I interrupt something?"

"No," Ryke replies coolly. "We were just talking."

Lo nods like he's trying to believe that. "If you were *just* talking, then why were her legs wrapped around your waist?"

"Lo," I try to cut in, but Ryke holds up his hand to stop me. This is between them, I guess.

But I do care about Lo a lot. He's always been another extension of my family in a sense. He started as Lily's best friend. Then her boyfriend. Now fiancé. And she always brought him on Calloway vacations. He was her plus one.

To say he's like a big brother to me would be accurate.

Which makes everything with Ryke a tiny bit weird, but at the same time, Ryke feels so disconnected from Lo—a barrier built between them from years of separation. So maybe it's not as strange as it could be.

"We're friends," Ryke tells his brother.

"Friends don't do shit like that," Lo retorts, pointing at my Ducati like it violated me. I would actually *love* to be violated on that motorcycle by Ryke Meadows. I wonder how rough he would take me.

Or if I would even be able to orgasm at all.

Ryke pinches the bridge of his nose in annoyance. "What do you fucking want me to say?"

"That what I just saw was a mistake!" Lo shouts.

Ryke doesn't speak, so I will. "It was a mistake," I tell Lo. "I wanted to see what it would be like to ride on a motorcycle backwards. I needed his help."

Lo glares from me to him. "That's the best lie you can come up with?"

I smile. "It's actually the truth."

This only incites Lo more. "This isn't a fucking joke, Daisy. He's seven years older than you. He's been with more girls than you probably even realize."

"No, I realize that he's slept with a lot of women, but his number is probably one that I would have easily reached at twenty-five too."

Lo grimaces like that image is disgusting. "I'm in an alternate universe right now."

"Really? Cool. Is it more fun here? I think it is." I turn to Ryke. "What do you think?"

"Tone it down," he tells me, his eyes fixed on his brother. "Lo—"

"You're not good enough for her," he says. "You realize that, right?"

Ryke's jaw locks, and his shoulders tense. "I care about Daisy just as much as you, if not more, so you don't need to pull this overprotective bullshit on me."

"It's not bullshit if you're fucking her."

"We're not fucking!" Ryke shouts.

More people trickle in the garage. Connor. Both of my sisters.

Rose is classily outfitted in a black high-collared dress, stomping through the doorway in five-inch heels. She looks like a perfect match beside the ever-confident Connor Cobalt.

Lily has on one of Lo's shirts and a pair of leggings, and she squeezes through the doorway to reach Lo near Rose's parked Escalade. I envy her short brown hair that's chopped at her shoulders. "What's going on?" she whispers to Lo.

"I caught them fucking on her motorcycle."

Ryke groans. "Come on! We were both on the bike, fully fucking clothed. We've *never* had sex!" He shakes his head. "How many times do I have to say it? You know what, we might as well fuck if you all think we've done it a thousand times already."

My eyes widen. Really?

"Whoa, whoa," Lo cringes, holding up his hands. "I can't stomach you guys doing it once. So please spare me the goddamn picture of it happening a thousand times."

"Both of you," Connor says, stepping down the three stairs into the garage. "Stop for a second." He stands between both brothers to mediate. "You're overreacting."

"I don't like being accused of things that I didn't fucking do," Ryke growls.

"Yeah? How do you think Dad feels?!" Lo yells.

It's like a bomb dropped, Lo's hostile voice echoing before the garage goes quiet. Ryke breathes heavily but makes no attempt to answer Lo. It's a loaded question.

Lo returns to the central issue. "She's eighteen."

"Here we go," Ryke says, throwing his arms in the air. "Let's fucking hear it, Lo. She's eighteen. She's like your little sister. Her mom hates me. I know. I know. I fucking *know*."

Lo's face contorts in a series of emotions, and Lily reaches out and wraps her arm around his waist. He calms down by the single touch.

Rose places her hands on her hips. "I don't see the problem here."

"Darling," Connor says with the shake of his head. "Don't make it worse."

She huffs. "They're both consenting—"

"I'm not consenting," Ryke suddenly says, not looking at me. "Because nothing is fucking going on." His eyes meet Lo's and they soften for him. "Okay?"

They both have trust issues.

I know it doesn't help that Ryke is lying to him about sleeping in my bed. If Lo found out, he would disapprove *and* find a way to separate us for the betterment of my health. But I think my health is the best when I'm with Ryke. Sleeping without him has been nearly impossible. I need the reassurance at night, the confidence of another person in order to sleep without fear. Otherwise, I can't even get an hour of shuteye.

But I'm not keeping Ryke at gunpoint. If he wants to leave, I'd let him. And I guess I'd have to find someone to replace him. I'm not even sure that's possible though. Maybe in my heart, I just know that I only want Ryke Meadows.

"Let's eat," Connor says. "The eggs are going to get cold."

We all wait for one of the brothers to make a move first. They have the power to reignite the argument or dissolve it.

Lo opens his mouth, needing the last word. "I didn't accept you into my life so you could bang my girlfriend's little sister. Don't make me regret letting you in."

That one stung. I felt it like a sharp kick.

Lo walks away, disappearing inside, and Ryke doesn't wait for me. He goes in right after him. Connor is next, leaving me alone with my sisters.

"Well," I say to them, "there are always fireworks at my parties, aren't there?"

"Do you need a hug?" Rose asks me. "Because if you do, Lily can give you one."

Lily looks at Rose like *really?*

"You give better hugs than I do. I know my weaknesses." Rose raises her chin at me. "But really, are you okay?"

I shrug. "Yeah." They think I have this massive crush on Ryke, and while I do like him, I understand more than anyone what we can and cannot do. I've accepted that reality for so long that the fantasy is always *us* being together.

I skip towards them and wrap my arms around their shoulders. "Thank you for the decorations, by the way. They're beautiful."

They both smile when I do.

That lights up any black spots that dotted my heart. But it's not enough to take away the panic that I'll feel come nighttime. Sometimes I wish it could be daylight forever. I wish that I could be with these five people and never have to face the world alone.

But Paris is my test.

I want to pass, but a part of me wonders if it's even possible to be that fearless girl again. Maybe too much has changed to go back.

< 7 >

Daisy Calloway

I wash the dishes after dinner, offering since Connor and Lo cooked. Everyone just acted like nothing happened in the garage, which was as expected. This wasn't the first time I've been too close to Ryke in front of them.

It's an exhausting fight and one that's strangely become predictable.

Ryke enters the kitchen, everyone else in the living room. I look up, expecting another body passing through the archway. "They know why I'm here," he says off my lingering gaze.

I frown. "You're going to help me wash dishes?"

He grabs a bowl from the cupboard. "No. We all watched you push your fucking eggs around for thirty minutes." He picks out granola cereal from another cabinet, his favorite brand. I'm sure he left a box here after early morning runs at Lo's house.

"I ate the fruit," I tell him. Fashion Week is coming up. I want to eat more than anyone. I just have a lot of self-control.

He opens the fridge for the milk. "Fucking fantastic," he says to me. "Now I'm really at ease."

"I also tried the bacon."

"Don't lie to me."

"Okay, I didn't eat the bacon, but I wanted to." I put the last plate into the dishwasher and then climb up on the counter. He makes the cereal beside me.

"You know what I fucking learned today?" he says, his features really dark. "Rose just told Connor, my brother, and me that you have irregular periods because of your weight."

Oh God. I groan. "She did not tell you guys that." Sometimes Rose being overly open is a bad thing. When it comes to *her* private life, she's a mouse. Or at least, she used to be.

"Yeah, she fucking did."

I didn't want her to share that info with *anyone* but Lily and maybe Poppy, our oldest sis. "It's only like that when I—"

"Starve yourself," he deadpans. Then he shakes his head. "You can't eat, you can't sleep..."

I smile wide at his words because I instantly recall a quote from a movie. I can't help it. I recite the lines, *"It's got to be that can't-eat, can't-sleep, reach-for-the-stars, over-the-fence, World Series kind of stuff."* Then I pause, waiting for his ah-ha moment. He just looks confused. *"It Takes Two."* It doesn't ring a bell for him. "A Mary Kate and Ashley movie. They were describing love."

His eyebrows rise. "Funny. But love isn't causing you these problems."

"How do you know?" I ask.

He extends his arms. "I'm sorry, where are all the guys you've been dating while I've been sleeping in your fucking bed?"

"I could be in love with *you.*" I throw out this line, wondering if he'll reel me in, but he just gives me a hard stare.

"Are you?" he taunts back, not stepping down from this.

He puts me on the defensive. I want to say yes. But am I in love with Ryke? How do I know? "I'm not sure."

"Well, be damn fucking sure about this," Ryke says, "any love that *I* fucking give will never hurt a woman." He passes the bowl to me, cold in my hands. "Eat your cereal."

Seriousness blankets the kitchen once more. "You heard my mom this morning." She bruised my hip she pinched my skin so hard.

"Yeah." His eyebrows rise. "Fuck your mom."

"Hey," I snap.

"Hey what? She's nothing but cruel to Lily. She fights with Rose constantly. And she treats you like you're a little fucking doll she likes to dress up and show off. It drives me *fucking* nuts watching you do things you hate just to please other people."

I'm not a fan of modeling, not when I have to stand still for so long. I just get restless. So I can't argue against his point. "It's different when peoples' careers are on the line. Fashion designers and agents are counting on me. If I can't fit into the clothes, then I'm not just disappointing myself but I'm hurting them."

I search his eyes, but all I see is that familiar stone that Lily talks about. She says his brother is ice. All sharp. But Ryke, he's like the rocks he climbs—just hard.

"Don't be a fucking mannequin."

"I'm not."

"Really? Because I see a girl who has another person's thoughts, another person's desires and dreams."

"I think that's a puppet."

"Don't be a fucking puppet then."

My eyes fall to the cereal. I've heard him speak with this conviction before, but this time, it barrels into me like the biggest truth of all. "Maybe after Fashion Week, I'll tell her how I feel again." Maybe I can finally stand up to my mom. "Why are you so passionate about this anyway?" I ask, expecting him to say something like *because I care about you.*

Instead he says, "I've been there with my own mother. It's not fucking fun."

He hardly talks about Sara Hale, mostly because of what happened a couple years ago. Mostly because she changed all of our lives. And I'm not sure it was all for the better.

"Eat your fucking cereal," he says roughly.

I do. Four spoonfuls later, Ryke looks pleased. I like when he's satisfied. I like when I do right by all people, but it's just hard when my mom stands at one end and my sisters, Ryke, Connor and Lo stand at the other.

They outnumber her, but my mom raised me. Isn't that a trump card?

He watches me eat, making sure that I'm not fibbing. "This cereal sucks," I tell him on the tenth bite.

"It's healthy, but if you want chocolate, there's ice cream in the freezer."

I practically moan. "Don't tempt me."

He almost smiles. "After Fashion Week, you promise you'll talk to her?"

I nod. "Yeah, yeah."

"Don't yeah me twice," he retorts.

"Why, because it's redundant?"

He leans close, his arms on either side of the counter, on either side of *me*. "Because it sounds fake, sweetheart."

"So if I moan twice—"

He covers my mouth with his large hand, enveloping my cheeks and jaw. "Don't go there, not tonight."

I do ride that line a little too much. We tempt and tease each other with knowledge that nothing more can happen. It's our dynamic.

I finish off most of the cereal, leaving the soggy clumps of granola floating in the milk. "I'm sorry about the garage. I pushed you too far." I set down the bowl and hop off the counter. He's right there, not moving from this spot. His hands still on the counter.

I'm closer to him than before.

"No you didn't," he says. "If I fucking wanted to be with you like that, I would have by now. You've been eighteen for six months."

This shouldn't hurt, but his words knot my stomach, the granola rising to my throat. I swallow it back down. I think *wanting* is a little different than doing. I thought he wanted to like me, but he knew he couldn't. But that's not right. He's never really expressed any attraction towards me. We flirt sometimes, but he's never gotten hard or aroused by me.

At least not that I've seen.

I want to test it.

I shouldn't, but I'm curious. I don't know how else to see if he shares the same attraction. He doesn't show it in his eyes the way I do.

He's close enough that all I have to do is wrap my arms around his chest for a hug. He's my wolf, and I seriously wonder if he'll bite me today. I don't think twice. I hug him, and his body goes rigid. I look up, neither of us retracting.

"Daisy…"

My long legs touch his strong ones. My hip bones press into his pelvis, a little shorter than him since he's six-three to my five-eleven. I become keenly aware of his flexed muscles and dark eyes that set on me. It's an R-rated hug, if there can be one. And yet, he's not hard. He's just tense, like he's waiting for me to draw away.

Instead of hugging me back, he sets a single hand on my head, hesitating.

I sigh. Well that test was inconclusive. "Thanks," I say. That single word relaxes his muscles. "I'm glad we can be non-fucking friends." It's better than nothing.

His dark eyes dance over my features. He stays quiet for a long time, both of us unmoving from this position. It's dangerous to be like this after the garage incident, but I think we're equally attracted to that danger.

His thumb grazes my cheek. "You look fucking exhausted."

"I napped."

"You don't fucking nap," he says.

"I shut my eyes this afternoon. What do you call that?"

"Shutting your fucking eyes," he deadpans.

A smile breaks through my face. I laugh, and then I lean forward and rest my cheek against his chest. I close my eyes, and his body stiffens again. He's warm. I listen to the faint sound of his heart for a second, and I swear it speeds. But maybe that's just me *hoping* that I have some sort of effect on Ryke Meadows.

"What are you doing?" he asks roughly. His hands return to my head, making me realize that I'm smaller than him. It's hard finding guys taller than me, which is why I've gravitated towards models in the past.

"Sleeping," I say with a smile.

"When did I become your fucking pillow?" he asks lightly.

"Shhh," I whisper, "it's safe here."

Just when I anticipate Ryke drawing away from me, he surprises me and kisses the top of my head. But it lasts only a second before his hands fall. His brows scrunch as he glares at something over my shoulder. I turn my head and follow his gaze, spotting a *Celebrity Crush* magazine by the coffee pot.

"Who still buys that garbage?"

"Lily," I say. "I think my sister's hoping people will forget about our family."

"She's dreaming." Ryke leaves my side to grab the magazine. He flips through it quickly, and I catch the main headline on the front cover before he trashes it. PHOTO! LILY CALLOWAY DATING HER FIANCÉ AND HIS BROTHER.

"What's the photo of?" I ask curiously, rinsing the cereal bowl.

"The three of us eating lunch at Lucky's downtown. The press can keep saying I'm banging your fucking sister, but we all know it's a load of—"

"Shit," I finish. "Bullshit." I mock gasp. "*Fucking* bullshit."

He stares at me with harshness that would intimidate most people. But I don't back down. My eyes stay locked on his piercing ones, and then his lips slowly rise. "When did your mouth get so fucking dirty, Calloway?" he asks.

"The moment I became friends with you."

"Good on me then," he says, messing my hair with a rough hand. "I'm tailing you when we leave, by the way."

"You're supposed to be my pillow, not my bodyguard," I remind him. "I already have one of those." His name is Mikey Black. He's in his forties and used to be a physical trainer in California. Unlike Lily's bodyguard who's a bit beefy and wears oversized suits, mine likes to dress in Bermuda shorts in the winter and cut-off shirts. He's pretty cool.

"He can't keep up with you," Ryke says, sidling next to me. He watches as I stick the bowl into the dishwasher.

"He taught me how to surf this summer," I refute.

"He only rides Harleys, and they can't go as fucking fast as your sportbike. I've never seen him pass a paparazzi's car when he's with you." That's true. I end up being flocked by SUVs. Like tonight. I tried to outmaneuver them, but they sped up behind me, forcing me to go a little faster. And Mikey was lost somewhere with my shift from eighty miles per hour to a hundred-and-five on the interstate.

"He smells like salt water and candy," I tell him. "Sometimes even cupcakes."

Ryke gives me a blank stare.

"Those are selling points," I say.

"Not for me."

"There's *nothing* better than cupcakes, except maybe chocolate cake, but that's still in the cupcake family."

"Sex," he says. "Sex is better than chocolate." He always tells me this.

"Not for me," I use his exact words.

His eyes descend to my lips. I swear they do this time. But it happens so quickly. Maybe it was just me wanting it badly again… I don't know why I torture myself. It's not like we can act on anything, even if he does admit to liking me as more than just non-fucking friends.

I let the moment go. Like I always do. "What makes you think that you can keep up with me more than Mikey?" I ask.

He leans close again. "Because," he says, "I'm the one who taught you how to ride a motorcycle."

I smile. Yes he did.

< 8 >

Ryke Meadows

"Watch me," I tell Daisy as I stand by her bedroom door. I jiggle the handle. "Locked."

She yawns, sitting on her bed, her legs tucked to her chest. Her eyes are deceivingly at ease, but her tense shoulders say otherwise.

I do the same fucking thing every night. I head over to the window next and pull back her green curtains, attempting to lift the window. She watches my biceps contract, my muscles carving into defined lines, to ensure that I'm actually *trying*. "Locked," I say.

I pass the foot of the bed and raise my eyebrows at her in jest, and I catch her small smile before I disappear into the bathroom. I check behind the shower curtain, just because I'd feel like a fucking ass if I lied to her by not doing it. And the percentage of someone breaking into her room again and hiding in the bathtub is higher than I can stomach. If I didn't check and that happened—I'd *never* fucking forgive myself.

Clear.

I fill a glass with water from the tap and then return to her room. Daisy holds onto her knees so tightly that her fingertips redden. Her spine is erect as her gaze transfixes on that window.

"Dais," I say, coming around to her side of the bed. "I just fucking checked there." I grab her pill bottle off the nightstand. I rest a knee on the mattress so I'm near her, and I block her view of the window. "Hey." My heart starts to hammer.

"Yeah…" She blinks a few times and then gives me the weakest fucking smile I've ever seen.

Aggravated, I throw the bottle at her face, and she catches it before it hits her. "Can you check again?" she asks.

"Sure." I hand her the water, and I go back to the window. Her eyes widen and her chest rises as I show her it's locked. The moment I try to lift the window, she flinches back in fear.

I don't know what's going on in her fucking head right now, but I know she has multiple reasons to be afraid. It tears my heart watching her recoil like that.

"You're okay," I tell her. "See, it's fucking locked."

She puts her hand over her mouth, and she nods, holding back tears. "Sorry. I'm jumpy when I haven't slept in a while."

"I know. You don't have to fucking apologize to me." I go back to her bathroom door and lock it from her bedroom. I installed a deadbolt on this door a week after she moved in, to give her peace of mind.

Her hands shake as she tries to uncap the pill bottle. I slide into bed next to her, wearing drawstring pants, shirtless. She's in a pair of cotton yellow shorts and a tank top that says: *Shut the Fucupcakes*. I dissed her fucking love of cupcakes three days ago, and I was waiting for her to bring out that shirt. I'm not surprised she chose the last night we have together to wear it. Tomorrow afternoon, she leaves for Paris. Six days later, I'll be gone to California.

Maybe it's a good thing we'll be separated. Connor and my brother think it's fucking weird that we both haven't dated in four months, and I guess we'll finally have the opportunity to change that.

I steal the bottle from her hands and open it with ease. I put two in her palm.

She hesitates. "You know, I didn't have night terrors or any other symptoms before I started taking these."

I run my hand through my hair. "Daisy, you've talked to your fucking doctor about this." For fuck's sake, *I* was there when she talked to three different sleep disorder physicians about her condition. She's taken EEGs. She's been through multiple sleep studies. They all advise her to take the fucking pills. Because without Ambien, she won't sleep at all. She suffers from insomnia, post-traumatic stress, and the only thing that can really help her is therapy, which she goes to routinely.

"It's not really sleeping though, is it?" she says, eyeing the pills in her palm. "I mean, it puts me in a half-sleep."

Parasomnia, the moments between wakefulness and sleep—yeah, I've learned all about it. She hasn't had anything better than that in over six months. "It's better than no fucking sleep."

She nods, takes a deep breath, and throws the pills back in her mouth. She chugs half the water before setting it back on her nightstand. I watch her slip beneath the covers and set her head on the pillow, staring straight up at the ceiling. Her eyes begin to glass.

"What is it?" I ask.

"I'm scared to sleep," she admits in a whisper. "I don't want to have a nightmare." Tears slide out of the creases of her eyes, too tired to hold them back. "But I'll be scared all night if I stay awake. It sucks."

I wish I could take away her problems. I'm not used to being unable to fix things, and it hurts, having to watch her go through this while I pretend that my presence is a fucking solution.

I lean over her so she's staring right at me. "Daisy," I say her name forcefully, wiping her tears with my thumb. "No one is getting in this fucking room." I don't normally do this every night, but she's worse today. I reach over to the end table near me and open the drawer. I take out a .45-caliber handgun and show her the ammunition. "Okay?"

I watch her breathe out again, and she nods.

Then I ensure the safety is on and tuck the gun beneath my pillow.

She shuts her eyes, and I near her under the covers so she feels my body heat. I've been doing this long enough to know what calms her down and what triggers her fear. We're a couple inches apart, and I already see a layer of sweat building on her forehead.

"Shhh," I whisper. "You're safe." I rub her arm, and she scoots closer to me. We're no longer a fucking inch or so apart. Her legs intertwine with mine like it's the most natural position. She turns, her back against my chest, my arm around her waist, my cock pressing on her ass, but she probably doesn't hone in on this last fact as much as me.

Do you want to know the kind of restraint it takes to be in this fucking position with this fucking girl almost every fucking night without doing one fucking thing?

More control than I even realized I had.

I FIGURED TONIGHT WOULD be a rough one, but I just didn't expect it to bypass a nightmare and hit on another fucking issue she has. Not sleepwalking. I haven't caught her doing that yet.

Daisy kicks me awake, which is the normal part. She squirms, her long, smooth legs moving back and forth, up and down, hitting my shins.

I don't try to stop her. She'll just be unresponsive until she wakes up fully.

She grips her pillow, her face turned into it, and she moans.

She's still asleep. This is a fucking side effect of her meds, and it's happened maybe five times in the past four months. I wasn't ever planning on telling her that she gets aroused in the middle of the night. She can't remember it happening, even when her eyes snap open and she looks pretty lucid, like a sleepwalker. I thought telling her that I've heard her moan in arousal would embarrass her, so I kept quiet. But during a sleep study, she did it anyway, and so she knows.

Daisy didn't look mortified when she found out. I forgot that she's not Lily. She's a lot less ashamed and a lot more brazen and probably five times as crazy. She just told me that if she does it again, I need to leave her bed immediately so she doesn't accidentally rape me.

She read that it could happen with sleepsex, and I told her that she's out of her fucking mind if she thinks she's going to rape me, asleep or awake.

Daisy tosses and turns restlessly, and then she stays still when her back faces me, one of her knees bent towards her body. She shudders, and then she moans again, the noise high-pitched and full of unbridled pleasure.

I sit up on my elbow and pause to watch her for a second. I start to harden, especially as she clenches the sheet by her waist. Her tank top has bunched to her chest, the bottom of her breasts peeking out.

Fuck. I have to go to the bathroom.

I'm about to tug her shirt down and leave, but her voice freezes me. "I can't," she moans softly, and then her noises turn into a series of breathless cries. "Ahh…ahhh…ahh…"

Fucking Christ. I wish I was so deep inside of her right now.

Her back arches. "Ryke!"

At least she thinks I am.

Frustrated, I toss the comforter off my body. *Fuck her shirt.* I glance back. Her breasts, even small, are killing me. I climb off the bed, my erection trying to burst through my fucking pants. Her body is skinnier than it's ever been. I want to fucking feed her first, and then I want to fuck her hard. Both of which seem improbable, and the latter can't happen.

"I…can't…" she moans. See, even in her fucking sleep, she knows it's wrong. So there we go. "Ryke…Ryke…" She cries again, feminine, high-pitched, and I lose it for a second time. "Ryke, ahhh!" I have to enter the fucking bathroom before I come right here.

It takes me a minute to unlock the deadbolt, and then I slip inside. I gently shut the door and tug down my drawstring pants to my thighs. *Fuck.* I find the lotion on the ground, along with hair spray (not fucking needed) and a tube of half-empty toothpaste (same). I didn't even realize it was fucking messy in here, but I guess it is. We both rarely clean up.

I used to make fun of Connor for masturbating like crazy when Rose wouldn't give up her virginity, and here I am, going through the same thing. The difference: there's no endgame for me. I don't have the girl at the finish. I'm not chasing after her. I'm just helping her, and when that's done, we're both supposed to move on.

I stand over the toilet and place one hand on the wall. I shut my eyes and stroke my hard cock that fucking begs to be inside a woman, but I've been saying *no* to that demand for months. Images start filling my head to increase my arousal, and the most prevalent is a girl with blonde hair, with that high-pitched cry and those long fucking legs.

I immediately stop rubbing.

I lick my lips and glare at the wall. *Why the fuck do you have to picture her?* Anyone else. Goddammit, anyone fucking else. I try thinking about a girl I've already fucked before, completely different from Daisy. She's big breasted, big assed, and big hipped. I like curvy. I like athletic. I honestly like everything. I don't think Daisy knows this either. I told her I had a type when she was fifteen—describing the complete opposite of her build, just so she wouldn't get any ideas.

And look where I am now, fucking imagining *her. Stop thinking.* I'm trying. I want to come, so I start again, and I keep picturing that other girl, my cock pounding between her legs. *Fuck...me.* I speed up my strokes, welcoming the friction with heavy breaths.

My hand on the wall turns into a fist.

And then the image of those big tits and large ass morph as soon as my brain remembers those cries again. *Ahhh...ahhh...ahhhhh...*

Ryke, Ryke! They turn into that delicate face, the one that bursts into a breathtaking smile, the one that can light up a city. Her lips part as she moans, and she smiles with each one.

Stop imagining her. I pause, my hand freezing in place. I can't fucking do this. I grab a magazine from the tile floor, some of the pages crinkled from being wet with shower water. It's a fashion magazine, and I have a hard time finding a girl without a ton of makeup on. I keep flipping, and then I land on a seven-page spread.

Of Daisy.

In black-laced lingerie.

Her small breasts look bigger, pushed up by the cups of her bra. She wears a thong that shows off her round ass, her shape slender. Her smoky-shadowed eyes only say *come fuck me*, which isn't helping. "Fucking A." Is the world against me tonight or what?

I toss the magazine aside, and I shut my eyes again, exhaling loudly. *Fuck this.* It's not like imagining her is a sin I can't live with. It's a line I've crossed before but not often, and it may force me a step closer to crossing another one.

I convince myself enough, and my hand resumes its natural course. *Ahh..ahhhh…Ryke!* A groan catches in my throat. *Fuck me.* I pulse my hips with the movement of my hand, picturing myself thrusting in between Daisy's thighs, her back permanently arched, in a constant state of pleasure that she can't contain.

It's an image that I'm not sure I'll ever be able to let go. I am so wound up, needing this release fucking hours prior to now. I hear her cries in my ears. I see her climax wash over her face. And her body is all mine, protected within my fucking hands, my long cock fitting entirely inside of her. All of it drives me to a new, intense place, giving me the biggest head rush of my life.

I come. If a simple fucking image is this good, it makes me wonder what the real fucking thing would be like. *Can't happen.*

Yeah, I know.

‹ 9 ›

Daisy Calloway

It takes a full minute to orient myself. I touch my temple, a little confused about where I am. I reach out and feel my comforter. My bed. Okay, I must be waking up, but I'm already in a sitting position. My limbs hurt like I thrashed all night. I rub my scratchy eyes and pat the mattress beside me. The sheets are tangled and twisted, no Ryke on the bed. Or even in the room.

Panic sets in, my heart shooting to my throat. My head whips towards the window, and I imagine a man crawling through with a bat or a camera or a combination of the two. My curtains stay still, not blowing, which means the window is firmly closed.

You're okay, Daisy. Stop freaking out. I repeat the mantra over and over as I stiffly turn towards the bathroom.

The door is ajar. The door is *ajar*. No. *It's just Ryke. It's okay.*

I glance at the other wall. The bedroom door…it's cracked open too. *It's just Ryke. You're okay.*

But what if it's not him? What if someone broke in and did something to Ryke? What if they hurt him and are setting a trap for me? It's a wild, crazed thought, but in the back of my head, I believe it's so true. I quietly sit on my knees, holding my breath as this cold adrenaline floods me. I lift Ryke's pillow and find the black handgun underneath.

With trembling fingers, I pick up the gun and point the barrel at the door. A clattering sound reverberates from my living room. I jump, a noise breaching my lips. *Shut up, Daisy. What if they hear you?*

And then the door slowly swings open.

Ryke stops short at the sight of me, his eyes filling with concern. "Daisy?"

What am I doing? The gun slides out of my unsteady hands and lands safely on my comforter. I can't breathe. Of course it's just Ryke. He's at my side the moment I blink. He rests a knee on the mattress and cups my face between two large hands. "Daisy, look at me."

I can't breathe. I gasp, trying to capture air for my distressed lungs. "Where…what…" I try to glance at the window. Why am I scaring myself? No one's there. It's all in my head.

"Shhh." He rubs my back. "Fucking breathe, Daisy." He towers over me, staring down as he studies my paranoid, anxious state.

I inhale deeply, and my body accepts it this time. *You're okay.* I can't stop shaking. He suddenly lifts me up beneath my arms, and before I exhale, he's on the bed, leaning against my headboard, and he's placed me on his lap. He peels off his clean gray Penn shirt, and I frown, but I'm too hot and exhausted to make sense of it or protest. His hair is wet, and he wears black jeans.

And then he wipes my forehead with his shirt. I'm caked in a layer of sweat. My tank top suctions to my stomach and chest. "I'm sorry," I whisper with a heavy breath. All the energy drains from me in a single instant. It's like I used everything I had in that moment of panic.

"What did I fucking say about apologizing?"

I hold onto his forearm, and he keeps me upright with his body and his other hand. "I was about to shoot you."

"No you weren't."

My eyes flicker up to his, and I only see that hardness in them. "You can't know that."

"The safety was fucking on," he tells me.

Oh. Good. A knot starts to loosen in my stomach.

He combs my damp hair out of my face and runs his cotton shirt across my neck. "I didn't think you'd wake up until later," he confesses. "I shouldn't have fucking left." Usually he nudges me awake before he goes on a run with Lo or to the gym early, so I know he was expecting to return to my bedroom.

"It's okay," I say, eyeing his wet hair again. "Did you take a shower?"

"I ran out of clean clothes in your room, so I went upstairs to my apartment." He shakes his head. "I took a shower up there. I thought I had time." He pauses. "Are you sure you can handle being in Paris alone for an entire fucking month?"

"I don't know…but I have to try. I don't want to be afraid at night anymore." I sit up a little straighter. "It'll be different," I tell him. "There'll be less paparazzi in France, less cameras, and none of my old friends will be there."

"I fucking hope you're right."

Me too.

After a couple minutes, finally catching my breath, Ryke slides me off his lap and gently leans me against the headboard. He climbs off the bed and snatches the handgun. I watch his fingers move quickly, checking the safety and ammunition in skilled routine. Then he bends down and opens the cupboard to his end table, revealing a safe. He types in a code, and the heavy metal door opens.

I really want him to leave the gun out, but I don't want to sound that frightened, so I let him lock the handgun out of sight. I stand and search my room for clean clothes. Shower. Energy drink. Check flight departure. Call my sisters to say goodbye. Have Mikey take me to the airport. Then I'm gone.

I can do this.

❀ ❀ ❀

I HATE THAT MY panties were wet. The only time I've *ever* orgasmed has been in my sleep. My *sleep*. And I remember nada. Not one little itty bitty moment. It's cruel.

At least the shower rejuvenated me. I feel like a new person, or at least, the kind of person I like to be. Fearless, ready for any new adventure. I draw open the blinds, sunlight streaming in, no longer dark and dreary in my room. After double-fisting two energy drinks, I'm wired enough to do anything and everything.

Ryke hands me another lime-flavored Lightning Bolt! after I asked for it. "Last one," he tells me. "Let's see if you can fucking beat me, Calloway." He sits at the edge of my bed beside me. These energy drinks are made by Fizzle, my dad's billion-dollar soda company, so it's my booster of choice.

"One," I say. "Two…" The lip of his can nears his mouth, as does mine. "Three." We both chug at the same time. The carbonated liquid slides down my throat, and from the corner of my eye, I watch Ryke's Adam's apple bob twice before he waves his empty can in victory.

Three seconds later, I finish my own.

"You're too fucking slow for me," he says.

"Is that a Ryke Meadows test?" I ask. "You only like the ones who can swallow quickly?" I break into a grin, and his brows rise.

"What do you know about swallowing?"

I shrug. "I know I don't mind it."

His muscles flex, and he drops his gaze from mine. He crushes his can in his hand and then tosses it into a faraway trash bin by my dresser. It lands perfectly. I sense the switch in his lighthearted demeanor, serious all of a sudden.

I crossed a line, maybe. *Good job, Daisy.* I try to recover by adding, "We don't have to talk about swallowing." *Shut up.* I bolt from the bed, preoccupying myself with cleaning. I start picking up sweaters and jeans and jackets from chairs and the floor, stuffing them back in drawers.

Ryke stays seated on the edge of my bed, his forearms on his knees, his hands clasped together as he hunches a little. His eyes fix on the ground in thought. "Can we talk?"

This isn't good. *Can we talk* never leads to righteous places. Before he speaks, I blurt out, "You don't have to do the whole awkward goodbye thing. We'll see each other again." I'll only be in Paris for a month. I'm not losing him as a friend. Right?

"I think we should both start dating again," he suddenly says.

I move a little faster, collecting a pile of clothes and trying to shove them into a drawer at the same time. *I think we should both start dating again.* What did I expect to happen? This wasn't going to end with us holding hands. He's just here to help me get on my feet. Still, we haven't expressed an interest in dating other people for four months. It's been just us, criticizing our previous relationships, no matter how brief or how long.

"Stop fucking moving for a second," he says roughly.

I slow down and concentrate on folding a sweater with block letters that reads: *Forever Young.* "If that's what you want." I shrug. "I can start dating again, I guess."

He runs his hand through his hair. "You can be single. I'm not saying that you have to get a boyfriend. I just…" he trails off in thought, and his jaw locks tight.

"No, I get it," I say with a nod. "We both used to date a lot, and you've stopped because of me. It's not fair to you." All because I've been an emotional train wreck at night. Now that he has a month apart from me—no longer sleeping in my bed—it makes sense that he'd want to have sex. He finally has the chance to do it.

"I'm going to be fucking honest with you," he says. I lean against the dresser and meet his dark gaze. "I'm not used to abstaining from sex for this long, and I think it's in both of our best interests if we start opening ourselves up to other people again."

His words shouldn't hurt me that much, but they feel like sharp knives sliding into my belly. "So I should find a number seven then?" I ask him. "Maybe he'll last longer than five minutes." I try to put on a smile, but it disappears pretty quickly.

I can't tell what Ryke is thinking. His features are hard as a rock. Brooding like normal. He stands up and takes a couple steps towards me.

I eye the ridges in his abs and the complex tattoo on his shoulder. I shouldn't suggest it—I shouldn't say it, but it leaves my lips before I can take back the words, "You could be my number seven."

"Daisy…" He shoots me a look.

My stomach twists. "You're really okay with me fucking another guy?" I imagine him with someone else, and it makes me physically ill. I don't want him to date another girl, and I know it's wrong of me to feel that way, but how do I change these emotions? How do I let them go? Maybe he's right. Maybe we do have to date other people to get over *this*.

"It doesn't matter what I fucking feel," he says. "I'm seven years older than you."

"You *just* turned twenty-five a week and a half ago." He has literally only been seven years older for four months. But once my birthday arrives in February, he's going to be all, *I'm six years older than you* with the same *I'm a fucking man and you're a little girl* tone that he likes to put on when he's making a point.

"I'm still seven fucking years older than you right now."

"Really? I should file a complaint to the woman who made me seven years younger than you. What a horrible, horrible thing."

He almost smiles.

"You know," I tell him, more serious, "I started modeling when I was fourteen, and right when I entered the industry, no one ever treated me like I was a teenager. I was doing things that people in their twenties would do."

I feel like I've already been to college, partying, drinking too much, experimenting, and I'm only eighteen. It's one reason why I don't want to go to a university. I had my fill when I was fifteen, sixteen and seventeen. And I can't picture myself sitting behind a desk all day either.

"I hear you," he says. "I do, but disregard our ages completely— you're still my brother's girlfriend's little sister. And there's no changing that."

I set the sweater on top of the dresser. When I look up, he's beside me. "So what happens when we're both back in Philly a month from now?" I ask. "Do we just pick up where we left off or are we going our separate ways from here on out?"

He rests an elbow on the dresser. "I don't want to lead you on, Dais. We can't fucking happen. I'm just here to help you until you can sleep better."

Maybe I should stop torturing myself then and just try to move on too. "I can find someone in Paris, and if not, I'll just fly solo. I've done that a lot. Maybe I'll make a lasting friend from New York," I say. "I can move out there when I come back, and I'll start over—"

"You would move out to New York?" He frowns.

"I don't know…maybe," I say softly.

He abruptly reaches out and draws me to his chest. He's hugging *me*. Willingly. But this feels more like a goodbye than anything else. A pain ripples through my body.

And then that cracked door to my bedroom—it whips open.

I turn my head with Ryke, and we both see my mother standing at the threshold of the doorway with her phone in hand. Her eyes grow to saucers, horrified at the sight of my embrace with a guy she finds unworthy of my time and affection.

Ryke and I slowly break apart, but he doesn't look guilty, only angry at her appearance.

"What is this?" my mom asks sharply.

"Ryke came over to say goodbye," I tell her, trying to shrug off the tension that builds with her presence. "I'm all packed, so Mikey should be here in a bit." I didn't think she'd stop by. I hugged my mom and dad yesterday at their house.

My mom scrutinizes Ryke's bare chest. "Why is your shirt off?" she snaps.

"Because I took it off," he says with narrowed eyes. He finds his T-shirt on my comforter and he pulls it over his head. But he makes no attempt to leave me alone with my mom, too worried about me to do so.

My mom walks over to my bed in her high heels. She fingers the pearls at her neck as she inspects the sheets, twisted like two people possibly fucked beneath them.

"I'm a bad sleeper," I tell her truthfully, but it sounds like such a lie. "I've been tossing and turning at night."

She ignores me, and her eyes set right on Ryke again. "If I *ever* find out that you're with my daughter, I will personally look into your past history, and if you've had sex with her when she was underage, you'll be in court so fast. Do you know what statutory rape is?"

Ryke has an irritated expression like *no, I'm a fucking idiot.*

"Mom," I interject. "He didn't do anything."

Ryke doesn't break my mother's gaze. "You want to act like it's a fucking age thing, that's fine, Samantha. Go ahead and do that. I don't give a fuck what you think of me."

She inhales drastically, the bones in her neck protruding. "I've *never* been around someone so disrespectful in my life." She purses her lips. "What did your mother teach you?"

"How to hate my father," he says without missing a beat. "How to hate my half-brother. Those didn't really come in handy, did they?"

My mom falters at that response.

"You think I'm the very fucking extension of my mom," he continues, "but I haven't spoken to Sara in over a year." And still, he can't shake the association. It's genetically written all over him.

"What about your father?" she retorts. "Jonathan would love to talk to you, but you've ignored *every* phone call, every text—"

"He really told you that?"

She touches her pearls again. "He told my husband, and my husband told me." I can see that happening. My dad is best friends with Jonathan after all.

"I'm not on speaking terms with my fucking father either. Let's leave it at that."

My mom lets out a vexed half-laugh. "He's going through the hardest time in his life with these accusations against him. Do you know what your word would mean to the press?" Jonathan was accused of abusing Lo, and Ryke hasn't brought it up to me at all. I'm not even sure if it's true or not. Out of our group of six, I'm the last to receive any info, the little dot on the outside of the inner circle.

"You need to fucking stop," Ryke says, truly getting pissed now. "Stay out of it."

"All you have to do is tell the press that it's a *lie*," she says. "Jonathan's name will be cleared—"

"You want me to protect that son of a bitch?" Ryke curses, his eyes blazing. "I'm *done* trying to wipe his reputation clean. He fucked it a long time ago, and it's not my job to make sure he comes across as a fucking angel to the press."

"What about Lo?" my mom asks. "He's hurting from this lie just as much as Jonathan." She lets out another hysteric laugh. "You're just like your mother, willing to take down *everyone* in your wake just to hurt Jonathan. When are you going to stop?"

Ryke looks like he's been slapped. It takes him a moment to collect himself. When he speaks, his voice is leveled and colder than usual. "I'm not actively trying to destroy my father. I'm trying to move on, and I want my brother to do the same. You want me to go defend Jonathan, but I fucking can't. I won't defend someone who may be guilty."

"He's *not* guilty."

"I don't *fucking* know that!" Ryke yells.

My mom scoffs. "You think that lowly of him? That he could do something that heinous to your own brother?"

"I've seen him grab Lo's fucking neck with pure malice," Ryke retorts. "He used to call me a pussy, and I won national track competitions, so can you even imagine what he called Lo, a kid who had *nothing* going for him?"

My mom's lips tighten even more, like she sucked a lemon. Her cheeks have reddened. "He's a better man than you realize. We're not all perfect." Before Ryke can say something more, she spins to me and says, "I came here to talk to you, not to have an argument with Sara's son."

Sara's son. That's what she thinks of him first and foremost. It's so stupid.

"Is it important?" I ask.

She nods. "I've talked to your agency, and they've booked multiple go-sees for you after Fashion Week, as well as a couple campaigns and ads while you're in Paris."

My heart beats crazily, and her words jumble together. It takes me a minute to sort through them. "Wait, I'm working after Fashion Week? But I thought…"

Her phone buzzes. She glances at the screen. "It's foolish to waste three extra weeks in France." She types a message. "You need to capitalize on the time you have there."

My free time.

I feel it slipping between my fingers. I feel the exhaustion pummeling me tenfold. I needed a break. I haven't had one in months. I dreamed of that leisure time in a beautiful country. This was supposed to be it. Glorified independence with a cherry on top.

I feel like she stuck my ice cream sundae under hot water.

But maybe I didn't deserve the sundae in the first place. I'm going to Paris, staying in a gorgeous hotel. Does it matter that I have to work? I'm being paid more a day than most people make in a year, and all I do is walk down a runway and pose.

Be grateful. I'm trying. I really am. But this sadness just pours into me no matter how much I want to smile and say *okay, thank you for the opportunity.*

"Daisy," Ryke says, coming to my side. He gives me a look like *speak the fuck up.*

"Mom," I call.

She's busy texting.

"Can we reschedule the go-sees? I'll meet with designers some other time. I just want a couple weeks to myself in Paris."

"You've already been booked. If you cancel, it'll look badly on you, and then other designers will hear about it." She pockets her phone in her clutch. "The month will go by before you know it, and then you'll be back home to do more American spreads." She kisses my cheeks. "Have a safe flight. Text me when you land." She checks her watch. "I'm late for a brunch with Olivia Barnes." She glares at Ryke as if he's the cause of her tardiness.

She leaves.

I don't stop her.

When the door shuts, my heart beats so fast, my lungs constricting, this pressure just mounting and mounting. I need to release it. I need to *breathe.* I look around my room, trying to find an escape.

"Daisy. Daisy, fucking stop for a second," Ryke says.

I grab my motorcycle keys out of a jacket pocket. "I'm going to go for a quick ride." Just as I pass him, he grips my wrist and pries the keys out of my palm. "Ryke—"

"You can't drive when you're like this. The last fucking time you did that, you almost highsided on the freeway."

I remember. I was really, really close to flying over the handlebars of my bike. I applied too much throttle around a curve. I've never seen Ryke so scared before, but when we met in a parking lot, he looked like he wanted to simultaneously hug me for being alive and kill me for almost making a fatal mistake.

I blow out a deep breath from my lips. "I really need some air."

"Run with me for half an hour," he says. "You'll feel better."

"How so?"

He draws me closer, my feet touching the sides of his. "You'll be able to fucking breathe." He studies my face quickly. "Or you could just cry and let it out for once."

My whole body hurts, and those words somehow pain me more. "What?"

"*Let it out.*"

I shake my head. "I can't."

"Why the fuck not? Stop trying to suppress your emotions, Dais. It's okay to be upset right now. What your mom just did was shit."

I shake my head again. *Who am I to complain?* I don't want to be that immature, selfish girl. I don't want to be what people probably think of me, the heiress of a billion-dollar fortune. Bitching over not going to Paris for fun anymore. How does that look?

"You have gone through hell since Lily's sex addiction went public, and you've told fucking no one about it but me. Stop trying to be strong. Just fucking cry, Daisy. Scream. Yell. Be fucking angry."

Everything crashes into me. Stresses that I don't like to confront. I'm not even ready to bear all of it right now. "Can we run?" I ask. "I'll race you down the street."

His features turn grave, but he nods. "Yeah. Get your shoes on—"

My phone rings, cutting him off. I look at the Caller ID. "It's Mikey. I guess..." *I have to go.* I meet Ryke's gaze, and he just shakes his head.

"I don't want to fucking leave you like this," he says.

"I'll be fine."

"Are you going to be able to last the whole flight, sitting in your fucking seat, not able to get up and move around that much?"

It sounds more confining now than it did a couple hours ago, only because my mom suffocated me with this news. "I don't have much of a choice."

"We all have choices," he says. "Some are just harder to make than others."

"Don't worry about me," I tell him. "I want you to go to California and climb those mountains." I pause. "And be safe." He can die out there. With no rope, no backup safety, he's relying only on his training, his hands and body. One wrong move and he can slip and fall. He doesn't talk about the risk that much, and I don't want to dissuade him from pursuing the three-mountain, free-solo climb in Yosemite. It's been his lifelong goal, and I won't keep him from that.

"You too," he says, his voice low and strained.

This is the part where we should hug again, but so many unresolved issues linger, things that my mom dumped and deserted.

We don't touch.

We don't say another word.

We just leave each other with a maybe—a sort of acceptance to move on. I can already see myself on that plane, visualizing him with another girl. Everything about this trip to Paris sucks, but I won't screw over a handful of designers just to come back to Philly.

I can't.

< **10** >

Ryke Meadows

Daisy is gone. With the time difference, I haven't even had the chance to talk to her. She's too busy to fucking call at a decent hour, and so I have no idea if she's sleeping or if she's been awake for two days straight. I can't stop thinking about the last look on her face—the one of pure devastation. Like someone physically ripped out an organ from her body. I've seen that expression before, and it only comes when she feels trapped.

I just have to trust that she's fine.

And I try to ignore the fact that I gave her permission to fuck other guys. I hated that, and even knowing that she may be hooking up with someone right now—it boils my blood. But I can't stomach screwing girls here while she waits for me either. Because she'll be waiting forever, and it's not fucking fair to her.

My brother lies on a weight bench, and I spot him. The gym is almost empty this early in the morning, the weight room desolate besides my brother, Connor and me. We always meet at 6 a.m. to avoid the paparazzi.

"How's Lily?" I ask, my eyes flickering over to Connor as he does leg presses while watching Bloomberg on the flat screen television overhead.

"Fine," Lo says, lifting the heavy bar off his chest with a grunt. I grab it from him and set it in the holder. He sits up, wiping his forehead with a towel. "How's not babysitting?"

"I wasn't babysitting Daisy." Since her going away party, I've been on the same rocky fucking road with my brother whenever her name is mentioned. It's not different. It's the fucking same shit over and over again. I'm used to it by now.

Lo stares at the towel in his hands. "I still don't understand how you're friends with her. Like…what do you talk about?"

He's fishing. "We're not fucking each other."

Lo glares. "I didn't say you were, but now I'm thinking it."

I roll my eyes. Maybe I'm overanalyzing everything. I don't fucking know anymore. "We talk about normal things. Motorcycles, sports…" *sleep, medication, siblings, parents.* "…food."

"She looked really thin at her going away party," Connor says, off his machine and heading towards us. He grabs his water out of his gym bag. "Rose fought with Samantha about it over the phone for an hour."

I pop one of my knuckles. "Her mom is putting too much fucking pressure on her to maintain that weight."

"Maybe she'll gain some while she's in Paris," Lo says, more optimistic than he usually is. I think he's just happy she's not around me.

I nod to Connor. "Hey princess, you want to compete at chin-ups?" Lo fucking hates doing them, so he can watch and count.

"I don't know," Connor says with a casual tone. "Will you cry when I beat you? If so, then yes."

"Just get your ass to the pull-up bar."

Lo stretches his arms. "Hey, don't talk about his ass like that."

"You're making my first love jealous," Connor banters, heading to the bar with me.

I've become used to their flirty fucking banter. They're best friends. They've lived together for almost two years. They have a much better relationship with each other than I do with either of them individually. Am I fucking jealous? Maybe a little.

"You two are so fucking cute," I say, grasping the bar underhand. I cross my ankles, and Connor does the same on the bar next to me.

"Ready?" Lo says, standing back to judge. "Go."

I pull myself up, my collarbones in line with the bar, and then I lower my body back to the starting position. *One.* I breathe out. *Two.* My muscles burn, but I'm nowhere near fatigued or strained. *Three.*

I keep counting in my head, Connor easily staying at the same pace as me. He's in really good fucking shape. I didn't even realize it when I first met him since he's always in preppy clothes or suits and button-downs. But he's kept his body healthy and at a physical peak like me.

Lo's mind must be wandering because he says, "I'm thinking about going to rehab again."

Ten. I falter a little, my muscles constricting in tight bands. I frown as I pull my body back up. "You don't have to decide this now," I say in a single breath.

Connor is more concentrated on the fucking challenge, so I think he's lapped me by two chin-ups.

"It helped me before," Lo admits. "I stayed sober for a long time, and Lily's in a good place. She'll be okay without me."

But it's different now. Back then, he wasn't famous. No one knew his name. Lily's sex addiction hadn't been publicized. He was just a rich kid from Philly.

"Do you think it's the right move?" Lo asks.

Fifteen. I usually can do twenty-two, but a nervous sweat drips down my forehead, and my arms go slack at sixteen chin-ups. I drop my feet to the ground. "I don't know," I say, undoing the Velcro on my gloves. I slip them off my hands.

Connor does his final chin-up, barely breaking a sweat. "Twenty-three," he exclaims, a smile behind the words. He knows he beat me. I smack his chest, hoping he'd flinch from the playful attack, but he flexes instead, and I hit muscle.

"Fuck you," I tell him easily.

He grins. "You love me."

"You say that to everyone," I tell him. "And I highly fucking doubt the entire world loves you, Cobalt."

"The entire world doesn't have to love me," he says, picking up his water again. "Only the ones that matter."

"That's cute. Did you write that in your diary this morning?"

"No, I read it from yours," he banters.

I flip him off, and then Connor turns his attention on my brother, never really forgetting what we were talking about. "When were you thinking of leaving for rehab?"

Lo shrugs. "Maybe this week since Ryke is going to California. It just seemed like a good time."

A lump lodges in my fucking throat. It's not a good time. I want to be around him while he's in rehab. I don't like knowing that he'll be separated for that long from Lily, from me and Connor, from the ones that truly love him. Last time he went to rehab, I was there. I went to meetings with him. And I'm honestly not fucking sure he can handle the criticism of the media, focusing on his stint in rehab. I worry that'll send him over the edge too.

Connor nods. "I personally think it's a good idea."

Lo's shoulders lift at that, taking Connor's opinion with high regard. And then his eyes meet mine. "What about you?"

He can't go to rehab. "I want you to come with me," I say.

He frowns with a glare. It's his normal fucking look, so I don't take offense to how hostile he appears. I don't know why I ever thought this kid had friends in prep school. He'd more likely chew them up and spit them out. "What?" he says with edge.

"To California," I tell him. "Fuck rehab, I'll make sure you don't drink. It'll be a road trip out west. You and me."

"The wind in your hair," Connor adds, smiling as he sips his water.

"Shut the fuck up," I say lightly.

Lo's face sharpens as he thinks about this. He glances at Connor, then at me before he says, "If I go with you, I think Connor should come too."

I glare because I can feel Connor gloating beside me. "Why?"

"*Why?*" Connor says like it's the stupidest question ever. I feel like he's about to say *Because I'm me.*

I have to stop him before I choke on his fucking arrogance. "Seriously," I say to Lo. "He has a wife that'll castrate you if you bring him back broken. What if he chips a nail?"

"Then I'll get a manicure," Connor quips. "There are solutions to everything. You just have to *think* to find them. Such hard work."

"Are we fucking friends?" I ask Connor, glowering. Lo just watches in slight amusement, but really, I think he's processing my proposal.

"I'm not sure what a 'fucking' friend is, so I can't answer you."

"Look at that, I know something that Connor Cobalt doesn't."

"When it comes to slang, made up words, and the best fire hydrants to piss on, yes, you do."

"Fuck you."

"You keep saying it, but you still haven't done it." His lips curve upward.

Lo cuts us off, "If you're both going to be this annoying the whole trip, then I'm choosing rehab."

"So you're coming with me?" I ask, internally letting out a deep fucking breath. I feel like I helped him dodge a bullet, and I'm waiting for the gun to reload.

"Yeah, but like I said, only if Connor comes. No offense, Ryke, but I'm afraid we're going to kill each other if we're together for that long." If we bring up our family issues, we just may.

Connor's a big peacemaker in our circle of friends. He may like to irritate me on purpose, but when everyone starts fighting, he's the one who calms people down. So I can understand Lo wanting him to come along.

"Fine with me," I tell him.

My phone buzzes in my shorts. I think it's Daisy. 1 p.m. in Paris. I check the message.

> I'd like to see you before you go kill yourself on a goddamn mountain. — Dad

I glare and delete the message.

"Who was that?" Lo asks. "You look pissed."

"My mom," I lie. Although, she did text me five times last night. I never answer her, even though it's the same plea:

> Come see me. I'm sorry. Ryke, please. I need to see you. I love you. — Mom

I'll always love my mom because she's my mother. But I can't ever forgive her for what she's done to me, to Lily, to the Calloway girls, my brother and inadvertently Connor.

She read my personal texts to Lo, where we talked about Lily's sex addiction. And she sold the information to the media with the headline: DAUGHTER OF FIZZLE CREATOR AND CEO IS CONFIRMED SEX ADDICT. Selling Lily out wasn't just for money. It was to hurt Lo, and that way, she'd hurt Jonathan.

But she also fucking hurt me.

Now, all six of us are famous because of Sara Hale.

Thanks Mom.

< 11 >

Ryke Meadows

Emergency! SOS! – Lily

I eat one bite of my fucking sub at Lucky's before Lily sends me an SOS. It seems too comical to be serious. I set the sub on the wrapper, tomatoes and lettuce falling from the bread. "Did you guys get a text from Lily?" I ask Connor and Lo across from me.

Lo freezes, clutching his Fizz Life can. "No, what does she want?"

It's unusual for Lily to text me before Lo. "I don't know yet."

I text back: What's wrong?

Connor scrolls through his phone, more agitation passing across his features than I think he'd want to show.

"Your shipment of handcuffs not come in, sweetheart?" I ask him before picking my sub back up in two hands.

"Hoping I'll cuff you to my bed?" he banters, his face returning to that impassive, unreadable state. "I'd make good on your fantasies, but Rose would be pissed at the claw marks on the headboard."

"Now I have claws?" I say with raised eyebrows.

He combats me by arching *one*. That fucker. "You're lucky, I don't usually let dogs sleep in my bed, but I'm willing to make an exception."

I flip him off, and Lo's leg bounces nervously beneath the table. He holds his hand up at me like *what the fuck?* "What's going on with my girlfriend?"

Right on time, Lily calls me. I answer, and before I even ask, she explains. "Rose got a flat tire, and she refuses to call a tow truck."

"I can fix it myself." Rose's icy voice bleeds through the speaker. She grunts a little, as though trying to lift the fucking spare tire.

"She's in five-inch heels," Lily notes. "I am impressed. I really am, but it'd be even more impressive if she knew what she was doing."

"I can read," Rose says. "I have the manual right here. I don't need a man to show me how to fix a fucking tire."

I scratch my jaw. Both Connor and Lo are glaring the hell out of me, hearing bits and pieces of both the girls' voices without understanding what's going on. I think Cobalt may snatch the fucking phone from my hand.

Off my gaze, he says, "Rose isn't answering my texts." That's where his agitation stemmed from—he can sense when things aren't right better than anyone.

"You want me to come out there?" I ask Lily. I'm going to anyway, but I figured that's why she called. I motion to Lo to ask for the bill. Guess I'll have to take my sub to-go. He flags down the waitress.

"Just in case Rose can't fix it," Lily says

"Doesn't she have a husband for these situations?" Even though Connor wears suits and rides around in a limo, I'm fairly certain he's smart enough to fix a fucking tire.

"She doesn't want him to rub this in her face."

I roll my eyes again.

"I can do this better than him," Rose insists in the background. "I don't need his help."

Lily sighs. "I'm afraid she's going to take an hour and then strangers are going to stop and try to help."

"That's why I handed you the pepper spray," Rose tells her. She lets out an irritated scream. "Why is this so fucking heavy?"

"Maybe because it's a fucking tire," I deadpan.

Lily says, "You're lucky she can't hear you." So I'm not on speaker then. She must turn to Rose because she adds, "And I'm not pepper spraying a nice person who tries to help us."

"You would if they tried to rape you," Rose retorts.

They're so fucking dramatic. "No one is going to rape the two of you."

Just like that, both Connor and Lo reach over the table to try and steal the phone from my hand. I hold it high above my head and lean further back.

"*Bro*," Lo sneers, "I'm not messing around. Let me talk to her."

"Is that Lo?" Lily says. "You have to come alone, Ryke. Lo will bicker with Rose and cause more problems. She's already in a bad mood." Anxiety pitches her voice, and I imagine her nervously biting her nails.

"I'll come help you. Just text me the address," I tell Lily before I hang up. Lo's eyes flash murderously at me, and even Connor looks pissed. Rose has been putting a serious fucking wall up between them lately. But they have a strange relationship already, filled with mind games that I can't keep up with.

"The girls have a flat tire," I explain. "Lily said Rose didn't want you there." I nod to Connor. "And since you get on Rose's last fucking nerve…" I nod to Lo. "She doesn't want you there either." I stand and open my wallet, throwing a hundred dollar bill down. "I'll drive."

There's no way I wouldn't bring Connor and Lo with me.

That's his wife and his fiancée.

I'm just the manual fucking labor.

WHEN WE ARRIVE, ROSE is crouched down beside the back right tire, the treads unraveled and the rubber flat, like they popped it somehow. She inspects the tire from a distance, careful not to grease her hands. Not because she's a fucking girl but because Rose is OCD. She freaks when a layer of dirt crusts beneath her nails.

She's also treating her black dress like it's a living creature she hopes to protect. That's not entirely right. If she had to pick between nurturing a stranded cat or saving a purse from the rain, she'd choose the fucking purse. She rests her ass on her ankles, supported by heels, very aware not to touch the ground and ruin her clothes.

I park the car behind her Escalade. The back road is quiet, no houses around, just one lane towards a hill, trees and grass. Lo climbs out first, heading towards Lily who unsurprisingly bites her nails and flips through an instruction manual, a canister of pepper spray in her back pocket.

The minute she sees him, her whole body lifts, and my brother—he wears a smile that's rare in anyone else's presence but hers. I've never really seen love until I saw them together, truly.

They kiss, and I go to help Rose just as Connor shuts his car door.

Lo has to say something. "This is the progress you made?" he asks Rose. "I thought you were supposed to be Wonder Woman."

She huffs, her cheeks reddening with anger. "Not now, Loren."

"How many geniuses does it take to change a tire?" Lo taunts with a smile. Lily punches him in the shoulder, and he mock winces. He rubs his arm. "That hurt, love."

"Be nice."

He kisses her temple. "I'm just happy you're okay."

This causes her to smile again. It's cute. All of it. But it's also annoying the hell out of me because I think of Daisy. Normally she'd be here too. Normally she'd be standing over my shoulder, peering at the car and helping me out.

Instead, I know I'm going to have to jack the Escalade by my fucking self and put in the spare. The couples are paired off, and I'm left alone this time.

Maybe a year ago, I would have been used to being the fifth wheel.

Not anymore.

Now it's frustrating.

I don't take Rose away from inspecting the underbelly of the car from afar. I let Connor do that.

He towers over her, six-foot-four, his hands in his pockets. "If you're trying to prove a point that you're better than me, you do realize that I wouldn't have tried to change the tire myself," he tells her. "I would have been smart enough to call a tow truck."

She shoots him a withering glare. "Don't make this about you, Richard."

"You made it about me the moment you didn't want me here." He grabs her wrist and pulls her to her feet with strong force.

She straightens out her dress, fire still in her eyes. I bend down and start working on replacing the flat, but they're close enough that I hear their whole conversation.

"What are you scared of?" Connor asks her with a frown.

"Je n'ai pas peur," Rose replies in fluent French. I translate easily: *I'm not scared.*

I act like I can't understand them. They think I'm just as clueless about the foreign language as Lily and Lo, but I've been fluent since I was a little kid. I just don't feel like explaining why I know French to anyone.

It's easier to ignore it.

"Alors, dites-moi ce qui ne va pas," he says. *Then tell me what's wrong.*

Rose jerks her hand away from him and raises her chin. "I wanted to do it myself."

"It's more than that," he says. "You and I both know this isn't about a tire. You've been shutting me out for weeks."

"If you're so smart, shouldn't you be able to figure out why?" She crosses her arms in challenge.

His eyes narrow. "Ne jouez pas ce jeu avec moi, chérie. Vous perdrez." *Don't play this game with me, darling. You will lose.*

I glance over my shoulder, and Rose looks a little nervous, inhaling a sharp breath. She is scared. But like Connor, I just have no fucking clue what it's about.

"Hey," I call to Rose. She looks at me and the tire like I'm not moving fast enough. I restrain the urge to flip her off. "Where were you and Lily going anyway?"

"Shopping," Rose says, way too fast.

I know a fucking lie when I hear it. "Glad I fucking asked." I shake my head and grab the spare tire.

Connor studies Rose's features, realizing she's not being honest either.

Rose says, "You knew what you were getting into when you married me."

"A lifetime of challenges." His lips rise. "Il n'y a rien de mieux." *There is nothing better.*

She almost softens at his words. He strokes her glossy hair and then kisses her forehead. Before I attach the spare, I spot Lo and Lily by my Infinity.

He has her pinned against the car. They aren't kissing, but he whispers in her ear with a smile that dimples his sharp cheeks. She's a giant fucking red tomato, so whatever he's telling her—it's dirty. I've never seen sex embarrass someone as much as it does Lily—and I know it's because she's an addict, more ashamed. But she's clearly turned on by my brother, giving him big bedroom eyes.

I shake my head.

I feel like the only normal one.

But that's a load of crap. None of us are really normal. We're all just strange pieces in the world. And the half that usually connects with me is thousands of miles away, in Paris.

I just hope she's sleeping.

If I picture her in a peaceful fucking slumber, I stop worrying. It's the only thing keeping me grounded, keeping me right fucking here. Without that image, I'd lose my shit.

< 12 >

Daisy Calloway

4:30 a.m.

Since I arrived in Paris three days ago, I've slept five hours, and I'm not really sure if it can be considered sleep. I woke up screaming and thrashing at an "invisible enemy" as Ryke calls it. I can barely even remember what was grabbing me in my nightmare, but that kind of sleep is something I don't want to return to.

Right now I am pumped full of caffeinated drinks and diet pills. I used to smoke cigarettes, the nicotine high fairly decent to keep me awake during long shoots. But when Ryke started teaching me how to ride a motorcycle, he convinced me to stop smoking. I haven't touched a cigarette since. I don't crave the nicotine at all. I just ache for sleep or at least a shot of adrenaline.

On the runway yesterday, I literally thought I was floating across the glassy surface in five-inch heels. I wore a peacock headpiece. I was *so* close to flapping my arms, and in my mind, I had already raced off the stage, down the street and jumped into an ice cold lake. I have no idea why that sounds so appealing, but it does. Anything but standing around, waiting. Sitting in chairs, waiting. So much waiting. I can't decide if I'm more bored or more tired.

I cup a steaming coffee while a stylist pulls every small strand of my hair into a braid. I look like Medusa or possibly a dreaded girl on Venice Beach. I'd think it was cool if it didn't take so long. I shift so much in the seat that the stylist threatens to take my coffee away.

This job would suit a million other people better than it does me.

People buzz around us, constantly moving, but it's usually not the models who are doing the buzzing. It's production assistants wearing microphone headsets, holding clipboards, and makeup artists and designers. I am stationary. Basically no more human than an article of clothing that a PA carries on a hanger.

A brunette model with a splattering of freckles across her cheeks sits in a makeup chair next to me. She's getting the same braid treatment. I met her about a month ago when she signed with Revolution Modeling, Inc. The same agency as mine. Our hotel rooms are across from each other. Christina is only fifteen and thin as a rail. She reminds me a little of how I was when I first began my career. Quiet, reserved, observant—just taking it all in.

She lets out her fourth big yawn.

"Here," I say, passing her my coffee.

"Thanks." She smiles. "My parents don't usually let me drink caffeine, but I don't think they'd mind if they saw how much I'm working."

"They didn't come?" I frown. My mom always supervised my time at Fashion Week. At first, I thought it was because she was protecting me, but later, I wondered if it was because she wanted to be a part of this world and was afraid of missing out. Now that seems more likely.

"No. They couldn't afford to fly here."

She's from Kansas, and she said it almost bankrupt her parents just to go to New York at the chance of landing an agent. Now she's the sole breadwinner for her family. I can't imagine that, and I think having Christina around has humbled me a little more.

"If someone offers you coke," I tell her, "I'd just say no, okay?"

Her eyes grow as she looks between both of our stylists, who don't even flinch, and then back to me. Cocaine is a lot of people's upper of choice. When I was fifteen, I tried it during Fashion Week. A guy shook a little plastic packet at me and said, "This'll help you stay awake."

Two lines later, I'd officially jumped into the deep end of adulthood—or what felt like grown up experiences.

Christina realizes that no one really cares that I admitted to cocaine circulating around, and she nods. "Yeah, okay."

I lean back in the chair as soon as a makeup artist decides to work on me. I'm getting double duty, two stylists at once. She pinches my chin to turn my head towards her, and she stares disapprovingly at the bags underneath my eyes.

My stomach makes an audible noise, gurgling. The stylist hands me a granola bar.

"Just eat a couple bites," she says. "You can throw it up later."

"I'm not into the whole bulimic thing," I say. "Or the anorexic thing." I sense the makeup artist listening a little too closely. Sometimes I forget that they can sell anything I say to a gossip magazine. They'll be identified as an "inside source" when they're quoted. "Thanks for the bar," I tell her. I'll taste it. I'm too hungry not to.

My body is already slowly eating itself. It's the main reason why I want to quit modeling. My health has been tanking from the sleep stuff—add this and I know I may do some damage.

I chew on the gritty bar that tastes more like tree bark than peanut butter and almonds. Christina is finished before me since she has less hair to braid. I'm going to be here for another two hours, I swear. At least the makeup artist has joined the other girl in the braiding. I tried to do a strand by my face, but the stylist slapped my hand away.

The chair fills quickly beside me. A male model slouches down, holding a whole bowl of fruit. He notices the granola bar in my hand. "Where'd you get that?" he asks enviously.

"The tree people," I tell him, taking another bite and passing him the granola. "What's wrong with the fruit?"

He bites the bar and sinks back in his chair like he's in food heaven. It makes me smile, one of the first times I've done so since arriving in Paris.

"Carbs," he says, answering my question. "Craft service only has fruit and raw vegetables." He takes a swig from his water bottle. "They told us we can eat whatever we want, but either all the waifs scarfed down the crackers and sandwiches or someone tricked me."

"They don't want anyone to overeat," I say. "Some years the selection is better."

"Last year," he says with a nod. "Last year was better. They had muffins."

I groan. "Don't talk about muffins."

"Blueberry *and* banana nut."

"You are a cruel, cruel person…" I trail off and get a good look at him, realizing I've never met this model before.

"Ian," he says, taking another bite of my bar. He has muscles, not a "waif" as he called the naturally skinny guys. His face is classically beautiful like a Greek statue. I've seen him in a cologne ad, I think. He holds out the granola to me.

"You finish it," I say.

"I'll trade you." He raises the fruit. "It's no muffin, but…" He smiles. And of course, it's gorgeous, full white teeth, bright and welcoming.

I like this guy. He speaks my food language. "I'll take it." We swap. "I'm Daisy, by the way."

"I know. I think I sat on your face at a bus stop today."

I mock gasp. "You sat on my face? Impossible. I don't let strangers do that."

He laughs. A stylist sprays *blue* dye in his hair. Fashion designers are crazy. I should know, Rose is one. Though she didn't get invited here. She's still back in Philly.

"So," he says, "I'm six-two, blue eyes, brown hair, twenty-five…" He tilts his head towards me as his stylist pauses to reach for hair spray. "I can list off my measurements, but something tells me you won't care about the size of my chest." This reminds me of a similar conversation that I had with Ryke once upon a time. He was trying to convince me to eat cake.

"Your hips also don't have to be measured in the morning," I told him.

"They can be," Ryke said. "Will you eat the fucking cake if I measure my hips?"

"And your ass."

"You want to know the size of my ass?" His brows rose.

"Yep."

"Eat the cake."

I smile more out of remembrance from that moment than out of attraction towards Ian.

I shake my head at Ian. "Only your ass."

He grins. "I only give that to girls I really like."

"Damn," I say. A pit sinks to my stomach. We're flirting. I don't want to taint that memory I had with Ryke by continuing this banter with Ian. It's starting to make me a little nauseous. Maybe that's the fruit or the one bite of tree bark. *But this could be a good thing.* He could be my number seven. This is what Ryke wanted, right? *Stop hanging onto what could be, Daisy. Let Ryke and the past go.*

Ian wears an easygoing smile as he checks me out. "You want to meet up later?" he asks.

Maybe commenting on his ass was a bigger signal than I thought. Ryke never acted on the flirty nature of our conversations. Sometimes I forget that not everyone is like him. Most guys will prod further, not stop at a point. They want the sex. All of it. Not just the dirty talk. *Maybe this is a good thing.* It doesn't feel that way.

But I think about going back to my room late tonight after runways. The balcony doors don't have deadbolts, so it'd be really easy for someone to punch through the glass and just unlock the door from the inside. I couldn't sleep the first night because I kept glancing at that door. Maybe having Ian around will help me calm down…and maybe sex will help me sleep without Ambien. I haven't tried it before, but I also never wanted to medicate with sex.

I didn't want to have Lily's problem.

These new possibilities sound better than my current situation. So I give Ian my cell number. I also didn't want anyone to know my hotel room, but I don't think it'll hurt to just tell Ian.

I feel like there's no perfect choice here. There are a lot of negatives, a few positives, and so I just have to pick.

"Know where I can find these tree people?" he asks, waving an empty granola wrapper.

I smile. He's not too bad.

I think I just made my decision.

‹ 13 ›

Daisy Calloway

By the time I enter my room, the clock strikes 2 a.m., and I only have enough time to wash my face and run a brush through my hair before Ian knocks on the door.

I peek through the peephole, ensuring that it's just him. I can smell his strong cologne through the door, but he looks casual, wearing jeans and a blue tee. I keep staring, hesitating for so many reasons. He knocks again. I flinch at the violent noise. *You can do this.*

I turn the knob, and when Ian appraises my jean shorts and baggy sweater, he smiles. "Nice," he says, motioning to the words across my chest: *Bulimia's so '87.*

He even understands a *Heathers* reference. Maybe he is perfect for me. "Welcome to my abode." I wave him inside. I haven't unpacked, so I had no time to be messy. My rolling suitcase rests by the television hutch, all zipped up. The hotel room has gold walls and red bedspreads, looking cleaner and more harmonious with the colors than any part of my apartment in Philly.

"Nice room too," he says.

"Yeah, it's pretty cool."

He heads deeper inside, going to the balcony door that I've spent a great deal of time locking and shrouding with the gold curtains. He pulls them back, and my pulse speeds. I hear the *click* of the single lock, and then he slides open the glass door, stepping outside to see the view of the city.

"Holy shit," he says, his voice louder so I can hear. "My room overlooks a parking garage. This is…"

I tune him out as I shut the front door, using every lock to ensure my safety and his. I even look through the peephole one extra time. The hallway is empty. *Good.*

And then I walk to the bed, waiting for him to come back inside. I don't want to attract any paparazzi, if they're here. On the chance that they spot me from the balcony, they'll count the floor I'm on and figure out which room I'm in.

"Yeah, the view is really pretty," I say.

Ian slips back inside, but he leaves the sliding door all the way open.

"Can you close it?" I ask, trying not to seem paranoid. I give him a small smile. "It's kinda cold tonight."

"Sure." He shuts the door and then closes the curtains back. No lock. But I'll just have to do that after he leaves. *What if he doesn't leave? What if you have sex with him?* Then I'll lock it when he falls asleep. No worries.

I sit on the foot of the bed and cross my legs, wondering where his head is at, what he wants to do right now. He eyes me a little more hungrily than before. His gaze travels across my legs, stopping at the place between my thighs.

He stuffs his hand into his pocket. *Condom*, I think. But he pulls out a baggy of white powder. "I thought you looked tired this morning. Want a boost?" He heads over to my dresser and begins to separate the powder into two lines.

"No," I say. "I've been chugging Lightning Bolts! and taking Ripped Fuel. I don't think coke will mix well with them."

I uncross my legs and then stand up, pacing anxiously before I reach his side.

"Yeah, I could tell you were on something," he says. "You were fidgeting all morning."

"Ripped Fuel only makes me fidgety when I drink caffeine with it. Otherwise they're just normal diet pills." But they're like a shot of endorphins, possibly the biggest boost I can get without heading towards cocaine and other illegal substances.

"Well, I'll help calm you down," he says, one of his hands reaching out and rubbing my shoulders. That's exactly what I wanted. Despite the coke, maybe my choices in men are improving.

With his free hand, he takes his rolled dollar bill and snorts both lines. He wipes his nose, and then when he turns to me, his glazed eyes trace my lips. He guides me to the bed, the back of my legs hitting the mattress, and my heart races.

"You're really beautiful, Daisy," he says. And then he plants his lips right on mine, waiting not even two seconds before his tongue chokes me. *It's not that bad.* I try not to gag for air, but his mouth overtakes my face, slobbering on my chin.

I hate kissing.

So very much.

I distract him by pulling off his shirt, forcing his lips to break from mine. He wears a crooked grin, his pupils like little pinpoints. I wait for Ian to hike me up on the bed, to set me by the pillow and press his body weight against me. The image flushes my skin.

But instead, he climbs onto the bed and pulls me down on top of his chest so that I'm in a perfect position to ride him.

And then he puts his hands underneath his head in relaxation. Maybe we should just skip all the awkward foreplay anyway. I did that with numbers three and four, and I saved myself an uncomfortable hour. But what's the point of all of this if we have a quickie and then he just leaves? I want him to spend the night, don't I?

So I begin to kiss his broad shoulders and suck on his hard abs and his muscular chest. He watches me and lets out a groan every so often. "Lower, baby," he urges. One of his hands has come out of hiding behind his head, but his fingers grip his hair, his mouth open as he gets off on what I'm doing. "Uhh, *yes.*"

I unbutton his jeans and unzip. His erection is visible through his red briefs. I stop touching him so I can yank off my sweater, no bra since my boobs are pretty small. I stand up on the bed, my body off of his, and I unzip my own shorts. He watches me with a heady expression, and I know he's feeling the effects of the drugs.

He sits and runs his hands up my legs, his palms coarse on my smooth skin. He brings me back down on his lap the moment I step out of the jeans. Everything seems more mechanical than sensual.

"I want you here," he says to me. He grabs my hand and brings it to his crotch, helping me find his penis. Not that I needed any help doing that. My head buzzes with erratic energy, the kind that has my skin all tingly and my heart pounding a little too hard. It's making it difficult to discern how I feel about this current situation, me on top, gripping his dick.

He plunges his tongue into my mouth again while he moves my hand up and down his shaft. Thankfully he breaks this kiss to groan. He stares down between our bodies, at the place where my small hand is underneath his large, where I'm touching his erection, warm to my fingers.

I rest my forehead on his chest. I think I just want something more than this. I don't even know what that *more* is. I keep searching and searching with guys. Is this really it? Maybe something's still off. I have no sense of attraction, no true nerve-spindling sensations yet. The only electrifying feelings are coming from my caffeinated concoction.

He forces my head back so that he can stare at my breasts while I give him a hand job. I don't think I'm being attentive or doing very good work, but I don't think that matters to him. I think the idea of me, a young blonde girl (famous), on top of him is all the stimulation he needs.

He kisses my neck now. But before he even sucks on my nape, his lips descend to my chest. His tongue flicks over my nipple, and then he bites it, *hard*. I wince, a high-pitched noise leaving my mouth, the sound so audible. Ow. Ow. *Ow*.

He must take my noise as approval or pleasure because he bites *harder*.

I shove him off with a push on his abs. But he grabs my wrist and brings my hand back to his dick. He guides my face into his shoulder, as though consoling me, but not really because his other hand travels to my backside.

"Have you taken it in the ass before?" he asks with a heavy grunt. He moves my hand lower on his dick.

"Once," I tell him. My boob throbs. I should end this. *But maybe it'll be better if I just wait a little longer.* Maybe I dislike sex because I don't try hard enough or I don't give enough effort. I convince myself to wait it out.

He grabs my ass, and then his finger slips into a hole that has *never* been penetrated by a finger before. I go rigid, my eyes wide and horrified. Okay, I don't like this at all. Is this normal? For once, I feel my age, and I'm more aware that I'm in bed with a twenty-five-year-old.

A guy as old as Ryke.

Everything about this feels weird. Physically, emotionally, mentally—I shift and find a way to adjust so he can't touch me *there* anymore. I don't even finish him off. I slide down to his ankles, crouching. "I'm pretty tired," I lie. "Maybe we can do this another night."

He gives me a long once-over. "Is it your first time? I didn't mean to scare you. I'll be more careful."

"I'm not a virgin," I say. "I told you, I—"

"You don't have to lie. I don't mind that you haven't been with anyone before. In fact, it's kind of sexy." He grins. "I'll go easy, I promise." He clasps my hand and pulls me back on his lap.

He's still hard, and he touches my panties, about to move them aside and then lift me up on his dick. I don't want to be on top. I don't want to have sex with him anymore.

"I'm dry," I tell him. "You'll hurt me." My first time, that's what happened. It was short and really, really painful.

"You'll get wet once I'm inside of you." He combs my hair out of my face.

A long time ago, Ryke once said, "What kind of asshole enters a girl on her first time without getting her aroused first?" *This asshole.*

Ryke's advice: "You should stay away from any guy who doesn't make you come at least twice before he fucks you. Keep that in mind."

Two and a half years later, I have kept it in mind, but I haven't followed it through. Not all guys are willing to take the time to get me off before the big show.

And maybe that's what he was saying back then. I shouldn't be with a guy who focuses on himself first and a woman last.

"I can't," I tell Ian. I climb off his lap quickly before he can grab me, and then I collect my sweater, tugging it over my head. When I look back, Ian still lies on the mattress, as though I'll return any second and straddle him. "I think you should go."

He licks his lips and then hides his erection in his briefs. He pulls his jeans back over his hips and slides off the bed. "I get it," he says. "You're not ready. Maybe tomorrow night?"

"I don't think I'll be ready by then. I'm sorry," I say, meeting his blue eyes.

He nears me a little more, and I try to appear more confident, like Rose. I pull back my shoulders and stand taller. I also paint on a face that I use when I have to look angry during photo shoots. Narrowed eyes. Tightened lips. A dark scowl.

He's not intimidated by me in the least. "You don't even want to finish?" he asks.

"I have a boyfriend," I immediately blurt, hoping that'll push him out. Maybe if he has morals…

He lets out a short laugh. "If you had a boyfriend, it'd be all over the news, especially if you were caught cheating on him."

"We're taking a break," I say. *What are you doing, Daisy?* "I just don't feel comfortable sleeping with someone so quickly."

"I can take a hint," he says, grabbing his little plastic baggy off the dresser. "If you change your mind, you have my number. Maybe I'll see you around." With this, I escort him to the door. He glances back at me and kisses me lightly on the cheek.

I give him a small smile.

And then he departs without another word.

< *14* >

Daisy Calloway

Lock. *Lock. Lock. Lock.* I speed through the room, checking behind the shower curtain in the bathroom, and then I prop a chair underneath that doorknob. When I finish securing the sliding balcony door, I head to the mirror and inspect my breast that keeps throbbing

I lift my sweater up. I'm *bleeding*. He bit me so hard that my nipple is not only red and raw, but it's trickling with blood. Why, *why* do things like this happen to me? He also sucked so hard that a yellowish tint of a bruise forms on the outside of my breast.

I'll have to cover it with makeup. Hopefully no one will notice tomorrow. Hopefully the clothes are modest, not too revealing or else the designer may be upset.

Good job, Daisy.

My room is quiet. No one talks. No one makes a sound. I am alone. I replace my sweater with a baggy night-shirt, and I climb onto bed, wearing boy-short panties. I don't want to take Ambien and experience another nightmare. So I lie awake, flinching at the *whoosh* of wind blowing into the window, as the ceiling creaks, as voices escalate in the hallway. Every little thing snaps my eyes open the moment they drowsily begin to close.

Okay. New plan. I snatch my laptop out of my rucksack, and I lean against the headboard. No, I will not open social media. But maybe… maybe porn will help. Maybe I haven't tried masturbating enough to find a climax. Surely I can do this right.

And the task is taking my mind off the possibilities of an intruder. That's the most important thing.

I pop open my computer…but I have no idea where to even begin. I check the clock. 3 a.m. in Paris. 9 a.m. in Princeton, New Jersey. She'll be up. I find my cell and make a quick call, putting it on speaker so I can search the internet too.

"Hey," Lily says with a yawn. "How's Paris…" Her voice softens, and I hear her whisper to someone in the background, "It's Daisy." Lo must be with her.

"Paris is pretty. So I have a question."

"For me?" she says in a little bit of surprise but also excitement. Rose is the knower-of-all-things, so I usually go to her with questions, but Lily is easier to talk to. When she has time to talk to me, that is.

"Yeah," I say easily. "So what's a good porn site that won't crash my computer?"

There's a long pause over the phone. She hesitates. "I don't know if…"

"Please." I hear the desperation in my voice. I glance at the clock, at each entrance to my room, and my heart accelerates. "I won't tell anyone that you told me." I think she just doesn't want me to turn out like her, especially since the media keeps saying I'm a little mini-Lily, with no other proof than dissecting my brief relationships with guys. I am young and more promiscuous than the average eighteen-year-old, but I don't enjoy sex like Lily. I've slept with a lot of guys because I'm trying to figure out how to do it right and to find the right one to do it with.

Now that doesn't seem as important in my life. Well, it wasn't until Ryke said we both needed to date more. I honestly just want a good night's sleep.

"I'll text it to you," she whispers a little dramatically. I can imagine her glancing back at Lo and reddening. I instantly smile.

"Thanks. Talk to you later?"

"Yeah. I'll try to call more, but the time difference…"

"I know, it sucks."

"Love you, bye," she tells me quickly before hanging up, probably distracted by Lo's presence. In only a second, a text pings on my phone.

Kinkyme.net – Lily

I log into the porn site, and I click on the most popular video. It takes a couple seconds to load. The screen is black at first, only heavy breathing, both male and female. I click the "play" button, hoping an image will reveal itself soon because this isn't doing anything for me.

Finally a picture surfaces.

Oh my God. A girl with silky brown hair is tied to a headboard by her wrists, her head tilted back in pleasure while a guy dominates her from the top.

But it's not the position that's freaking me out or the fact that it's *porn.*

I know this girl. I know this guy.

It's Rose and Connor.

Oh my God. *Click out. Click out!!* I try to press escape and leave these images behind, but it won't disappear. A popup keeps flashing *SUBSCRIBE!* I don't want to subscribe to my sister's kinky sex videos with her husband!

They never even meant for these to hit the internet, so I *highly* doubt they'd be comfortable with what's happening right now. Last year, they were screwed over by a producer who filmed their intimate bedroom sessions without their knowledge and put their videos online. Legal issues ensued, and what it boils down to is this: the videos are here to stay.

And now I have accidentally stumbled upon one of them.

I try not to look at the screen. I shut my eyes, close the computer, open it, and the video is still playing, the breathing is still heavy. I can hear and see everything. I fill in the subscription box, which seems to be the only solution right now.

As I type in a fake name and email address, I catch Connor slipping his fingers beneath Rose's diamond studded collar. He lifts her head to meet his lips, and she lets out a sharp cry as he keeps thrusting between her legs with rough force. Then she comes. He pulls out to switch positions.

OH MY GOD! I have just seen Connor's ginormous penis.

I am scarred forever.

Please, someone *burn* my eyes. I fill out the rest of my info, and I click and click.

It's gone.

Thank you baby Jesus. It's disappeared. I let out a breath. As if my world couldn't be stranger—I have just seen my sister have sex with her husband. And she was tied to a headboard. I will *never, ever* look at Connor Cobalt the same way again. I think…I think I need rehab for this.

As I collect my sanity, a noise chimes from my laptop—a Skype call. Someone's calling *me?*

The Caller Username: RYKE_MEADOWS

Not very creative, but it's still very Ryke. Mine is flowerchild20, which seems almost obnoxiously colorful compared to his. I wonder if that's how we are together—mismatched, uneven. Or maybe he's the ying to my yang. Lame but maybe perfect for us.

The longer I stare at the incoming call, with his name, the more my stomach somersaults. I nearly had sex with another model tonight. I gave him a pretty horrible hand job. Should I really be talking to Ryke after that? *It's not like you're together. He told you to date another guy.* My conscience gives a good argument.

So I click, and before the screen pops up, the guilt replaces with this nervous excitement. He called *me*. That means he's thinking about me, right? I try to hide my smile that begins to hurt my cheeks. *Stop smiling. Be cool.*

I take a deep breath.

A new screen pops up, and my lips slowly fall.

A raspy feminine voice blares through my speakers, "Yes, yes, right there! God, yes. Holy…!" Even in the darkened room, I can distinguish limbs. The girl's tanned legs are split apart by the edge of the bed, her back curved upward. She clenches Ryke's hair, his head between her thighs as he kneels on the ground, his body hidden by the bed frame.

He didn't mean to call me. It was a mistake. She must have hit the laptop with her flailing arms, too overcome with pleasure to notice that she Skyped someone.

In the span of five minutes, I have witnessed three of the closest people in my life having sex. Although, Ryke's just going down on her…but it's morning in Philly. This is probably just round two after going at it all night.

The disappointment, the uneasiness and hurt tries to sink my mood.

Before I close the computer, I become distracted by the girl's build. She looks so much older than me—full breasts, probably close to Ds, defined hips (an hourglass shape) and wavy brown hair. I wish they looked odd together, like an ill-fit match, but they go together better than I do with him. Even though she's most likely twenty-eight or twenty-nine, he pleases her so easily.

She is practically melting on the bed.

Jealousy assaults me, and my face is frozen in a permanent cringe.

My joints won't unhinge to close the computer. I am torturing myself watching this, but somewhere in my head, I want to see it, maybe to solidify the fact that I need to move on too. *You should have just fucked Ian.*

My conscience is mean.

She lets out a pleasured scream as she reaches her climax, gripping the sheets. She must hit the computer again because a text box flickers that says *MUTE*. I can't hear anything. She smacks it again. *UNMUTE*. There we go.

She breathes heavily, coming down from a high that *I* long for.

"Oh my God," she says to him with the shake of her head. "That was…"

He lifts his head, and I see him for the first time as he kisses her knee. My insides twist. The look he's giving her—it's filled with *I want you* and *you're beautiful*.

If that's not a sign that he's moved on, I don't know what is.

< **15** >

Ryke Meadows

Emilia catches her breath. I stand at the foot of the bed, and she eyes the buttons to my jeans. She's naked, sprawled on my sheets in my apartment, a layer of sweat coating her skin. Normally, I'd fucking take her right here, without much hesitation.

But what happened last night unsettles my fucking head, and my body responds by staying completely still.

I met Emilia a few months ago at the gym, and last night, I called her to go to a Philadelphia Eagles game. That was my first fucking mistake. I've only either taken my brother or Daisy to go watch football with me. Yesterday, I turned towards Emilia in the stands, caught off guard by the brown hair, the big tits, everything that I haven't had in months.

I thought I'd want it. I thought my body would respond in complete fucking joy.

It didn't.

Not even a little.

A couple guys with cameras snapped photos of us during the game. So Daisy's going to fucking see Emilia hanging onto my arm, the pictures posted online already. And I shouldn't care how Daisy feels—we're not together—but it's been tearing up my fucking lungs.

For fuck's sake, *I* told Daisy to go screw another guy. Yet, I *still* hope that she can't find someone, even if that someone is good for her.

I glare as a horrible image flashes through my head. Of some model fucking Daisy. Of her hands on his back, nails digging into his flesh as he pounds against her. It's wrong. It looks wrong, even if she's getting off. Because she's not getting off by me. I want to rip the guy from her body. I want to fucking punch him in the face for separating her from me.

Really—I should be fucking punching myself, shouldn't I? *Why would you ever tell her to go fuck another man?* I can't fucking be with her. I can't. That's why I'm here with Emilia. That's why I have to date again, even if it kills me inside.

But that fucking picture—of her being intimate with someone else—it's *so* fucking painful. Someone is drowning me, my throat burning with salt water and rage.

"Ryke," Emilia coos. "You okay?" She sits up, her legs dangling off the bed and she touches my hand. *No I'm losing my fucking mind. I need to go outside, run eight miles and then go climbing. But if I told you that, you'd want to come with me or you'd say I was crazy.*

I didn't screw Emilia last night. She fell asleep right here, too tired to go home, and I crashed on my couch in the living room. She woke up about a half hour ago, appearing buck naked, and then she pulled me into the bedroom.

My cock didn't even harden.

Even now, there's nothing. This has never fucking happened to me before. I'm so knee-ass deep in my fucking head that I can't enjoy this.

She looks confused, and a wave of insecurity starts coating her face.

My gaze hardens, and I lean forward and stroke her hair. "Hey," I tell her. "It's not you, I fucking promise." I even kiss her cheek so she understands that she did nothing wrong. *It's just me. For however fucking cliché it sounds, it's true.*

"We can take it slow," she says. "I really don't mind, Ryke."

"No." I shake my head at her. "I'm not in the fucking mood for slow." *Just fuck her.*

She bites her lip, and then she slides one of my fingers in her mouth, sucking on it. I unconsciously imagine those lips as pale pink, that hair as blonde, that smile as bright, and that laugh as energetic and full of fucking life as Daisy's.

I harden. *Fuck me.*

I feel like utter shit, and Emilia is grinning from ear to ear, my finger between her teeth. She lets go. I'm still hesitating, which is so unnatural for me.

"What do you want me to do?" she asks.

Just fuck her. "Lie on your back," I say with edge.

She scoots towards the headboard. My laptop slides down towards me as she accidentally yanks the sheet. She said she was checking her email this morning, but she should have fucking closed the computer before we started fooling around.

I pick up my laptop, about to set it on my dresser. I glance at the screen—

What the... Daisy. I see Daisy in a Skype window, but she closes out the moment our eyes lock.

What the fuck.

Did she...

How much did she fucking watch? I almost chuck the fucking laptop at the wall, angry at this situation that I'm in, angry at myself. What the fuck is going on? Why the *fuck* does this shit have to happen? The one day that I try to preoccupy my mind with something other than Daisy's wellbeing and it backfires. I just don't understand what I'm supposed to do anymore.

I don't understand why bad shit has to happen to people with good intentions. I feel like I'm serving an eternal sentence of bad karma for not meeting my brother as a teenager.

"What's wrong?" Emilia says.

"I need to fucking call someone. Rain check?"

"What is it?" she asks.

"It's too fucking hard to explain." I point to the living room. "I have to call a friend. You can take a shower, and then I'll drive you home."

She wavers before she says, "Fine." She leans in for a kiss, but I end up planting one on her forehead. I don't wait to contemplate whether or not I've hurt her fucking feelings; I just shut the door behind me and sit on my couch, the computer on my lap.

I Skype Daisy back, waiting for her to answer my call.

She doesn't.

I dial her again and then take out my phone.

I text: Fucking answer me. The reply comes almost immediately.

I'll call you on the phone. — Daisy

No. I need to see your face.

She rejects my third Skype session, so I'm forced to fucking call her by cell. She answers. "I'm sorry," she immediately says. "You called me on Skype like three minutes ago. I thought you wanted to talk. I didn't see much at all, I promise. Just…go back to doing what you were doing—"

"I can't. We need to fucking talk about this."

"There's nothing to talk about," she says quickly.

I rub my eyes. "Daisy…" What do I say? *I'm sorry for going down on another girl?* Daisy isn't my girlfriend. I also warned her that I would be dating again. If this is the right path, then why the fuck do I feel like I need to explain myself?

The answer is there, I just don't want to fucking accept it. It can't be my reality.

"Look, I'm sorry you had to see that. Believe me, this is the last fucking thing I wanted to happen."

"It's okay. It's just the cherry on top of a really, really weird night. So weird, that I think it's going to take years to scrub it all from my brain."

I frown, my eyes narrowing at the floor. "No one broke into your room, right…" *Fuck, Ryke.* I run my hand through my hair. I can't suggest shit like that. "I didn't think they would." I don't want her to think that someone can get in.

"Not weird like that," she says, her voice high-pitched. Her paranoia practically ekes through the phone line. Her breathing shallows for a second.

"Hey," I snap. "Have you taken Ambien tonight?"

She clears her throat to calm down. "I will after I get off the phone."

"Fucking promise me."

"I *fucking* promise you," she says. I hear the smile in her voice.

There's a soft knock on the door frame to my bedroom. I look up. Emilia stands there, wearing one of my T-shirts. It barely covers her thighs. "Towels?" she whispers.

I point to the hall closet, and she tiptoes there, my shirt riding up to her waist. I don't look at her bare ass. Mostly because it feels like I'm cheating on Daisy. The guilt just keeps on coming.

I wait for Emilia to return to my room so she can't hear my conversation. I've been in the media long enough to know that friends can fuck you over quickly. Strangers even faster. Eavesdropping on one of my conversations and selling whatever the fuck I said to a magazine was the easiest paycheck five of my old college friends have ever made.

I don't necessarily hate them. I just don't go on snowboarding trips and to birthday fucking parties when I'm invited anymore. Two years ago, when the Calloway girls, my brother and Connor were swept up into this publicity mess, I realized we had to band together to survive. From that moment, I knew it was going to be hard trusting anyone beyond the six of us. How can you when a simple fact like *I hate Justin Bieber* could be worth a grand to a magazine?

The phone line is quiet.

"You still there?" I ask Daisy.

"Yeah." She pauses. "I don't want to ruin your time with your... date. We'll talk later."

"Fuck that," I tell her. I haven't been able to get Daisy on the phone in days. She won't even let me look at her face. I have no idea the amount of sleep she's been actually getting. I just want to make sure she's okay. "What was weird about tonight?"

"You really don't want to know."

"Now I *really* fucking do."

She lets out a short breath. "I saw Connor's penis."

What? "Excuse me?"

"I was looking at porn, and I accidentally stumbled upon Rose and Connor's sex tape. Hence, his penis. To think, I managed to dodge the explicit version for a whole year. I thought I was going to get away without seeing it *forever.*"

I lean back against my couch and pinch the bridge of my nose in a cringe. Not a lot can make Connor Cobalt fucking uncomfortable, but learning that his girlfriend's little sister saw him having sex—that may do it. My face has hardened in a wince.

And I have a hard time imagining her seeing anyone's dick but mine. Nausea barrels through me.

"Are you going to say something?" she asks.

"I haven't even seen those videos."

"Jealous?"

"Not in the fucking slightest," I tell her. The shower turns on, the pipes groaning through the walls. I glance at my closed bedroom door and then back at the floorboards. "Daisy, you weren't looking at porn to try and fall asleep, were you?" It's a fucking path that no one would want her to go down.

"No…" She sounds like she has something else to add, so I wait for her to speak again. I can hear her shifting on her bed. "I had a guy over tonight."

The temperature drops ten degrees. My head is fucking submerged beneath an ocean again, that gritty salt water sliding down my throat. I see an older guy fucking the hell out of her, and I almost kick the coffee table. I calm down with a deep breath. "Yeah?" I run my hand through my hair a couple times, messing up the already disheveled strands.

"Yeah," she says, leaving it at that.

"Did you look at porn together?" I shoot up to my feet and head to the fucking kitchen, the phone to my ear with one hand. I open the fridge, nothing in there but a case of water and a leftover sub from Lucky's. *Don't punch the fucking wall.*

"That would definitely be another weird thing for the night, but no, we didn't watch it together."

"Is he still there?" *Don't fucking think about it.* I open the freezer to distract me. It's just as bare as the fridge. A package of freezer-burnt chicken and a tray of ice. In the last four months, I've spent almost no time in my apartment. Maybe to grab some clean clothes and my climbing gear. Other than that, I've been at Daisy's place.

I've been sleeping in the same bed as her. I've been taking care of her. She's mine. She feels like she belongs to me. I don't want to share her with any other fucking guy. And I don't want to be with any other fucking girl.

Anything else feels like a sickening betrayal. How the fuck did we get to this place?

"No," she says. "He's gone. I thought maybe I wasn't doing it right, so I was going to look at porn."

"What's *it?*" I ask, finding a packet of oatmeal in a drawer. I tear it with my teeth and pour it into a bowl. I uncap the water bottle as she answers.

"Sex. I can't orgasm. I think it's a physiological problem," she states matter-of-factly. I remember a time when she claimed that she orgasmed before. We were in Cancun for Spring Break, and she said she skipped foreplay, just went straight to sex and experienced something more. I should have been happy for her, but I felt more fucking joy when she admitted that she got it wrong. That she thought she climaxed, but after talking to her sisters, it didn't seem euphoric enough to be that heightened peak.

"You *can* orgasm," I tell her. "I've fucking heard you, sweetheart."

There's no answer. I called her sweetheart—I do it unconsciously, and I know every time I say it, her lips rise.

"Daisy?"

"Huh?" She laughs a little. "Can you say that again?"

"No." I realize I've overflowed my fucking oatmeal with half the water bottle. "Shit," I curse. I have to dump all of it in the trash.

"Sorry," she says.

"No, it's not you," I tell her. After scraping all of the oatmeal out, I toss the bowl too hard in the sink and it cracks. What the fuck is wrong with me today? I shake my head. "I fucking hate talking to you on the phone."

"Me too."

I lean against the cupboard and stare at my bedroom door, keeping an eye on whether or not it opens again. I have to be fucking cautious with people I bring over. I had a one-night stand steal a pair of my fucking boxer-briefs a year and a half ago. She sold them for three grand on eBay. "Were you careful with this guy?" I ask her.

"We didn't have sex," she says.

I shut my eyes and take a deep breath. *Thank fucking God.* "Was he a part of your weird fucking night?"

"Oh yeah," she says. "I just don't understand why I meet people and they seem so perfect for me, and then I get them in bed, and they're just…wrong." She pauses. "I think it's me."

"I already hate this fucking guy." That's a real understatement.

"You would hate him more if you saw him last night. He thought I was a virgin, and he was happy to deflower me upon a first-time meeting."

I glare. I want to rewind time and take everything back. I want to tell her to *not* date a single fucking soul. I wish my brother's claims hadn't gotten to me. "Stay away from him."

"I plan on it."

The shower cuts off. "Hey, Daisy?"

"Yeah?"

"It's almost four in the morning where you are. Take a fucking Ambien and go to sleep, okay? Call me when you have time."

She hesitates. "I have time to talk more now."

"You need to sleep before you go to work."

"It's pointless. I have to be in for hair and makeup at five thirty. Ambien may knock me out for hours, so I might as well just stay up."

My door swings open, and Emilia stands with a towel wrapped around her chest, her hair dry. "You're out of soap," she says. "I couldn't find any in your cabinets." She hasn't even taken a shower yet.

Fuck. I grab my keys off the kitchen bar. "I'll get you some. Wait here."

"You don't have to go buy more," she says.

"I'm not. There's some in my friend's apartment. She lives below me."

"I'll come with," Emilia says. "Hold on a sec." She disappears back into my room, and I catch her slipping on her blue dress from last night.

I still have the phone pressed to my ear. "Daisy—"

"I'll go."

"No," I suddenly say. I don't want to stop talking to her, not if she's just going to spend the next hour paranoid. I can distract her from her fears. Even thousands of miles away, that's still fucking possible.

"Are you sure?" she asks.

Emilia comes out and gives me a smile.

"Yeah," I tell her. I point to the door, and Emilia heads out first. I lock it, and then we enter the elevator. Emilia looks from me to the phone that hasn't left my ear. It won't either. *My friend*, I mouth to Emilia.

She nods and then tries to concentrate on the elevator as it descends. I hit the fucking button a couple times, even though it's already lit, hoping it'll go faster to save me from this awkward tension.

< 16 >

Ryke Meadows

" I talked to my therapist yesterday," Daisy tells me over the phone, the elevator still dropping. "She wanted me to describe what happened at Lucky's again. She said it would help stop the nightmares."

"Did it?" I ask briefly, feeling Emilia's body stiffen the longer I ignore her. But Daisy, a lonely, frightened girl in Paris, is going to trump Emilia. Every fucking time. Especially when it involves the past and the multiple events that have fucked her over psychologically.

"I don't know," she says. "It hasn't helped before. I can say the words just fine." She recites with an even tone, "*Some angry guy outside of Lucky's called me a cunt and destroyed my bike. I've moved past it.*"

I cringe at the sound of *cunt*. Ironic that I fucking hate a swear word—I know. But it's grating, like someone's scratching my fucking eardrums. In the back of my head, I hear my father calling my mom it, over and over. It makes me sick to my stomach.

"You're leaving out a big fucking part," I tell her, "and it's not something you can get over in a day."

"It hasn't been a day," she snaps back. "It's been *over* a year." For that one incident, yeah it has been that long. But it's not the only thing that she's gone through after the media attention. Some people were bound to hate the Calloway girls because they're socialites, wealthy, entitled. The media likes to show them as privileged snobs, so that's what people think. But it didn't give this fucking guy the right to beat the shit out of her Ducati. And as she tried to stop him from wrecking her bike, he turned around and assaulted *her* in broad fucking daylight. I wish I had been there.

I would have fucking killed him.

I ended up taking her to the hospital because she wouldn't tell anyone else about it. She didn't want to worry her family.

They found out anyway, but they never learned about her broken rib. Or the fact that the trauma of the event has stayed with her past that single moment. They think it was no more than a few bruises.

I don't fucking blame her sisters or my brother for not noticing the change in Daisy from that point on. She likes to make it seem like she's okay, even when she's not. She hates whining, crying and throwing tantrums because she thinks she'll come across as immature. When she's hanging out with all of us, people in their twenties, she'd do anything to avoid that label. God fucking forbid she act her age.

And *fuck that*, when a guy assaults you, you're allowed to have every moment to scream. You're allowed to talk it out and ruin everyone's week by burdening them with your emotions.

"Don't try convincing me of anything else," I tell her. "I'm going to be fucking stubborn on this subject."

The elevator doors slide open. I slip into the hallway, Emilia following close behind.

"Okay," Daisy says, "what about you? Have you been training?"

"I beat my time the day you left," I tell her, stopping by Daisy's apartment door. 437 in gold iron on the dark wood. I fit the key inside and glance at Emilia who stares at the number.

"By how much?" Daisy asks. "Was it the same mountain you took me to?"

"Yeah, can you give me a minute? Don't hang up."

"Okay."

I pocket my phone so I have use of both hands. I push open the door, and Emilia slips inside with me. She scans the apartment quickly. It's the same layout as mine, but Daisy has a yellow couch, green pillows and multicolored lanterns hanging from the ceiling.

"This friend is a girl," she says, eyeing the clothes that are scattered on the hardwood floors.

"Didn't I say that?" I'm almost fucking positive I did.

"I must not have heard."

I lead her across the living room, bypassing the small kitchen where dishes are stacked in the sink. I should wash those for Daisy. I'm pretty sure half of them are mine. I step over a skateboard. "Watch your feet."

"She's a slob."

To be honest, I don't usually fucking notice. "She's cleaner than me."

Emilia bumps into a wicker chair, and it knocks over a purple surfboard that was leaning against the wall. I catch the board before it hits her in the head.

Her eyes widen. After she exhales in relief, she says, "She surfs and she lives in Philadelphia?"

"She's learning, and she flies out to California when she has free time, which is rare." I don't add that I go with her so I can climb at Yosemite while she's on the coast with Mikey.

Understanding washes over Emilia's face. "This is Daisy Calloway's apartment." She nods to herself. "She's rich." Her lips tighten, and she's now glaring at every piece of furniture, every article of clothing. "You have keys to her place?"

I don't answer her. I just walk into Daisy's bedroom. The bathroom door is already unlocked, and I point to it. "After you." I don't want her fucking dawdling in Daisy's room.

But she does anyway.

Her eyes float to Daisy's bed, the green comforter tucked in with half-assed effort. On a chair next to her, she lifts a white bra by the strap and twirls it around her finger.

I grab it out of her hand with a glare. "Don't touch her shit." I toss the bra on her bed.

"Why not? I'm about to use her soap, aren't I?" She waits for me to refute.

I stare at her hard.

Her eyes travel around the room again and land on the bathroom. "How about I just take one here?"

"Why does that interest you?" I ask with narrowed eyes. "It's not any different from my shower."

Emilia shrugs. "Do you know how many girls would love to be her? Billion-dollar heiress. A supermodel at seventeen—"

"She's eighteen," I retort. I rest my elbow on the fucking chair. "Look, she's my friend. She's nice enough that she won't fucking care if you use her soap or touch her things. But I fucking care if we spend more than a few minutes here."

"I'll be quick," Emilia says, and then she moves her feet and enters the bathroom. I trail her, and I shut the door. She's already out of her dress before I look over. She waits for me to appraise her. I don't. I'm not fucking sorry either.

She steps into the shower, closing the curtain. "Couldn't she afford a glass shower?" she asks, standing in the tub.

People forget that I have almost as much money as the Calloway girls, all pooled in my trust fund. I just never break into it for more than I need. The most expensive thing I own is my fucking car.

"It wasn't high on her priority list," I tell her, speaking loudly as she turns the water on.

I put the phone back to my ear. "Hey, you there?" I already know she's caught that whole conversation through the speaker.

"Yep," Daisy says. "Tell her not to use your shampoo. It doesn't smell as good as mine."

I end up smiling at that. She'd probably grin so fucking hard if she saw my lips lift this much too. "Mine does its job. That's all that matters."

"Normally, I don't care about prices, but it's a ninety-seven cent shampoo. The only job it does is *pretending* to smell like lemongrass."

"Ryke," Emilia calls. "She has men's shampoo in here."

I move the phone from my ear and say, "I know, and I don't fucking ask."

"You don't care?" Emilia wonders.

"No." *Because it's mine.*

After a moment's pause, she asks, "Does she have an extra razor I can use?"

I'm about to say, *I thought this was going to be a quick fucking shower.* But Daisy's voice sounds through the receiver. Only I can hear her. "Cabinet behind the box of tampons."

For some reason, I gravitate towards high-maintenance, jealous, out-of-their-fucking-mind girls. I'm used to the impulsive, the rash, and the confusing as all hell. My mom used to chastise everyone I brought home, saying that I look for the "crazy" in people. Maybe she's right.

Maybe I like a little crazy.

I dig though the cabinet, knocking over the tampons to find a package of razors. Just as I grab one, I spot a plastic circle with bubbled capsules. I know what it is. I just don't fucking understand what it's doing in Philly and not Paris. I take Daisy's birth control and inspect the dates. It's almost all full, except for a couple pills missing. It looks like she stopped taking them weeks ago, which would be fine if she didn't admit to almost fucking a guy in France.

"Did you find it?" Daisy asks.

"Yeah," I say with a steel voice. I can't talk to her about the birth control with Emilia right here.

"What is that?"

I go rigid.

Emilia peeks from behind the shower curtain, water dripping off her arm. She squints as she scrutinizes the pills. "Oh shit," she says with a laugh.

I pocket them and glower at her as hard as I fucking can. "Here's your razor." I throw it at her. She catches it, but instead of finishing her shower, she shuts off the water and steps out, wrapping the towel around her body.

"Let me see that," she says with a smile.

I hold the phone to my ear and say, "I'll call you back."

"What's going on?" Daisy asks.

"Is that her?" Emilia's eyes brighten at the phone.

I don't like that look on her fucking face.

"Hey, Daisy," Emilia calls loudly so she can hear, "thanks for the shampoo. It smells like teen spirit."

"She's fun," Daisy says to me, a humored smile to her words. She usually doesn't take digs at her age to heart.

"No she's not," I say blankly, staring hard at Emilia.

She's quick. In a swift second, she steals the birth control out of my pocket.

"Oh my God," she laughs and waves the packet. "Male shampoo *and* she stopped taking the pill." She glances at the phone. "Hey Daisy, you need to tell your fuck-buddies to wrap it, honey, or you're going to be sixteen and pregnant."

"I'm eighteen," Daisy says flatly, but only I can still hear her.

I glare hard at Emilia. "You need to fucking go."

Her smile fades. "I'm just joking around, Ryke." She tosses the pills back to me. I catch it with one hand. "Daisy knows that."

"*I'm* not fucking joking."

I hear Daisy's voice go hysterical in my fucking ear. "Stop, Ryke, you can't kick her out. She may sell that info to the press."

She probably will anyway. I roll my eyes and shake my head. "I'll drive you home. Just don't make a big deal about this." I raise the pills between two fingers to show her what I'm referring to.

"Yeah, sorry." Her eyes drift to the counter. "Is that her brush?"

Fucking A. "I'll wait for you in the bedroom." I don't care what she does anymore, as long as she's on her way *out* in five minutes or less. I sit on the mattress while Emilia combs her hair. "You there, Dais?" I ask her for what feels like the millionth time.

"Yeah, about the pills...I don't like taking them around Fashion Week. My mom says I gain too much weight when I'm on them. So... don't be mad."

If I didn't tell her to date other fucking guys, I wouldn't be so concerned right now. My nose flares, and it takes me a moment to answer. "It's your body. Just be fucking careful."

"I will," she says. Silence stretches over the line. "Hey, Ryke?"

"Yeah?"

"Don't fuck her in my bed."

I grimace. "I would never do that."

"Just making sure."

I let out a deep breath. "I miss you." *Fuck me.* Why do I say shit like that to her?

Because it's the truth.

She says, "It's only been four days."

"Feels longer than that."

"Yeah, it does," she says softly. "So what was your climbing time?"

I almost smile. She remembered that I said I beat my last record. "Two minutes, seventy-three seconds, eighty feet of ascension."

"I'm proud of you," she says. "Did you scream, 'I am a Golden God' when you reached the top?"

"Only you do that, sweetheart."

There's a long pause again, and I can't keep my smile from filling my whole face.

When she collects herself, she laughs and says, "I did it once, and it wasn't even a real mountain."

It was a gym rock wall. And it took her a week to complete the hardest course. By the end, she pumped her fists in the air in triumph and shouted that quote from *Almost Famous*. The entire gym clapped.

It was really fucking cute.

"Do you feel better?" I ask her. She doesn't seem as paranoid or fucking antsy.

"When I talk to you, yeah, I do."

"Then call me. I told you I wouldn't fucking mind if you did."

"I didn't want to bother you…the time difference…"

"I'll answer your call if it's at four in the morning or midnight, Dais. It's just fucking hard for me to call *you* because I don't know when you're on the runway."

There's a long drawn out pause, and I can tell she's trying to find the right words. She settles on these: "Thanks, Ryke." She says my name with this genuine, heartfelt affection. "I mean it."

"I know you do."

"I have to start heading over for hair and makeup. Call you later?"

"I'll answer."

For you, I always fucking will.

< **17** >

Daisy Calloway

Stylists and publicists with walky-talkies and headsets dart around the backstage area with crazed eyeballs. Mine aren't bugged. I rub them, dry from the lack of sleep.

Models swarm the congested backstage, hurrying into their clothes. I sit in another makeup chair while a stylist twists my long blonde locks into an intricate shape of a humongous ribbon. The more hairspray she uses and bobby pins she pokes, the more weight gathers on my head.

When she finishes, I wander over to the racks of clothes and find my garment. It's nothing more than black hefty fabric, draped to form an indistinguishable bow. Yes, the dress is a giant bow. *I* am a bow, really, and my hair is also a bow with a ribbon.

I start undressing in order to put the garment on.

"Ladies in the Havindal collection, hurry up!"

Uh-oh. Finding the armholes has proved troublesome, even if I've tried the dress on before. Just discovering where to put my head takes ten solid minutes.

I stand beside Christina, who's not doing much better. She tries to jump into a pair of gray slacks that accompanies a bow-styled blouse, which is hanging on the rack beside her. As she hops into the right leg, the fabric suddenly tears.

"Oh no," she says with wide eyes, whipping her head from side to side to see if anyone saw. "What do I do?" Her freckled cheeks redden.

The designer, an eccentric skinny lady, inspects each model with a narrowed, judgmental gaze.

"Step out of them," I tell Christina before she bursts into tears. I flag down the stylist that just did my hair and show her the rip before the designer notices.

"I have a sewing kit at my station. Stay here," she tells us.

Christina wears a bra and a nude thong. I'm no more dressed. In fact, I don't have on a bra because my bow-gown has a bit of side-boob. My breast still hurts from Ian mauling my nipple, but I used some concealer to hide the yellowish hickies. It's not that noticeable, and no one has said anything about it.

People try not to stare as we change, and most of the crew backstage are women. But when I look up, just once, I catch a couple men lingering by the doorway.

One has a camera.

My heart thuds. A *camera*. I freeze, my limbs crystalizing. They're not allowed back here. Not with cameras.

Not while we're changing.

Maybe it's okay though. No one kicks them out. It's not like we're used to being naked. I mean…I haven't done any nude shoots yet, even though I'm allowed to be topless now that I'm eighteen. I just don't want the world to see my boobs, high fashion or not.

But what if they're paparazzi, hoping to snap a quick pic of me for a magazine?

That's not okay. I glance at Christina, whose fifteen and innocent and new. She's me three years ago. Nausea roils inside my belly. My skin pricks cold, and I instinctively step in front of Christina. If they're snapping photos because of me, I don't want her to be caught in the background. I block her from the men that have breached what I always thought was a "sanctuary"—a line between the onlookers and the models. I guess there is no line. Everyone sees all of me.

I don't like feeling this gross.

Christina fumbles with her blouse, her eyes glassing as she believes her runway has ended with the torn pants.

I've already wrangled my dress and put it on. "Here let me." I help her into the blouse that has many loops and detached fabric pieces. I keep glancing over my shoulder at the guys, my ass in direct view of their lenses.

The camera clicks.

There's an actual flash.

They have a picture of me. Not naked, but there are a couple other girls still dressing. It's a picture they didn't ask for, one they didn't get permission to take. Maybe a year ago, I wouldn't have noticed this. Maybe I would have just shrugged it off. Now I just want to scream at the photographers, but the backstage commotion tugs my mind in several directions.

"Twenty minutes!" a woman with a clipboard yells. "Models, line up. Line up!"

Just as Christina pulls her brown hair through the collar of her blouse, the stylist arrives with the mended pants.

I feel the hot lens on my body again. Clicking.

The stylist fixes my hair that I messed when I was putting on the gown, the heavy fabric an extra ten pounds on my body.

"Those guys," I say, her hands quickly fixing a loose strand by my face, "they're not allowed to be in here."

"Who?" She glances around, but she doesn't see what I do. They're *right there*. Not even twenty feet away, snapping pictures of all of the models, not just me. My heart is racing. *They're probably just going to write an article about Fashion Week with some backstage pictures. It's okay.*

But it doesn't feel that way. I am worth less than the clothes I wear. I have always known this. A dress is treated with more humanity and kindness than I ever am. One of my shoots, I was told to stand in a swimming pool for four hours without a break.

It was thirty degrees outside.

The pool wasn't heated.

And I was fourteen.

The gown, though, that was the first priority. "Don't drop the dress, Daisy. Whatever you do, it can't touch the water."

Then why the *hell* did the photographer want to do a photo shoot in the pool, in the middle of winter?

It was one bad experience out of many. I was lucky that my mom was around, supervising, but she disappeared to network, to schmooze most of the time. Sometimes her presence really didn't make much of a difference.

I am dazed, exhausted and hollow by the time the designer reaches me. She scrutinizes the fabric on my body, the way the dress hangs and hugs in unison.

"No," she suddenly says.

"What?" My shoulders drop, my stomach gurgling—the sound incredibly audible. "What's wrong?"

"Everything!" the designer shouts at me. I flinch. "You gained weight since last I saw you."

"I didn't," I say. My pulse kicks up another notch. *I didn't. I know I didn't.*

"We can measure her," the stylist suggests.

"This is wrong," the designer touches the sleeve. "This is not on you right." She tries to adjust the gown, but it looks right to me. I don't see how my head is supposed to go where she's pointing. That's not how I wore it in the fitting.

"No, no, no." The designer pinches my slender waistline and then her hands fall to my ass. She stretches the fabric down and then squeezes my butt. "This is too tight. Her thighs, too fat."

I try to grin and bear it, the designer's hands going wherever she pleases, in places that I would prefer her *not* to touch.

I haven't eaten real food in days. I don't see how I could have gained anything other than hunger. The designer just dislikes me. I must have offended her somehow.

"I want another model," she declares. "Get her ready, the hair, the makeup. *Now.*"

My eyes grow big. "Wait, please, let me fix this. Don't pull me out of the show." I've walked more than one runway this week, but being fired from even a single job will displease my mom.

"The dress looks hideous on you," she says. The models in the line watch the designer berate me with more insults. "You're overweight. I don't even know why others are booking you."

Christina's mouth has permanently fallen open.

I take each word with a blank face, but my eyes begin to burn as I hold back more emotion. "So there's nothing I can—"

And then the designer physically pries the dress from my body. It's all I can do to not teeter off my heels. She strips me bare.

No bra. Just a nude thong.

In two quick moments, I stand naked in a room of now fully-clothed people. The cold nips my arms and legs, but the embarrassment is hot on my neck.

The designer focuses on a new model. Blonde. Tall. Wiry.

The exact same size as me.

The nice stylist combs the new model's hair. I'm alone, and no one's going to tell me what to do, where to go, or even give me a robe to cover myself with.

When I turn, I meet the intense gaze of the camera. *Click, flash. Click, flash.*

It's in this moment—eighteen, being photographed bare and nude without consent—that I feel violated by my own career. I could be fifteen right now, okay with this, told that this is what's supposed to happen. I could be fourteen. But what difference does it make now that I'm eighteen? I'm just more aware. I see the wrongness, and the blow strikes harder and hurts greater.

I spend the next ten minutes trying to find my clothes, passing people with my arms over my chest. Trying not to cry. But tears build, and the hurt of the whole situation weighs on my chest like a brick drifting to the bottom of the ocean.

I don't want to be here anymore.

I just want to go home.

< 18 >

Ryke Meadows

I take off my helmet in the parking lot, switching off the ignition on my bike, and I notice Sully's forest-green Jeep parked by the Information Center. I dial his number, quickly putting on my climbing shoes and tying my chalk bag around my waist.

The wind blows hard today, the trees rustling together in Bellefonte Quarry. It's not so fucking bad that I can't climb. The sky is clear, and that's more important.

An incoming storm can fucking kill me.

The moment the line clicks I say, "You flirting with the receptionist again, Sul?" Last week, I had to drag him out of the Information Center before dark clouds rolled through. He was leaning over the desk with his mop of wavy red hair, throwing out the cheesiest fucking pickup lines to Heidi, a blonde twenty-something girl at a community college nearby.

"Now look who's slow," he says. "Mission accepted and completed an hour ago, man. Late, late, late should be your first, middle and last name."

"Did she reject you again?" I ask, heading towards the sheer side of the cliff.

"Not this time. I have a date on Saturday, so every naysayer can suck my balls."

I smile as I pick up my pace into a run. I don't want to be that fucking late. He's going to solo climb beside me, placing gear up the rock face as he ascends, and then he'll have to repel back down to clear all of it. Free-soloing doesn't have any of those luxuries. I have powder chalk and my fucking shoes.

That's it.

A gust of wind ripples the brown water that runs through the quarry. I've climbed most of the traditional routes you can in Bellefonte. But before I leave for California, Sully wants me to climb the first route I've ever free-soloed before. As some sort of last fucking hoorah in case I die.

So I rode three hours out here. It's not far away considering the places I'll travel to for this sport. If I'm not hanging out with my brother or with Daisy, I'm climbing. Finding really good rock faces is hard in Pennsylvania. There aren't many routes higher than 200 feet.

And one of the three I plan to climb in Yosemite is 2,900 feet. I've been flying out to California the past year to train with Sully, using trad gear—with him always as the lead.

I've trusted him with my life too many times to count.

We had to path out my course, and even though it's all planned out—climbing all three rock faces with a harness and my childhood friend—it's still fucking terrifying to do it without both. No amount of confidence can extinguish that lingering fear. It'll always be in the back of my head.

I reach the bottom of the flat rock face within another minute, my breath even. I look around, and I don't see Sully's ratted blue shirt he wears with his khaki shorts. His pasty white skin is almost always burnt from the sun. "Where the fuck are you?" I ask him, pressing the phone back to my ear.

"Vanished with magic. I'm a descendant of the Weasley clan. I got powers."

He was never proud to be a redhead as a fucking kid until *Harry Potter.* I remember meeting him at six-years-old at Rock Base Summer Camp and he was scrawny and quiet. That fucking changed fast. "You're fucking cute today," I tell him.

"Because this is a special moment," he reminds me. "Look up."

I crane my neck, my eyes grazing the flat limestone, and then I spot Sully waving at the top of 120 feet of ascension. "You climbed without me?" I frown. "I thought you wanted to do this together?"

"That was the plan until I got here." His legs hang off the cliff. "I was just going to scope out the face, but I saw weeds and dirt in the cracks. I cleaned the route for you on my way up." I can almost see him shrug. "I didn't want you to die in Pennsylvania on a hundred and twenty foot ascent. If Ryke Meadows is gonna go out, he's gotta go out big."

"Thanks, man," I say with as much appreciation as my voice will allow. If I climbed and found loose rocks in the cracks and handholds, it would've been a bad time. I'm thankful for a friend like Adam Sully, especially after all my college ones were shit when I became famous.

Sully never really cared. He doesn't even mention it that much. We met at summer camp, climbed together, and we've done it ever since. Some months I don't see him since he backpacks a lot, skipping college. For cash, he's a climbing instructor at a gym. When we meet up, it's like no time has passed. It's like we're at summer camp again, picking up right where we left off.

He's the kind of friend I'll have for life. Not because we share deep fucking secrets or our heartbreak—we don't do either—but because we have a passion for the same thing. And even though I know I may die alone while I climb, I've been lucky enough to share each accomplishment and triumph with someone else who understands what it means to reach the top.

"I'm timing you," Sully tells me. "What's your first record?"

"You fucking know all of my times." He always told them to kids at camps, gloating about my speed climbs each year. And then when we were instructors, he'd fucking tell the pros. And then when we were considered pros, he'd tell anyone who'd listen.

"Remind me," he says.

I dip my hand in the chalk and then begin scanning my path upwards, a grid that I see laid out with each crack and divot and precipice in the fucking rock. "The first time I climbed this, it took one brutal fucking hour," I tell him.

"And what's your latest time?"

I smack my hands together, the chalk pluming. "Six minutes, thirty-eight seconds."

I know he's smiling. I don't even have to see him. "I'll see you at the top."

My lips rise.

And I climb.

I DIDN'T SET MY stopwatch since Sully's timing me, but the ascent feels different from the last time I did it, which was over a year ago. I feel lighter, freer. Stronger.

I'm near the top, clinging to the rock, my hand slipping between the smallest crack in the mountain, a fissure just deep enough for my fingertips to rest. I support my body with this single grip until I reach for the next handhold, a space where two rocks meet.

I move fast and precisely, not stopping to catch my breath or to consider an alternate path. This is where I'm fucking going, and I just go.

My muscles stretch, every inch of my body used with each new position. At one point, I have all of my body supported by two fingers. I find good footing to adjust my weight.

I look down once or twice and grin. I don't have a problem with heights. I also know if I fall, I'll die, but people don't realize how confident I am. If I didn't think I could do it, I wouldn't.

"Oh my God, he doesn't have a rope!" I hear a woman yell the closer I am towards the top. She wears a helmet and stands beside her instructor, coming off a route with bolts.

"I know," Sully says, still sitting on the cliff. "That's my friend." His smile reaches his scraggily hair that covers his ears.

"He's crazy," another man says.

"He's a professional," the instructor tells them. "We also don't advise anyone to free-solo."

And then I reach the last ten feet, the easy part. My muscles barely ache. I have a lot more left in me, and it bolsters my fucking confidence to go after my other goals in Yosemite.

I hike my body onto the ledge beside Sully. The people behind me just stare, and I try not to make eye contact in case they're into celebrity news, reality television, all that shit. They congregate together, looking like they'll keep their distance.

I turn to Sully, who wears a squirrely looking smile.

"What?" I ask.

He unzips his backpack and pulls out a store bought cake, all the white icing smashed into the plastic lid from the climb. "It said *Climb that bitch*." He pops the lid and sticks his finger in the icing. "I guess we'll have to settle for *limb that itch*." He grins. "That's even better."

It's hard to joke around when you're overcome with foreign emotion. I squeeze his shoulder.

He pats my back and then nods to the cake. "This half is mine by the way. You can take the itchy piece." He uses a plastic fork to cut the cake in two.

We eat quietly at first, staring out at the expansive view of the quarry. I can hear a guy scream in terror and excitement as he jumps off one of the jagged cliffs, splashing into the water below.

After the long moment of silence, he says, "You didn't ask for your time."

I know it's shorter. I could feel it the moment I had thirty feet left. "Six minutes flat?" I ask him.

He shakes his head with a smile. "Five forty."

"Damn." *That's really fucking good.* I look back out at the tree tops. My progress, my journey—from being a curious six-year-old, to a punk teenager, to a determined adult—it just flashed quickly before my eyes. I think that's what Sully had intended to happen all along.

"So you're probably wondering *why did Sully bring me to the top of this cliff and serve me cake?*"

"Not really," I tell him.

He smiles. "Besides your foul-mouth and that intimidating scowl thing you do, you're probably the nicest person I've ever met. And I've been around for twenty-five years." He laughs. "In climber life span, that's a long ass time. I've already neared my halfway-point."

I grab his water bottle and take a swig. I wipe my mouth on my shirt sleeve. "I'm only nice to you because you carry my gear when we climb together, and you're the lead. If I anger you, you can turn around and cut my fucking rope."

He snorts. "Right. I don't believe that for a second."

"Why?" I ask, seriously this time. "You're always the one protecting me from a fucking fall."

"Yeah, and I'm pretty positive I'm the only person who has that job when it comes to you, climbing, not climbing, doesn't matter. I know you've been going through some *heavy* shit with your brother, and you still make time for other people and this sport." He means I make time to meet up with him.

I nod. "Yeah," I say, not knowing how else to respond.

"I remember you telling me that you had a brother when we were in Lancaster." He shakes his head. "That seems like such a long time ago."

My gaze darkens, recalling that day. I was too angry to climb, and it was one of the few times I opened up to him about my family. I didn't civilly talk about it. I yelled. And the only person who ever heard the pain in my voice was a summer camp friend. "I called him a fucking bastard."

Sully gives me a look. "We were fifteen. You were pissed." He shrugs like it's no big deal. "It's what you do later that matters. Making mistakes and correcting them, that's life."

"We make a mistake on a mountain, Sul, and we die."

"Here I am, being all metaphorical, and you have to go and be all literal." He shakes his head at me with mock disapproval. He lifts the cake, acting like he may smash it my face. And just like that, we let the heavy shit go. Our friendship is the easiest one I've ever had.

"You do that, Sully, and I'll push you off this fucking mountain." We're sitting on the edge, and if we start hitting each other, we could go over quickly.

"I was just going to tell you to take this back to Daisy." He dips his finger back in the icing and licks it off. "I've never seen a girl melt over cake like she did."

I took her to the gym to teach her how to rock climb, and Sully was there, instructing two ten-year-olds. I could never do his job full-time. I have a harsh way of speaking when people aren't giving a hundred fucking percent, but that shouldn't come as a surprise. He went with us to a café after his shift, and she ate three pieces of cake, all chocolate.

"She's not in Philly," I tell him. He doesn't keep up with the gossip, so he wouldn't know that she's left for Fashion Week. "And she hasn't eaten sweets in practically a month. She'd probably fucking drool if you put cake in her face."

"Aww," he says. "Poor girl. Where is she?"

"Modeling in Paris."

He whistles. "She's always all over the place, isn't she?" He gives me another look, this time with a growing smile.

"What?" I snap.

He shrugs. "You two have a little thing. Not as cute as what Heidi and I have, but you know, you'll get there."

"We don't have a thing," I tell him.

He ignores me. "Don't forget to invite me to the wedding, okay? I don't have to be a groomsman or anything, but I do expect to be in the wedding pictures. I'm not against photo-bombing either."

"Fuck off," I say.

He touches his heart. "I love you too."

My phone vibrates in my pocket. I pull it out and check the caller ID.

DAISY CALLOWAY.

Sully looks over my shoulder. "Think she heard us talking about her?"

"I wouldn't be surprised."

"Your voice is louder than mine," he refutes, knowing where I was going with that.

"I have to take this."

"Don't take her too hard. She's young and impressionable."

I flip him off, standing to answer the call while he laughs.

I press the green button and walk further onto the peak of the rock. It's flat, and up here, people gather to repel back down, the chatter echoing from one side to the other. I check my watch.

8 a.m. here. 2 a.m. there.

The line clicks and then dies. I frown. I look at my phone. She fucking hung up on me? Maybe it was a misdial. I call her back.

Her answering machine cuts on this time. "Hi, it's Daisy. Not Duck and not Duke. Definitely not Buchanan. I'm a Calloway. If you haven't misdialed then leave your name after the beep, and I'll call you when I return from the moon. Don't wait around. It may take a while." *BEEP*.

"Call me back or text me that you're okay," I say tersely before I hang up.

I'm about to return to Sully, but my phone rings again. She's being fucking weird. "Hey, what's going on?"

She sniffs and tries to speak, but her voice falters.

She's been crying.

My chest tightens. "Fuck. Daisy, what's wrong?"

She lets out a breath that shakes the sound from her lips, and then she inhales sharply and chokes like she's unable to exhale.

Fuck. Fuck. I rest my hand on my head. "Dais…"

"I…I can't…"

She cannot have a fucking panic attack while I'm here and she's there.

"Shh, shh," I tell her in the gentlest voice I can. Calming someone— that's not a skill I possess. I jump after girls who dive off of cliffs. I accompany crazy chicks on their illogical adventures. I teach them how to stand back up. I hold them while they fucking cry.

But I'm not there to do any of these things. I'm thousands of miles away with no room for error.

"Take deep fucking breaths. Relax," I say roughly, dropping my hand and clenching and unclenching my fist.

"I…feel sick…" She coughs, dry heaving until I hear her really fucking vomit.

Fuck.

Sully is by my side with concern. He looks at me like *what's going on?*

I just shake my head at him. "Daisy," I say, running my hand through my damp hair. "Hey, you need to talk to me right fucking now. Take deep breaths. You're not dying, so stop acting like it." Being a jackass is the only way I can think to get her to calm down. It's the only fucking tool I have to work with.

She pukes, but it turns back into a violent cough. Then she begins to breathe *somewhat* fucking normally.

"Good girl," I say.

She exhales shortly. "They took pictures...of me...and no one cared..."

What the fuck is she talking about? She's a model; of course they take photographs. "You're not making any fucking sense." I can't just stand on top of this fucking cliff. I can't just fucking *talk*. I head over to Sully's backpack, and he keeps up with my hurried stride.

"I was naked," she says, a tremor in her voice. "The designer...she threw me out of her show, and she stripped me..."

You've got to be fucking kidding me. I freeze, gripping my hair with one hand. "And no one did anything?"

She chokes on another cry.

I almost kick the fucking cake off the edge. I almost lose my shit. I bend down to a crouch to stop myself from screaming. I fucking hate people. I hate that the ones I care about most are the ones that get shit on.

"Hey, fucking talk to me," I say, realizing she's completely silent now. "Daisy?" Nothing. "Daisy?!" I check my phone. *Signal lost.* The call dropped. I try again, but I have no more range. I look to Sully with panic.

"No signal," he says, tapping at his iPhone screen.

I stand up quickly and switch into a new gear called *Get the fuck off this rock.* "We need to go down now." I pick up his backpack and find the extra harness that I use when I descend with him. I put each leg through the fucking straps while Sully collects rope, repel devices and locking carabineers, his hands moving in a flash.

"Is she hurt?" he asks, his eyes flickering to me.

I tighten the straps on my legs. It's not a physical hurt. It's not like she crashed her motorcycle, but it fucking feels like she got into a head-on collision. "I don't know," I tell him. Truth is, I think she's always been hurting. It's just different when I'm not there to take care of her. "I need to get her back on the fucking phone."

"Double your rope so you can get down faster." He tosses me extra rope for my descent, and I tie two together with a Double Figure-8

Fisherman's knot. Then I tie an extra knot at the end of the rope in case I fucking fall. It's the last safety I have to catch me.

"Ready," Sully says. "I only have one anchor. You take it. I'll go after you since I have to pick up my gear."

I nod and hook into the anchor. I take a breath to relieve the pressure that bears down on my chest. As I stare at the 200 foot drop, everything fucking clicks.

I am so emotionally involved with that girl. If someone told me she was crying two years ago, I would have called Lily or Rose to deal with it. But I want to be the one to protect Daisy. I want to be the one to hold her in my arms. I want to comfort her until she reanimates in pure fucking happiness.

I don't want to miss a day with her. I don't want to be here while she's there.

And I can't take back these feelings.

I can't go in reverse.

I just drive forward at a hundred and fifty miles per hour. I'm racing towards her when I should be slamming on the fucking brakes.

I know how to stop.

But I'm not going to.

I don't want to.

That's the fucking truth.

< 19 >

Daisy Calloway

The paparazzi found my hotel.

I peek out of the balcony door once, just to confirm that the SUVs lined on the curb are in fact cameramen and not kickass secret service. The flashes blind me. *Click, click, click* in a wave. I shut the door instantly, my heart beating wildly.

I tried to lose them every time I exited my hotel for work, but with Mikey riding a moped next to me at a leisurely pace, we couldn't exactly dodge all of them. Now he's back in his hotel room, and I'm in mine.

It's been one day after being thrown out of the runway—which has made headlines—which is why I've now become bigger news than before. One day after Ryke talked to me—calming me down by recounting his time at the quarry.

It almost felt like he was here.

But he's not.

And now I have my mom rapidly texting me: You need to go talk to the designer right now and make it up to her. Apologize. Buy her something...

And she goes on and on. As though I can march to the designer and *bribe* my way back into her good graces, demanding her to like me. That's not how this works.

The rejection is harder to accept when my mom won't let it go.

And I can't even think about the pictures of me undressed backstage. If they surface...they haven't so far, but it makes me sick. The thought caused me to cling to the porcelain toilet yesterday night.

I twist my hair into a high bun, pacing anxiously in my room, peeking through the curtains again. My stomach tosses, and a layer of sweat gathers across my forehead. It's midnight, and I can't do anything. I can't go outside without being swarmed, but I can't stay here and be a prisoner in this hotel room, suffocating in my extreme paranoia.

I have to get out. I have to breathe.

I pocket my wallet in my jean shorts, change my tank top into a long-sleeve sweater that says *keep it surreal* and hightail it out of the room on impulse. I can ride my moped as fast as it'll go without Mikey and lose the paparazzi. I can go somewhere. A lake, a river, whatever, and take a freezing cold dip. Something. Anything.

I settle with this spontaneous plan, and I open the door to the stairwell. I dislike riding in elevators without someone I trust beside me. Like Ryke or Mikey. Without them, I'll rock back and forth on my heels, staring with bugged eyes at the lit numbers, praying that the elevator doesn't stop to let anyone on.

Stairs are better. It's more private, less chance of running into someone I know, like an old friend. In Paris, that possibility is slim to none, but the fear still propels me towards the staircase.

My heart never slows from its quick panicked pace. Because even though stairs are better—it's not by much. I haven't been attacked in a stairwell, but in movies, it's the first place villains go, right? It's the place where the bad guy chases the hero.

But the hero usually escapes up the stairs. I think I could too.

I'm on the fifth floor, so I hop skip some steps as I head down to the lobby, fluorescent lights blinding in some corners and dim in others. The levels are painted on the walls.

4.

I pause for a second, listening. A door bangs above me. *Oh God.* Someone followed me here? From my floor. They sound close.

I sprint.

3.

The extra footsteps echo loudly, and they start to quicken, matching my stride. My breathing is so off-kilter. I exhale deeply just to ensure that I'm not holding it in.

2.

My hand glides along the railing, my feet moving in a blur.

"Daisy!"

I freeze. I go cold. It can't be...

I turn around and my mouth falls. I'm losing my mind.

"You can't be real." I pause. "You're in Philadelphia."

‹ 20 ›

Daisy Calloway

Ryke stands four stairs above me, wearing a leather bike jacket and dark jeans. "I flew in after you called me. I just fucking got here." He scrutinizes me from head to toe, a long once-over with stone-hard eyes that heats my body, snuffing out the cold. He looks real. "When I got off the elevator on your floor, I saw you going into the stairwell. I didn't mean to scare you."

Relief tries to surface. He's here. For me? "I'm not scared," I tell him.

"You look petrified," he says flatly. I watch his eyes dance over my features again, his chest falling and rising in a deep rhythm. He bridges the gap between us, descending the four stairs. He still has height on me, staring down to meet my eyes.

"I'm not anymore," I say softly.

He nods a few times, processing this, and then he asks, "Were you going to meet up with that weird fucking guy?" His eyes darken.

I sense a hint of jealousy. Or maybe he's just trying to protect me from Ian. Not jealous at all. "Didn't you hear? He was a very uncomfortable pillow."

"I thought I was your fucking pillow."

I stiffen. "You didn't want to be my pillow, remember? In fact, you told me to find a replacement."

"How's that going for you?" he asks roughly. I can feel him tapping into his asshole side pretty fast.

"Amazing," I say. "Sleep has never been better."

"Must be why you have dark circles under your eyes."

"You caught me," I say with a shrug. "I haven't found a decent pillow replacement, but I'm still on the hunt, per your request."

With a deep inhale, his muscles flex, and anger shrouds his gaze.

I add, "You replaced me too." A lump rises in my throat. "It looked like you enjoyed going down on her." He stares unflinchingly, that rage brewing. When he doesn't reply, I just shrug and add more, "Which is good, you know. You're dating other people, I'm dating other people—"

And then his lips meet mine, kissing me with abrupt, forceful passion that explodes my chest. A breathless moan leaves me before I can catch it.

Our bodies connect like they've been dying for this affection for years. He hikes *both* of my legs around his waist, pinning me to the wall, to this place, to *him*. His tongue effortlessly slides into my mouth, wrestling with mine in the most natural way possible. My fingers slide into his thick, soft hair, gripping and exploring in ways I've only dreamed of.

He breaks away once, his hand above my head as his whole body weight melds against me. He says in a low masculine voice, "You don't need to replace me. You can have me, sweetheart."

I pant for air. "Say that again."

His lips brush my ear, hot breath warming me. "How about I just fucking kiss you?" He finds my mouth again, and we attack like we're thirsty for each other. I drink him in with every kiss, my body curving towards his chest and his hardening against mine.

I cross my ankles around his waist, dying in this heat, in this insane pleasure. I don't stop to think about what all of this means. I just focus on the feelings, some I've never even met before.

He breaks away again, this time to suck on my neck, his lips soft but the pressure hard and aggressive like him. My next moan sounds like a piercing cry. The spot between my legs has found his cock, only the fabric of our clothes separating us. The more he sucks, trailing a line to my breasts, the more my back arches, bucking against him. And in turn, his crotch drives a little harder into me.

I barely notice that he's untied my hair, the band around his wrist. The long blonde strands stick out wildly. The intensity between us stirs our need, and I thrust forward while he grips my ass, lifting me off the wall. He suddenly spins me around, and my back digs into the stair railing.

He kisses me again. I cry out as he hoists me higher, my bottom resting on the railing now. I sense the forty-foot drop behind me in the stairwell, the danger present, the risk quickening my heart.

He holds me securely, his arms firmly on my hips. And then he grinds forward, his dick right up against the spot that begins to ache and pulse. I have never been so wrapped up in a single person, in a single moment.

Ryke Meadows has invigorated my body and soul.

He is more than just my pillow.

My wolf.

My bodyguard.

He's my everything.

Every time our lips meet, it's like a new burst of energy between us. Our hands find new tantalizing places, mine slipping below his jeans, resting on the top of his toned ass. He skims my bare, sensitive skin along my ribs. His incredibly high stamina surpasses mine, and he has to stop kissing to let me catch my breath.

He runs his finger over my tingly lip. "Every theory you've ever fucking had about men, I'm going to prove wrong," he tells me.

My chest collapses. I may pass out from this moment. I truly thought it would never come. "I had a theory that not kissing is sexier than kissing." I was so stupid. I could do this forever with Ryke.

"I know," he says. "And now?" His eyes fall to my lips.

I smile bright. "Just fucking kiss me."

And he does, a grin lifting his lips. But the embrace turns just as sensual, just as intoxicating as the last. His hand rises up my shorts, underneath my panties, landing on my ass. He squeezes and I cry into his shoulder.

I dig into him and clench his hair harder, and then I kiss the corner of his mouth, denying him my lips for a second. He tries to go forward to kiss me fully, and I resist, drawing back an inch. He stares at my mouth, his lips parted as he watches me with a lustful gaze. When I close the gap between us, my tongue runs against his, and his muscles harden.

A groan catches in his throat.

He's heated every ice cold crevice. Nothing about being with him is uncomfortable.

It feels right.

I toy with him again. And I lean back, subconsciously thinking a wall will brace me. There's nothing. Air rushes out of me as I fall backwards, but Ryke supports me with his hands on my bottom. He lets me hang upside down, the blood rushing to my head.

These electric sensations heighten by ten more notches. I laugh, and he lifts me back up. My hair drapes messily in my face like I forcefully came to a stop on a roller coaster.

My voice reverberates off the cavernous stairwell. "I have a theory that skipping foreplay makes sex better, remember that?"

We've crossed one boundary, and I know we're both the type of people to never slow down, to run around the bases at high speed. I want that with him. To freakin' make a home run like we're track stars on a baseball field.

He kisses my cheek, which almost restarts us all over again, but we restrain ourselves from attacking full force. "Not now," he says. His eyes flicker to my canvas watch.

"I'm not tired," I tell him. "If anything, I'm…" I can't even say it.

"Wet?" He takes his hand off my ass and slips it down the front of my shorts. Holy shit. His fingers don't go beneath my panties. He cups my heat, his eyes never leaving mine. "You're not nearly soaked enough for me, sweetheart."

Ahh. I breathe heavily and I wrap my arms around his neck. *Take me there.* Right when I think he's going to brush my panties to the side and slip his fingers into me, he retracts his hand from my shorts.

"Why stop?" I frown. "Is it because we're in a stairwell?"

His hard gaze soaks in all of me. "Calloway, I'd fuck you in every corner of every hallway and then do it over again for good measure."

My jaw unhinges.

"And I'd be more likely to fuck you in a stairwell than on a bed."

"Why?"

He combs his fingers through my hair and holds the back of my head. "It's more fucking fun." He kisses me strongly again, my whole body pulling towards him. My hips roll into his pelvis. He turns his head from me and grips my waist hard. "Fuck," he groans. His eyes fall to the way we're pressed together, his cock rubbing along a throbbing place of mine.

"How big are you?" I ask with heavy breath. I can feel him through his jeans. I know he's big. I know he's hard. I know he's everything that I want.

"You're not finding out today."

I stick out my bottom lip.

"Don't flash those green doe eyes at me."

"They don't melt your heart of stone?" I banter.

"Stone can't fucking melt," he retorts. "It just grows hot."

"Are you hot now?"

His brows rise. "What do you think?"

I smile again. "So…" And then my lips slowly downturn as I realize something. He never answered me about his "girlfriend"—not really. "Are you going back to that girl when we return to Philly?" Is this some Paris hookup while we're both away from our families?

He glares. "Fuck no."

"Would you be upset if I dated the model from the other night again?"

His reaction says it all. He sets me on my feet with firm hands, and he clenches the railing on either side of me. Anger laces his dark eyes. "Do you want to date the other model?" His words sound stilted like he tried pretty hard not to swear.

"Wow, you managed to say that without cursing."

"You're killing me."

I poke his chest with my finger. "You *crushed* my heart when you told me to go sleep with another guy."

"I didn't fucking—" He growls in frustration and runs his hand through his hair. I love, love when he does that, even when he's upset. It lights my core on fire. "I never wanted you to screw someone else! For fuck's sake, it broke my heart telling you to even pursue another guy." He glances at his jacket pocket and groans with more irritation. He takes out his vibrating phone and ignores the call, putting it back. "Look at me," he says.

My eyes meet his. He cages me back against the railing. "I can't watch you flirt with another fucking guy."

I shouldn't bring it up again, but I do. "I watched you go down on another girl." Pain wells inside me again, my stomach tightening at the image. "You kissed her knee. You looked at her like she was beautiful—"

He covers my mouth with his large hand. "Fucking stop." He breathes heavily, a guy that runs marathons, a guy that scales mountains in minutes. "I never slept with her, but I can't take back what you saw. I wish to God I fucking could."

He never slept with her. This almost brings tears to my eyes. I see how much this moment is tearing him up, and the torture that I feel reflects equally in his rigid posture and cinched brows.

He keeps his hand over my mouth. "I've ignored a lot of bad shit in my life, but I don't want to ignore this one good thing anymore. It's too painful." He stares at me deeply, my chest rising with something pure and warm. "I kissed you tonight because I want your lips to only touch mine. From now until forever. That's the fucking truth." He drops his hand.

My heart can't stop slamming into my chest. *From now until forever.* I skim my hands down his arms. He doesn't withdraw. He's serious. He wants to be together, no more dating other people. "What about your brother?" I ask the million dollar question, the crux. "And my mom... my dad?" They're the biggest roadblocks.

"It's up to you," he says. "We can tell them, or we can do this in private and wait until the age gap isn't a big deal to them anymore."

"When will that be?"

He shakes his head. "I don't know. Maybe when you're twenty."

A year and a half. I think I can wait that long. If we tell everyone now, I see my mom tearing him away from me. I see too many headaches and more heartbreaks. I just want something good. Something right without anything abysmal attached. So I say, "I don't want to tell anyone."

He nods and looks relieved by my answer. I don't think he was ready to confront his brother. He backs up a little, but as he watches me, he grimaces. It's the same expression he had when I brought up Ian. "I'm going to spell it out for you," he says, "because I'm still fucking worried you don't understand what I want."

I smile. "Okay."

"We're together," he says pointblank. "I'm not going to be with anyone but you, even if no one else fucking knows that. We don't date other people for show. They just think we're single."

I nod. "I like it."

I hear his phone buzz. He takes out his cell again, annoyed. He ignores the second call. "We need to go upstairs to your room."

I tilt my head with a playful smile. "How forward of you."

"Cute," he says. "But we're not fucking. We're meeting two people there."

I frown. "What?"

"I didn't fly alone."

The bottom of my stomach drops and my eyes grow to saucers.

"You think I could leave Philly to check on you without worrying anyone else? They read the tabloids too." They learned that I was thrown out of the Havindal collection.

"Who?" I ask. "Who came?"

He touches the small of my back and guides me up the stairs. "Surprise."

I do like surprises.

But this one will be bad no matter what. Being alone with Ryke sounded like a hot, steamy vacation. Add in one of my sisters or his *brother*, and it turns awkward and uncomfortable...but definitely more dangerous.

Danger. That is alluring. And it's what partially drew us together in the first place.

I realize, right now, that this is the beginning of something new.

< **21** >

Ryke Meadows

L o raises his arms as we walk down the hallway towards him. "I called you ten times. What the hell were you doing?"

I point to Daisy beside me, a normal amount of distance between us even though I'd rather be back in the stairwell, with her wrapped in my arms. "I was trying to find this one. She wasn't in her room."

"I went for a vending machine run," she says, masking the lie with a bright, overwhelmingly beautiful smile.

Lo relaxes some. He wears a backwards baseball cap, looking like a fucking '90s kid. But it's partly to disguise himself from people, not that it's doing a good job. He has striking features that bring attention, even among male models.

"So you came to check up on me?" Daisy asks with an even larger smile, bouncing on her feet as we stop by her hotel door. She looks to the other person next to my brother.

Two inches taller stands Connor Cobalt.

We're the only ones who hopped on Connor's company jet.

And it's a new situation that none of us are used to—the three of us alone with Daisy. Usually it's Lily, not the youngest, wildest Calloway with us.

"Yeah," Lo says. "How are you doing?"

"Better." She fits a strand of hair behind her ear.

Daisy looks fucking terrible. And I don't say anything about it, but I think we all can tell that she hasn't been sleeping. She's really fucking pale, her body frailer, and all I want to do is hold her and tuck her into bed. I wear my concern outwardly, and I don't give a shit if someone hounds me for it. I'm fucking concerned, and I'm going to stay that way.

"Right…" My brother says, not believing her at all as he scrutinizes her features.

I asked Lo to come along. I've been so fucking worried about his state of mind that it'd be just as hard leaving him as it was leaving Daisy.

But the tension builds in the room because we all know his feelings about my friendship with her. Now that Daisy and I have moved beyond that title, the lie weighs heavy on my chest.

Lies.

I'm used to being wound tight by them, and the guilt will come later. It always does.

"Bad news," Lo says, turning to me. "Connor fucked up."

I let out a short laugh. "I never thought I'd hear those magic fucking words."

"So much of what you just said, I hate," Connor tells me causally, as though he doesn't really care, but I see that he does when his lips twitch.

Magic—Connor fucking hates magic.

He also hates being wrong. "What'd you do?" I ask.

"Nothing," Connor says. "Which is why I didn't fuck up."

"He forgot to book a hotel room," Lo explains. "And with the Rugby World Cup happening in Paris this weekend, plus Fashion Week, there's nothing here or close by available."

Fuck. "How'd you forget to do something?" I ask Connor, cringing the moment I give him that much credit. But honestly, he has a photographic memory. He has charts and alerts and fucking notes everywhere to remind him of things too.

"Not that it's any of your business—I'm having a fight with my wife," he says. "My mind was somewhere else." He's still fighting with her?

"Is she okay?" Daisy asks, pulling her phone out of her pocket to text Rose.

"She's how she normally is," Connor says vaguely.

"Bitchy," Lo clarifies. "High-strung, obsessive compulsive." He smiles. "God, I'm so glad she didn't come."

Connor's eyebrow arches. "I'm starting to be thankful too. Truthfully, I'm not in the mood to handle two five-year-olds." He pauses. "And in case you didn't catch that, I was referring to her and you."

Lo laughs, not taking the insult to heart. See—that shit is fucking annoying. If I said that to Lo, he'd give me the cold shoulder. But for Connor, he can say whatever he wants in this mellow, chill way and get any reprieve from my brother.

It irritates me so much that I turn to Daisy and hold out my hand. "Your key card." She takes it out of her pocket and passes it to me. I unlock the door, hearing their conversation continue without me really in it.

Daisy asks, "She's not texting me back. Should I call her?"

"No," Connor says as I walk into Daisy's room. They follow close behind.

She has a chair propped underneath the handle of her bathroom door. I set it back on four legs before any of the guys notice and ask questions.

"I'm worried though," Daisy says. "She usually answers me within the second."

"Don't take offense to this," he begins. "You're younger than Rose by seven years, and while I don't take that much stock in ages, she still feels weak if you console her. In Rose's mind, that's her job."

"But you can console her?" Daisy asks.

"I'm her husband, her equal."

I can sense Daisy reading into that last word. Her shoulders fall at the idea of not being equal to her sister, at being *less* somehow.

"Hey," I nod to Daisy and shake my head at her. "Don't overanalyze what he's fucking saying."

She barely looks at me. Then she asks Connor, "If it's her job to console me, why isn't she here?"

This shadowed anger passes through his features. "She's challenging me." Connor stuffs his hands in his black slacks. "She wants me to figure out whatever's been upsetting her, and she'll do anything to beat me."

"I thought she said that she had meetings all week," Lo says with a frown.

"Maybe she does." Connor stuffs his hands in his black slacks. "But Rose would drop any meeting for her sisters. She should be here. She *would* be here otherwise. But she wants to win, and winning means putting an ocean between us." Their relationship is so fucking weird.

"What do you think she's hiding?" Lo asks.

"If I knew, the game would be over and she'd be here," Connor says easily.

"Maybe I can get it out of her," Daisy offers.

"Unlikely," Connor says. "Lily is probably the only one who knows." Even though Connor is being honest—that Daisy isn't the sister Rose would turn to for anything—it still hurts her. She tucks her hair behind her ear again and then disappears into the bathroom.

Connor notices her quick exit.

I take a step towards him and lower my voice. "I swear to fucking God, you need to work on your tact around Daisy."

"First off, don't swear to God around me. He's not listening when I'm in the room. And secondly, I thought she could handle it. I'm misreading a lot of things today. I admit that." He clenches his teeth, something he rarely does.

"If you need to go home, go home," I tell Connor.

Lo crosses his arms. "But Lily is there with Rose, so whatever she's going through, you know her sister will take care of her."

Lily had to stay back because she has class at Princeton, the only one of us that's still in college.

And I can tell Lo wants Connor to be here for the duration of the trip. We're starting our drive to California after this. If Connor bails now, he won't be coming with us.

"If you go back home," I say, "Rose isn't going to tell you regardless."

Connor nods. "It's better if I'm here. We'd tear each other apart if we were together right now."

After a couple minutes of setting down our bags and getting a look around the hotel room, Daisy slips out of the bathroom in pajama shorts and a tank top, her hair still in a high bun. She doesn't appear upset anymore. While my brother bends down to his bag, digging through a pocket, she approaches me with a coy smile that lifts the corner of her lips.

I remember those soft pink lips on mine, my tongue in her mouth. It seems like a fucking dream. My eyes flicker to my brother, still searching through his bag.

I run a hand through my hair, suppressing that image. While I stand in the middle of the room, she comes close. I watch her carefully as she stops only an inch away. I look down at her.

She whispers softly, "Did you bring my birth control?"

Her eyes flit to my brother for a second, but his back is turned to us. I try not to worry about him right now.

"You willing to gain five fucking pounds by taking it now?" I ask her in the same hushed voice.

She nods, and her breath shallows. She's not wearing a bra—she rarely does—but her nipples harden, visible with the form-fitting top.

I struggle to stop thinking about taking it in my mouth, my tongue at work. I know we just had our first kiss, but I want to do so many things to her, with her. One of the reasons why I'm glad we're not telling anyone—it forces us to go slow.

I would have fucked her in the stairwell if Connor and Lo weren't here right now.

And then I'd fuck her again on the bed.

But this heightens everything. Drawing it out will make our first time even better. And I want it to be so fucking amazing.

I glance from her breasts to her eyes. She registers the signal and crosses her arms over her chest, her face heating already. "This almost never happens to me," she says under her breath.

"Stop imagining me fucking you," I breathe, "and maybe it won't." I brush a flyaway hair out of her face.

She smiles like I guessed her thoughts correctly. "That doesn't sound fun." She glances at my brother again who stands up with his toiletry kit. "Birth control?" she asks.

"Front pocket of my bag." I take a couple steps away from her, and I flip through a room service menu on the end table.

My brother leaves the bathroom door open while he brushes his teeth, and Daisy unzips my duffel bag. Connor watches her, glancing from his laptop screen to Daisy kneeling on the ground.

Before he asks questions, she says, "Who's sleeping in the bed?"

"You," he tells her.

"That's stupid. Ryke and Lo can share the bed, and I'll take the chair tonight."

"No," I say at the same time as my brother, who shouts from the bathroom.

"I don't want to waste the *whole* bed."

Connor adds, "Ryke can share the bed with you. Problem solved." He types with speed, his eyes not leaving his computer screen. "What talents I have."

Lo peeks through the doorway, his toothbrush in his mouth. "Did you smoke a bowl on the plane? Because you've got to be goddamn high to put her in bed with my brother *while* we're in the room."

"I didn't say anything about sex." He stops typing. "I don't want to watch that any more than you do."

Daisy's cheeks redden. *Fucking fantastic.* I forgot she saw his porn tape. I shut the menu. That's not particularly something I want to imagine.

I run my hand through my hair. "I'm going to sleep on the floor. It's not a big deal."

"Of course. You probably feel at home lower to the ground," Connor says with a growing smile.

Lo won't stick up for me where Connor is concerned. If someone else said that to me, maybe. But I'm just supposed to take Connor's shit because he's Connor. "Fuck off," I tell him, not even wanting to waste time on a good retort.

This just makes Connor gloat more.

Lo retreats to the bathroom, turning on the faucet.

I watch Daisy. She keeps her hands within the fucking duffel pocket, and the only time it comes out is to pop a pill in her mouth. She quickly zips it back and stands up.

Connor catches her, and he stares between us in suspicion. "What'd you just take?" he asks her, his voice quiet, which means he's at least nice enough not to alert my brother.

"Advil," she lies too easily. "I have cramps." She slides into the bed without another word. I can tell that Connor doesn't believe her. If there's anyone who can see through Daisy like me, it's him. But he goes back to his work, not uncomfortable by anything she said. But my brother is. I watch him linger in the bathroom a little longer.

I find her Ambien in the end table drawer, and I dole out two pills and hand them to her. She glances at Connor, but he's busying himself, no longer interested.

I pass her a water bottle, and she hesitantly accepts it. Her paranoid gaze flickers to the balcony door.

"I'll lock up," I whisper so Connor can't hear. "But you have to fucking trust that no one is going to hide in the bathroom." There's nothing I can do about that door.

She nods. "Okay." She sits up on her elbows, her gaze on my lips.

I can't kiss her right now. Because I can already tell with us, a kiss won't stop at one fucking kiss. It'll last five minutes, and we can't afford that with my brother here.

I surprise her by running my hand slowly from her hipbone to the side of her ribs to her breast—all above her thin tank top. My muscles tighten as she stiffens in arousal, especially as I skim my thumb over her hard nipple.

I've suppressed myself from doing something like this for so long. It's a fucking one-eighty to even go this far. The adrenaline rush is dizzying my fucking head. I watch her slender body, on the bed, lighting up underneath my hand. It grips my cock, and stopping is harder than ever before.

But I imagine my brother.

Beating my face in.

It helps. Somewhat. But I also imagine her with another guy. And *that* stops me from thinking *this is so wrong. Turn back now, Ryke.*

I won't ever turn back.

This is it for me. I want to make this fucking work as best I can.

Her mouth falls, a heavy breath escaping. And then she smiles so fucking bright.

I take my hand off her as soon as I sense my brother returning to the room. Daisy is so flushed that she turns into her pillow to collect herself.

I love watching her feel those sensations—especially after hearing how much she's been denied them. I want to put her in a state of euphoria more than anything.

I leave her so I can secure the balcony door. The lock is pathetic, nothing more than a turn of a latch. *No wonder she hasn't been fucking sleeping.* After that, I head to the entrance, locking the deadbolt and sliding the chain across. When I turn around, Connor's eyes flicker up from the computer.

"I don't know if you've heard, but Sara is making waves again," Connor says.

"My mom has already caused a fucking tsunami, so whatever waves she's making, I don't really want to hear about it."

Connor flashes me his phone, not letting me ignore this. I grab the damn thing from his hand. The headline of an article reads: TELL-ALL INTERVIEW WITH SARA HALE COMING SOON ON 60 MINUTES.

"You've got to be fucking kidding me," I say, glaring at the image of my mother, sitting with her legs crossed on a chair against a navy blue backdrop. I have my father's dark hair, not hers. She's been described as a Julia Roberts lookalike with golden-brown locks, her nose a little sharp. She's originally from a poor town of New Jersey, a fighter, she used to call herself when she yelled at my dad on the phone.

"Do you *know* where I came from?" she would sneer. "If I got here from nothing, you think I can't stay here and protect my son from *you?* I'm a fighter. I'm going to do everything I can to keep my head above water. If you don't believe that, then think again, Jonathan. Think again!"

She's a woman who can't let go of a fucking grudge.

I examine the fine print of the article, detailing the interview to come.

Sara opens up about her marital problems with Jonathan Hale, her recent fallout with son, Ryke Meadows, and her plea to reconnect with Ryke. She also discusses the allegations regarding Loren Hale, and in a preview clip, she says, "Through the twelve years that I was with Jonathan, he was nothing but verbally and mentally abusive. The trauma my own son went through with his father…I won't ever forgive Jonathan for what he's done."

"Don't break my phone, please," Connor says in a controlled voice. "That's my lifeline to my wife."

I'm gripping his cell so hard that I do almost crack the screen. I toss it back to him, my muscles on fire. "Now they think Jonathan traumatized me," I say with the shake of my head. How can this be my life?

Connor slips his phone in his pocket. "The article could have spun one of her lines. It's fragmented. Don't get upset until you watch the interview."

I shake my head. "Whatever." I take a few trained breaths, and it returns to normal. But I'd love to go fucking hit something right now. I need the gym, to just pour my energy and this pressure somewhere healthy instead of keeping it in my chest.

I glance back at Daisy. She tries to force her drowsy eyes open, watching me from the bed, her head on the pillow.

"I wish people were nicer," she says softly before yawning.

Me fucking too.

< **22** >

Ryke Meadows

I can't sleep.

Not when I know what's going to happen.

She tosses and turns underneath her covers, kicking an invisible fucking enemy. And then around 5:00 a.m., she starts screaming. She shoots up, her eyes snapped open, and she thrashes, scurrying back towards the headboard and swatting at the air.

Her high-pitched shrieks blister my ears and instantly wake up Connor and Lo. I'm already on my feet, by her side while she stares off, focused on something that I can't see, on something that's not there.

She's still asleep.

That's the scary fucking part.

"What the hell?" Lo says, rising with Connor.

"Daisy, Daisy," I try, but I know it's fucking useless. She'll wake up when she's ready. I slide on the bed, kneeling, and I reach out to hold her, but her fist flies at my shoulder, punching me hard, like I'm the attacker.

"Get away!" she screams, fear pulsing in her big green eyes. "Leave me alone! Just leave me alone! I don't want this! I don't want this!" Terrified fucking tears pour down her cheeks.

Fucking A.

Lo rushes to the bed. "Daisy?! What the hell…" He climbs on the bed while she screams and cries, kicking back so quickly that the sheets bunch at her feet. She clutches the mattress beside her. Lo stands up on the bed and tries to pick her up underneath the arms.

She wails on him the moment he touches her, kicking and whipping her fists every which way. Lo raises his hands in the air in surrender and glances at me. "What the fuck?"

I stand up with him on the bed, towering over her. I smack his chest slightly with my hand. "She's still fucking asleep."

His brows furrow. "Her eyes are open." He kicks a pillow at her and she freaks out again, tears running down her cheeks. My heart is racing.

"Daisy, you're okay," Lo tells her. "No one is in here." She's still unresponsive, and Lo turns to Connor who's beside the bed, on the ground unlike us.

He wears an unreadable expression, watching Daisy's hysterical fit.

I'm afraid she's going to fucking hurt herself. Her nails start digging into her palms. So I grab her ankle and drag her back down onto the bed. She rolls over on her stomach like she's crawling through barbed wire.

I bend down and flip Daisy onto her back. She thrashes. "No, no!"

I hate how wrong this looks. I want her to wake up so fucking badly, especially before someone hears her screams through the walls and calls the hotel staff.

I press my knees onto her legs, pinning her down. And I hold her wrists on either side of her body, and she screams bloody fucking murder at being trapped like this. I end up having to use one hand to cover her mouth, and she slaps me *hard* across the face. The sting burns, and I taste blood, my lip busting open.

Lo kneels and grabs her hand, not letting her go.

She's stronger in these nightmares than she is awake because she's driven by fear, an adrenaline rush that I can't fucking begin to imagine.

Her tears well and redden her eyes. I lean forward, my face close to hers, my fingers digging into her cheek. "Wake up!" I shout. "Daisy, wake the *fuck* up!" *Come on, sweetheart. Fight this.*

"Her pulse is out of control," Lo says, his voice flooded with worry.

I take my hand off her mouth and touch the top of her breast, her heart practically pounding through. She has to fucking wake up and calm down.

"No!" she cries like she's dying, like someone's killing her. Sweat beads her forehead, hot tears dripping off her jaw. "*Please,*" she cries, shaking her head from side to side. "Please…"

"Wake up," I growl in her ear, combing her damp hair out of her face. *Wake the fuck up.*

"Be careful," Lo tells me.

I'm not hurting her. Whoever's tormenting Daisy in her head is. I glance over my shoulder at Connor. "Can you hand me a glass of water."

Daisy is about to start screaming again, so I muffle her noises with my hand once more.

"You shouldn't pour water on her face if she's having a night terror."

Lo glares at Connor. "You know what's going on and you didn't think to share?"

I stare hard at the mattress, ignoring the guilt that tries to fuck me over. *You've known all along what's going on, Ryke. For months.*

"She's asleep," Connor starts to explain.

"Just give me the fucking water," I tell him. "I'm not going to drown her." *I've done this before.*

Connor's brows pinch as he scrutinizes me, and then he hands me her water bottle—I think more out of curiosity of what I'm about to do.

I pour some water on my free hand, and then stroke her hair out of her face again, cooling her down and hopefully waking her up soon.

She jolts at the new sensation and thrashes again. But I keep her pinned in the same position. Lo clasps her whole arm as she tries jerking out of his grasp. My muscles burn the longer I watch tears squeeze out of her eyes and fear wash over her face.

"How can she still be asleep?" Lo asks. "She's looking at Ryke."

"It's a state between REM sleep and wakefulness," Connor explains. His eyes meet mine. "How long has she had this problem?"

I shake my head, and Daisy's leg slips beneath my knee, trying to fucking kick me again. I shift her back. "I wouldn't fucking know."

He doesn't believe me. "You haven't seen her like this before?" he questions with an arched brow.

"Why would you think I have?" I retort with a dark glare.

"Because you're the closest person to her, and you don't look surprised by this."

"I am fucking surprised," I retort.

Connor shakes his head, still disbelieving.

"I just fucking reacted, Connor," I retort, my brother frowning between me and him. He's trying to give me the benefit of the doubt, which is making this fucking painful. "Stop turning it into a thing."

And then Daisy's eyes slowly focus on me. Her tense limbs slacken, but the panic stays in her gaze.

I peel my hand off her mouth. "Daisy?"

She blinks a few times, and Lo releases her arm. I sit up off her body, and she touches her head in confusion. When she truly meets my eyes, her face breaks and she starts crying again.

I immediately lift her into my arms, and she hides her face in her hands. "They were here," she says. "They were stabbing me—"

"Hey," I say roughly, stroking the back of her head. "You're safe. No one's here but me, Connor and Lo." She's on my lap, in my arms, where she's been so many times before.

But it's fucking different now.

We've never been in front of other people. And we've never called ourselves anything other than friends.

Lo climbs off the bed. "Daisy, who's *them?*"

Her hot tears wet my gray shirt, and she mumbles into my chest, "Bad guys."

Lo frowns. "What'd she say?" he asks me.

"Bad guys," I say. "It was a fucking nightmare." But no matter how imaginary her dream was, to her, in those three minutes, it felt real, more so than any kind of bad dream I'm used to.

I understand why she'd rather not take the medicine at all, but she has to sleep some. It's trading one bad place for another.

Daisy's arms wrap underneath mine, clutching onto me tightly. My brother gives me a single warning look like, *You can't lead her on.*

His concern is warranted. I would feel the same fucking thing if I was him in this situation. But no part of me wants to disentangle her from my body.

Still, I know I have to.

I whisper in her ear, "I'm going to tuck you into bed, and you're going back to sleep."

"What?" she breathes. She glances up at me with wide eyes, and she shakes her head. "No, Ryke. I can't go back…"

"You'll be fine," I tell her, prying her arms from mine and setting her back against the mattress.

"No," she cries. She springs up immediately. "No, please don't do this…I need you—"

"Daisy," I say her name forcefully. My lips find her ear. "You have to fucking try to sleep again." I rise off the bed, and she hugs her legs and rests her forehead on her knees, sobbing.

I turn to my brother, my heart clenching, and I throw my hands up like, *What do you want me to fucking do now?*

His brows are furrowed in concern. "Daisy? What can we do? I can get Lily on the phone."

She shakes her head and wipes her tears. "I'm sorry I woke you."

While my brother keeps conversing with her, Connor suddenly rests a firm hand on my shoulder. "I need to talk to you," he says quietly.

He looks angry. His deep blue eyes pierce me in accusation, and his fingers are digging into my skin. He rarely shows this kind of emotion—and he's letting me see it on purpose.

He knows.

He knows I've been keeping her problems a secret, and he probably gathered that they stemmed from a traumatic event.

I don't want to talk about her issues with him. "Maybe later," I say, stepping out of his hold.

"Ryke, this is *serious.*"

"You don't think I fucking know that?" I growl under my breath. I glance back at Lo who's looking between us, but he doesn't say anything and Connor and I shut down the conversation.

Lo hands Daisy a water bottle. She takes small sips, leaning against the headboard. "How many times has this happened?" my brother asks her.

"Not that much." She rubs her eyes with the back of her hand. "It was just a nightmare."

"Not according to the smartest guy in the goddamn room."

"The world," Connor corrects him, hiding his anger from my brother. "Being smarter than the three of you really isn't that big of an achievement." He pauses. "No offense."

"I'm fucking offended," I retort.

"Oh, sorry," he says flatly. "I don't really care about your feelings."

Lo shoots us a look. "Now's not the time for you both to go at it." He takes the water from Daisy when she finishes with it. "Are you going to do something about your night terrors or whatever they're called—or are you hoping it'll magically go away?"

She smiles weakly. "Magic," she says. "I've consulted with three blue fairies and Tinkerbell. I think they've got me covered."

Lo glares.

"Joking," she tells him. "I've been to a doctor. It hasn't been as bad as tonight. I think with what happened at the runway the other day, my head as been all screwy." She downplays the degree of her illness. I would believe her in this moment.

I know Lo does.

I know Connor can't.

The facts that he just acquired disprove her words, and he can easily look past Daisy's sweet-natured voice and bright smile. He's talked to me a few times about Daisy being depressed—and if she needed to go see a therapist. He diagnoses people from afar and only fucking brings it up when he wants to.

Daisy rests her head on the wooden headboard, her shirt stained with sweat, her limbs sagging like she just ran a marathon. I watch her foot cramp and her calf muscle spasm, and she brings her leg to her chest and massages it herself with a wince.

Normally that'd be me.

But I stand at the edge of the bed, close to coming clean about everything right here. I just want to hold her. Even if I told my brother the truth, I can see Lo kicking me out of the room, tossing my bag in my face, telling me to get on a plane.

Like he said before, he let me into his life, and it seems like I went after his girlfriend's little sister like a predator.

That was never my fucking intention.

Sure, I want to fuck her. But it's more than that. It's always been more than that.

I stay quiet and rub my jaw, so much taken out of me tonight. If I do right by her, I do wrong by him. I wonder if the only way to move forward is to unearth my past with my brother.

I don't know if I'm ready for that shit storm.

I just want to forget with him—but I wonder who's been the stronger brother all this time.

Lo has confronted our father. He's worked out his feelings. He's rebuilt a relationship with him *while* trying to stay sober.

I'm the one who can't deal.

Maybe that has to fucking change.

< 23 >

Daisy Calloway

"Ryke, what's with the busted lip?" Cameras flash, and paparazzi swarm me. Mikey has his arm braced out, standing in front of me with his dirty blond hair and Bermuda shorts. Ryke grips my shoulder, guiding me towards the glass hotel doors.

"Did you get in a fight with one of Daisy's ex-boyfriends?"

"Ryke, did your brother punch you?"

"What happened?"

They all ask roughly the same questions, and Ryke says nothing. A bruise has begun to form on his cheekbone from my thumb ring hitting him. I wish I could rewind time, shake my half-coherent body and tell myself to stop freaking out.

I've hit him before in a night terror, but not this badly.

Once we enter the sanctuary of the hotel, the noise dies down. Mikey spins towards me. "I'm going to grab something to eat before the buffet closes, but I'll escort you to your room first just to be safe."

"You can go eat now," Ryke tells him. "I'll watch her."

Mikey looks to me for affirmation since, technically, I'm his boss. "Go," I say. "Eat something yummy for me."

"Squid." He rubs his stomach in mock hunger.

Right now, that actually sounds delicious.

"Hey, stay outside!" a hotel concierge yells at a cameraman that opens the door. The lenses are pressed to the tinted glass, still trying to capture photos of us.

"We better go," I say. We split from Mikey and wait for an elevator in the hotel lobby.

Ryke watches Mikey disappear and then nods to me. "It's good that he's here, even if he can't keep up with you most of the time."

A camera flashes in my eyes, a large body behind the lens. I blink, and my heart jolts. I look around for the source, but there's nothing around us but people rolling their suitcases to the lobby elevators.

"Daisy," Ryke says. He holds my face, trying to get me to look at him.

Sweat gathers on my forehead. "It wasn't real," I whisper. That flash was in my head.

He stares at me with more concern. "What'd you see?"

I take a deep breath. This has happened before. "I think it was when the cameraman broke into my room." The incident was when I didn't have Mikey, when all six of us were rooming together in Philly for a period of time. We were under a bigger spotlight than usual, and pictures of us were worth a lot of money.

"Can you tell me about it?" he asks, his hands warm on my jaw. I hold his wrist to keep him here, not wanting him to break away from me just yet.

"You know what happened," I whisper. "You were there." I've repeated it to my therapist before, and it still feels the same. It still feels like the past, but why does it constantly creep up to scare me? I want to let it go. I've tried to let it go, but it won't let go of me.

"Just two sentences, Dais."

As I remember the event, cold washes over me, and I shiver. He draws me closer to his body. I swallow hard and say, "He started taking pictures while I was sleeping, and I woke up from the flashes. I called you, and you arrived from across the hall and beat him up. The end."

"Not the end," he retorts.

All of my sisters and their significant others think it's the end. It should be. The cameraman got fined for trespassing. Ryke bruised two knuckles. And my dad hired more security outside of the townhouse we were living in. It all turned out okay.

Except maybe my head.

"Oh yeah," I continue with a weak smile, "after that, you used to watch movies with me every night."

He rolls his eyes.

But he knows that one night he spent with me turned into a week and then a month. And we never really looked back. Every night, the television would play in the background, and I'd drift off. When I woke up, a blanket would be tucked around me and Ryke would be gone.

He says, "And then you moved back to your parent's house and everything was a fucking mess."

I had ten months left until I graduated prep school, until I could move out. I thought my mom would fight me on it—the idea of me living in an apartment alone so young. But she saw how much I wanted this.

It was her greatest kindness. One that I won't ever forget. She let me live on my own, and in doing so, I was able to live close to Ryke. I could have stayed with Rose, but she was already so worried about Lily and Lo's addictions. I knew if I lived with her, she'd be consumed by my problems too.

And I wanted her to live her own life. I didn't want to be the center of attention or cause anyone more grief. Pulling Ryke into my mess was enough of a burden. I couldn't imagine doing that to more people I love.

Ryke runs his thumb beneath my eye. "Those ten months when you moved back home—they drove me fucking insane."

"Why?"

"It was ten months I couldn't placate your anxiety, I couldn't shield you from anything that came through your doors. I wasn't a hallway away, not a floor, not a room. I was a half an hour from you, Dais." He pauses. "And we both fucking know it was those ten months that changed you."

Something happened that I don't like to talk about. It's the one thing that tightens my throat.

It was when my simple fear of nighttime turned into waking up screaming. It was when every horror in my life met me repeatedly in my dreams.

The elevator chimes. I flinch, but the noise cuts into the tension.

We let a family of five on ahead of us, the small children tugging their suitcases through the doors. I eye Ryke's bruise again and my stomach flips. I slide the gold ring off my finger and put it in his hand. "Here. You can have this back." I've already apologized for hitting him. And he did what he always does when I say I'm sorry for things I can't control.

He glared.

Ryke appraises the ring, and his features darken. "I gave this to you. I don't want it back." He grabs my hand, and instead of just handing it to me, he slides it slowly on my finger.

We're about to be alone together for the first time since the stairwell.

If the elevator would ever get here, that is.

"You didn't give it to me," I rebut. "I won it in a poker game."

"Same fucking thing."

I wear the ring a lot. I had it resized to fit my thumb, and the jeweler told me that the design on the front was an Irish coat of arms.

A family crest.

I never brought it up, but now that we're together, I kind of want to. "You told me it wasn't an heirloom," I say while he watches me closely.

"It's not."

"It's an Irish coat of arms, Ryke," I say. "Your dad is Irish."

He shrugs. "So it was my father's. It's not like it was passed down generations to fucking generations. It was his, and he gave it to me when I was eleven or twelve. I don't even remember. It means nothing."

"I know," I say, "because people don't put family heirlooms that mean something to them in poker kitties." He's so detached from his dad, and this proves it. He's also so unlike Lo, who has an antique pocket watch from his father that he keeps in a safe. He brought it out once to prove to Connor that he owns something historic.

Ryke ignores his mom and dad like he's trying to erase them from his life. Maybe it's easier for him to just forget the past than be consumed by hurt and hate.

Ryke hits the "up" button again. He rubs his lips and then stares down at me with that swirling darkness. "Truth," he says, "I don't want you to take off the ring. I've fucking loved that you wear something of mine."

I smile. *Loved.* I wonder for how long. We played that poker game on a flight back from Cancun.

I was sixteen.

I take a step towards him, despite being in semi-public. I scrutinize his bottom lip, cut from where I slapped him.

"Does it hurt?" I ask.

"No," he says, looking at me with those brooding features, reminding me that of all the guys I've dated, no one has been as dangerous and mysterious as him.

The elevator chimes again. I drop my hand and slip inside, Ryke behind me. Thankfully an old couple with luggage waits for the next one.

We stand a few feet apart, and I realize that the fifth floor is just too close. We'll have time to make out for *maybe* thirty seconds. He leans forward to press the button, but instead of hitting my floor, he taps the 28.

"Are we going for a ride?" I ask him, my lips pulling higher.

"You are."

The doors shut, and he turns on me with this masculine power that draws me towards him in curiosity and need.

He's my wolf.

And instead of biting me, he kisses my lips passionately, our bodies igniting as soon as they connect. I moan the second his tongue meets mine, and his hands possess my ass, lifting me around his waist. The air leaves my lungs. And I grip the back of his hair, yanking hard.

A deep, throaty noise escapes him.

"Ryke," I cry, my head knocking into the wall as he pins me to the corner of the elevator. His kiss slows, eking out the tension that clenches my core. And I shut up, being consumed by his tongue, his hold, his experience.

His hand dips down between my legs, on the outside of my jean shorts. He cups that spot, and my legs spasm. *Ahhh!* The smallest nerves react like he drove his dick right into me.

I'm usually told to give hand jobs and go down on guys. I love that I now have choices, able to do whatever my mind wants. So I kiss his neck, lightly at first while his other hand rises underneath my shirt.

And then I suck deeply, clenching his hair with two hands. He stops going towards my breast, and he uses that hand as a support against the wall.

"*Fuck*," he breathes.

I cry again.

His favorite word is so overused, but I melt every single time he says it like that. Our lips find each other, as though they can't be apart for long. If he had more time, I wonder if he would go beneath my shorts.

I think he would.

He pauses so I can control my breathing. "What floor are we on?" he asks me.

I look over his shoulder. "Twenty-four."

He kisses my cheek, which turns into our lips locking again. As soon as we part, he drops me on my feet, and he hits the fifth floor button. The elevator stops on the twenty-eighth floor, and unfortunately, a hoard of female models slips in, laughing loudly and wearing clothes to go clubbing.

They speak in Russian and barely acknowledge us.

Ryke comes back to my side. "So you like my hair?" he asks with raised brows.

I stand on the tips of my toes and run my fingers through it, knowing he'll let me now. But even so, the tension winds between us, causing my body to curve towards him like a magnetic pull. We really need to find more time together. "It's soft, and I love that it's long enough for me to grab."

His muscles tighten, and his eyes flicker cautiously to the Russian girls, who've begun to whisper even more, their eyes flitting to us. He grabs my hands, forcing them down to my sides. I frown, confused. But he suddenly speaks, not to me though. To *them*.

In Russian.

I can't understand a word of it, but he has a lilt that matches theirs.

The tallest girl looks over her shoulder and laughs. "You make cute couple," she says in chopped English.

Ryke replies back in fluent Russian, his eyes narrowed.

She nods, says something else in the same language, and then leaves with her friends on the twentieth floor.

As soon as the doors close, I punch his arm. "Why didn't you tell me that you can speak Russian?" I knew he was fluent in Spanish, but Russian isn't a language commonly taught in schools.

He leans his arm on the wall. "Shouldn't your first fucking question be: *what were those girls saying?*"

I shake my head. He glared at the girls after we started talking in English, so I figured they must have been eavesdropping and whispering about us. "You accused them of listening to our conversation, didn't you? And then she said something snarky back." I smile wide and wag my brows. "Am I right?"

He tilts my chin up. "When did you get so fucking smart?"

"Didn't you hear? It was my second wish when I fell upon a magical lamp. *Be smarter than Connor Cobalt.* He doesn't know it yet."

"Don't pad his fucking ego," he tells me. Connor's ego is practically its own life force.

I run my hand up his arm, and then I keep it on the back of his neck. "Tell me," I say with a playful smile. "Did you learn Russian in prep school or are you like a secret badass CIA agent?"

He draws back, any talk of his past like a repellent. But I'm curious. He can't just speak Russian and act like it's no big deal. "Yeah, I learned some at Maybelwood." He shrugs. "I had an easy time picking up languages."

That's definitely not the whole story. "And?" I prod.

He struggles to open up, but after a long moment he says, "And when I was six or seven, my mom hired tutors. They were the ones that taught me." He stares at the ceiling and then shakes his head. "I curse so fucking much that people assume I'm just an idiot, a good athlete, but a fucking idiot. And I don't really care to prove anyone differently. There's no point."

I think it takes a really strong person to be that way, to not care what people think, even when you're better than they say. I have no idea why he'd be satisfied with doing that. "Why Russian?"

"Because she wanted me to learn it," he says. "I also know Spanish, Italian and French."

I gawk. "Wait, what?" I punch his arm again. "You know *French?!*" Rose and Connor speak French, and he's kept this knowledge to himself. "Oh my God." I smile deviously. "You know what my sister and Connor have been saying this whole time?"

"Most of it is stupid."

"Do they speak dirty to each other?" I've always been curious.

"Sometimes," he says. "But when they do, I try not to fucking listen. Trust me."

The elevator numbers blink from 10 to 9 to 8 in such a short period of time.

Ryke harbors so much inside his head, and he's kept so much to himself through the years. He's more solitary, more alone than I thought. Maybe he prefers it that way.

"Does Lo know?" I ask.

He frowns. "About what?"

"Russian, French, all of that."

He shakes his head. "No. It doesn't matter."

"But...it makes you, you," I say. "It's a part of who you are, isn't it?"

His jaw hardens. "It's not a part I like to fucking remember, Daisy."

Being controlled by his mom, he means. I think he chooses to forget so much from his childhood that it's made him into some shadowy figure that's just as tormented as his brother. I stand on the tips of my toes and kiss his cheek. "Thanks for telling me the truth."

The elevator doors open, and I head out of them. He catches my hand, intertwining his fingers with mine as we enter the hallway. It was a quick, impulsive gesture, one that has my heart on fire.

< 24 >

Ryke Meadows

I press the phone harder to my ear, thinking I've heard Connor wrong. "Excuse me?"

"I stepped out for maybe ten minutes to talk to Rose. I didn't think he would order anything but a Fizz and some fries."

"You're telling me you turned your back for ten fucking minutes and my brother downed *what?*"

"I don't know. But I can tell he's had something. He won't look at me, so I think he's drinking a Fizz and rum."

"Take the fucking glass from him." I pace across the hotel room, running my hand quickly through my hair.

"He's upset," Connor says. "We were bombarded by paparazzi all day, asking questions about your father. He couldn't handle it."

They were just supposed to be shopping along Rue St-Honoré. Lo texted me earlier that Connor bought out Hermes for Rose, having to ship most of the items back to his house. My brother seemed fine, but I should have fucking called him and asked.

"Don't fucking try to rationalize my brother's addiction," I growl. "He's sick, Connor."

Daisy watches me with concern, putting on a maroon turtleneck over her tank top. It's stitched with three gold Quidditch hoops and the words: *I'm a Keeper.* She mouths, *You okay?*

I can't answer her. I just glare at the carpet. "Connor, I'm being fucking serious. Grab the fucking drink from him right now."

"We're at the pub beside the hotel."

It clicks. Lo has no idea that Connor knows he's drinking. "You want me to be the bad fucking cop?"

"He has to have someone on his side, Ryke," Connor says. "He can't feel like everyone's ganging up on him."

"He's a fucking alcoholic!" I yell. "He's not even supposed to be *in* a bar. You're telling me you're the smartest guy in the fucking world, and you can't even pry a drink from his hand."

"I'm smart enough to know that it won't do any good coming from me. You've already proven to be the hard ass. I'm not taking that role."

"I sincerely hate you right now." I'm shaking I'm so fucking mad, and I don't know if it's because Connor accidentally turned his back on my brother or because I did. "You want to be his best fucking friend while I get shit on, fine. I don't care anymore."

I hang up, breathing heavily. "We have to go." I look up at Daisy, and she has a purse across her body.

"Ready," she says.

I grab my jacket, and we're fucking out of there.

I HAVE MY HAND on Daisy's lower back while we try to navigate through the crowded streets, filled with cameramen and sports fanatics, wearing red and white rugby jerseys.

"Go England!" a drunk guy shouts with an English accent, pumping his fucking fist into the air. That fist also has a beer in it. His friends chant a victory song, even though they lost to their South American rivals.

Daisy watches the sports fans in curiosity, her eyes lighting up at all the chaos. If there weren't cameras flocking her, I think she'd go up to one of them and start a conversation just for the hell of it.

I try calling my little brother for the third time, but he's not answering his phone. I'm going to kill him. No, I'm going to kill Connor and then I'm going to fucking kill him.

"Are you two dating?" a cameraman asks us.

"How long have you been a couple?"

"Kiss her, Ryke." That picture would be worth so much fucking money.

Daisy and I are always spotted out together, so that rumor mill has been churning for a while. It just makes her mom hate me more, and it makes my brother more cautious of us. But there's never been proof beyond my hand on her shoulder, my hand on her back, hugging—nothing serious.

Daisy locks eyes with one of the cameramen, her lips curving. "I don't kiss boys who ride motorcycles."

I almost smile, but her one quote shoots off ten more questions from each cameraman. We walk forward, and people keep congregating around us.

"Daisy, someone weird is behind you," a cameraman suddenly says.

"Yeah, there's a creeper. You better watch out, Daisy!"

I turn my head and find a leering guy who edges too close to her. No camera in his hand, but he's touching her fucking hair. And a scissors sticks out of his pocket. I immediately push back his fucking arm, giving him a warning glare. I've been to court three times for smashing cameras. I even punched a "pedestrian" and was charged with assault. Even if that fucking pedestrian was peering into Daisy's apartment window with binoculars. I couldn't prove it. He said he was bird watching. And he was on the street, public property.

Such bullshit.

He throws up his hands like I've infected him or something. *Fucking A.*

I stand behind Daisy and usher her forward, gripping her shoulders. "What was it?" she asks me, trying to catch a peek.

"Just a fucking guy."

She puts on a good front when we're outside. She's not alarmed or scared like Lily usually is. She's just energetic and lively. At night, when she's alone, that's a different story.

She spins around and walks backwards so she's facing me. Her eyes start at my hair and descend to my feet in the slowest fucking once-over known to man. If that doesn't fuck with my head and my dick…

The camera flashes are blinding at this point.

There's something hypnotic about the light going in and out on a beautiful girl. One second I can see her fully, the playful smile and bold green eyes. The next second, she hides in the dark of the night completely.

It also scares the fuck out of me. There's three feet in between us. For every step I take forward, she takes one back. And in those dark moments, I wonder if she'll be gone for good. I imagine the light flashing and she's no longer smiling. And then with the next burst of light, I picture fear in her eyes.

That one possibility pushes me to Daisy like a soul-crushing force. And I grab her by the waist, about to spin her around, but she suddenly stops. Our bodies knock into each other. Everyone is watching. The tension is enough to choke us.

"Move," I tell her roughly. "Or I'm going to throw you over my fucking shoulder."

She stays put, her smile growing. And I'm fucking glad I now have an excuse to carry her. Daisy annoying the fuck out of me—that's a common back and forth we have in front of the paparazzi.

I swiftly pick her up, my hands on her hips, and I toss her over my shoulder. She lets out a laugh, and I rest my palm on her ass.

Yeah, her father doesn't really fucking like me.

This won't help.

Connor thinks I'm an idiot to do things that put me in a bad light—especially since I don't bother to clarify my intentions. But in the end, they're going to think what they want to think. I can't empty my soul to every person who thinks I'm an asshole. I can't even empty it to the people who matter.

When we reach the doors to the bar, I gently set her down, and the cameramen are shoved back by some bouncers. We're let in almost immediately, passing a long line of people who've probably been waiting for thirty minutes to enter.

The moment the door closes behind us, the noise only intensifies. Boisterous drunk people—not my favorite fucking setting. Some of them are models, beautiful features, thin girls.

And there's my brother. He actually looks like a model, easily fitting among them with his sharp cheekbones.

His ass is on a *fucking* barstool, the pub smoky. Connor is right beside him, drinking a glass of water like nothing is wrong.

I'm going to kill them.

"Daisy!" a girl exclaims. A freckle-faced model, really young, hugs Daisy with a big smile.

"Christina!" Daisy grins. "What are you doing here?" Her eyes flicker to me once like *I'll be okay. Go to your brother.*

So I let her catch up with her friend while I make my way to the bar. "Hey," I say, putting a hand on Lo's shoulder. He sips his Fizz, acting like there's no alcohol in the dark-colored soda. "How was shopping?"

"Boring," Lo says, eating a fry from a plate that he shares with Connor. He glares at the shelves of liquor behind the bar, looking like a murderous little fuck. I don't know how else to describe my brother when he starts drinking. He always has that *I hate you and everyone in this fucking place* look. The difference is that now it's intensified by a thousand.

I nod repeatedly, my eyes flashing hot. I grab the fucking stool beside him and drag it over to fit in between him and Connor. I'm not going to let Connor near my brother right now, consoling him. Lo doesn't need a fucking safety net, so I cut it off in one move.

Connor stays quiet, not arguing with me.

I flag down the bartender, a young French girl. "What can I get you?" She speaks English well.

"What he's having." I point at the glass.

Lo finishes off his drink in one swig. "I'm done. Let's just get out of here." He stands.

I clamp my hand back on his shoulder. "Sit your ass down. I want a fucking drink." I force him back in his seat.

"You sound like Dad, you know that?" he retorts, shooting a bullet my way to get me to stop.

That's not good enough. I need him to tell me what he just did. I ignore him, watching the bartender make my drink. She puts in the ice.

"Ryke," Lo snaps.

I turn to him. "What?"

I think he's going to come clean, but I realize he's watching the bartender out of the corner of his eye. Then he says, "Let's go."

"I told you. I want a fucking drink."

He goes quiet, and the bartender squirts Fizz into the glass. I'm guessing she's already added the alcohol while I was looking at Lo.

He clenches his teeth and rests his forearms on the bar, deep inside his head as he stares off. I wonder if he's going to stop me. I want him to admit that he drank. Instead he continues to stay silent, even as the bartender slides the glass over to me.

"Refill?" she asks Lo.

He shakes his head. "No, I'm good."

"Cheers." I raise my glass at him, and he watches me with narrowed fucking eyes. I put the rim to my lips. *Stop me, Lo.*

This is a high stakes game of chicken.

And he doesn't move a muscle or say a fucking word.

I tip the glass back, and the sweet taste of Fizz mixes with the sharpness of *whiskey.*

Scotch whiskey.

He drank alcohol.

The more I repeat it, the more irritated and concerned I become. I drink half the glass, waiting for him to say something, to grab it out of my hand. But no matter if regret flashes in his eyes, he watches with a cold, dead gaze like I deserve this shit. Like this is my penance for ignoring him for over twenty years.

I set the glass down.

And it takes me a moment to process the weight of what happened.

I just broke my nine years of sobriety.

I stare right at him. "I hope you enjoyed that."

"Which part? Me drinking or watching you do it?"

I am trying not to explode on him. My muscles are on fucking fire. I grab the glass again, about to down the last of it, but he surprisingly steals it from me, passing it to the bartender.

"He's done," Lo says. When he turns back on me, he adds, "If you're this big of an asshole sober, I can't imagine what kind of asshole you are drunk."

I grab his arm before he jumps off the stool and disappears through the tightly packed crowd. "You can't do this shit," I growl. "You're supposed to call me if you have a craving to drink. I could have talked you out of it."

"Maybe I didn't want to talk to you!" Lo shouts all of sudden. He hops off the barstool, and I follow, having only an inch height advantage. We face each other, unresolved hate strung between us.

He doesn't know anything about my childhood, and I don't expect him to ask. All I wanted was a chance to undo what I had done wrong. To be there for him, to be his brother, and Lo makes it so fucking hard. He never gives me a reprieve like Connor.

"Then call Lily," I say, "your fucking fiancée, who would be in tears if she saw you right now. Did you fucking think about her when you drank? Did you consider what this would do to her?"

Lo's face twists. He won't punch me. "I'm done with this shit," he says. He's about to walk away.

I grab him by the arm, not letting him go that easily. "You can't run from your fucking problems. They're there twenty-four-seven. You have to deal."

"Don't talk about *dealing*. You won't even text Dad back. You're ignoring him like he's not even alive." He shakes his head, venom pulsing in his eyes. "You're doing the same thing to him that you did to me. So why don't you just do what you do best and pretend that I don't fucking exist."

His words slice cleanly through me, the pain like a fucking swift punch to the gut. Lo never needs his fists to fight. He shoves past me, and Connor stops him before he leaves the pub, calming him down.

I hold onto the bar, training my breath to normalize. When it does, I scan the crowds for Daisy. I spot her with Christina and another male model, his jaw chiseled. He leans in close to Daisy, licking his lips as he talks.

What the fuck?

Not tonight.

Seeing that—it's enough for me to start weaving through the fucking people to reach her. I don't like her body language that's angled towards Christina, away from the guy, silently telling him to back off.

They stand by a high-table littered with beer bottles and spilt liquor. The taste of scotch still lingers on my tongue, making me nauseous. Some people recall the perfume their mom wore with fondness, the cigar smell on their late father's shirt, the cologne, the shampoo—but for me, I smell and taste scotch and I remember my father sitting across from me in a fucking country club. I remember his sharp gaze, his fingers tapping the glass in annoyance, as though the world moved too slowly for him.

I feel like I ingested my past, full of bad memories. It's a sickening nostalgia.

I try to ignore it as I approach Daisy. The moment she sees me, her face brightens, but it dies down when she absorbs my features. "Do we need to leave?"

"Not yet," I tell her, my hand finding the small of her back. "Who's your friend?" He's been sizing me up this whole fucking time, a beer clutched in his hand. His pupils are also dilated.

"This is Christina," Daisy says, her arm hooking with that young model. She sheepishly meets my eyes, her cheeks already reddening. "She's in the same agency as me."

"You're Ryke Meadows," she says with a nervous laugh.

"Yeah," I tell her. "Cool necklace." She wears a sapphire on a chain, shaped like a dolphin. She bites her lip to hide her full smile. I raise my brows at her, and she has to look away from me, too giddy. Daisy has never been like that around me. I thought she would be flustered by me when she was fifteen, but instead, she had no trouble holding a conversation. It always felt like we were meant to be friends.

"This is Ian," Daisy introduces. "He's a—"

"Ford model." Ian extends his hand. I shake it, both of our grips firm. *He's slept with her.* I can see it in his eyes. And if not that, they've fooled around. A territorial rage consumes me for a minute. I want to wrap my arm around Daisy, but we can't exactly do that in public.

He nods to her. "I was just telling Daisy that we should go to a salsa club after this."

She looks up at me. "And I was telling him that I'm rhythmically challenged. Lily is the good dancer." Daisy is right. She's not good at dancing, but that has never stopped her from doing it. And I fucking love that she doesn't give a shit.

Ian laughs. "I don't believe that at all." His eyes graze over her hips, as though imagining them shaking side to side against his dick. *Fuck you, you fucking fuck.*

I glare at him, and he smiles as he sips his beer like *Yeah, I've got the fucking girl. Be jealous, asshole.*

"I'd try to salsa," Christina says, raising her hand.

"See," Ian says to Daisy, "you have to at least try like Christina. I'll teach you." *Over my dead fucking body.* He reaches out to wrap an arm around her shoulder, to bring her in for a fucking hug, and I step between them.

"Sorry," I say, "you're not teaching her how to grind on your fucking ass."

Ian lets out a short laugh. "I don't think she needs you to tell her what she can and cannot do. She's a big girl."

"Yeah," I tell Ian. "She's also *my* fucking girlfriend." I don't break his gaze, but I can feel Daisy's smile fill her whole face beside me. She grabs my hand, restlessly bouncing up and down on her toes like she wants to kiss me but realizes she can't. Even though I said the fucking words, it's different than someone having photographic proof.

That evidence is enough to overturn our world.

Ian stares between us. "I thought you said you were on a break?" he asks Daisy.

I'm not that surprised she lied to him—before we were together—telling him that she had a boyfriend. She's done more impulsive things than that.

"We got back together," she declares.

Ian begins to smile again as he stares at me.

Don't bring up your night with her, you fucker.

But he does. "Did she tell you that we hooked up during your break?"

"Do you want me to rip your head off?" I ask. "Because I'm close to breaking your fucking neck."

Ian licks his lips again. "I'm just laying it out there. You deserve to know the truth. She even moaned when I stuck my finger in her asshole. Did you know she liked that?"

I fucking punch him, my knuckles socking his jaw hard. He knocks into the high-table, beer bottles shattering on the floor. He raises his hands in surrender really quickly.

"Whoa, whoa," he stammers.

"I don't know where you fucking come from," I tell him. "But where I grew up, a guy would get more than a sucker-punch to the fucking face for what you've said to me."

"I didn't think you were seriously together," Ian says, touching his reddened jaw like I've damaged his career.

My body is begging my mind to go and claim Daisy with more than just words. *Fucking kiss her.*

But people have whipped out their camera phones, recording our confrontation for the internet.

I can't do a fucking thing. I can't solidify this relationship in front of the whole fucking world. Not without huge consequences.

"Let's go," Daisy says, tugging me towards the door. "Christina, come on."

"She wants to stay with me," Ian speaks up. "Right, Christina?"

Daisy wraps her arm around Christina's shoulder. "We're partying together, sorry."

"She has a voice," he tells Daisy, waiting for Christina to make a decision.

She timidly points towards the door. "I'm going to stick with Daisy." She tucks a piece of hair behind her ear, and Daisy squeezes her shoulder.

"Girl power," Daisy exclaims with a bright smile that carries so much energy. It lights up the whole room. "Come on." She lets go of my hand and clasps Christina's, swinging her arm as they reach the door. Christina immediately looks relieved and smiles with this newfound happiness.

Ian takes a step forward, and I put my hand on his chest.

"Don't even fucking try." That girl has to be fourteen or fifteen, and from what Daisy has told me about her weird night with him, I doubt he cares about that girl's age.

He stays put, and then I follow the girls out, spotting my brother and Connor on the congested street already.

"Everyone is a giant!" Daisy howls into the night sky. Literally, like a wolf. "We're in the land of tall people!"

Christina can't stop laughing, and Daisy turns her head to see me watching.

I raise my brows at her like *what the fuck are you doing?* And she howls again and points at the full moon. "Like my mating call?" she asks me.

"I don't see any fucking guys responding to it."

"I do," she says with a smile, staring right at me.

"Right. If that's true, then I'll be humping you later, sweetheart." My eyes lighten a little more because this time—there is fucking truth to our banter.

"Doggy-style or are you just going to be grinding on my leg?"

"Not your leg."

"Higher?"

"Well what's the other alternative? I'm not going to fuck your ankles."

She raises her hands in defense. "There are some people into feet."

"I'm into pussy. Now you know." My unfiltered response causes her to flush.

She grins. "I should howl more often then." She's cute. She always is. I'd kiss her if I could, but I need to check on my brother.

I glance over at Lo. He's staring at the sky like he wishes he could settle among the stars for fucking eternity and never have to live this life. I hate that look. It's one that I used to wear when I was fifteen, kicking shit over and screaming at the top of my lungs. I'd end up exhausted, collapsed on the grass of my yard, and I'd look up at the fucking sky and think *what am I doing here? Why the fuck am I in this world? Living shouldn't be this painful.*

My life had no meaning until I decided to turn around and meet my brother.

I can't lose him to this disease…or because of the choices I've made.

Connor has his hand on Lo's shoulder, his lips moving like he's talking him down from a fucking cliff. I feel like I put him there.

The traffic is gridlocked, taxis barely budging. We have a short walk back to the hotel, and most of the paparazzi have dispersed. Instead, the streets are full of sports fans, those red and white jerseys everywhere.

In the distance, the Eiffel Tower glows green. The screen on the front of the fucking mammoth structure plays footage from the Rugby World Cup.

When I glance back at Daisy, her smile is gone. She shrugs at me and then turns to Christina, whispering in her ear. I wish she had no affiliation to my brother. I wish they never knew each other—then all of this would be so fucking simple.

The girls start watching a couple guys bicker by the curb, fighting about women or maybe the rugby game. I can't tell from here, but they're drunk, spitting out their insults and puffing out their chests.

The construction nearby forces people to draw closer than they normally would. Scaffolding juts out from the pub next door, losing space, and plywood and other materials are thrown around the cement, covering divots and potholes.

"Hey, let's head back," I tell Daisy.

She nods to me but doesn't take her eyes off the growing fight. More and more people push onto the sidewalk, separating me from my little brother. I weave in between guys to reach him. Most are models and beefy fans. I even spot a portly guy doing a keg stand, his feet held up by his friends. His jersey falls to his neck, and his large stomach lolls over his jeans. His friend jiggles his fat while they all laugh.

When I near Lo, Connor steps aside a little, but my brother looks pained as he meets my eyes. "You shouldn't have had that whiskey," he says, his eyes glassing with remorse. Not *I'm sorry*. Those two words barely exist in his vocabulary, so I wasn't fucking expecting them.

"One glass isn't going to make me fucking addicted, Lo."

He rubs his lips and lets out a bitter, dry laugh. "Lucky you." He cringes at his sharp words and just shakes his head.

"We should go back to the hotel—" An elbow digs into my fucking back, the force pushing me into someone else. I look up and realize a new fight has broken out behind me, between two blue-collar looking guys with beards.

Screaming pierces the fucking air, and I'm being pushed in every fucking direction. Fights break by the curb, shoving people into the slow traffic, ramming bodies into the hoods of cars. Stumbling between vehicles. I hear the smash of glass as people start shattering car windows.

People are yelling about the rugby game, about England's loss. Angry fucking drunk fans are storming some of the bars, thrusting people aside. I'm trying to grab ahold of my brother. My heart runs wild as my mind catches up with me.

They're rioting.

And we're stuck in the middle of it.

I turn my head, and a taller guy decks Lo in the face. Lo snatches his shirt and hits him back in the stomach. The guy doubles over, and someone is pulling at my fucking leather bike jacket, trying to drag me to the ground. I spin around and shove him off me.

Daisy. Where the fuck is, Daisy?! My head whips from side to side. I don't see where I left her. Christina is gone too.

There are too many people running around, screaming. Fire. Someone started a fire in the pub we were just at. Flames licking the windows.

Fuck. Connor ducks as someone swings at him, and he catches a terrified girl around the waist before she face plants on the cement.

"Daisy!" I yell. *Where the fuck is she?!* I push people away from me with hostile aggression. Why did I leave her alone? "DAISY!"

Everyone is fucking screaming. Like she said, it's the land of the fucking giant people. With models taller than her, she doesn't stick out like she usually does. I start looking at the ground, at fallen people, and I lift up a young girl who cries in pain, her leg bent in the wrong direction. I carry her towards a street lamp and set her beside it, out of harm's way.

And then just as I go back in, I spot Christina clutching onto the same iron lamp, flinching as a guy punches another man right in front of her, their bodies starting to drift this way.

"Christina," I call. Tears streak her cheeks.

She meets my gaze and cries harder.

"You okay? Where's Daisy?"

Christina shakes her head over and over. "She pushed me out, and then she got swept in it. I couldn't find her…" She sobs into her hand and then points at the center of the riot, where so many men are brawling.

I don't think twice. I just go back in, another elbow ramming my back. A head knocking into my jaw. I shove and push and dig my fucking way through the people.

And then I see her.

She shakily stands. Blood trickles down her forehead, the source by her hairline, like someone ripped the strands, like they could've been caught in something. She teeters, disoriented. I try to reach her, but a couple guys shove me back and punch me in the face. I'm too fucking concentrated on her to feel the pain.

I tear through them, hitting them back with as much force.

Daisy touches her forehead, blinking a couple times to clear her vision. And then she meets my gaze, and relief floods her eyes.

"Ryke," I barely hear her say over the noise, but I see her lips form my name. Sirens blare in the distance, but no cop or ambulance will make it here anytime soon, not with this fucking traffic. Not with this madness.

She stands on the curb. And out of nowhere, some guy comes up from behind her. I watch in slow fucking motion, and I scream as loud as I can. "DAISY!!" I shove against so many fucking people, but it's like a current draws me back, pulling me under. *"DAISY!!!"*

He holds a two-by-four, part of the construction waste on the sidewalk and street, bracing the piece of wood like a bat.

I can't see his face. It's shadowed by the blur of bodies. But I do see him swing. Just as she turns her head to the side, the board smacks hard into her cheek.

Her body thuds to the cement with the force—limp and motionless.

I fucking lose it.

I barrel through whatever's keeping me from her, shouting more expletives than necessary. I worry about people trampling her body. And then I *finally* fucking reach her, the fastest and slowest moments of my life.

I instantly lift her unconscious body in my arms. *I have to get her out of here.* That's my only thought. I edge through the masses, glancing down at her once. Her face is turned into my chest, but I feel a wetness seep through.

It's not tears.

It's blood.

So much fucking blood, beginning to turn my white shirt into something red.

My heart is in my throat. I can barely breathe. I make it into an area where people frantically try to find their friends, calling out to them in French, German, English, Russian, pressing their phones to their ears.

I can't even look for my brother. I just think *hospital.* She needs a fucking hospital.

I take a trained breath, cradling her in my arms. Someone taps me on the shoulder, and I spin around on him, about to go on the offensive, but I realize he's older, grayed hair with glasses.

He has a phone to his ear, his features grave. He points to Daisy and then to the street. "L'ambulance est coincée dans les embouteillages." *The ambulance is stuck in traffic.*

"À quelle distance se trouve l'hôpital le plus proche?" I ask. *How far is the nearest hospital?*

He points in the direction. "Hôpital de l'Hotel-Dieu, environ 5 kilomètres." *About 5 kilometers.*

3 miles.

With Daisy in my arms, I can fucking run that in fifteen minutes or less. I mumble thank you, and I just fucking take off.

Her head bounces against my chest only a couple of times before I adjust her.

I have carried this girl so many times in my life.

But this time—this is the absolute worst.

I run.

One hundred and fifty miles per hour.

I don't fucking stop.

Not for anything.

I just keep going. *It's what your good at Ryke.* It may be the only thing.

< 25 >

Ryke Meadows

The moment I step through the emergency room doors, a gurney is brought out, and doctors and nurses pry her from my arms, setting her on the white sheets. The fluorescent lights burn my eyes, and sweat drips down my forehead. I try to follow the gurney back through these double blue doors, but a couple nurses block me, holding up their hands.

"I can't leave her," I say. *I can't fucking leave her.*

It takes me a moment to realize the nurses' lips are moving—that they've been talking in French. They switch to English, thinking I can't understand them. My mind is all over the fucking place.

"Sir, you need to sit down. We'll get you cleaned up and looked at."

"Come here," the other says.

She leads me to a chair in the hallway, out of the waiting room and next to a large white scale and counter.

"I can't leave her," I say again. "I have to go back there."

"She's being admitted," the forty-something nurse tells me. Her tawny hair chopped at her shoulders. She wears pink scrubs, and I glance at her nametag. Janet. "They're taking care of her right now. She's in good hands."

The other nurse, in teal scrubs, is a little younger and brunette. She dabs a piece of wet gauze on my eyebrow. I didn't even realize it was fucking bleeding.

I stare at the floor, holding back a scream that so badly wants to rip through my body. *Why?* I want to know why her. Why did this have to fucking happen? This is a nightmare. I'm going to wake up. Any fucking second now.

But I don't wake up. I'm here, in a foreign city, at a hospital, covered in blood. "Arms up," Janet orders. I mechanically do as she says, and she pulls off my shirt. I glance down at my hands once, finally registering how red they are, my palms stained with Daisy's blood. My stomach overturns.

"Margery, a bucket," Janet says quickly.

The brunette nurse puts a cream tub underneath my chin, and I vomit.

"What's your name, honey?" Janet asks, rubbing my back.

I wipe my mouth with my forearm. "Ryke."

She shares a look with Margery, as though recognizing me now, from television and the news. Thankfully they don't make a big scene. My hands shake as I take out my phone and dial a number. I press it to my ear, and the line doesn't even fucking ring. My brother's cell just shuts off.

Not him too. I can't lose these two people today. I can handle a lot of fucking shit, but not this. I don't know how to handle this. I shoot up from the chair, and I dial the number again, my hand on my head. Both nurses watch me with even more concern.

"I have to find my brother," I say aloud, my heart pounding.

"Let me show you to the bathroom," Margery says. "You can wash your hands—"

"I have to find my little brother," I say with the shake of my head. I dial again. *Nothing.*

"You're in shock," Janet says slowly so I understand. "Please, you need to calm down."

I think I'm being pretty fucking calm right now considering. Hot tears well in my eyes, and I ignore their requests. I call Connor next.

He answers on the second ring. "Where are you?" he asks, his voice spiking with fear. *Fear*—from a guy who's composed at every fucking moment.

"The hospital. Where's Lo?"

"He's fine. He's with me."

I try to breathe normally. I try to accept this, but it barely lifts the weight off my chest. "Why wasn't he fucking answering?"

"Someone stepped on his phone. It's trashed. We're coming to you. Is Daisy with you at the hospital?"

"Yeah." My voice chokes at the word, and I pinch the bridge of my nose to stop from breaking down and crying. I rarely ever fucking cry. I can count on one hand the number of times I've shed a fucking tear.

There's a long pause before Connor asks, "Is she alive?"

The question sends me to my fucking knees. I breathe heavily, no amount of training preparing me for this agony. I shake my head and I say, "I don't...I don't know."

I could have been carrying a girl without a pulse for three miles. I didn't check.

I just ran.

< 26 >

Ryke Meadows

It's been five hours. Connor has argued with the doctors for four of those, trying to persuade them to let us see Daisy, but it's been "family only" visiting hours, so we have to wait until the morning before friends can enter her room. They won't say if she's brain dead. All we know is that she's in a room and she's breathing.

For once, Connor Cobalt can't talk his way through a bad situation. I really fucking wish that wasn't the case tonight. When I tried speaking to the doctor, I started yelling, and they called security out, so I've sat my ass on a maroon leather chair in the carpeted waiting room. Watching the clock barely move. A television is on a news channel, playing footage of the riot that continues to destroy Paris and local stores.

I can barely watch it without feeling sick.

My brother is passed out beside me, a purpled shiner on his right eye. He didn't say much when he arrived, but he wore a similar haunted look that I had. Janet gave me a clean white T-shirt, so at least he didn't see the blood on me.

Now I'm in a new stage of grief, my body numb, my mind starting to slow down. And I know partly it's from being stabbed in the fucking ass with a sedative. I have to thank Janet for that too.

My phone buzzes for the seventh time. I read the caller ID: DAD. I contemplated changing the name to "Jonathan" a few times, but he's still my father. No matter how much I wish that wasn't the case.

He hasn't texted at all, so I figure he's goading me to answer with each irritating ring. It works. I'm too emotionally exhausted to reject him this time. I put the phone to my ear. "What do you want?"

He exhales in relief. "You're successfully trying to give me a fucking heart attack, Ryke." He mutters a few more curses under his breath before asking, "Is Loren okay? His phone just cuts off every time I call."

"He's fine." I glance at my brother again, his chest falling in a heavy sleep, induced by alcohol.

This may be the worst night of my life. I failed the two people that matter most to me.

"The news has pictures of you near the riot before it started. I thought you might have gotten caught in it." I hear the clink of a glass hitting the lip of another, as if he's pouring a drink.

"I have to go," I say.

"Wait for a goddamn second," he says. "I want to know how you are."

How am I? Numb, but my emotions try so hard to surface and pour through me. I could scream until my voice leaves me. I could run until my legs buckle beneath me. I could hit the wall until exhaustion defeats me. And my fucking *father* is asking me this. I swallow a rock in my throat. "You're the last person I want to talk to right now."

"We do need to talk, Ryke."

"Why? Are you going to fucking accuse me of taking Lo away from you again?" When Lo went to rehab for the first time, our dad acted like I brainwashed him. Like rehab was the bad fucking choice. Like Lo wasn't even an alcoholic.

"That was a long time ago," he tells me. There's a long pause, and at first, I think he's taking a sip of his drink. But he clears his throat like he's having trouble producing words.

"Listen, my…" I pinch my eyes. I was about to say *my girlfriend*. I take a deep breath. "Someone I fucking care about isn't doing well, so I don't have time to rehash the past with you."

"Okay," he says, giving up much more easily than I thought he would. "Be careful, Ryke. And if I don't talk to you before you climb that ridiculous rock, I just want to say…" He clears his throat again. "I love you, and if you don't believe me, then check the name on your license. Stay safe." He hangs up.

He tells Lo that he loves him all the time. And all the bastardly things our father does—that is out of fucking love too. I'm not surprised he said I love you or that he mentioned my first name, *his* name, as evidence of his feelings. Part of me wants to embrace that paternal affection. The other part sees him trying to get me to speak to the media. If we become friendly, then maybe I'll stick up for him.

It's all a wicked game that I never asked to play.

After a couple minutes, I shelve my father, my mom, my brother— all of the family drama in the back of my head.

Connor appears around the corner of the waiting room, holding two coffees in paper cups. He fucking dodged most of the flying fists and brunt force of the riot. No bruises, just a small cut on his forehead. He hands me a cup, and I nod at him in appreciation. His expression is still morose, not unreadable like usual.

"When are the girls landing in Paris?" I ask him, taking a sip. Lo was on the phone with Lily for a while, but he didn't tell me their conversation. I know Connor talked to Rose for an hour.

"They're not," Connor says tersely.

I frown, thinking I've heard him wrong. "What?"

"They are not coming to Paris," he emphasizes each word.

"Their sister is in the hospital," I say. "I don't fucking understand. If this was Lily, Rose would be here in a fucking *heartbeat*." I squeeze the coffee too hard, and the lid pops off, spilling on my jeans and burning me. "Fuck," I curse, standing up and drinking the coffee quickly before tossing it in the trash.

Connor sidles next to me by the trashcan. "I'm just as angry as you."

I look him over. His muscles are relaxed despite the sadness in his eyes. This is a lot of emotion for Connor to fucking show, but I highly doubt he's feeling what I am. "I don't think you are, Cobalt. Not even fucking close."

"My wife is upset, and she's too prideful and stubborn to tell me why. Rose is the type of woman who would die with a secret if it scared her to reveal it, if it contributed to any type of weakness. So my mind is fucking reeling."

"Then go," I tell him. "No one is keeping you here."

"Lo just drank alcohol," Connor says flatly. "Daisy is in the hospital. You're a mess. I'm not leaving the three of you."

"I'm not a fucking mess."

He points at the hallway. "I watched two guys who probably weigh two-fifty drag you to the ground. You spit in one of their faces."

I glare. "He tried to kick me." It was a low fucking move. "It doesn't matter. Stay if that's what you want to do. Leave. If I need to, I'll call Lily later to ask why she's not here—"

"Lo already tried," he says. "Lily and Rose said they'll take a flight out tomorrow."

I extend my arms. "Then why are we fucking arguing? They're going to be here."

Connor shakes his head. "I already know how this plays out. If Daisy is awake and coherent, the minute they talk to her on the phone, which they will, she'll convince her sisters to stay back. She won't want to ruin their day, week, not even over a serious event like this."

He's right. If Daisy liked to burden people with her pain, she would have told her sisters about her insomnia, about her horrible fucking prep school friends. About what happened during the ten months that she was living with her parents—when I was at my apartment. She doesn't think her problems measure up to Lily's addiction, but they do. They're just as important.

I stare at the ground, my eyes burning again. I just have this mental picture of Daisy waking up in a strange place, in a foreign country, with no familiar face in the room. It's fucking horrifying, and I want to save her from that. "Has anyone called her mom yet?"

"No," he whispers. "Samantha doesn't know anything, and Rose wants to let Daisy decide whether they tell their mother now or later. Especially since Daisy is going to miss the rest of Fashion Week, and we all know Samantha won't take that well."

"Her mom loves her though," I say. "She'd be concerned. We should at least fucking call her."

"Ryke," he breathes. "She'd kick you out of the hospital. I looked online, and someone already uploaded your fight with Ian from the pub. Somehow Samantha is going to blame you for Daisy's injuries, then cause a scene and upset Daisy even more. It's delicate. So we need to ask her first."

I nod. I just hope Daisy is coherent enough that she can respond to anything. What if she can't talk? What if she's fucking blind? We know nothing.

Connor studies my reaction for a while and then adds, "And *Celebrity Crush* posted a photo of Daisy thrown over your shoulder." He pauses, and his deep blue eyes narrow at me. "Your hand is on her ass, by the way. You should care more about what her father thinks if you want to have a real relationship with her, and if you don't, then I'm telling you now, as her brother-in-law, back *off*."

This is a new side of Connor. Protective of Daisy. I do appreciate it, more than I'm going to let on. "How do you know what I want?"

"I can read people really well. I'm almost a hundred-percent positive you've kissed her, based on seeing her in Paris. Her lips were red. She was a little flushed. You were too."

I open my mouth, but he cuts me off.

"Lo didn't pick up on it. He wouldn't. I don't think many people can see what I can."

"Why do you have to fucking compliment yourself when you prove a point?"

"I'm stating truths."

I cross my arms. "Well, here's one for you, Cobalt. It doesn't matter if I grab her around the waist, if I kiss her chastely or if I kiss her roughly. No matter what I fucking do, her father isn't going to like me. Her mom is going to *hate* me. Fuck *you* for thinking I need their approval to have a real relationship. What I feel is fucking real, and I don't need her mom to verify that for me."

Connor shakes his head like I'm an idiot.

I want to fucking hit something right now, so him standing here, being a smug prick is not helping the situation. The sedative that has kept me at ease is quickly wearing off.

"How is it real?" he asks. "If you have to hide it from your friends and family, that makes your relationship pretend, Ryke."

"Fuck you," I say again.

"No, *fuck you*," he retorts, pretty uncharacteristically. So much so that my muscles tense. "I stuck up for you. When Lo was against you and Daisy, *I* was the one who tried to convince him that you're both mature adults. I supported any idea of a relationship you two might have in the future, I still do, but after this trip, I'm reconsidering how much faith I had in you."

I can tell this is more than just my hand on her ass in a fucking picture. It's the "talk" he wanted to have in her hotel room after she woke up screaming. Why does he have to pick this moment to tear through me?

I miscalculated how pissed Connor is tonight. He was right. He's truly fucking angry, and he's on the offensive. "You should have told someone about her sleeping issues," he says. "I thought you, out of all people, would be more concerned about her health. I thought you would have run to her sisters with the news. I thought you'd do *anything* to ensure Daisy's safety and protection."

"I fucking did!" I shout. Some people sleeping in the waiting room begin to stir.

"Then why does no one know?"

"She didn't want to tell a fucking soul," I say. "Rose and Lily had their own shit to deal with. She didn't want to worry her mother or you or anyone with these problems. She wanted to fucking deal with it in private."

Connor processes this for a second before he asks, "And how long has she been dealing with this, Ryke?"

I shake my head at him. "It wasn't one singular event. It's been an accumulation of things."

"How long?"

I can't hide it from him. "Over a year."

His eyes begin to glass, but he nods repeatedly. "It was all the media, wasn't it? The paparazzi that broke into her room, the guy that destroyed her bike and assaulted her—it all got to her more than she let on."

"That was the start of it."

"Rose is going to be so upset that she didn't pay enough attention to her." Connor blows out a deep breath, as though he can feel his wife's pain from this and she still has no idea. "I can't believe I didn't see it sooner, to be honest."

I roll my eyes. "This stays between us. Daisy has to be the one to tell her sisters."

He nods in agreement. "Has she been to a doctor?"

"Before she left for Paris, she was seeing a therapist regularly, and she's been through her fair share of sleep studies." I list out all the information I know he'll ask. No one has given her much of a solution to resolve her insomnia besides medication and therapy. She just has to cross her fucking fingers that one day she'll grow out of this.

Connor takes out his phone and starts typing. "I need the names of all her doctors and her therapist."

"You sound like Rose."

"I'm serious. I want to make sure you took her to the best—"

"Connor," I cut him off, "she's *my* fucking girlfriend. I've triple fucking checked every person she's been seeing. I don't need you to do my job for me. I'm more than capable of taking care of her."

He hesitates before pocketing his phone, and then he stares at me with more respect than when this conversation started. "So you put a label on your relationship?"

I nod. "Yeah, we did." My nose flares as I hold back emotion. *She's in a fucking hospital room, maybe fighting for her life. What wrong decisions did I make to put her there? Where did I fuck up?*

Sometimes I wonder what life would be like if I chose to never meet my brother. If I chose to keep my head buried in the sand.

My mom would have never known about Lily's sex addiction.

She would have never shouted it to the fucking world.

No media.

Daisy would sleep peacefully.

Lily wouldn't feel so fucking ashamed.

Connor and Rose wouldn't have their sex life distributed online.

And my brother—I think he'd still be drinking.

I take a deep breath, the night saddling me with more regret than I'm used to bearing. "I haven't always done the right thing, Connor," I say. "I'm not perfect. But I'm trying so hard to look after my brother and her. But if I'm hurting them, then you need to tell me right now." I meet his gaze—no pretenses. No jokes. The severity in our postures makes it hard to breathe. And I tell him something from my fucking soul. "I don't want to ruin anyone's life by being in it. That was never my intention."

Connor lets out an exhausted laugh, and tears actually brim his eyes. "Ryke…" He shakes his head and rubs his lips. He drops his hand. "You *ran* with her in your arms for over three miles. Your brother's existence caused your parent's divorce, and yet, you gave up most of your time and energy to help him through his sobriety. How can you possibly think you're a pain in their life? What you've done for them, it's nothing short of heroic, and if you can't see that, then you're blind, my friend."

A hot tear rolls down my cheek.

I'm so fucking tired of being alone. I was scared that he'd tell me to fucking leave. Because that means going back to a life I can't see for myself anymore. Daisy has changed that for me. She made me comfortable to share my life with someone else, to live for happiness in the company of others. My solitary future looks bleak. But my future filled with my brother, my friends, *her*—there's nothing fucking brighter.

She's the sun. I'm the dark.

If she's gone, I can kiss that fucking light away.

Without her, I know I'll never see it again.

‹ 27 ›

Daisy Calloway

I open my eyes, disoriented. My vision blurs, everything out of focus. I blink sluggishly, my arms and legs heavy. My mind hasn't processed anything beyond my physical abnormalities—the lightness of my head, the numbness along my face, the tingling in my fingers.

I make out shadows, dark and light, first. A figure rises from a chair, standing closer to me.

I'm not waking up after a night terror.

This feels so different.

I try to recall my last memory, the last picture I had before this— before lying down.

It's not coming as quickly as I'd hoped. It's just fuzzy.

Thankfully my ears are working. "Daisy," the deep familiar voice says, still rough but full of unbridled concern. "Can you hear me?"

I try to nod. I think I'm nodding. I blink two more times, and then my vision clears. Ryke towers beside a hospital bed. *My* hospital bed. But I focus on his features, the scratches along his cheeks, the bruises that blemish his eyes and jaw. The stitches on his eyebrow.

"Ryke," I whisper, raspy.

Tears build in my eyes. I've never seen Ryke so battered before. My hand instinctively goes to my mouth to hide my emotions, but the movement tugs an IV stand. I glance down to inspect the source. Tubes are stuck in the top of my hand, running across my lap.

Ryke takes a seat on the edge of the bed, by my legs. He rubs them, even though they're underneath a light blue blanket. "Do you need water?" He's just as overwhelmed as me, his features hardening to hide that burgeoning emotion.

I shake my head. "Can you…come closer?" I reach for his hand, but I grasp air. I try to sit up in the bed so I can see more of him, but my whole body is sore like I was hit by a truck. *Was I?* Did I accidentally run into traffic? *Please tell me I didn't do something stupid that got him hurt too.*

I burst into tears because I'm terrified that's what happened.

"Daisy, don't cry," he says. "We're going to get through this." *We.* I focus on this one pronoun while he presses a button on a remote. The bed groans as it rises to a sitting position. Then he scoots forward so he's beside my thigh.

I let out a breath to stop the waterworks, and then I reach out, my fingers skimming his cheek. He watches me inspect the damage with a trembling hand, and I zoom in on the stitches. "Your eyebrow…"

"It's fine." He clasps my wrist to stop me from poking at it.

"It's going to scar," I murmur.

His face almost breaks. He shakes his head repeatedly. "I don't fucking care."

I smile weakly, but the motion stings. *Why does that hurt?* My lips fall. "What happened?" I ask.

His Adam's apple bobs. "You can't remember?"

"No," I breathe. "Did I…did I do something stupid? You didn't… you didn't follow me into traffic, did you?" The fact that this could be a possibility, I realize that reflects poorly upon me. I can be unthinking and selfish when I try to live fully. But I've always loved that Ryke never stops me.

Whatever wild thing I do, Ryke Meadows does too.

Down a ski slope.

In an ocean, caged with sharks.

Off a cliff.

Off a cliff. I was fifteen. I dove into the water. He jumped in after me. I couldn't imagine any other guy willing to do that for someone they hardly knew. In that moment, I had fallen for Ryke. Literally, figuratively—I knew, if we couldn't be together, he would be my friend.

Here we are now.

In a hospital. "Maybe I should have left you alone," I whisper.

"What are you talking about?"

"You wouldn't be hurt…" I scrutinize the way his muscles tense, sitting rigidly. I grip the bottom of his white T-shirt—that doesn't look like one of his.

He holds my hands, stopping me. "Daisy," he says with force. "I'm fine."

"Take off your shirt."

"No."

I smile again. *Ow.* "I must be the only girl you've rejected."

"That's so fucking *not* true," he growls. He glances at the hospital bed, me in it, and then he sighs heavily, giving in. He lifts the shirt off, and my mouth plummets.

My hands zip across the yellowish purple bruises that mar his abs and chest, some bleeding into his phoenix tattoo. "Turn around, please," I say softly.

He rotates only halfway, and I see even worse ones, deeper yellow, deeper purple. I want to kiss the wounds, but as soon as I lean forward, he puts a hand on my collar and leans me back against a fluffy pillow.

"What's the last thing you remember, Dais?" he asks me seriously.

I strain my mind. "The bar." *We went to the pub next to the hotel.* "Lo…" *He drank alcohol.* "Christina—I saw her in the pub and…" *Ian.* "You didn't…did you guys…" *Did they fight?* "Ian…" I blink a few times, the picture starting to form. No, that fight ended early. That's not what happened. "I was outside with Christina. We were about to go to the hotel."

Flashes of the next events ripple through my mind. I was watching these two big guys screaming on the sidewalk, pushing each other in the chest. One punch flew, and then I was swept in a hurricane of drunken men and violent acts. I immediately shoved Christina back, and someone's jacket zipper caught in my long hair. I was dragged backwards.

"Ryke…" The fear as I fell on the pavement returns, and the heart monitor's steady *beep, beep, beep* picks up pace. Feet clobbered around me, on my stomach, my legs, and finally I yanked my hair free, only for it to snag in something else. This time, it pulled hard near my forehead. The pain seared beneath adrenaline. *Beepbeepbeepbeep.*

"Daisy, look at me," Ryke says, his hand sliding on my thigh, holding me tightly.

I meet his concerned gaze just as the last memory hits me. I picked myself off the concrete. "I saw you," I whisper. "You were right there." I remember meeting his eyes. And they were full of anger, full of desperation, full of gut-wrenching pain.

He screamed my name. I heard it only once before something hard met my face.

My face.

For the first time, I raise my hand to touch my cheek. All I feel is tape, gauze, maybe. But whatever lies underneath it—that's what hurts each time I begin to smile.

BEEPBEEPBEEPBEEP!

"Take deep fucking breaths," he tells me, rubbing my arm.

Someone knocks twice, and then the hospital doors open. A nurse in pink scrubs sticks her head in. "Daisy, you're awake." She smiles, and then she turns slightly to whisper to someone else. "Can you go let her friends know?" She shuts the door behind her and pads closer to me. "My name is Janet. How are you feeling?"

She pours a cup of water and passes it to me. I take a sip and hand it immediately to Ryke. "Can I have a mirror?" I ask her.

Beepbeepbeepbeep.

I can't articulate my feelings beyond panic. I just need to see my face first to understand these emotions that blow through me.

"Do you want me to call the hospital psychologist first?"

What? "Ryke." I turn to him with widened eyes.

"Can you just give her a mirror?" he asks Janet with a hard gaze.

She nods. "Okay." Janet tentatively picks up a handheld mirror from a drawer, and I take it from her.

I raise it up to my face. *BeepbeeepBEEPBEEP.*

Bandages cover my left cheek down to my jaw. But my lip is swollen, and dark purpled bruises sit beneath both eyes. I look...so much worse than Ryke, no wonder he stared at me like *stop fucking talking about my injuries.*

I start picking at the tape, to uncover the bandage, and Janet swats my hand away. "Don't touch."

"I need to see it." I don't even know what *it* is.

And then another nurse in blue scrubs waltzes in with Connor and Lo.

"Hey," Lo says with a weak smile. "How are you doing?" He touches my feet above the blanket. I want to return the smile, but it hurts too much to do so.

"Okay," I say.

Connor just nods. "Has anyone told you what's happened?"

"Sort of," I murmur. "I want to see what's wrong with my face."

"She doesn't know?" Lo frowns and glares at Ryke like it's his fault.

"We're fucking getting there."

"Let me help," the other nurse says, sidling to the bed. "We have to put new dressings on the wound anyway."

Ryke stands up while both the nurses hover over me. He joins Lo and Connor at the foot of the bed, and my heart rate stays at the same *beepbeepbeepbeep* pace.

Janet slowly removes the tape, peeling back the bandage that clings to a few stitches…no wait, a *lot* of stitches.

"It was a deep gash," Janet explains in the kindest way possible. "You've had an MRI. Everything came back normal. The doctors said you may have a slight concussion, but otherwise, you'll be fine in about two weeks, no more stitches. Just a—"

"Scar," I finish for her. They free my face of gauze and tape, and there it is: a reddened gash that runs from my temple, across my cheek, to my jaw. I move my tongue in my mouth, along my gum, feeling the backs of the stitches, as though my cheek was cut open at one point.

"How…" *BEEPBEEPBEEP.* I look up at Ryke, my eyes like saucers.

"You were hit with a fucking two-by-four. The doctors think there was something sharp on the board that sliced you."

"You were given a tetanus shot," the blue-scrub nurse assures me.

Janet says, "We can get the psychologist in here."

Because I'll have this scar forever. Because I'll never be the pretty Daisy Calloway in magazine spreads or down runways. I am no longer a model.

I am no longer the person my mom aspired me to be.

But I am more me now than I was before.

I shut my eyes and lean my head back. And my heart rate—it slows. I take a deep breath. What feels like my very first one ever, and silent tears fall. A pressure so heavy begins to rise off my chest.

"It's okay to be upset," Janet tells me.

I open my eyes and shake my head, a weak laugh escaping. "I'm not upset." My chin quivers. I wipe the tears and I say, "I'm relieved." My gaze meets Ryke's. "How sick is that?" And then I burst into tears because I know I shouldn't feel this way.

He's by my side in seconds, and I wrap my arms around his chest.

I didn't realize how trapped I was until this very moment. Until something so horrifying could actually feel good.

And I know I'm partly to blame. If this doesn't tell me that I need to stand up for myself, then I don't think anything could.

‹ 28 ›

Daisy Calloway

Pain medication conks me out. It's been a new type of sleep. Not exactly better. I always feel lethargic, drowsy, and I still ache for that perfect sleep that I used to have before the media. Luckily Ryke supplies me with an energy drink on my last day in the hospital.

I sip the Lightning Bolt! while I dig through my suitcase that he brought. The guys have already checked out of the hotel for me and gathered our stuff.

"Did you call your agency?" Ryke asks.

"Yeah, I quit last night." The final day of Fashion Week, I called Revolution Modeling Inc. and said, "I don't want to model anymore. I'm sorry, but you'll have to find someone else for the runway tonight. And I won't be working for the next three weeks or in the future." My voice wasn't as confident or ballsy as maybe Rose's would have been. But I look at it as a trial run for the phone call to my mom.

They asked why.

I said the biggest truth of all: "I don't love modeling."

No cop outs. I've had two days in the hospital—of quiet nights left with my endless thoughts—to come to this conclusion. My career has ended because of my face, but it should have ended so much sooner because of my health, my emotions, my happiness. It has taken a near-death experience and the end-all of modeling for me to realize this. Blaming it on the scar—it seems like the easy way to deal. I know I won't feel better unless I do it the way I was always meant to.

I find a pair of jean shorts and a shirt that says: *I'm a fucking mermaid.* "How's this?" I ask Ryke, flashing the V-neck at him.

He almost smiles, which sells it for me.

I zip up my bag. "Can you close the curtains while I change?" I give him a single look like *you don't have to leave.*

His features are hard to gauge. I can't read much behind his brooding eyes. I've tried not to question if he's going to break up with me over my face. He did say, *We're going to get through this.* I just wonder if he'll be helping me as a friend or as something more.

These thoughts tear holes inside my stomach.

I guess I'm about to find out where his head is at. Connor and Lo are waiting in the rental car for us. So we're alone for the first time since I initially woke up. I don't think Lo is worried about leaving us together. I can tell he's trying to trust his brother, especially after screwing up and drinking.

I also talked to Rose and Lily, stopping them before they flew out to Paris. I don't want Lily to miss college or Rose to cancel meetings for her fashion business just to see me. It took some convincing and a two-hour argument, but I won out this time. Although, Rose made me Skype her, but I refused to show the wound beneath my bandage. I told her that she'd have a good look at it every time she saw me for the rest of my life. So she can wait a few more weeks.

I watch Ryke whip the curtain around the ceiling track, enclosing us in the room for extra privacy. I set my jeans and shirt on the end of the bed, the hospital gown hanging on my body like a thin sack. The silence speeds my heart. Luckily I'm no longer hooked to any machines, but my shallow breath replaces the *beep beep beep*.

I can't tell what he's going to do, and that mystery instantly draws me to him. I take a couple steps forward and then stop halfway, a few feet separating us. He stands tall, his masculinity so apparent in his build and hard jawline. I think I could live underneath Ryke Meadows, under his weight and protection, and be satisfied for life.

The thought pulls my lips upward. I ignore the pinch in my cheek, the slight pain of the motion. I want to smile, dammit. So I'm gonna smile.

He watches me closely, all my small movements under scrutiny, and then he steps forward. One foot near. I inhale strongly, smelling his woodsy scent, like water and earth. I'm too curious about his thoughts and actions to touch him first.

His eyes meet mine and then fall to the collar of my hospital gown. He never looks at me like I'm half of myself, too beaten to love, too fragile to handle. Instead, his gaze rakes me like it's our first time being this close again.

One more step and his chest brushes against mine with each deep breath. He leans forward, and I go rigid. His lips tickle my ear. "You're so fucking beautiful."

I smile wide. Those words mean so much more now than they ever did before. "Say that again."

"How about I just fucking show you?" His hot breath warms my neck, and then he kisses that very spot, deeply right away. Just like that, my body responds by curving towards him. He holds the back of my head, sucking the nape of my neck with such diligence that every nerve lights.

"Ryke," I breathe softly, a high-pitched moan following.

My arms slip underneath his, holding his back like he belongs to me. I can't believe I'm turned on after being cooped up in a hospital. But my sore limbs loosen like jelly at his possessive touch.

He unties my hair, slipping the band on his wrist. Then he messes the long locks with a rough hand, as he's done so many times before. It dizzies me, and my heart palpitates.

His lips return, trailing my collar. He fingers the ties on the back of my gown. I only wear panties, having put them on as I started dressing earlier. The hospital fabric slips off me, the cool air nipping my skin. Goose bumps run along my bruised arms and legs. I stiffen, thinking he's going to pull away at the sight of all the purple blemishes, but he only gently kisses around them, being careful with me but not so much that he'd let me go.

I wish I could kiss him back. Even if it didn't hurt, Ryke would never allow my lips to near him, not wanting to cause me pain. But his kind of TLC is the best kind. His hands slide along my hips, edging towards my yellow cotton panties, daises printed on the backside.

My mouth opens as I watch his kisses descend to my boobs, already exposed for him, no bra to unclip or fling off. His head lowers to the top of my right breast, and as he nears my nipple, I have a flash of what happened with Ian. The sharp pain. Biting. *Blood.*

I jerk back in fright, and Ryke says nothing about the panicked flinch. He just lifts me up to his waist, my legs wrapping around him, and then he brings me to the bed. I lie on the soft blue blanket, and Ryke hardly misses a beat. He splits my legs open, kneeling between them before he kisses the same spot beside my nipple.

Only this time, he watches my expression as he sucks the sensitive skin, his eyes on me the whole time, studying my response. So that's why he moved me. I like this position better. His pelvis is right up against my pelvis, and I hook my ankle around his to secure me to him.

I hold my breath as he kisses my nipple, his tongue skimming the hard bud with only a desire to light my body. It works as soon as his other hand kneads my left breast, and a sharp cry entangles with my gasp.

He sucks a little harder, and I tense, so he slows, which feels… "Ahh," I cry again. *Wow*. His forceful passion stays, pulsing the spot between my legs with new need and want. I ache for something harder. An ache I've never experienced to this degree.

"I want you so badly," I say with another gasp. I claw at his back, his shirt riding up. My hips are thrust upwards against him with so much pressure that he groans, the noise deep in his throat.

He strokes the sweaty hair off my forehead, and then he sits up, his hands running along my long slender legs. He stares at the length of them with a newfound hot and heavy lust. "I love so many fucking parts of you," he says huskily.

I clutch the blanket on either side of my hips, grinding harder into him. "Take off your jeans," I practically whimper. Usually I want the guy to keep them on, for the uncomfortable moment to end faster. This is so foreign. And I adore every single second.

"We're not having sex yet, so store that fantasy for later, sweetheart." *Sweetheart.*

I smile. No pain. It's drowned beneath my arousal.

Ryke says sweetheart with so much force that it conflicts with the mildness of the word. I wonder if that's us. Soft to his hard. Sweet to his rough. Wild to his stone.

I like it.

He grabs my ankles, unhooking them from him, and he bends my legs. He pauses once, listening for the silence, hearing my breath, and I think he's discerning how much time we have before someone catches us. We are in a hospital. A public place. But he has a way of making it feel like the most private, safe place on Earth. Thankfully he looks satisfied to continue.

He kisses the top of my knee, and then his intense gaze meets mine. He takes two of his fingers and slips them in *his* mouth for a short moment. Just watching that—my hands dig harder into the bed. With my head on the pillow, he's too far away to clutch.

His hand glides underneath my panties, and his two warm fingers enter the pulsing spot, I clench around him almost immediately. I moan, my mouth permanently open. The corners of his lips rise, and he unlatches one of my hands from the bed.

"Have you been this wet before?" he asks me. He presses my fingers to the same spot that he's inside, and my cold touch feels worse than his warm. I am not *just* wet. I am soaked. And I feel so swollen with need.

I shake my head. "You've done what I have trouble doing to myself."

"It's time for that to fucking change, don't you think?"

I smile wider.

"Don't smile," he says. "I don't want to fucking hurt you."

"There's no way you can." He's only ever been the opposite in my life. The most positive force there ever was. He's like that to everyone he meets. I'm sure of it.

"Still," he retorts.

I bite my lip to keep from grinning, and he lets my hand go as soon as he begins moving his two fingers inside me, finding a sensitive place that I've been searching for, for years. I wish I could see his hand beneath my panties, his fingers so deep in me. That's a visual I'd keep planted near the front of my brain.

I don't want him so far away. I slowly sit up while he fucks me with his fingers, and he gives me a stern look like *you can't fucking kiss me.*

I rest my forehead on his chest and stare down at the way his hand moves beneath the cotton. He has to adjust a little inside me, but he finds the right place again. He holds the back of my head with his other hand. Out of need and instinct, I rock my hips, driving him deeper. I cry at the new sensations.

"Easy," he whispers, but now that I'm so close, he pulls my panties down to my thighs, showing me what he's doing.

Just seeing Ryke, his hand, right between my legs, his fingers all the way inside me, it nearly sends me over. "Ryke," I gasp. "RykeRykeRyke."

I clutch onto his back and keep rocking my hips in sync with the movement of his fingers. I am climbing a gorgeous mountain that I have never even neared before. And he's the one taking me there.

He leans my back on the blanket again, but he doesn't pry me off him, so in result, I've taken Ryke with me. He hovers over my body, so close to me. Even if he's fully clothed and I lie naked, I feel safe in his possession.

"Don't stop," I cry. "Ryke." I grab his bicep for support.

I meet his wanting gaze once before my toes curl, my spine arches, and my eyes roll back. Every part of me explodes like a thousand fireworks inside my head and body.

I go off.

And I come for the very first time.

Finally.

He keeps me full while my breath slows and I clench a few more times.

I laugh because that was one of the best things I've ever felt. Period. And he hasn't even pushed his cock inside of me yet.

"Better than chocolate?" he asks, wiping my lips that stay parted. His forearm rests beside my head, propping up his body as he stares down at me.

"I don't know," I pant. "I think I need to test this out five or six more times to make a definitive answer." I smile playfully.

"I have a strong fucking feeling that we'll hear your answer quickly."

"I love your strong feelings," I tell him.

"I love watching you come," he says like it's a simple fact. But it's not simple at all.

"How much?"

He kisses my good cheek and then whispers, "More than you'll ever fucking know."

Damn. He slips his fingers out of me, wiping them on the blanket, and then he slides my soaked panties off my legs at an extremely slow rate. So slow that my body clenches all over again. When they're off my feet, I turn on my stomach and moan into the covers. "Just take me now," I say into the muffled blankets.

He's on his knees, and he lifts me by the hips so I'm on mine too. "That's not how I take women," he says, squeezing my ass.

"You torture them," I say, turning my head. "I can't come twice before we have sex."

"Want to fucking bet?" he says with narrowed eyes.

I grin. "Yes, I do. Let's test it out now."

"We don't have time," he says, shutting it down. It was worth a shot. He wipes between my legs with the blanket, and then he swiftly grabs me around the waist and sets my feet on the floor. Completely naked. I watch as he grabs a clean pair of panties from my bag.

He dresses me, helping me step into them. And once the soft cotton touches my hips, he puts the shirt on over my head and lets me step into my shorts. He's taking care of me to a new degree. It makes me feel more than just loved. I feel like I'm truly his.

I hold onto the back of his neck while he zips my shorts, his body so close to mine again. He fishes the button through the hole, tension constricting his muscles. My breath is ragged. How is this possible? I *just* orgasmed.

I look up at him as he finishes. "I guess that answers my question."

"What question?"

"Before, I was going to ask you if this was it for us."

He frowns. "What are you fucking talking about?"

I don't back down to the darkness in his features. I cling to every dangerous quality he possesses. "I just thought you'd want to go back to being just friends after what happened with my face."

His confusion turns into a hard glare. "I'm not with you because you're a fucking model."

"I know."

"Clearly you didn't."

"I do now."

He's not happy with that answer. "I didn't think I was going to have to spell it out for you, Calloway."

"Now I'm confused."

He shakes his head. "I've never met a fucking girl that I wanted to stick around for longer than a month, and then I became friends with you—"

I cut him off, "And I thought that you could go back to being my friend."

"No, you thought that I'd *want* to. You think I'm with you just because you're fucking gorgeous? Daisy, I could have been with you the *moment* you turned eighteen. Having sex with a hot fucking girl that gets me hard isn't worth risking the relationship I have with my brother."

I breathe heavily. "What's worth the risk then?"

"What we fucking have," he says. "I love you beyond physical attraction." He cups my smooth cheek, looking deep into my eyes. "I love you, Dais, because you're the wildest fucking girl with the biggest fucking heart. And without you in my life"—he shakes his head like it's an inconceivable picture—"I'd be the unhappiest fucking guy."

His words flood me with so much emotion. For however ineloquent they are, they sound perfect off his lips—because they're one-hundred percent Ryke Meadows. I focus on the three most important ones of the bunch.

"You love me," I breathe.

He lets out a short laugh. "You're such a fucking girl."

"Say it again."

He smiles, a full blown one that tingles my body all over. "I fucking love you, sweetheart."

I lean in to kiss him, forgetting I'm hurt, but he holds my jaw, controlling the touch of our lips that desperately wants to be something more. Before it turns wild, he kisses my forehead and murmurs, "I'm not going anywhere."

I never knew that a relationship could be so mental, so emotional before all the physical. I wonder if we're doing this backwards or if this has been the right way all along.

Right. I've found the one person who makes me the happiest, but I just wonder how long I'll be able to keep him. I wonder if there are too many outside forces pulling us apart for this to last.

I'll take each day as they come.

Live in the moment with Ryke Meadows.

If I ever die, I want that across my headstone.

‹ 29 ›

Daisy Calloway

Janet hands me a plastic bag with all my valuables and the bloodied maroon turtleneck I was wearing that night. I slip the gold ring on my thumb while Ryke heads down the hall, talking on the phone and waiting for me to leave.

"You need to go over to that cashier's window and they'll give you the hospital bill."

I nod. "Will the ambulance fee be added with that?" I don't know how the French medical system works.

Janet frowns. "There is no ambulance fee. Didn't you know that?"

I shake my head. "No, but I…" I blink as I wrack my brain. The pub isn't even close to this hospital, so how…

"He carried you," Janet says, a hand to her chest, like that night was emotional, even for her. "You were in his arms when he reached the hospital doors. He arrived about ten minutes before anyone else from the riot."

Tears well, and I suppress them as best I can. My voice trembles. "He ran here?"

She nods and reaches out to touch my wrist in comfort. I glance down the hallway at Ryke who speaks with force into the phone, like he wants the person on the other end to fully listen to him. He's the hero of my story, but he refuses to claim any of those moments, as if they don't matter.

They do matter. Everyone sees partial sides to Ryke, and he lets them think he's just an athlete with no brains, an aggressive asshole. It's like he's been alone for so long that he's lost any interest in showing off his worth.

I think I've hit the lottery—to have him in my life.

To me, he's worth every loud moment, every peaceful silence, the crazy and the sad, the restless and the quiet. I would trade it all to be with him, but I have a feeling there will be no price for my mom. She'll keep us apart at any cost.

I feel it in my bones like a bad, bad omen.

< 30 >

Ryke Meadows

"What the fuck is Rose hiding?" I snap at Lily on the phone. I decided to call her while I wait for Daisy to finish sorting through her belongings.

Daisy looks up at me with a plastic baggy in her hand and then points to a cashier's window, standing in the line.

I nod to her and listen to Lily's response. I'm not expecting much.

"Like I told Lo, I've made this pact with Rose not to talk about it, like a Ya-Ya Sisterhood thing, and I can't go back on my word. And just so you know, Rose is scary. She took out a knife and was saying something about blood oaths, and before I knew it, she *slit* my palm." Her voice lowers, almost comically that it's hard to take her serious. But she is. "And this comes from a girl who *cannot* walk on the hardwood without shoes. You don't have to say anything, it surprised me too."

I roll my eyes. "Lily," I say forcefully. "If it's something serious, you need to tell my brother."

"The pact," Lily hisses. "What if Rose put a curse on me? I can't say anything."

"You can't be that fucking superstitious."

"Rose might as well be a supernatural force when she's upset. You haven't seen her truly angry, so you can't say anything."

"I've seen her so fucking pissed that she almost tased my brother, how's that?"

"This is a different kind of upset," Lily says. "We're handling this, okay? I think it's good that Lo is with you, and I'm here with Rose for a little bit."

I frown, never thinking I'd hear Lily say that. She's usually glued to my brother's side and vice versa. "You're really okay without him?"

Silence stretches before she says, "I mean, I miss him *a lot* more than I can articulate. It hurts without him here. But I'm better than I was when he first left for rehab. I'm at a better place."

"I know you are," I tell her. Back then, she was almost in tears every time I called her. It was kind of fucking pathetic, but I didn't understand their relationship. I didn't understand that kind of unconditional love. And then Daisy left, and I felt out of my fucking mind for three days. I yelled at Lily for bitching after only seven days without Lo, so who's the hypocrite now?

"We're meeting you in two weeks right?" Lily asks. "It won't be too long."

"You sure you want to keep it a fucking surprise from Daisy?" I ask. Rose has been calling me non-fucking-stop, trying to find ways to see Daisy *without* upsetting her. I told them that they should just meet us on the road, but to wait until her face heals a little. They agreed.

"She likes surprises," Lily says. "Otherwise, we would have told her."

She's right about that. "Just don't come early. I can't spend thirty days in a car with all of you. Eighteen is already too fucking much."

"Weren't you the one who wanted to start the road trip in New York?"

I groan in agitation. "You're annoying me, Calloway."

"All I'm saying is that you could have picked a closer place to California, and then we wouldn't have to be in a car for so long."

"That defeats the fucking point of a road trip. If it was up to you and Rose, we would have started *in* California."

She pauses and then says, "Now that sounds like a good idea."

I roll my eyes again. I let out a deep sigh. "Can you promise me something?" I ask her.

"That depends. Does it involve breaking a promise to my sister that will unleash her diabolical wrath?"

"Promise me that whatever it is, you'll be fucking safe. And be careful on your way out to us. My brother can't live without you. I'm expendable, you aren't."

"You can't honestly think that about yourself," she says softly.

"Just promise me, Lily."

"I promise, but Ryke—he needs you. You're his brother."

I shake my head. To Lo, I'm equal to Connor. We met Lo at nearly the same fucking time. In fact, Connor has some months on me. For fuck's sake, Lo made us flip a coin to determine who would be his best man at his wedding. I didn't get it by fucking default because I'm related to him. In less than a year, I'll be standing by his side as he's about to get married, all because of *luck*.

A flip of a coin.

He can so easily push me out of his life, and the only reason I'm still here is because I refuse to go, no matter how hard he shoves.

But Daisy...I know in my heart she's something that can drive me away from him. I'm going to fight against the moment, but I also mentally prepare for it. "Sure," I tell her. "Listen, do whatever Yada Sisterhood thing—"

"*Ya-Ya*," she corrects me.

"Whatever," I say. "Just don't let Rose fucking cut you. Stick up for yourself."

"Is that what you've been telling my little sister?" she asks, flipping the switch.

"I tell her a lot of fucking things," I say. "And yeah, that's one of them."

"Good," Lily says. I can practically see her nod with resoluteness, in this goofy fucking way.

"Are you wearing an animal on your fucking head?" I ask her.

"You know what it's called."

"No I don't."

"It's a Wampa cap."

"That Star Trek shit?" I say, knowing that it's Star Wars. I like to give her a hard time.

"*Star Wars.* Lo would kick you for that."

"Good thing he's not fucking around." My brother, a fucking comic book geek with looks that could murder and simultaneously melt women. It's so fucking weird. Who would have thought? Nine years ago, not me.

There's a long pause before she asks, "How is she doing?"

I glance at Daisy who rocks on her feet, antsy as she stands in one place for so long. Her bandaged cheek is on the other side. The only marks visible are the bruises beneath her eyes. I remember her smile as she came, her laugh and the genuine happiness that blanketed over her. I wish this bad fucking thing didn't have to happen for her to make these hard decisions about modeling, but I am glad she's finally made them.

"She's going to be okay," I tell Lily. "She looks good." *She looks fucking beautiful.*

"Thank you, for what you did," Lily says. "We all appreciate it, you know."

I don't pick my words that carefully. I just fucking say them. "I'd do anything for her."

"Is it different this time?" she asks me.

"What do you mean?"

"In Cancun a couple years ago, you kind of saved Daisy back then too. I just wondered if you feel differently now." *What is she getting at?*

"Say it fucking bluntly or don't say it at all."

She sighs. "Why do you have to be so mean?"

"I didn't think I was," I snap.

"Do you like her more now than you did then?" she says straight out.

"She was only sixteen back then," I tell her. "I didn't hang out with her that much." The truth is way more complicated than that.

"Just say it bluntly or don't say it at all," Lily rebuts, with ten times *less* force than me.

I almost smile. "She means a fucking lot to me, Calloway." It's still not much better but it seems to appease Lily.

"Have you told this to Lo?" she asks.

"What would it fucking matter? He sees what he wants to see." I'm the intruder, the fucking guy he opened his arms to, the guy he let in his life. If I stick my cock anywhere near Daisy, he will be affronted as though I fucked with his family, his friends, his *world*.

"He sees what you give him," Lily says softly, "and you're not giving him a lot to work with, Ryke."

I run my hand through my hair and sigh. I'm so fucking scared to open up about my history with my own brother. That's the fucking truth. I did wrong by him for so long, and if I start talking about it, I feel like I'll just push him away more. I'll give him no reason to be close to me. I have *years* of hate underneath my belt, no fucking love.

So why express that? What fucking good will that do?

I just want to forget it all and move on.

Daisy reaches the front of the line.

"I have to go," I tell Lily.

"Was she happy that she's able to go with you guys to California?" she asks before we hang up.

"Yeah," I say, my chest rising with the fucking fact. "I'll keep her safe."

"*You* be safe," Lily emphasizes. "You're the one climbing. I'm packing a first-aid kit, just in case you fall, so you know."

"Your fucking Band-Aid isn't going to save me."

"Wolverine is printed on the front. He can save *anyone*."

I roll my eyes for the fifth time it feels like. "Let's just hope we all make it there in one piece."

Daisy starts walking over to me.

"Gotta go."

"Bye." We hang up, and I slide my arm over Daisy's shoulder and carry her duffel. Mikey is going to stay in France for another two weeks as vacation, hopefully distracting the paparazzi and leading them off our trail. For the first time in a while, we should be free of the media.

"You ready for a fucking adventure, sweetheart?" I ask her.

She hugs me close and says, "Does this adventure contain cupcakes, Ryke Meadows and motorcycles?"

"Substitute the last one for a fucking rental car."

She smiles. "I'm ready for this awfully big adventure then." She pauses and adds, "With you."

I kiss her temple.

30 days until Yosemite.

The fucking countdown begins.

< 31 >

Ryke Meadows

Seven days into the road trip, and I'm already fighting with my brother. "Do you know how fucking inappropriate you are?" Lo is half-turned around in the front seat of the SUV, his jaw clenching as he lays into me. The surprising fucking bit of all this: it's not even about Daisy.

It's about Lily.

His fucking fiancée.

"I'm pretty fucking inappropriate," I admit with a shrug. "I thought we all already knew that. So why are you hounding me about this?"

Lo gives me a look like *are you serious?* "You can't talk about that shit with her. She's a fucking sex addict."

Connor's eyes flicker to me in the rearview mirror, his hands tight on the steering wheel. Whether he sides with Lo or me, he doesn't let on. Daisy twists her hair into a long braid beside me.

I groan loudly. "She's so embarrassed to talk about sex. I was doing her a fucking favor, and secondly, I don't know why you're yelling at me now. This conversation happened months ago." *Thanks,*

Lil, for bringing it up right now. When I'm in a confined space for fucking hours with my brother.

Lily and I talk often, but I don't remember how we arrived onto the topic about public sex, maybe because she mentioned how she missed it. It's one of her restrictions now that she's in recovery. I was sitting on their couch, waiting for Lo to change for the gym, and I asked her all the places she's done it.

Her face flushed red and she stumbled for answers. I thought it'd make her more comfortable if I listed my sexual fucking adventures.

Beaches.

Bathrooms.

Golf courses.

Woods.

Parking lots.

Elevators.

Parks.

Malls.

Gym locker rooms.

The list really just goes on and fucking on. I like screwing everywhere, especially outside. Lily started to open up a little bit. It wasn't my fucking intention to share our sexual exploits with each other, but I just wanted to make her feel less ashamed about her sex life. So fuck me.

She told me she had sex with Lo in a movie theatre once. And how she did it at an amusement park when she was eighteen, on the fucking Ferris wheel.

My first thought: I have to give her some credit for that one. It sounded fucking fun.

And then she told me it was with a random guy she met at the cotton candy booth.

My insides kind of twisted. For her. For my brother. I wish she could have just enjoyed sex like me, but instead it was something else entirely for her. Something darker.

"I appreciate you trying to make her comfortable," Lo says in a way that sounds like he really doesn't appreciate it. "But for Christ's sake, she's texting me to clarify public sex to her." He shakes his head and looks down at his phone and reads her text. "*Is tent sex considered public sex, if the tent is owned by us? Because some people live in tents. Therefore that would be a house, and a house isn't public, it's private. Therefore, tent sex is private sex.*"

Connor tries really hard not to make a sound (at least I think he does) but he ends up bursting into laughter.

"I know," Lo says. "It's insane. It's like reading a text from someone trying to convince you that cocaine isn't a drug."

"And how do you know this is my fucking fault?"

Lo raises his brows. "Because I told her that it's public sex and she immediately responded with: *Ryke has a lot of public sex. Maybe he's a sex addict.*" He looks up to me. "And then we had a long fucking talk about the conversation you had with her."

Daisy eyes me with a grin. "You like public sex? Like in grocery stores?"

"Yeah, right in front of the fucking cantaloupes and produce," I deadpan.

"I prefer to do it in front of the baking goods. Chocolates chips. Cake mix." Her smile grows.

Lo looks between us. "No," he says sharply. "Don't even go there." His eyes land on Daisy. "And don't have sex in public. It's fucking gross."

"Hey," I cut in. "Let her do what she wants."

"Yeah, sure, get arrested, Dais," Lo tells her. "Or better yet, screw in a grocery store and then some cashier will be peeking in from the aisle over and film you on his cellphone. Great story to tell the world."

I expect another sarcastic comment from her, but instead, her face turns serious. "Do you think it's gross that Lily has had public sex?"

Lo's face contorts and he starts shaking his head. "Of course not. She's not gross."

"But it'd be gross for me," Daisy says, touching her chest. Confusion wrinkles her forehead.

I glower at Lo. He did just say that.

"That's not what I meant," Lo says, cringing. "You're just…you're you, Dais. You're young."

"Lily had sex on a Ferris wheel when she was eighteen," I refute coldly. "Don't make this into an age thing. Say the fucking truth, Lo. It'd be gross for *you* to think about Daisy having sex. It doesn't matter where the fuck it is."

"It's okay, guys," Daisy says quickly, "I'm sorry I brought it up." She slides over to the window, her face sinking in guilt at stirring more confrontation between my brother and me. But honestly, anything she fucking says is going to rile Lo. It's just the way he is.

Lo gives me a long stare. "Just be more careful with Lil next time. You, ranting and raving, about losing your fucking virginity on a golf course is not going to help. She's going to want to try it, and I have to tell her no."

"You can't even do it outside the bedroom once? I thought she was getting better," I say.

"She can't ask for it," Lo tells me. "And she's starting to fucking ask. You see the cycle here?"

"Yeah." He's not getting laid. But I know it's more than that. He worries about her. He always has.

"Who locked the windows?" Daisy suddenly asks.

I glance over and see her flicking the button on the door handle, nothing happens. Dais cannot sit still for longer than thirty fucking minutes. Put her in an SUV for an hour, and she'll stick her head, arm, legs and eventually her whole body out of the window. Lo had to drag her back onto the leather seat three or four times already.

I slide next to her.

"I did," Connor says. "I'm not getting my first ticket because Ryke won't restrain his puppy."

"Hey," Lo interjects. I frown. He's going to stick up for me? "Don't be calling Daisy *his* anything."

I roll my eyes. "Just unlock the fucking window, Connor."

"No, it's cool," Daisy says, scooting closer to me. "I don't want to get anyone in trouble." She tucks her long blonde hair behind her ear, and her leg brushes against mine. Her bruises are gone, and this morning, she had her stitches removed by a doctor in Ohio. The gash along her cheek is closed but reddened.

Still, it looks ten times better than it did. I untie her hair that's in a bun, and I playfully mess the strands. They lie tangled on her head, frizzy like she rolled out of bed or ran through the woods.

She tenses as she watches me look her over closely. I act the same in front of Daisy as I did before we got together—which means my brother shoots me a warning glare every half hour for overstepping and walking a thin line.

"Do you like my hair long?" she asks me.

"No because I can tell you fucking hate it." I wonder if she was waiting for my opinion before she grabbed a scissors. I thought cutting her hair would be one of her first spontaneous acts after she quit modeling.

"Then why do you always untie my hair when I put it up?"

I'm going to have to fucking generalize because my brother is in the front seat. So I say, "I like when girls have messy hair."

"Like '*we just fucked*' messy?"

She went there anyway. I try hard not to smile.

"Daisy," Lo interjects with a grimace. "Don't say that to my brother."

"You're right," she says to Lo. "The f-word is a bit abrasive." She tilts her head at me. "How about '*we just had sex*' messy?"

Lo shakes his head a couple times, puts on headphones and balls his sweatshirt in the corner of the door. "Wake me up when you stop flirting with a guy seven years older than you. It's disgusting."

Her smile fades.

I love Lo, but he can be a real fucking asshole.

Connor stays quiet, concentrating on driving, and I take the opportunity to cheer up Daisy. I grab her waist and set her between my open legs. The surprise causes her to smile again, and I slip one hand beneath her shirt, rubbing her back while I massage her shoulder with the other.

Her tense muscles can't loosen with me this close. The more I knead my fingers into her shoulder and skim her back with my palm, the more she stiffens and holds onto my kneecaps for support.

She purposefully scoots her ass harder into my crotch. *Fuck me.*

I remove my hand from beneath her shirt and comb my fingers through her hair. "I like your hair down because of how wild you look, but you could do anything to it and I would still love it." I want *her* to choose the length and color based on what she wants. Her mom and agency have dictated her appearance so much. I'm not fucking replacing them.

She spins around, my hands falling off her shoulders. And in effect, she half-straddles my lap. Her ass is on the edge of the seat, not on me.

"Can I have your knife?" she asks.

I stare down at her and cup her face, brushing my thumb along her smooth cheek. "What knife?"

She reaches towards my ankle, and I grab her wrist to stop her. A smile plays at her lips, mischievousness dancing in her eyes. "The knife you used to wear to bed," she whispers in a silky voice.

I'm wearing that knife now, but I stopped strapping it to my ankle at night because I thought it would lessen her anxiety—for her to see that I wasn't worried about someone breaking into her apartment anymore. "Don't talk about my knife, Calloway," I deadpan.

She eases forward, straddling my lap. "I like your knife."

She's a wicked fucking girl. There's a reason why guys haven't been able to last with her. In bed, she probably won't lie still while a guy dominates her. She doesn't beg to be in full control either. She wants to be a part of the experience, so when I fuck her, she's going to fuck me with equal intensity. It's a back and forth between us that I didn't expect to translate to sex, but I already know it will.

My gaze hardens, giving her a look that intimidates most women. Instead her eyes brighten, hypnotized by the darkness inside of me. The *I don't give a fuck what you think* mentality scares some people, but it attracts her. It always has.

She breathes deeply and runs her hand through my hair before her lips touch my ear, "You're my wolf." Her hands fall to the back of my neck, watching me watch her.

"Cute," I say.

"The cutest?" She smiles.

I shake my head, lean forward, and whisper in her ear, "The cutest is you, wrapped in my arms, coming three or four times before you fall asleep."

Her fingers grip my neck tighter. "I can barely come once," she whispers.

My eyebrows shoot up. "You came pretty fucking quickly with me," I breathe. She stares at my lips while I reach down in my boot and pull out my serrated knife.

I hand it to her, and she touches the point of the blade to her finger, not drawing blood but just inspecting the sharpness.

"It can cut through hair," I assure her.

She still scrutinizes the blade with a faraway look. Then she says under her breath, "I've never had sex with a guy like that."

I frown. "With someone holding you?"

She nods. "Usually they have their head on a pillow, watching me while I'm on top."

That really fucking bugs me, and the irritation passes through my features.

"I shouldn't have brought up other guys I was with. I know it's like a relationship faux pas." She slides off my lap and steals back her hairband from my wrist.

"I'm not upset because you were talking about your past hook ups,"
I tell her. I glance at the front of the car. My brother is fast asleep while
Connor switches lanes, acting disinterested in everything. I don't think
he can hear us, and if he can, he'll probably keep everything to himself.
I look back at Daisy who ties her hair in a low pony.

"You looked pissed," she says.

"I fucking am," I whisper. "You deserve better."

"What's better?" she asks.

"Someone who pays attention to you," I tell her. "Someone who
can tell what you like and dislike without asking." And then I lean
forward and whisper in her ear, "Someone who makes you so wet that
you scream when you come."

Her face flushes a little and she ties her hair off and whispers back,
"Where were you three years ago?"

She was fifteen. I was twenty-two.

"Three years ago," I whisper, "I met you at a New Year's Eve party
where you got roofied and I carried you to my car."

She shakes her head. "You met me before then at my house. You
waved at me."

I remember that. "I didn't know you were Lily's sister. Honestly, I
thought you were twenty-two and one of Rose's friends."

When Lily pointed at the tall blonde eating a pomegranate in the
kitchen, I thought she was fucking gorgeous. So I waved. Her face lit
up and she gave me a quick once-over, her lips curving in a cute smile.

I immediately wanted to fuck her, to start something, wondering if
she was the kind of girl who did long term, short term, or one-night
stands. I planned to do any of the three, just based on the way she was
smiling, her carefree nature where she radiated with energy, and her
beautiful fucking features.

I was going to walk over and see if I could ask her on a date, but
then Lily said something that burst my fucking plans.

She said, "Oh, that's my youngest sister."

My face hardened. "She looks older than you."

"I know, but she's only fifteen."

Fifteen. A weird feeling washed over me, like I did something really fucking wrong even though I hadn't done it yet. I closed off to Daisy instantly, burning every thought and image I had constructed on a fucking impulse.

"You really thought I was Rose's friend?" she asks.

"Yeah," I say. *A big fucking mistake.*

She lets this sink in with a faraway gaze.

My phone buzzes on the seat. I sigh with more frustration as I check the message.

My interview with 60 Minutes airs tonight. I hope you can watch it. I love you. — Mom

I delete the text before I let the words affect me.

"How's this length?" Daisy asks. The hairband lies right above her chest. It's a length between Rose's long hair and Lily's short shoulder-length.

"If you want to go shorter, I won't care," I tell her roughly, just making sure it's not staying this long because of me.

"No, this is what feels right." She hands the knife back to me, and she sits on her knees. "I want you to cut it." She inhales strongly, as though preparing herself for the moment.

"How many times have you envisioned cutting your hair?" I ask her seriously.

"A million."

And she's asking me to do it. Out of all the things we've done together—ridden motorcycles, swam with sharks, snorkeled, skydived, rock climbed—this is the most intimate. Not because we're dating but because this means so much to her.

She's waited for it to happen for years.

My hand wraps around the hilt of the knife, and I hold her pony in my hand. She watches, her palm sliding on my thigh.

I cut right above the hairband, and her smile grows as I slice through her blonde strands quickly. In a matter of seconds, the ponytail is in my hand, and her hair is chopped raggedly near her collarbones.

She grins as she touches it, like it was cut by a professional and not hacked by someone with coarse hands. I slip the blade back in my boot, sheathing it on my ankle strap.

She kisses my cheek and rushes to the window, flicking the button. "Connor, can you unlock it? I just want to see how my hair feels in the wind."

Connor looks at her through the rearview mirror. "That depends, are you going to howl again?"

She shakes her head quickly. "No. No howling, I promise." She flicks at the button repeatedly with the widest grin, knowing she's going to get what she wants this time.

"We're on backcountry roads," I tell Connor. "There aren't that many cops around." We're heading towards the Smoky Mountains in Tennessee, and trees border either side of the one-lane street.

Connor gives in and unlocks the windows. As soon as Daisy hears the *click*, she bounces on the seat. The window is already rolling down, and she hoists half her fucking body out of the SUV. She sits on the windowsill.

"I don't know who's a worse influence," Connor says, "her with you or you with her."

I almost smile. I grip her ankle, letting her do her thing. "If she falls, I'll pull her back in," I tell him. I have confidence in my strength. If I didn't spend almost all of my life building it by rock climbing and running, I wouldn't be able to keep up with her.

She raises her hands in the air and laughs, the wind whipping her shorter blonde hair. She shuts her eyes and inhales deeply.

Freedom doesn't come with age. It doesn't magically appear when you're a legal adult.

It comes when you stand up for what you believe in. Right now, I see a semblance of that peace for Daisy.

But she called her mom three days ago, and when Daisy told her that she quit modeling, Samantha hung up. She just shut her out. She didn't listen to Daisy explain why. And then her mom called Rose, and she bitched about the whole situation to her other daughter. My name was slung through the fucking mud by her mom.

It's my fault Daisy isn't modeling.

I forced her here.

If Samantha thinks my friendship with Daisy caused her to quit her career, then I wonder what she's going to believe when she sees Daisy's face.

I have no doubt that'll be my fault too.

< 32 >

Daisy Calloway

"Don't eat anything heavy," Ryke tells me. I sit cross-legged in a booth, moose and antelope heads chopped and mounted on the walls of John's Backwoods Smokehouse. We stopped in the Kentucky Mountains for dinner, and now that I'm without stitches and no longer modeling, I can eat real freakin' food.

"I don't like that suggestion." My eyes glaze ravenously over the pictures on the giant menu. Juicy steaks. Baby back ribs. Barbeque sandwiches. Greasy burgers.

My grumbling belly wants it all.

"You're going to be fucking sick. You can't go from eating fruits and vegetables for months to eating red meat."

I stare at him over the menu. "I have this theory." I pause for dramatic effect. "That my stomach is made of steel."

Ryke crumples his straw paper and throws it at my face. It sticks in my hair. I smile, but he can't see it behind the menu.

Lo doesn't notice our exchange, even if he sits next to me. He's busy scanning the other full tables and booths, wondering if anyone notices us. So far we've stayed anonymous.

He tips my baseball cap lower on my eyes to hide me from sight. My scar is facing the wall, so on the off chance that someone photographs us, they won't catch the cut. And it's not really *my* hat. Ryke gave me his.

Connor sips his water across from Lo. "If you act like you're hiding something, generally people are going to think you are," Connor tells him.

Lo glares. "I just don't want to be hounded the whole trip." He squeezes a lemon in his water, glaring at that too like it affronted him in some way. I guess it has by not being whiskey.

"No one's picked up where we are," Ryke says. "We're good."

Lo nods, trying to believe this.

I keep looking at Ryke above the menu, only my eyes visible to him. He had his stitches removed too. A cut slices through the corner of his eyebrow, small but noticeable. It'll turn into a scar after it heals fully.

He catches me skimming his features, but I don't shy from him. We play a dangerous game of *who's gonna look away first*. Not me. I eye him like I want to crawl into his lap and lick his face. He stares at me with an intense hardness—rugged and alpha and a tad bit assholish. That's Ryke Meadows. The singular look forces my heel into the spot between my legs. The pressure is nice against the throbbing place.

I fear that I'm going to break first. So I say, "My scar is bigger than your scar." I smile behind the menu again.

His dark expression never falters. "And my cock is bigger than your cock."

Ohhh. Burn. I laugh, and Lo cringes. He's past scolding Ryke for feeding into my inappropriate talk. He just shakes his head and flags down the waitress to come take our orders.

I give Ryke another look like I want to fuck him, my eyes softening but still narrowing. I can speak through my gaze pretty well after practicing different expressions for modeling.

Even with the *fuck me hard, come hither* stare, he stays fixed on me, unwavering. It's a game between us, but his penetrating gaze is seriously heating my body past its normal temperature. I think it's different now that it can go further than just flirting. It can progress to kissing and fondling and fucking since we're together. Just not in front of his brother and Connor.

The waitress stops by our booth. "Ready to order?"

"Yeah," Lo says. I vaguely pay attention to his burger order, along with Connor's salmon. Ryke raises his brows at me like *you have to look away sometime, sweetheart.*

Fine. I lose. Maybe next time it'll end with us tangled together. I mull over my food options quickly and then smile at the pretty blonde waitress. "I'll have the sirloin steak with a baked potato."

Ryke shakes his head at me, but he doesn't force me to switch. He looks at the waitress. "I'll have the same thing." We pass her our menus and as she walks to the kitchen, Ryke says, "Just so you can see why I'm not sick and you are."

"My stomach is made of steel," I repeat.

"That theory hasn't been fucking proven yet."

"True."

Connor types on his phone and then slips it in his pocket. He looks at me. "Now that you're done modeling, are you going to apply to college?"

I knew this topic was going to surface, and I'm not surprised he's the first one to bring it up. "Do you want me to go to college?" I ask.

"We all want you to do what you love," he says. "College is a good place to figure that out, but it's not for everyone." He looks at Lo, who lets out a bitter laugh.

"Sure, turn to the guy who dropped out his junior year," Lo snaps.

Connor shrugs easily. "You're a good example. Don't be ashamed. It's a fact."

"Fact," Lo says, "you're a conceited prick."

"Fact," Connor retorts, "you're a good looking asshole."

Lo touches his heart mockingly. "A compliment and an insult. Fuck me now, love."

Ryke rolls his eyes. He balls up my straw paper while I smooth the corners of my napkin, making a rose out of it.

"No college," I tell them. "I don't want to sit behind a desk all day and be lectured."

Connor nods understandingly.

"Maybe down the road I'll go," I say. "Just not anytime soon."

"So what are you going to do then?" Lo asks me.

"I don't know yet," I admit, twisting the stem on the paper rose. "I thought this trip could help me decide." I wish I was like Ryke. His job is his sport. He's been in so many rock climbing magazines because of successful free-solo climbs he's done. While he does live off his trust fund, he's been in three commercials where he's climbing and they paid him *millions* because of his celebrity status. He's the face of some kind of men's razor—which is pretty funny considering he's always unshaven. And he did a couple ads for REI and Under Armour.

Basically, he's balling. And I don't have a talent to capitalize on.

I guess that's a lie.

I did have a talent: Modeling.

What happens when the thing you're good at isn't the thing you love?

That's where I am now. Stuck.

Someone's phone vibrates on the table. I check my cell, thinking it may be my mom. Maybe she's ready to talk to me. I want to explain, but she's not giving me much of a chance.

No texts.

I look up, and Ryke's jaw locks as he stares at the screen of his phone. He presses a button. I know he's deleted a text from either his mom or dad. I've seen him do it before. He slips his phone into his leather jacket pocket.

I can't help but sympathize with his parents in this moment. I know what it feels like to be ignored, and it hurts. But it's not really my place to say something, is it? All of that business with his mom and dad and Lo, it's too messy for me to jump into.

Connor starts asking Lo about Superheroes & Scones, his duel comic book and coffee shop that he owns with Lily. I tune out at the words *taxes* and *profit margin.*

Ryke nods to me. "Where'd you learn how to do that?" His eyes fall to the paper rose. He's watched me make them over the years, but this is the first time he's asked.

Sometimes I don't even notice that I'm playing with the napkins. I just do it out of habit. "When I was a debutante, the instructors made us sit at a table for hours. I was really bored."

"You taught yourself?"

"Yeah," I say. "I found an article online on how to make cool shapes." I finish the napkin flower and hold it out to him. "Ryke, do you accept this rose?" I tease. He knows *The Bachelor* reference. When we were living with everyone, I made him watch taped episodes with me while I tried to fall asleep.

"That implies that you have many fucking guys dating you."

I mock gasp. "But you're my number one." I raise the baseball cap on my head so I can see him better.

"If I'm seriously dating a girl," he says, "I better be the *only* fucking one."

He knows he is. I smile and pinch the stem of the rose. I slip it behind my ear. It's not long after that our food parades towards us. The plates slide on the table, and the steak looks *exactly* like the picture.

"Need anything else?" the waitress asks.

"A dessert menu," I tell her. I'm already anticipating a piece of chocolate cake. And if that doesn't exist, then I'll settle for a warm brownie.

"Sure thing, honey." She leaves, and I cut my steak into large slices, not wanting to waste any time. My brain is screaming *eat, eat, eat!*

I take my first bite and shut my eyes. Delicious.

Magic.

I love food. After four more bites, I sip my water and say, "Told you, steel stomach."

He chews, and his brows rise again, not as optimistic as me.

< 33 >

Daisy Calloway

Theory disproven.

One hour after we left John's and the steak forced its way back up in my throat, knotting my stomach. I even passed on the dessert back at the restaurant, already feeling queasy at that point, but I didn't want to make a scene. I just mentioned that I was "full" from the sirloin and skipped it.

For Ryke, that must have been the first sign that I was going to be sick. The second, he said was me not moving in the back of the car. I was painfully still.

And then I puked.

On the side of the road thankfully, not in the car.

I'm less upset that Ryke was right, and more bummed that I can't gorge myself on sweets and savory foods. I hate taking things slow. But my stomach is obviously not made of steel. More like plastic.

Not fun.

Many hours later, my stomach has completely settled, and we've crashed at a motel in the mountains, no Hilton or Holiday Inn in sight. Just a quaint little place called Big Cove Motel with yellowed wallpaper, kind of moldy bathroom tiles, but fox-printed quilts that look clean.

We checked into two rooms. One for me and one for them. Lo wanted to be nice by giving me some privacy and alone-time, I guess. I'm not used to being around Lo without Lily, and I think he's uncomfortable by a lot of things. Me around his brother. Me around three guys and no sisters. Me on the road in a confined space.

But he doesn't realize how paranoid I get when I'm alone. Even still on pain meds, I was wide awake when Ryke snuck in here at 2 a.m., and his presence just shifted the temperature in the room, lighting me on fire.

And then we kind of went at it.

We've been fooling around for the past twenty minutes, all fingers and kisses. He stares down at me, his lips raw. I only wear a shirt, Ryke's favorite of mine. A baggy one that says: *fuck you, you fucking fuck.*

My eyes linger on his erection that stirs new feelings in me. It's hard to wait. Especially since I feel like we've been waiting for years, not just a few weeks. If our relationship began normally—not secret from his brother and my sisters and basically everyone—we would have had sex that day in the stairwell. We're both a little impulsive.

And I wonder if tonight will be the night.

I hope so.

"How big are you?" I already kind of know the answer. His thin pants leave very little to the imagination.

He leans me back against the mattress, and I counter by propping my body on my elbows. He towers above me on his knees, slowly lowering his pants. I sit up again, wanting to be closer to him.

His cock springs out. Fully erect. And I unconsciously file through all the guys I've been with, all the dicks I've seen, and my heart thuds. He's bigger than anything that's been inside of me. And I have a flash of Connor's porn tape. Oh God.

My brain wants to fry the knowledge, but it's here to stay. I think they're around the same size. I only caught a glimpse of Connor, but yeah, it's kinda weird I know this at all.

I focus on Ryke's cock though. The one in front of my face, begging for *my* attention.

Ryke holds my jaw. "You're going to be insanely fucking wet before I push into you, sweetheart."

He doesn't want to hurt me. He cups my heat, and I think he's going to fuck me with his fingers. "I want to get you off," I say bluntly. "Or I want to watch you get off. You've seen me come twice. It's only fair that I see you."

I really want to try and suck him—the challenge really alluring, but I have a feeling he's been postponing showing me his dick for that very reason. Knowing I'd want to and knowing he may choke me.

He doesn't say much, not that I expected him to. Ryke is a guy who speaks through his dark eyes. The heavy silence tightens all of me. He takes off his pants, completely naked. I rake his body with my gaze, every single muscle defined and cut hard. He seems unreal. And I've been with models.

I tell him in a raspy, needy voice, "I want to fit you all in my mouth."

"*Fuck...*" He says the word in a heavy breath, his eyes on my lips. I have good practice in blow jobs, so I know I can pleasure him as well as he has me. I just wish he'd let me try.

And then, suddenly, he rises to his knees, the mattress undulating beneath us. I'm too excited to wait for him, so I scoot off the bed myself and lower to my knees on the carpeted floor.

He gives me a look. "We can do it on the bed, Dais."

"I know, but I like this way." I want to be able to look up and see his face. And it's easier in this position. His eyes grow dark and heady and he sits down on the edge of the bed, his legs hanging over. He reaches out and combs my hair out of my face, and then he holds the back of my head, guiding my mouth to his erection.

I smile before I lick the length of him. His abs sharpen, and I rest a hand on his muscular thigh that flexes beneath my touch.

Right before I take him, he says, "Remember this isn't a fucking contest."

I nod with a brighter smile. I open my mouth as wide as I can, and he grips the base of his cock, helping me. He can't hold back the low groan that leaves his lips.

The deeper he slides along my tongue to the back of my throat, the closer I am to his body. Ryke moves off the bed so he can stand up, and his length immediately deepens into me. I put both hands on his ass and tilt my head back while the last two inches of him remain. I can't even describe how full of him I am. I wish I had the visual that he does, of his cock around my lips.

"*Fuck*," he groans.

I reach the base of his shaft, all of him in my mouth. And I look up into his eyes, and he stares down at me, engraining this image. His ass tightens beneath my hands, and I gently ease out of him by an inch. He thrusts forward, easing me back in. We repeat the motion, and the spot between my legs pulses again. Especially as I watch his face break in hot pleasure.

He grabs my hand off his ass and he lowers it as much as he can. "Touch yourself, sweetheart."

I've never been successful touching myself before, but in this position, with him naked right here—in my mouth, I'm already incredibly sensitive *everywhere*. It doesn't take much to start a routine that he's done before, the circular motion and the interchangeable speeds from fast to slow. It immediately heats me up.

I can't believe I'm going to come for the third time in one night. I never thought this was possible.

I feel like I'm on the brink, and maybe he is too. Right when I think the fireworks are about to explode in my head, I hear the door open from the adjoining room.

And those fireworks transform into sudden hysteria, and I react on impulse.

I pull away at the worst possible moment.

Because as soon my mouth leaves his dick.

He comes.

On my face.

< 34 >

Ryke Meadows

W hat.
    The.
Fuck.

I can't stop looking at her face. Normally, this is something that might turn me on, my cum all over her cheeks, on her lips, even on her eyelids. Fuck, it'd make any guy harder than rock. But not now. Not when Connor Cobalt stands in the room, closing the door as Daisy tries desperately to wipe it from her face.

She uses both of her hands, only making it worse. Her face flushes with embarrassment.

"Dais…fuck." I pull up my pants quickly and squat down, ignoring Connor.

Concern floods me immediately. I find my shirt on the ground and use the soft fabric to wipe her face gently, trying to care for her and not make her feel like a fucking porn star.

I can't believe she pulled away right then. Bad fucking timing.

Connor clears his throat.

"Um…I can explain," Daisy says.

"There's really no need," he says with a tense voice. "I'm well aware of what a blow job is."

I grimace as Daisy's cheeks turn redder. *Thanks a lot, Cobalt.* Way to make this more fucking awkward.

I don't turn away from her as I say, "What the fuck do you want?" I try to brush her hair out of her face, but it's useless. Strands are already wet, and they stick to her cheeks. My dick actually threatens to clench and harden but every time I see her eyes, mortified, my fucking arousal returns to reality.

I can't imagine what's going through her head.

I clean her as quickly as I can, but we're both too stunned to move from this spot, not able to rise to wash her off in the bathroom.

"You're both crazy," Connor says, his deep blue eyes pinging from me to Daisy. "You needlessly heighten the risk of your relationship every second you do things like this. Talking about sex in the car, screwing *one* wall away from Lo and me—it's like you're begging to be caught. So I'm going to give you both a friendly warning." He sets his gaze on me. "Tell them before they catch you or tone it down. I could have *easily* been Lo, and I can promise you, his wrath will be ugly."

I thought we were being fucking careful, but in the moment, we don't pay much attention. We're used to flirting with boundaries, and now that we've kicked some over, it's messing with my fucking head. I know this can't last forever. Definitely not the year and a half like we planned. But maybe for a few more months at least. We just need some time—especially before we have to deal with all the people who hate the idea of us together.

"And you couldn't wait until the fucking morning to tell us that?" I growl.

"You were getting loud," Connor says flatly, not smiling. "You can thank me later." He looks down at Daisy, making her whole body stiffen. I notice I missed a spot by her hairline. My stomach knots as I use my shirt to wipe at it, knowing she's going to fucking hate that it's still on her.

"I hope this is different than your other relationships," Connor tells her sincerely. *Fuck him.*

"You're really going to fucking go there?" I ask, my body pulsing with anger. I'm not like those other douchebags. The first time she goes down on me and he walks in. It makes me seem like a fucking dick, but it's also bad fucking luck.

"Yes," he says, "I've actually seen her leave a bedroom after doing something similar with Julian."

Her ex-boyfriend's name literally lights my core. I clench my fists, wanting to punch the shit out of him. I don't want to think about his cock in her mouth or even his cock fifteen feet from her body. I want that image fucking *gone.* And of course, Connor brings it up just to rile me. I shake my head, restraining the urge to throw a fist in the wall. I decide to leave for the bathroom instead, my anger spinning around me as I grab a washcloth and run it under the sink.

When I return to the room, I hear Daisy say, "Ryke's not like the other guys, Connor."

I shoot Connor a glare. "Can you just be fucking embarrassed right now? How are you still standing here?"

"I've never been embarrassed in my life," he says. Everything that comes out of his mouth—I'd like to strangle. He's so fucking annoying.

I bend down and start rubbing the warm washcloth on her cheeks, holding her chin steady with my other hand. "Oh yeah?" I ask, my eyes flitting to Connor's. "What about if Daisy saw you fucking? How embarrassed would you be then?" This isn't going to lead anywhere good, but I'm so fucking sick of him thinking he's a god. Like he can't be touched. I want him to feel at least an ounce of the embarrassment that he's caused Daisy.

Her eyes go wide. "I'd be embarrassed," she says to me, kicking my ankle hard. She mouths, *Stop*.

So that plan wasn't fully fucking thought out. I grit my teeth, fucking pissed by everything. Julian being brought into the conversation did not help.

Connor raises his brows. "Did she watch those tapes?" He sounds more surprised than affronted.

I keep my mouth shut this time, rubbing the cloth along her forehead, concentrating on her.

"On accident," she blurts out. "I tried not to look, I promise." I haven't even seen those tapes, but I'm sure it'd be more awkward for her. It's her sister and her brother-in-law in them. She clutches my shoulder like all of these facts are going to shrivel her from humiliation. I console her the best I can, caressing her head with my right hand and wiping the rest of my cum off her face with the other.

Connor stays quiet, unreadable, which makes this so much worse for her.

When I finish, I stand to scrutinize Connor's reaction. But it gives me nothing, so I have to ask, "How do you feel now, Cobalt?"

"Disturbed," Connor says calmly. "A little worried too. I didn't think it'd be that easy to stumble onto our porn." He looks to Daisy, his brows now furrowing. "What site were you on?"

"I fucking hate you," I deadpan. "Seriously." I wanted that satisfying moment where we arrive on an even playing field. She saw him naked. He saw *this*. But Connor refuses to give us that triumph. We're left with this fucking awkwardness, no matter what.

Connor pulls out his cellphone like he's going to make a note of the site.

"I can't remember, Lily suggested it," she mumbles.

I freeze with Connor. Lily shouldn't be watching porn, and if she is…well that would be considered a relapse in the sex addiction recovery handbook.

Daisy's eyes widen like *what did I say?*

"Is she watching porn again?" Connor asks.

"No. She just recommended the site when I asked. No need to go postal, guys. You know she hates when everyone overreacts. Last month, *you...*" She points at me accusingly, defending her sister. "... barged into her bathroom just because she was taking a little longer. Do you know how embarrassing that is?"

Yeah, I know, I was there. Her face turned into a giant fucking tomato and she screamed at me. But I'd rather embarrass her ten times over than have the alternative happen—relapse or worse...suicide. It'd kill my brother. It'd kill all of us. And I've seen her at her worst, when she was in a bathroom out of her fucking mind, and I often wonder what would have happened if I didn't barge in.

None of us will take that chance.

Connor lets out a sigh. "I'll text her later. You." He looks at me. "Return to our room. I don't want Lo finding out about your quasi-relationship like this. You." He turns to Daisy. "Don't let Ryke come on your face again." *Fucking A.*

"Fuck off, Cobalt." I push him out the door, aggressively, wanting so bad to remove that fucking smile on the edge of his lips. I settle with closing the door on his face. When I spin around, Daisy stands to her feet.

"Has this happened to you before?" she asks, her eyes rising to mine. My cum on a girl's face. *No. Never.* And I never even thought about it until now.

I'm so fucking sorry, Dais. I know she didn't like it. I know it's not something that should have happened tonight.

"You're the fucking first," I tell her.

"Me too," she says, trying hard not to smile. Now that Connor is gone, there's a lightness in her eyes, a laughter that bubbles up and tears away the tension from the situation. I walk over and cup the back of her head, my fingers running through her hair. She lets out a breath. She likes this.

"I'm sorry, Calloway."

"I like you on me."

I give her a look. "Not like that."

"Not like that, but…it was an experience." She grins.

Connor may not believe we're in a real relationship, but I'm glad we're starting out like this, to relish in all these little fucking moments before we get to the one she's waiting for—the one I crave. But despite what anyone says, this fucking works for us right now.

< 35 >

Daisy Calloway

I exit the motel shower, basking in the warm water before we start camping-camping. With real tents and campfires and everything that makes my heart flutter in excitement. As I pull on a shirt that says *this ain't paris*, I glance up once and meet the television. My smile fades, and my whole body goes rigid.

Sara Hale is on the screen.

Ryke's mom.

A news segment shows clips of the *60 Minutes* interview that aired last night. Ryke's mom faces a reporter, her golden-brown hair straightened. I strain my ears to pick up her words. "What I did was not a malicious attack on the Calloway family."

"But you sold the information about Lily Calloway's sex addiction to magazines, did you not?"

"Yes, but I wasn't trying to hurt that girl. I was just tired of hiding the truth. You have to understand that I spent *years* protecting Jonathan Hale's infidelity. The only way to expose him was to put Jonathan under a spotlight. I only saw one way to achieve that, and I apologize for whatever emotional hurt I caused Lily. But she was linked to Loren, his son. She was tangled in a very complicated family dispute."

"You sound as though she was cannon fodder."

"Again, I apologize if it seems that way." Sara pauses and stares at her hands with solemnity, but she has a hardness behind her eyes, a toughness that combats the softness. "As a mother, I was torn daily. I had to hide my real son, and I was forced to act like Loren was my child. I just wanted to be free of Jonathan, and I wanted my son to be free too."

"But were you really forced?" the reporter asks. "You signed the divorce agreement. You knew what you were complying to."

"At the time, I was a single mother, young and confused. I was scared, and I did what I thought was best for my son."

"Ryke."

"Yes, Ryke."

Someone shifts in the open doorway that connects the adjoining motel rooms. I look over.

Ryke. His eyes are dark and set on the screen like he's been watching for a little bit. His hair is wet from taking a shower in the other bathroom. After Connor's warning last night, he went back to their bedroom. And I didn't even make him check the locks before he left. I'm trying my best to overcome that fear.

It must be almost time to hit the road again, and I'm sure he came to fetch me, but his gaze stays on the television screen.

Sara straightens up in her chair. "I realize now that I only hurt him through the divorce agreement."

Ryke runs a hand through his wet hair and walks further into the room, his eyes falling to the ground as he searches the floor for the remote.

"Don't you want to listen to what she has to say?" I ask him, packing my comb in my duffel.

"It's a fucking media ploy to make herself look better."

"How can you be so sure?" I ask.

Ryke turns to face me. I'm not scared of him at all, and I don't think he wants me to be. But his eyes flash hot, with anger so deep-seated that it's hard to look at. "She sounds like she rehearsed her answers. She doesn't fucking talk that formal."

I frown. "Really? My mom sounds like that."

"Mine doesn't. She's emotional. If she was real, she'd be crying or yelling. She wouldn't hold back and be stone-faced." He gestures to the television. "The only time I've seen her like that is when she's trying to impress her wealthy fucking friends."

This is the most he's ever talked about his mom with me. I watch as he searches for the remote, but it's with less diligence, his gaze faraway as his thoughts spin.

"Do you miss her?" I ask him.

He finds one of my shirts on the ground and tosses it to me. "Sometimes, but it doesn't fucking matter, Dais."

I stuff the shirt in my duffel pocket. "But she's your mom…" I can't imagine never talking to mine again. Even if there are times I'd like to run away from her, running away forever sounds painful.

He shakes his head. "I can't live in your fucking optimistic world where everyone is kind and holy. I've seen too many bad people to believe there's that many good."

"She can change though—" I start, wanting something better for him. I wish I could take his problems and uncomplicate them, even if I can't. It hurts to feel like I have no control over it.

"Change what, Daisy?" He shrugs. "She already ruined Lily's life," he states matter-of-factly, but his eyes are dark. "She ruined *your* life and Rose's. And she broke my fucking heart. It's fucking over."

I swallow hard, a lump in my throat. "She didn't ruin my life," I say softly.

Ryke glares. "Don't even fucking start." Because he's seen me scream at night, he's watched me turn into a scared, frightened girl. And the catalyst for everything was Sara Hale.

"I wouldn't be upset if you tried to have a relationship with her," I add. "I just need you to know that."

He surrenders his search for the remote and walks forward, his hands brushing my cheeks. "Thank you," he says with a short nod. "But it won't change anything."

I nod back, not sure what else to say. My throat closes.

Off my silence, his features darken, his brows furrowing. "I just can't forgive her," he tells me. "For some fucking reason, it feels more like a weakness than a strength to open my arms to her."

"Even if you miss her?"

He nods. "Yeah. Even if I miss her. So that's where I'm at." He kisses my head. "Don't worry too much about my family problems, Dais. It's my shit. I really don't want you in the middle of it."

I look up at him. "I'm glad that you want to talk to me though."

He gives me a confused look. "Why wouldn't I want to?"

My age.

The pieces must click because he says, "We wouldn't be together right now if I thought you were too immature to talk to about this stuff."

My lips begin to rise, but a reporter at a news desk cuts into our conversation, "Sara Hale has no evidence that either Ryke Meadows or Loren Hale was sexually or physically assaulted by their father. Although, she did say it's possible both happened to Loren during his residence at his father's home in Philadelphia. You can learn more about this ongoing case on our website..."

Ryke is on the hunt for the remote again, and before the reporter gives any contact info he finally finds it and shuts the television off.

I don't ask what he knows about the whole ordeal. I can tell that he's through talking about it. I was lucky enough to get what I did out of him today.

< **36** >

Ryke Meadows

We've made some progress towards California. Not much. But we're getting there.

Before the sun fell, we arrived at the heart of the Smoky Mountains. Like I said, we're still fucking far away. But the point of this trip isn't to speed to California. It's for my brother to relax, breathe, and try to find some inner-fucking-peace.

I could use some of that too.

Connor spins on his expensive loafers that sink into the muddy dirt. This image is so priceless: Connor Cobalt in a fucking suit standing in the middle of the woods and looking—probably for the first time in his life—like he doesn't belong.

If he was trying to schmooze an advertising exec and planned a wilderness retreat, he'd put on a fake fucking smile and dress down to fit in. But there isn't any reward in pitching a tent for him right now. He just has to do it because we're friends and we told him so.

"You okay there, Cobalt?" I ask.

He shoots me the middle finger. I see the annoyance flicker in his eyes. It's easier to catch his emotions the more you know him.

Lo smiles. "Hey, look at that. Connor has adopted Ryke's native language."

"Why aren't we staying in a hotel again?" Connor asks me. "Not that I don't love to see how you like to live, Ryke, but some of us prefer a bed to the ground."

"It's called camping," I retort.

Connor gives me a look. "I'd forgotten the definition of camping. Now that you reminded me, the whole world is clear." His real irritation, however, comes from his phone. He raises it at the sky, trying to achieve cell signal. He's already worried about Rose, and now that he's losing communication with her, he's becoming a bigger asshole.

Good thing I can handle most personalities, even Connor Cobalt's conceited one.

"For someone so fucking smart, you sure as hell love to act stupid around me."

"Like Lo said," Connor says, half-distracted as he presses buttons on his cell, "I'm trying to tap into your way of living." He just called me dumb. He lets out a frustrated sigh and pockets his phone. "So far it sucks." And he hightails it back to the car to help Daisy unload the supplies.

Lo kicks some rocks and twigs away from the place where we're setting the tents, clearing anything sharp that'll dig into our backs. He does so with a distant gaze, lost inside his head.

"Hey." I come up beside him. "You want to go to a fucking hotel too?"

He glances at the thick woods that surround us and gestures towards the pines. "Don't act like you didn't see an RV past those trees." He points at the tall ones that seclude us from the other campsites.

It's a national park. There are other campers. I can't change that. But at least we have some privacy. I recognize his fears though. This trip is supposed to be paparazzi free. For us to live off the grid and be absent of the media.

That's what I promised him.

If some road-tripping family recognizes us, snaps some pictures and posts them to the web, we're fucked. But this is the best I can do.

"They're not going to find us here, Lo."

His eyes darken, not completely trusting me. I don't know if he ever will. "In rehab they had a five-star gourmet chef on call. Your pseudo-rehab isn't really living up to my expectations."

"I'm sorry I didn't hire a fucking butler or maid, and I forgot to pack those scented toilettes you use to wipe your ass," I snap. He's not a rich snob that he makes himself out to be. He just likes to poke people until he sees a reaction. "If you want to go to rehab in New York, I'm not fucking stopping you, Lo. I'm just giving you another option." I outstretch my arms. "Open air. Freedom from the media. A normal fucking life for a month. Something that the rehab center isn't going to provide you with." At least not when everyone there will know he's Loren Hale. Another celebrity checking themselves into the center.

Like clockwork.

I wait for his response, and Connor returns, watching my brother as well, seeing what his decision will be. I can support either choice, but I want to be available if he goes to rehab. I can't be on the road with shitty cell reception while he's back in New York.

So if he chooses rehab, this trip to California is over. For Daisy, for me. I'd pick my brother in this instance. I have to.

After a long moment of silence, Lo looks at me. "Hotdogs and hamburgers tonight?"

My limbs loosen in relief. "Yeah," I say with a nod. "You okay with that?"

"As long as Connor doesn't cook them. He doesn't understand that medium-rare means red and bloody."

"No, I understand the meaning of medium-rare," Connor counters. "I just also understand the meaning of Escherichia coli."

"Why the fuck can't you just say E. coli?" I ask.

"Because abbreviations are lazy and I'm clearly not."

I shouldn't have asked.

Daisy tries to carry a stack of fold-out chairs in her arms all at once. I take a step forward to go help her, but Lo puts his hand on my chest. "I've got this." He pats my shoulder with force, silently warning me, and then sprints to catch Daisy before she falls.

She laughs while he takes two chairs off her pile.

"You're glaring," Connor tells me.

"Fuck off." Though I do try to lessen the agitation that tenses my jaw.

"Maybe try acting like you don't want to murder your brother for stepping in your way."

"It's hard," I say truthfully. I scratch my neck. "What would you do if you were me?" Maybe it's masochistic of me to ask after what happened at the motel. But I want to hear his answer anyway.

"If I were you? You mean if I was screwing an eighteen-year-old girl who's my brother's girlfriend's little sister, whose mother hates me because I'm the spawn of Sara Hale, and whose father dislikes likes me because he's protective over his youngest, wildest daughter?"

I open my mouth to chew him out, but he cuts me off.

"But if I'm you," he says with the tilt of his head, "I've also been there for that girl. When she had an ape of a boyfriend, when she was alone and all backs were turned, when she was going through heavier things than all of us realized." His calm tone soothes any anger that threatens to rise. Just like that. "If I were you, Ryke, I'd stop letting people see the worst parts of me, and I'd finally show them the good." He shrugs. "But I'm clearly not you." He stares around at the forest landscape. "And you're not me."

"I just don't see what good it'll do to have those fucking arguments." I don't want to fight. I just want to leave it all behind. I watch Daisy unfold all of the chairs with Lo. He motions to her messily cut hair, and she shows him the back, the blonde strands uneven. He shakes his head, but her face has never been brighter, even with a scar.

"Why does there have to be an argument?" Connor asks.

"You think people are just going to accept any explanation that comes out of my mouth? I can talk to her mom until she's blue in the fucking face. She won't accept me, Connor. Her dad let Daisy date *Julian*, a guy my age who thought more with his cock than his head, and *I'm* the one who receives threatening looks when I stop by her parent's house."

"First off, he didn't let her date Julian," Connor notes. "He was furious. You weren't there when Jonathan and Greg were trying to plot ways to have him fired from his modeling agency."

"That clearly didn't work."

"I said *tried*," Connor says easily. "I never said they were successful." He presses a few buttons on his phone again. "Greg is a smart guy, Ryke. Even though you aren't dating Daisy out in the open, he's known since she was fifteen that she's had a crush on you. He's just worried you're going to lead her on and break her heart."

I wish I had a better relationship with her parents, but I don't. In order to be Greg's friend like Connor is, I'd have to start talking to my father. Greg and Jonathan see each other all the fucking time. Greg used to stop by the country club on Mondays when I was a kid. He was the water to my father's scotch. Nice. Cool, even. Sometimes I used to wish he was my dad.

"I know this is going to seem like such a foreign concept to you," Connor says, raising his phone in the air again, "but if you *actually* show that you're invested in a girl beyond sex in front of people that matter, you'll gain more respect from them."

But he forgets that I don't speak with an even-tempered voice. I'm rough. I'm abrasive as hell, and the moment I try to talk, everything comes out coarse. Nothing comes out how I really intend. I gave

Daisy sex advice when she was fifteen because I was trying to steer her towards the kind of guys that would treat her right. And I got shit on for that conversation for the next two fucking years.

"Hey," Lo calls. He holds up a package of hamburgers and then points at the tent that Daisy tries to set up alone. "You two helping or is doing five things at once part of my rehabilitation?"

I'm about to walk over to him, but Connor inhales and puts the phone to his ear. "Rose?" He frowns. "What? Wait, darling…you're breaking up." He looks at the cell, actually glaring at the technology. He turns to Lo. "You better set out two more chairs."

"No." I groan. "Lily promised me she wouldn't arrive early." All three Calloway girls for twenty *long* days in a confined space—shit.

"She broke it then," Connor says, trying to sigh in relief, but he still looks worried. "Rose said they're ten minutes out before the line dropped."

Fuck me.

‹ 37 ›

Daisy Calloway

Rose and Lily are here.

At the beginning, I was too stunned to do anything but smile, a full-blown one filled with genuine happiness. I didn't realize how much I wanted them here until they arrived. Lily hugs me tight, and I try to convince them to sneak away with me. Girl time, no boys.

But they have to reunite with their respective partners.

I back away from my sisters while Lo wraps his arms around Lily. She's wearing her Wampa cap, a white furry hat that has flaps for her ears. Lo whispers to her, and she blushes bright red. As I keep backing up, I bump into something hard and two pairs of hands rest on my shoulders.

I crane my neck. "Hey you," I say to Ryke. He stares at me with those brooding eyes. I wish he could kiss me the way Lo bathes Lily in his love. Out in the open, passionate beautiful kisses that seem to make them float off the earthen floor. But even in the darkened night, the campfire flickers close by, illuminating our features.

We can't hide with everyone around.

Rose and Connor talk in French. He kisses her forehead, rubbing the back of her neck with tender affection, and her nose crinkles. "What animal died beside our tents?" She puts her hand to her mouth.

"Are you burning the burgers?" Lo asks Ryke, and I feel his hands drop off me, cold air replacing the spot.

"No, I just started cooking them." Ryke checks the burgers just to make sure, leaving my side.

I sniff the air. "I don't smell anything except wood smoke." I hike over to where Rose stands, her five-inch heels sinking in the dirt. Connor has his arm around her waist, and he tries to kindly take her purse from her, but Rose swats him with it.

"I'm not lying," she says. "It smells foul."

"It's probably the fucking pit toilet," Ryke tells her. "You passed it in your car on the way here."

Rose shakes her head. "It's closer." She pinches her nose and gags dramatically.

"Maybe it's your own stench," Lo says, holding Lily to his chest like she's a part of him, a piece that had been missing this whole time. He seems happier. "Bitch No. 5."

Rose points a threatening finger at him, manicured and blood red. "You insult Chanel and my heel will find your asshole in a millisecond, Loren."

"Oooh," Loren mock cringes. "I didn't know you could move that fast with your she-devil hooves."

Rose shrieks, and I flinch at the violent noise, coming out of nowhere. She tries to catapult herself at Lo, but Connor is really fast. He grabs her around the waist, holding Rose tightly. And I jump again when pine needles and dried leaves crunch beside me. Ryke stands there and gives me a look like *you okay?*

It's nighttime.

I hate nighttime unless I'm wrapped in his arms.

I nod, trying to play it cool and not act like a scared teenager.

Rose kicks her legs out, while wearing a pleated black dress, even as her husband restrains her. She looks more unladylike than I've seen her in a while. I know she has meltdowns. Lo has mentioned them before in their spats, but she almost always keeps these moments hidden from me.

My vision of Rose is this solid iron fortress that won't let anyone in, not even Lo's snide comments. She just bulldozes right over him with ones of her own.

Right now, his few words are crawling underneath her skin faster than usual.

Connor whispers in her ear, and she screams something in French. I turn to Ryke. "What'd she say?" I whisper.

He stares down at me. "*I'm not overreacting,*" he translates under his breath.

She shrieks again. I don't flinch this time.

"Is that your she-devil cry?" Lo continues to antagonize. Lily slaps his arm, seriously telling him to quit.

Connor actually glares at him. "Lo," he warns. "Stop."

Rose is tearing at Connor's hands, manically trying to free herself from his strong hold. His lips return to her ear, and I think she's on the verge of a panic attack, inhaling sharply. How did this happen over a couple comments?

Guilt washes over Lo's features, and I catch Ryke watching his brother closely. "Lo," Ryke says, nodding to him. "Help me with the burgers?"

Lo nods and they break away from us, nearing the fire.

I trudge over to Lily, who's biting her nails as she watches Rose's outburst. "Is she okay?" I ask Lily. Clearly she's not, but I don't know what else to ask. "Is she PMSing or something?"

"I guess," Lily says.

I reach out and hold her hand so she stops biting her nails, a bad habit of hers. She gives me a weak smile and I return it.

When I look back at Rose, she's no longer thrashing in place. Connor points to me while his lips move fiercely against her ear, and then Rose's gaze peels off Loren and fixes on me, as though just now noticing my presence. I think she's about to cry.

I've never seen Rose cry before.

She wipes her teary eyes quickly and nods while Connor keeps talking. His flexed muscles start to relax and then he kisses her forehead. She hands him her purse, straightens her dress, raises her chin and walks calmly over to me, as though nothing just happened. As though she did not have an epic meltdown.

"Let's go somewhere," Rose says, "just the three of us. I need air that's not polluted by Loren Hale." She waits for my answer, and then her eyes linger on my scar. Both of my sisters have been avoiding my cheek since they saw me, looking anywhere but there. She catches herself and tries to force a smile.

"I know a perfect place," I say with a sly grin. I scoped out the area and woods before they arrived.

Five minutes later, I've navigated Lily and Rose through the mountainous terrain, filled with fallen logs and wet moss the closer we near the small waterfall. The moon and flashlights guide our way there. The trees break into a clearing, and stone surrounds what looks like a deep swimming hole, the waterfall collecting in the pool and then running into a tinier stream.

I sit on the stone and shed my long-sleeve shirt, the air nippy in mid-October.

"No way," Lily says. "It has to be freezing."

Rose shines her flashlight at the murky water. "It's brown."

"It only looks that way because it's dark," I insist.

She inspects the area a little more, her beam of light whipping from tree to tree, checking for visibility. It's private for the most part.

Lily hesitates, crouching and dipping her finger in to test the temperature.

"Come on," I smile at them. "You're not going to make me beg, are you?" I stick out my bottom lip and bat my eyelashes. I will totally play the I-was-just-in-the-hospital card if I have to. I have to use it to my advantage while I can.

"Are we going in like naked, naked?" Lily asks.

Rose points the light at her face. "What other kind of naked is there?"

Lily blocks the beam with her hand and squints. "Partial nudity and full nudity."

"I'm going full," I declare, standing while I unbutton my jeans. I snap off my bra, and I'm out of my panties in seconds.

Rose shuts off her light. "Daisy," she says my name with severity while Lily takes off her Wampa cap and starts shedding her shirt. "We should talk about what happened in Paris, the runway and the riot."

I do the immature thing and take the opportunity to escape that discussion. I jump straight into the swimming hole, the ice cold water shrinking my lungs and plunging me into pure darkness. But I don't want to kick to the surface just yet.

I know what awaits me.

Feelings that I've dug through since… never. I've tried to take one thing at a time. The hospital. The scar. My mom. The runway rejection. Quitting my career. Everything just piled up on each other. I didn't have time to really process. It just happened like a domino hitting the next one in line. I had no chance to go backwards and recount all the pieces that knocked over.

Ryke says I need to let it out.

To scream.

But I just saw Rose's meltdown, and all it really did was worry her husband, guilt Lo and cause Lily's eyes to bug out of her head.

Why scream if it just hurts everyone around you?

When my lungs beg for air, I pop to the surface. Rose is in her black panties and bra, peering into the water from the edge of the rock. The moment I come up, she splashes me. "I thought you drowned," she says icily. "I was about to jump in after you."

"Jump in now," I say, the freezing water pimpling my arms and legs. I float on my back. "It's so warm."

Rose's eyes narrow. "You're shivering."

Lily's completely naked, and she slides in the water really slowly. Her boobs are totally bigger than mine now. I glance at my breasts. Did mine shrink? *Damn.*

"Are your boobs bigger?" I ask Lily. "Or are mine smaller?"

Lily blushes deep red, still not used to talking about sex and all that jazz. I was never really close to her like that growing up. I went to Rose for any female-related advice. "Uhhh…" She touches her cheek. "Am I red?"

"Yes," Rose and I say in unison.

Lily glances at my boobs as I float. "Uh, yours are smaller. You got really skinny, Daisy." She plops all the way in the water and actually hisses like a cat. "Cold, cold." Her breath smokes the air and she clings onto a warmer rock for refuge. I'm sure she's wishing for Lo's body right now.

I could use a Ryke Meadows pillow.

I smile at the thought.

Rose hops into the water, keeping her underwear on. "Motherfucker," she gasps when she breaches the surface. Her glossy hair is wet around her cheeks. Her teeth chatter, and she nears Lily, who deserts her rock to swim closer to Rose.

"Huddle, huddle," Lily says.

I laugh as they hold onto each other for warmth. I know they're suffering through the cold for me, and I appreciate it a lot.

Rose looks at me, and her eyes land on my scar.

I stop floating and tread water.

"Are you worried about what mom is going to say?" Lily asks me first.

I tremble. I'm not sure it's just from the cold. "I want to move on from this, and I'm afraid she's going to turn it into such a big deal that I won't be able to."

"Tell her that," Rose says.

"How?" I ask. "She won't talk to me. I called her five times."

Rose holds onto Lily like she's her personal heating blanket, almost dunking her under the water a couple times. But Lily keeps her chin above the surface and elbows her. Rose concentrates on me, or at least tries to. "She doesn't take change well," Rose says. "By the time you go home, she'll be ready to talk to you about your career change."

"What if I don't have a good backup plan?" I ask.

"You may need one," Rose says honestly. "Mother likes plans, and if all you have is *I don't know*, she's going to start filling out college resumes for you."

So in order to escape my mom's control, I have to figure out what I want to do with my life. That shouldn't be so hard, but it sounds terrifying to make that decision at eighteen.

I need like five more years at least.

Maybe ten.

A decade sounds good. A decade of preparing for what I'm going to do for the next fifty years. How do other eighteen-year-olds solidify their dreams and career paths right before college? How is it possible to *know* what you're good at and what you love so young?

What if you never find out?

What if you spend a lifetime searching with no real answer in the end?

The future is depressing.

Maybe that's why I've never thought about it before.

"You and Ryke," Rose suddenly says, waking me up from my melancholy stupor. Maybe she realized the topic of our mom was a downer. "Have you fucked yet?"

I gape. Wow, my sister said that so blasé-like. "We're not together, so…" It's weird. I've said these words before, but now they've become an actual lie.

Rose rolls her eyes. "When you do have sex, please make sure he's safe with you. I would have a talk with him, but Connor forbade me. He said it wasn't my place," she scoffs. "You're *my* sister. It's most definitely my place to threaten his testicles and penis."

Lily frowns. "When does Connor forbid you to do anything?" Rose does have equal footing in her relationship with Connor. Except probably in bed. God, I balk at the memory of him dominating her as they had sex. I restrain the urge to disappear beneath the water.

"He threatened to return all of the Hermes clothes he bought for me." She inhales deeply. "It was low. But I've moved past it."

"Right," I say with a smile. "Well you don't need to worry. I'm not having sex with him." *Yet.*

This should be the moment where I open up about my very first orgasm, where I share all the details. I've told them about these troubles before, so telling them about my success would be natural. But I keep that inside. Not just because it involves Ryke but because it feels attached to more things I can't express to them anymore.

Night terrors. Sleeping.

I have no more pain medication, which means no more sluggish sleep for me.

I'll be taking Ambien tonight, a pill that combats my insomnia but brings me to a dark realistic dream-state.

I'm nervous about screaming in the middle of the night, waking and worrying them. How do I explain myself?

Do I say: *I can't sleep at night because I think about the man who crawled into my room to snap pictures. I think about the paparazzi who've cornered me. I think about all the friends who hate me, scorned me and terrified me. I think about all the men who believe I'm Lily. And you're the cause, big sis. You're the reason I can't sleep. If it wasn't for your sex addiction, I'd be free. So fucking free.*

You've hurt me.

I can't say those words.

Not tonight.

Maybe not ever.

No one brings up Ryke again, but after one minute, Lily winces. "Ow. Don't pinch," she tells Rose.

"I didn't," Rose snaps. "Stop rubbing up against the rock." And then Rose's gaze drifts to me, and her eyes slowly grow.

"What?" I say. "I know you don't like my haircut, Rose—"

"It's not that," Rose says softly. "Lily, get out of the water."

"What?" Lily says, and then she follows Rose's gaze. "Oh...shit." Lily motions to my neck and then she turns and crawls onto the rock. The moment she does, I see, on Lily's back, what Rose is internally freaking out about.

Leeches.

We're swimming with leeches.

‹ 38 ›

Ryke Meadows

I chug a water bottle after finishing my burger.

Lo tosses his dirty paper plate into the fire. No one mentions how long the girls have been, but with every pause in our switch of conversation, it's the unspoken thing that's said. We ate without them because none of us wanted to eat cold fucking food.

"Lily looks like she's gaining more weight," I tell Lo. She's always really bony, naturally skinny and gangly, so it's a good sign when she's bigger. It means she's getting healthy, not so consumed by her sex addiction.

"Her boobs are bigger," Lo says, taking a sip of his water. He twists the cap, lost in thought for the hundredth time since the camping trip.

"Or Daisy's are smaller," I add.

Lo glares. "I shouldn't even have to fucking say it."

"What? That I shouldn't be looking at her boobs? It's not like there's anything there," I say the fucking truth, but I realize immediately that it sounds bad. I don't need a girl to have big breasts in order to love her or find her attractive. None of that matters.

Connor arches his brow at me.

Yeah, this is exactly what he told me not to do. Fucking A.

Lo waves his *plastic* butter knife at me. "How many times in two years do I need to remind you *not* to talk about her boobs? Seriously? It's fucking weird."

Now I feel like shit. I keep reminding myself that she's my girlfriend, but it's really fucking hard when Lo is looking at me like I'm another Julian. "You were the one who brought up Lily's tits. I didn't say one fucking word about them until you did."

Connor wraps aluminum foil over the plate of leftover burgers. "You just used a kindergarten argument," Connor says. "The *he did it first* isn't a good rebuttal."

I swear they love to fucking gang up on me—probably because they know I can take it. "Thanks for the opinion, Cobalt."

"Always," he says. Then he checks his watch, glancing at the woods where the girls disappeared off to. It's been a fucking long time. I start to worry about Daisy. I don't know where she was taking Lily and Rose, but she could have easily climbed a tree and fallen off a branch. My heart plummets to my stomach.

And then Lo shoots off of the chair, tossing his water bottle on his seat. "I'm going to go find Lily." He spoke the fucking unspoken words, and just like that we're all standing, following Lo's trail. We can leave the fire for a few minutes without putting it out.

Walking in the general direction of where the girls went, we hear the rush of water and figure Daisy would've been attracted to it. Voices echo the closer we near the stream or waterfall.

"It's leeching all my nutrients!" Lily shouts. And Lo takes off, his walk turning into a sprint.

"Hold still," Daisy says calmly.

Rose winces loudly. "I'm going to murder every one of these disgusting things!" Connor matches Lo's pace, and I stay behind them, thinking Daisy's fine.

When we come into the clearing, Lily looks like a deer caught in the headlights.

A naked fucking deer.

I try not to look, but black leeches are stuck to her abdomen and arms while Daisy tries to pry them off…who's also naked.

This isn't the first time I've seen her completely undressed. Last year. New Year's Eve at Rose's house in Princeton, Daisy had a scheming look on her face with this really playful smile. The countdown to midnight happened, and while her date, some fucking Abercrombie model, was about to kiss her, she avoided his mouth by starting to strip, backing up towards the kitchen with each discarded article of clothing. She said that the new year couldn't start off right without someone streaking.

Her eyes were on mine.

Mine were on hers.

And then the model she was with—he cut in and helped take off her bra.

I grabbed him by the shoulder, instinctively, a gut reaction out of irritation and anger. I didn't want her with this fratty fucking guy, a grade A douchebag. She finished undressing, and I caught a glimpse of her body before she sprinted outside, laughing in the cold. And then her date went off on me, yelling in my fucking face, and my date—she shot daggers at me from across the room, holding a champagne glass in a tight hand.

I can't even express how many months we both tried with someone else. But even seeing her now naked another time, it's different. My concern is at a fucking peak, heightened, revved to the max.

My brother has blinders on. He just goes straight to Lily without looking at anyone else.

Connor is already beside Rose while she stubbornly tries to pull a leech off her shoulder blade, refusing his help at first, and so Daisy is instantly pushed to the side.

Or rather, pushed towards me.

I grab her wrist and tug her to the tree line, away from the rocks, creek and waterfall. I spin her around so I'm blocking her from my brother and Connor's view. If there's any girl comfortable in her skin, it's Daisy Calloway. The only time I've heard her freak out about being naked was during the fashion show, when she was stripped in front of complete strangers.

That fucking violent act would've affected anyone.

I'm not even sure how much it's left a mark on her. Maybe she doesn't either.

"Don't they just suck the blood and then fall off when they're bloated?" Daisy asks, eyeing the two leeches on her arms and the one that sucks her neck. Blood drips from underneath the leech's belly. I glance at the other girls, and they don't seem nearly as fucking bloody right now.

Connor answers Daisy, "You girls have too many on you."

"I told you!" Lily shouts. "It's taking our nutrients."

"It's not, actually," Connor says.

Lo focuses on Lily's back which has five fucking leeches attached. "How many diseases do these carry?"

I fucking swear Lily yelps in fear, like a wounded animal.

Rose squirms more fiercely now. "Get it off, Richard!"

He holds her shoulder firmly now that she's conceded, and he pries the leech off with the pinch of his fingers. "Leeches can be used for medicinal purposes. Think, Rose," he tells her. "You know this."

She breathes through her nose.

To reassure everyone, Connor adds, "The girls are fine."

"Should we burn them off?" Lo asks.

"No, their stomach contents will explode on the wound."

"Gross," Daisy says, poking at one on her abdomen. She slowly starts peeling it off and then stops as her skin pulls with it, the leech not detaching easily.

I scan her body quickly, my eyes falling to her back. Two on her shoulder blades, one on her lower back, none on her ass, but one on her calf. My stomach twists because I can tell she's in pain—that these actually hurt to remove.

"I'm going to rip them off like a fucking Band-Aid, okay?"

She nods a couple times, not complaining. I start with the one on her calf, squatting, and she clenches my hair while I grip the leech and tear it off in one motion. The spot bleeds profusely. Fucking Christ. I wish I brought my water bottle to wash the wound.

I rip two more off from her stomach and her arms.

Tears brim her eyes. "Sorry," she apologizes, wiping the corners.

I fucking hate when she says she's sorry for her feelings—for stupid fucking things that don't ever need apologies. I stand up and kiss her temple, knowing my brother is consumed with his girlfriend's wellbeing. And I hold the back of her head and whisper in her ear. "You can cry if it hurts, sweetheart. It doesn't make you a little girl."

She lets out a deep breath. And her arms tighten around me. She places her forehead on my chest, and I reach over her shoulder to take off the last three on her back. She flinches, and only one of them bleeds after removal this time. I rub her head before pulling off my long-sleeve gray shirt. Cold washes over my bare chest, and I realize that she must be freezing. I fit it over her head, and it falls to her thighs, the fabric soaking some of the blood.

I rub her arm, creating friction to warm her body. "We'll clean and bandage those at the campsite," I tell her.

She nods, and then glances over at Lo, checking to see if he's watching her.

Fuck it.

I lift her in my arms, cradling her. She smiles, despite her tears drying in the corners of her eyes. "We'll meet you guys at camp," I tell them.

Lo glances at me once, clearly noticing Daisy in my arms. This isn't the first time I've cradled her. Nor will it ever be the last. I stare at him with a hard, unflinching gaze.

I did nothing wrong.

I just helped someone who I love—the same fucking way Lo is taking care of Lily and Connor is taking care of Rose. I'm tired of being shit on for doing the right thing with the wrong girl. The biggest kindergarten response pops up in my head.

It's. Not. *Fucking*. Fair.

And then Lo does something surprising. He nods at me, almost like an approval, not quite, but almost. He gestures with his head towards the campsite. "Go."

I do.

I leave with Daisy in my arms.

As I've done so many times before.

Maybe that's why it's not so fucking hard for him to accept this moment. When everyone pairs off, I become the only option for her. There's no one else but me.

That's how this all started.

But I think about Julian. I think about all the other fucking guys she's been with. All the other women I've dated.

And I'm certain that's not how this ends.

There's no way I'm with her out of circumstance.

We chose this because nothing else felt right.

Nothing else felt as good.

Our greatest happiness has always been with each other.

< 39 >

Ryke Meadows

We helped the girls clean off their wounds with soap, and we bandaged them. Now they're in sweatshirts and baggy pants, grouped around the campfire. Lily sits on Lo's lap, her head to his chest. She keeps dozing off, but faraway howls from the woods and rustles in the trees startle her awake.

"What was that?" she asks with wide eyes, glancing over her shoulder.

"A big bad wolf," Daisy jokes, her legs kicked up on my lap. Before we were together, she'd playfully do this, but I wouldn't touch her. So I can't put my hands on her ankles or pull her closer to me. I just have my hand on the back of her camping chair, watching her pick at a hot marshmallow on a stick. "Oh wait," Daisy gasps, "he's right here." She tilts her head at me.

I raise my brows at her. I can feel my brother watching, and I'm not fucking sure what's going on in his head. His expression has been unreadable for most of the night.

She leans forward and licks gooey marshmallow off her finger. My arousal heightens as she quickly grabs my attention. Her eyes lock on me, and she whispers, "Big bad wolf, are you going to eat me?"

You're a dirty girl, Calloway. My gaze drops to her mouth. "Until you fucking scream."

Her lips curve upward.

"It's dead, Rose," Connor says. His voice pulls our gaze towards him. Rose is curled on a chair beside Connor, his hand on her thigh, her fingers intertwined with his. In her other hand, she fries a leech on the tip of a stick, her yellow-green eyes murderous.

"Not nearly enough," she retorts. "This little bitch took my blood."

"And here, I thought you were roasting it for dessert," Lo banters.

Rose holds up a hand at him, as though to say *silence*. She squishes the blackened leech against a log, stabbing it over and over.

Lo looks around at us like *what the fuck?* He nods to Connor who sips a Fizz Life, a grin at the corners of his lips. He finds his wife fucking amusing—even if she's half-crazy. "How are you not scared to bite her in bed?" Lo asks. "If you draw blood does she grab a fire poker?"

"I'm not a leech," Connor replies with ease.

Rose tosses the stick into the fire and cleans her hands with a wet wipe. Then she reaches into a grocery bag by her side. "So I bought these on the way here." She pulls out a tall stack of tabloid magazines. "I wanted all of us to burn them together and purge the bad energy."

Connor says, "As long as we don't have to chant afterwards, I'll participate."

Rose stands, trying to hide a smile that's clear to me. She fucking loves him, arguments and all. "I'd rather you not. Your pessimism is already clouding the process."

"Realism and pessimism are two very different things, but I'd be happy to explain it to you."

She covers his mouth with her hand. "Thank you for defining arrogance. You can keep your other definitions to yourself." She spins around, dropping her hand. "Now where were we?" She starts passing out the magazine, and Connor's eyes fall to her ass. Even though he acts like he's better than every horny bastard, he's still a fucking guy. Case in point.

Lily holds her marshmallows over the fire, and a flame engulfs it almost immediately. She shrieks and waves it around, as though that'll snuff it out.

I shake my head at her. "You're going to fling it in the woods, chill the fuck out." Last thing we need is to start a forest fire.

"It won't extinguish!" she defends. "Extinguish, you mallow! Extinguish!" She flaps it around some more and tries blowing, but she more or less just spits on the thing. And then from behind her, Lo easily blows out the flame himself, leaving her with a burnt marshmallow.

Daisy smiles wickedly. "Wow, who would have thought—Lo blows better than Lily."

I rub my lips to keep from smiling. Everyone else looks fairly uncomfortable by that statement—only because it came from Daisy. If I said it, it would've been fine. If Lily said it—everyone would have fucking laughed.

Lo glares at me.

I extend my arms. "I didn't do a fucking thing."

"You're a shitty influence."

Daisy acts nonchalant, but her gaze flits all over the forest. Every time she tries to be one step closer to us, someone in our group has a way of pushing her back out. It's unintentional, I think. But it happens, regardless.

"It was a fucking joke," I tell Lo. He's about to open his mouth, ready to chew me up and spit me back out. I mentally start putting on my armor to withstand him.

But then Rose snaps her fingers, cutting off Lo and regaining everyone's attention. Her eyes meet mine briefly. I know she did that for my benefit. I'm grateful, but I don't show it. "We're supposed to be purging bad energy not creating it." She drops a magazine on my lap. "Here, you can burn this one."

I read the headline: RYKE MEADOWS CONTINUES TO PLAY GAMES. The front page picture shows Daisy hanging over my shoulder outside of the pub in Paris, my hand on her ass. But I can't get over the smile on her face. The camera caught her mid-laugh.

She's gorgeous. And she's mine.

I don't want to burn this picture. I want to frame that happiness and revisit it every morning and every night for the rest of my life.

But the headline definitely taints it.

They think we're flirting. We are. But they also think I'm fucking Lily. So I'm a player. I'm fooling around with both Calloway girls. It's just so fucking absurd.

My jaw locks, and I don't waste another moment. I fling it into the fire.

"You have to wait!" Rose yells at me. "We're doing this as a group." She slaps my arm with another rolled up magazine and then tosses it at me.

"For fuck's sake you're high-strung tonight."

"Talk to me when you've had a worm suck your blood off your ass," she retorts, walking past me to Lily and Lo. I read the headline of my new tabloid: SARA HALE AT WAR WITH HER FAMILY.

Fucking fantastic.

Daisy rolls up her magazine, hiding the headline from view.

"Everyone," Rose says, sitting back in her chair and crossing her ankles. Connor is the only one without a tabloid. Rose is sticking to her earlier claim, refusing to give him one. "Take your magazine and read something you find particularly offensive before tossing it into the fire."

"And what is this supposed to fucking do?" I ask.

"Ward off evil spirits," Lo says, sipping his Fizz Life while hooking his arm around Lily's waist. She leans against his chest again. "Too bad it won't cure your obsessive compulsive personality, Rose."

She shoots him a scathing look, the flames reflecting in her eyes. "Too bad it won't cure your alcoholism, Loren."

He raises his soda can. "Look, it's already working. You're practically a licensed witch....shit, I meant bitch." He snaps his fingers. He might as well have said *aw, shucks*.

She opens her mouth to argue and Connor cuts her off. "This is all very fun, but the more we talk about witches and spirits, I find myself becoming stupider and stupider. So please, for the sake of all humanity, shut up."

I shake my head while Lo grins, finding this hilarious.

Rose combats her husband almost immediately, "You really think your intelligence benefits *all* of humanity? You own a diamond business."

"And I give a large percentage of my money to charities and research, darling."

They start to bicker, and Daisy leans closer to me. She folds a napkin into an origami swan, glancing from it to me every so often. "Want to know a secret?" she whispers.

"Sure," I say, my arm stretching across the back of her chair again.

She smiles and says, "You're my favorite four-letter word." Her bold green eyes flit up to me.

She makes the corniest pickup lines sound like the sexiest things I've ever heard.

"The word *fuck* didn't do anything for you?" I ask, my muscles tensing.

"You've desensitized me to it. It might as well be as powerful as the word *foot*."

I lean into her ear and lower my voice. "You won't be saying that when I actually fuck you."

A blinding smile fills her face, and it stirs my need even more. I want her in my fucking arms. I want to kiss her so deeply that air has trouble reaching both of our lungs, gasping with wild, arresting pleasure.

One day, it'll happen.

Just not this moment.

"I'll go," Lily announces, cutting in Connor and Rose's bickering. She stands up with her magazine in hand. "Um…so there's this picture of me in this one that really bugs me." She flips a couple of pages and then nods. "Yeah, so I'm buying condoms and they captioned it with *Lily's spiraling out of control again*."

Rose claps, excited to have a willing participant. "Okay, now throw it in."

Lily tosses the magazine into the flames. It falls against the logs and burns quickly.

Connor stands next, snatching a magazine off the towering stack beside Rose.

"Oh so now you believe in it?" Rose asks.

"I believe in you," Connor refutes. "Not your superstition." He flips open the magazine. "*Connor Cobalt's seventh sex tape has grossed over twenty million dollars. Making Scott Van Wright, the owner of the tapes, one of the world's richest pornography distributers.*" Scott Van Wright is the reason Connor and Rose have sex tapes leaked every few months. He screwed them over. After Connor dropped the lawsuits and used the publicity to grow both Rose's fashion business and his own, I offered to personally beat the shit out of Scott. But Connor said that he didn't want to see me in jail—even if the offer was appealing.

I hope someday that son of a bitch gets what he deserves.

Connor throws the magazine into the fire, hate actually passing through his blue eyes.

Rose is next. "*Rose Cobalt is a bitch.*" She nods and tosses hers in.

"That's it?" Lo asks when she sits down. "That's all you could come up with?"

"Those are hurtful words," Rose replies.

"I call you a bitch five times a day and you don't bat an eye," Lo reminds her. Then he remembers her outburst tonight and corrects himself, "Well, not usually."

"They're not hurtful from you," she refutes. "That was *Vogue*." She touches her chest. "I cried for two days straight when I read that."

"*Vogue* is her Bible," Lily says.

"Does that mean I'm like your saint?" Daisy asks with a smile. She was in *Vogue* a few months ago. On the front of the fucking magazine.

"You'd be more saint-like if you participated," Rose says.

Daisy brightens and then stands on the seat of her canvas chair. "*Daisy Calloway 'the baby Calloway',*" she reads and adds air quotes, "*has been spotted with another male model at a Gucci fashion shoot. Close sources have confirmed that she's been seeing him. This is the third guy this month for Daisy. Could this be a clear sign that she's following in Lily's footsteps? Only time will tell.*" She flings the magazine and it spins to the fire like a Frisbee.

Hearing that—it hardens my face. The Gucci shoot was months ago, and even though I know she couldn't be with those guys—we slept in the same bed every night—the accusations piss me off. Rose wants to expel bad energy, but I don't read these tabloids for a reason.

"You go," Daisy tells me. She tries to kick my chair over with her foot, but she doesn't have enough strength when she's standing up high. I don't rise. I just look down at the magazine in my hands after finding the center article. "*Ryke Meadows in another fight with a photog.* And they show a picture of me yelling at some cameraman." I lazily toss the magazine in and lean back in my chair.

"Do you feel any different?" Daisy asks as she hops off her chair.

"Nope."

Daisy gasps and looks to Rose. "It didn't work on him. Can we cast a spell to protect him from evil?"

Rose rolls her eyes now and then she looks at my brother. "Loren, please go."

He reluctantly rises, but only because Lily climbs off his lap and physically pulls him from the chair. When his eyes fall to the magazine I see how they change. They sharpen and turn cold. "*Another source confirms molestation rumors. Jonathan Hale and Loren Hale continue to deny them. Jonathan's first son has yet to comment.*"

No one speaks. An uncomfortable tension blankets our campsite. I wait for Lo to throw the magazine into the fire or curse me out or both. But his eyes remain on the tabloid and his brows furrow as he continues to read silently. He starts shaking his head.

"What is it?" Connor asks.

"*A psychiatrist specializing in sex addiction was interviewed,*" Loren reads, "*and confirms that most sex addicts experience sexual trauma. We have confirmation that…*" He rubs his lips to hide emotion, his eyes reddening. He shakes his head. "*We have confirmation that Lily Calloway spent much of her time with the Hales. It's suspected that Jonathan Hale might have bene an influence in her addiction.*"

They're implying that Jonathan abused her too.

I can't see that happening. I shake my head as much as Lo. My dad may be a bad fucking guy, but he wouldn't do that to Lily, to his best friend's daughter. It's something unthinkable.

And if Lo saw that happen, he wouldn't roll over and stay quiet. He would go absolutely crazy. He would have, without a fucking doubt, killed our father.

"What?" Lily says, gaping. "Lo, that never happened."

Lo looks up at her and his gaze immediately softens. "I know, Lil." He doesn't even hesitate. Doesn't question her or think otherwise. There's complete loyalty between them. But it doesn't break the pain that they share between their gazes. They're both being dragged through this.

"Throw it in," Rose says quietly.

He does it. And I watch it burn, right along with my thoughts.

I don't know what or who to believe anymore.

Everything's just dark.

< 40 >

Ryke Meadows

I am alone with Daisy. In a tent.

"I'm not surprised," Daisy whispers. I attached a flashlight at the top of the three-person tent and it dangles like a lamp. I can see all of her as she sits cross-legged. I lie on my back, watching her twist her hair into a bun. "Rose thought the shadows were bugs, and she rolled on top of Lily, she was so grossed out." Daisy smiles at the image. "She's never been camping."

"Really? I hadn't fucking noticed," I say. Rose was the first to ditch the all-girls tent. She unzipped the one I was in, bracing an axe in her hand like she was ready to murder all of us. I think the thought seriously crossed my brother's mind.

But Connor reached out for her, and she melted, like a feral cat turned into a soft kitten. Before I left, his arms were wrapped around her, and she seemed content. Lily showed up next, too frightened to be alone with just Daisy in the all-girls tent. In Lo's words, Rose could scare off a "wildebeest" and without her, Lily decided to seek comfort with her boyfriend.

Which left Daisy all by herself.

And it gave me a necessary excuse to sleep in her tent. No one really wanted her to be alone in the middle of the woods. Not even my brother.

"Lie down," I tell Daisy. I can tell she's having trouble sleeping. She doesn't want to take Ambien tonight, and I can't push her to take that pill anymore. The side effects are too intense. There has to be another way to combat her insomnia.

Instead of lying down, she straddles my waist. She's wearing my track sweatpants that are baggy on her legs. I fucking love her in my clothes. "I can't sleep," she says.

"It's two in the morning," I whisper, sitting up fully. I'm taller than her in this position. Being this close to her, my chest an inch from hers, strains the air and stiffens my muscles. "Have you ever imagined me fucking you?" Curiosity compels me to the question. My fingers glide along her bare hips, underneath my Penn shirt that she wears.

Her breathing shallows, probably wondering if tonight will be *the* night. "Yes."

"When?" I prod. I pull the T-shirt over her head, leaving her topless, her nipples already erect. It's over for me. I harden in a fucking instant and a large breath catches in the back of her throat as she feels me underneath her.

"A bunch of times," she says in a whisper, the air tensing. She tugs on my shirt, wanting me bare as much as she is. I help her pull it over my head, and then she starts to trace the outline of my tattoo with her fingers. "By myself. But usually…" She pauses, her green eyes flitting up to mine. "When I was with other guys. I thought it'd help."

She thought about me when she was screwing other guys.

Not just masturbating to the idea of me.

I just want to fuck you harder.

My surprise sits beneath an intense arousal that literally forces my body to hers. I grab the back of her head. She grabs mine, and I kiss her hard and urgently. I think about every night I spent in her bed. The restraint. Every time I pictured Daisy underneath my body, my muscles cloaking her in safety and so much fucking power. Driving into her. Releasing. *Fuck.* I need inside of her.

Our lips and hands and bodies connect like a bomb goes off between us, nerves screaming, lungs barely fucking breathing.

I move roughly with her and she moves wildly with me.

Our legs tangle together, and her hands roam my abs with eagerness, settling on my back, gripping my flesh while my weight bears down on her. She cries out as I grind into her. *Fuck...* I want to hear her again, but I have to stifle her noises. So I cover her mouth with my palm, and I keep grinding against her, my cock throbbing. *Push into her.*

Not yet.

She mumbles against my hand, trying to speak while I slide the track pants off her long legs. I remove my hand and shed down to my boxer-briefs.

"Push into me," she whispers, her lips swollen from our embrace, her breathing ragged. The flashlight swings above us. We must have knocked into it, and neither of us attempts to turn it off. I want to see all of her, every reaction and every limb.

Instead of outright answering her, I undress Daisy, slipping off her panties and shirt. We kiss again, just hammered with these intense feelings. She rolls her hips against me, and I slam my weight back into her. She cries out, and I grip her hair.

She lies on her back, her shallow breaths slicing the silence. Her eyes pin on my dick, and I can tell she's imagining every inch of me inside of her.

"Please," she breathes.

I comb my fingers through her hair and then hold her face in my large hand. She's small beneath me, fragile. Even if she thinks she's experienced, she's not experienced with me. Not yet, at least. I kiss her while my other hand descends to her clit. She bucks her hips up to meet me as my fingers move up and down and then circular.

She writhes beneath me, her nails clawing into my back. Just as her lips part, I slide my hand over her mouth, her hot breath heating my palm.

I scan her from head to toe, the way she unravels in pleasure, the way her legs spasm, and her body arches towards me, her hips thrusting to try and find a pressure that I have yet to give her. Watching Daisy come is like watching a person discover a new world, seeing fireworks for the first time, lit up and awed. Knowing I helped her achieve it—I fucking ache to be closer, to fill her with happiness and me.

Her toes curl and her fingers press deep into my back, her head tilted, my hand enveloping her face to muffle the cry.

I sit up and let her catch her breath, which is all over the fucking place.

She watches me, but my dark gaze lets little through besides *I want you. You're so fucking beautiful.* She quickly matches my position, sitting, and I spread her legs wider around me.

Her mouth starts to descend towards my cock, and I lift her chin up quickly and kiss her. I move on impulse—what feels right. And my fingers slip inside of her. She's so fucking wet. She climaxes within a couple minutes, and I take them out and grip the base of my cock.

Daisy inhales sharply, realizing what's about to happen. She edges closer to me, holds the back of my neck with both hands, and rests her forehead on my chest. She likes the visual, and I'll gladly give her one.

I brush her hair away from her ear and whisper, "Ready to have all of me, Dais?"

She answers by running her hands through my hair near my neck. I smile, and I slowly slide into her. She clenches around me, and my mouth opens. I force a fucking groan to stay in the back of my throat. My muscles cut into hard lines, and I hold the back of her head to my chest.

I can't imagine a more intimate way to fill Daisy, with her on my lap as I sit up, clung to my chest, giving me possession of her body and heart.

She's swollen around my erection, soaked and so much tighter than I anticipated or expected. Underneath these nerve-splitting sensations, I'm acutely aware of how much she can take of me. She gasps, learning how to keep her voice hushed, and I stop midway from fitting into her completely.

"Ryke," she cries.

"Shh," I coo. She rocks her hips, attempting to put all of me inside of her. My hand falls from her head to her hip. I steady her, and then I push in further. *Fuck.* My eyes shut as the pressure overwhelms me. I haven't even started moving in her yet.

I grip her ass while she stares at the way my long cock disappears between her legs. She breathes short, choppy fucking breaths, and when she's engrained the image, I tilt her back against the dark green sleeping bag.

My hand slides from her knee to her thigh, and I begin to thrust with slow, deep strokes, milking every fucking movement. I want each one to last for eternity, no rushing, no speeding up this cliff. My ass tightens as I push forward, and I kiss her, combing her damp blonde hair away from her forehead.

I'm inside the girl who has begged for this type of pleasure for years.

And I'm the one finally giving it to her, showing her that sex can be so fucking good.

Fucking Christ, I've wanted this for so fucking long.

"Ryke," she starts saying. So much that I have to put my hand over her mouth again. She rocks her hips upwards each time I thrust down, creating friction and extra depth that blinds me with adrenaline. I rest my forearm beside her head, my six-foot-three body hovering over her small frame.

Her eyes fix on mine as I thrust, my pace increasing by a notch. Her hips can't keep up with me. Her legs hook around my waist. She's limber enough that I bring one of her legs over my shoulder while my chest is close to hers.

She moans into my palm, and I restrain from coming right there. I hold back, grunting and pushing. *Fuck.* I don't feel her breathing, and her eyes flutter.

"Breathe through your nose," I say roughly, instinctively quickening each thrust. I don't want her to fucking pass out.

She finally exhales, and her gaze returns to mine. I slow for a second, but I can tell she's nearing the end. Her whole body is tense beneath me; her eyes threaten to roll back at any moment. I pound into her in fast spurts, a thin sheen of sweat coating my skin. *Fuck.*

Fuck.

She's so tight.

I can't slow down, even if I wanted to.

My parted lips touch her forehead, and I move until her body lifts against mine, until her head tilts back and her eyes close. Her moans breach my hand, but they're soft cries that only I can possibly hear. And they're so fucking beautiful.

I grunt as I force myself not to come yet. I take my hand off, and I lift her from underneath her arms.

"Ryke," she says, her tense muscles all softened and melted after that climax. Her eyes fall to my erection, and she frowns.

"Catch your breath fast, sweetheart." I spin her on my lap, her back against my chest, and I grip my cock, sliding into her easily. She gasps as she has the best visual of me moving up and down inside of her.

I suck her neck, lifting my pelvis up into her in a deep, pulsing rhythm. I knead her breast, my finger flicking over her hardened nipple.

She leans back against me and clenches my hair, letting me fuck her how she deserves to be fucked. With attention and so much love. Long minutes pass, and I know I could build her up for hours. I could make her come until exhaustion shuts her eyes, but I want her to be coherent afterwards. As she clenches around my cock, I focus on her body in my grasp, me deep inside of her, and her shallow noises.

I push upwards hard, and I come with her, white lights flashing in my vision, my head fucking spinning. I exhale a couple times before I slide out of her. I gently lean her against the sleeping bag, and I lie next to Daisy, my body at peace with hers. The flashlight swings above us like a pendulum.

Fucking finally.

Nothing has ever compared to that.

She kisses me, before I can say anything. I smile and kiss her back. Then I cup her face, my legs magnetically finding her smooth ones, tangled once again. "Better than chocolate?" I whisper.

She breathes like I took her on a marathon, not a sprint. "You're in another league."

I skim her cheek with my fingers. "Yeah?" I smile. "You've finally found the league you're supposed to be playing in, Dais."

"I like it here," she whispers. "The *better than chocolate* league." She wraps her arms around me, and I press my lips to her head. "How long do you think this'll last?" Her voice turns serious, fear creeping in. Now that we've slept together, we could lose so much more if someone pulls us apart.

"As long as we want it to," I tell her. "I'd fucking fight for you, Dais. You just have to let me." She can't be worried about hurt feelings. We're going to upset people eventually, but if they love us, if they want us to be happy, they'll accept this.

"Even your brother?" she whispers, her eyes closing as she dozes off.

"Even him," I breathe, watching her begin to fall asleep. How long it'll last, I'm not sure. I sit up and turn off the flashlight. I zip open one flap that faces the woods, the moon bathing our tent in a serene glow. I lie back, not closing my eyes. She eases into a peaceful slumber.

And I stay up and recount what I have with her and how much more I want.

One day can change everything.

So I keep hope that one day we'll finally be there.

❀ ❀ ❀

AN HOUR MUST PASS before she wakes up, unable to sleep. She notices that I'm already awake, and she rolls onto my body and traces the outline of my tattoo again, grazing her finger over the dark ink. I hear the faint sound of crickets outside our tent.

Her finger trails the inked chain on my side that's bound around the feet of a phoenix.

"Am I the anchor?" she asks, skimming the tattoo on my waist.

My eyes darken. "Why would you think that?"

"You never told me what the tattoo meant when you got it."

She was with me almost every time I went to the tattoo parlor to have more of the design filled in. She asked only a couple times what it meant. I would give her a look, and she'd drop it. I didn't think she'd draw this conclusion. Not back then, and definitely not now.

"I've weighed you down the past couple of years," she elaborates off my dark gaze. "I just thought—"

"I'm the fucking anchor," I tell her suddenly.

"What?" Her brows furrow.

I know I need to give her the whole explanation. I can barely meet her eyes as I do. "When I was seventeen, my dad came to one of my track meets. He tried to watch as many of my competitions as he could."

I stare at the top of the tent, remembering the heat of the summer in May. Jonathan Hale in the bleachers, wearing a suit and nodding at me as I met his sharp gaze. He smiled. Genuine pride.

"My mom was there. She wouldn't look at him," I say. "And when a lady leaned in to ask my father who he was there for, I heard his answer." A bitter taste fills my mouth. "He said, 'my friend's kid. That one.' He motioned towards me."

I remember flipping him off, and that pride vanished from his eyes.

I didn't care anymore.

Daisy places her hands on my abs. "What happened?" she asks with a frown.

"I still had to run, and I had two fucking choices. I could reach the finish line or just walk away. I took my fucking mark, and right when I started the race, I began to slow down. And then I fucking stopped on the track, took a couple deep breaths and walked off." My heart beats faster at the memory. "My coach pulled me aside and he told me something…" I shake my head. "It's stayed with me for so many fucking years. It changed me."

I meet her eyes that are filled with my pain, sensing the hurt that travels through my body, thinning the air.

I can practically hear my coach in my ear, see him standing on the sidelines, one hand on my shoulder. "He said that I could be anything and do anything, and no one can stop me but me." I say what he did, "You are your own anchor, Ryke. When you fail, you hurt yourself more than anyone else. Do you want to keep burning or are you going to let yourself rise?"

My brother—I don't think he ever had someone to tell him this. He just kept failing until there was no way he could ever succeed.

I reach out to Daisy and tuck a piece of hair behind her ear. "So I'm the anchor and the phoenix, and it was around this time that I learned to run for me. I stopped winning for my fucking mom, for my dad. Every achievement, every good grade—that was mine. I started living my dreams and I stopped living theirs."

She smiles, tears in her eyes. "That's beautiful, you know."

I sit up with her and kiss her cheek. It feels good to finally share that with someone. I never thought it would matter, but I can see that it does.

"How did you know that you loved running and rock climbing?" she asks me.

I think about this for a second. Take away all of my trophies, all the success, would I still run and climb? My lips rise at the answer.

"Because when you find something you love, you can't quit. Every failure pushes you harder. It's in your soul and in your fucking heart."

"And what if I never find what I love?"

"You have to try some things," I say, not worried about this as much as she probably is. She's only eighteen. She'll figure it out. She has time, even though her mom makes it seem like she has none. "I got lucky." I kiss her temple. "Try to sleep with me, Dais."

She smiles and opens her mouth to make a very fucking obvious quip.

"Real sleep," I say, lying back down with her. I hold her to my chest, keeping her safe.

And I wait for her to start dreaming.

< 41 >

Ryke Meadows

I unzip the tent, running my hand through my hair while the birds chirp. I can tell it's early. Probably around six, and Daisy only fell asleep an hour ago. I didn't close my eyes at all, and honestly, my body isn't that tired. Fucking her was the best adrenaline rush I could have. I'm still living that high.

I immediately find Connor and Rose around the campfire, both dressed in inappropriate fucking clothes for the morning. A suit and a dress. And they're drinking coffee from Dunkin Donuts paper cups.

I outstretch my arms. "You're a bunch of fucking cheaters."

Rose scoffs as though I punched her in the face. "We did not *cheat*."

I slouch in a chair across from them. "You can't buy coffee while you're camping."

"I've never heard of these rules," Connor says. He sips his store-bought coffee with a pompous grin.

"You camp and you make instant coffee with boiled water and powder packets." I shake my head at them. "Running to the store is like excusing yourself to go to the bathroom during a test, checking answers on your phone."

Rose's eyes narrow at me and then she takes a larger sip of her coffee too, not backing down. Connor looks like he could fuck her right there.

Whatever.

"You're glowing, by the way," Connor tells me. I don't like that knowing expression on his face.

"Fuck off, Cobalt." I kick my boots up on the cooler.

Rose plants her fierce fucking yellow-green eyes on me. "Did you wear a condom?" she asks in a hushed but forceful voice, pretty careful not to wake up my brother.

My face hardens. There's no way they heard us last night, but Connor puts details together to find facts, so I'm not that surprised he's figured it out. Or that he's been keeping Rose updated on my relationship with Daisy. "Did you wear one when you first fucked Connor?" I retort.

Her neck reddens. "That's not the point."

I roll my eyes. "Okay then." I have nothing else to say. I'm not about to explain how I always wear condoms with other women, but I honestly don't see the fucking need to with Daisy. We're in a serious relationship. I trust her. And I trust me. The. Fucking. End.

I'm about to stand up, but Rose says something that keeps me here.

"Be careful with her, Ryke. She might be experienced, but she's still *my* sister. If you hurt her, I'll personally snip off your balls and hang them on the Christmas tree this year."

I internally cringe. "I wouldn't fucking hurt her, I promise you, Rose."

She nods. "Okay *then*," she repeats what I did, and I almost smile.

"I'm going to get more wood," I tell them.

Connor follows me with his coffee in hand. "I'll help."

"Feel guilty for cheating?" I ask, heading towards the forest.

"No," he says, his expensive shoes crunching the leaves. "I just thought you needed an extra pair of hands."

I wait for the punchline. My brows rise when it doesn't come. "No insult?" It's weird not hearing a dog joke. Even with the constant badgering, he's always been my friend, but like most of my relationships, it's complicated. "You didn't tell Rose about Daisy's sleep issues, did you?" I stop about twenty feet from the woods, our camp still behind us.

"I thought about it," Connor admits, "but you're not giving me all the information, and I'd rather not spread around partial truths." He waits for me to divulge more.

I won't.

"She's going to talk to her sisters," I say. "She needs time."

"Man's greatest excuse to delay the inevitable."

"Can you not fucking talk like your auditioning for the role of Confucius?"

"*If you make a mistake and do not correct it, this is called a mistake.*" Of course he goes and actually quotes Confucius. *Fuck me.*

I shake my head. "You're such a fucking prick."

He doesn't even blink, not affected by the insult. Maybe because he knows it's true. "You know, I never really liked Confucius. I always thought his principles were a bit basic, common sense."

"Fascinating," I deadpan.

He continues casually. "But there is one quote I appreciate from him." Connor looks at me and his eyes turn serious, no pretense or humor. "*Wheresoever you go, go with all your heart.*"

I don't know if he meant for this to be about Daisy. But she's immediately what comes to mind. After what happened last night, bringing up some of the past, all I want is to go full fucking throttle. No more slowing down. No more hiding. I want to believe that I control my fate, that I'm the one who chooses to stop and start.

I want everything that my friends have. Out in the open. *Real.*

I have to tell Lo.

The resolution lifts this weight off my chest.

And then something rustles a bush twenty feet away. I see it out of the corner of my eye. A movement that crashes the weight back down tenfold and twists a chain around my ankles.

"Connor," I whisper, a pit in my stomach. "Nine o'clock."

He calmly sips his coffee and turns a fraction. Into his next sip, he says, "I can see two lenses."

They found us.

I run a hand through my hair. I promised my brother freedom from this bullshit. I've failed him. Then the cameraman peers out of the bush, noticeable, and I lock eyes with him, my body blazing with anger. I start to charge forward, and Connor grabs my arm and forces me back by his side.

"You can't go to court again," he says.

The fucking cameraman no longer cares about "candid" shots that sell big to tabloids, he's taking a video instead.

"Fuck them," I tell Connor. "They shouldn't be here."

"This is public property," Connor says. "He can legally be in the woods."

"I said *shouldn't*. How'd they get tipped?"

"RV," the cameraman says. "I'm friends with the two guys camping next to you. Called me last night. Flew in this morning."

I shake my head. It'd be more of a coincidence if the paparazzi didn't get their tips like that. But mostly it's from fucking friends and connections.

"Fucking fantastic," I snap. I made a mistake. We should have gone to a fucking hotel. I shouldn't have tried this. I head back to the campsite, ready to pack up. Rose is already folding chairs and pouring a water bottle on the fire.

The cameraman follows us like a shadow, entering the campsite as though we gave him permission to come hang out with us. Oh wait, we fucking *didn't*.

"How many more of you are coming?" Connor asks.

He just smiles, and that's when I hear tires and an engine groan up the hill. And then two more photographers pop out of the bushes in addition to however many are in the car. *Fuck me.*

"Ryke," the guy says, his camera pointed at me as I head to Daisy's tent. "What were the sleeping arrangements like?"

Before I unzip it, I spin around and the camera guy almost runs straight into my chest. He rights himself while a glare sears in my eyes. My fists clench. "Back the fuck off," I growl. "You came into *our* campsite and disrupted *our* vacation. Don't act like this is for your fucking job."

"I'm allowed—"

"You're allowed to breathe because I'm letting you," I refute. "Back up and give me ten feet before I put you in the fucking ground."

"You can't touch me."

I near him, and he takes a couple steps back. "You think I care about going to jail for a few hours? Fucking test me, and your thousand-dollar camera and those fucking pictures will be gone in an instant."

He stays put where he is.

I'm so heated I can barely see straight. I open Daisy's tent and duck my head in, careful not to let the cameraman have any view of her. She yawns tiredly, barely awake and really fucking naked. I crawl in and zip the tent back. Her spine straightens as she gets a good look at my pissed expression.

"We're leaving," I say, grabbing my shirt that she was in. I pull it over her head quickly.

"What's going on?"

"Paparazzi."

"Uh-oh." She hurries to put the baggy sweatpants back on. They fall at her waist, and I tighten the string so they stay up. "What's the plan?" she asks, trying not to appear scared. But she still hasn't told anyone about the cut on her face, and I'm sure she'd rather tell her mom instead of letting her find out from the tabloids.

"I'm carrying you out," I tell her. "Front piggyback. Put your face to my chest, okay?"

"Like how Lo carries Lily?" she asks.

I didn't realize…but yeah, that's how my brother carries Lily in front of the paparazzi. "Yeah, like that."

"How many are out there?"

"A fucking lot."

She smiles. "What's a fucking lot? Ten? A hundred?"

I give her a look.

"What?"

"Just get in my arms." I hold them open.

She grins wider. "Say that again."

"Get in my fucking arms, Calloway."

She mock gasps. "I thought you'd never ask."

I don't smile, but my nerves slowly start to subside. She does that to me—calms me. Makes me feel like this worry is one that should be smaller, less significant.

She crawls towards me, and I lift her in my arms, her legs wrapping above my waist and her cheek pressed to my chest. I rub my fingers through her tangled, messy hair. "Hold tight, sweetheart."

I open the tent and the lights go off like a neon bomb.

< 42 >

Daisy Calloway

We've split up.

I'm in a black two-door sports car that Rose had rented with Lily, heading down a freeway with Ryke. Rose, Connor, Lily, and Lo took the SUV. The paparazzi parted. Some following us, others following them.

Ryke shook off the three vans on our ass in under thirty minutes. Our sports car is manual, and Ryke switched gears and cut corners sharply, driving like he owned the road. He wasn't scared to slam on the brake at the last minute, go in reverse or hit hundred-mile-per-hour speeds. If we didn't just have sex, I'd think it was the sexiest, hottest thing he's ever done with me.

Now the open freeway is less exciting, but it is peaceful. And I am thankful for no tail and the crazed paparazzi.

With a bit of decent cell signal, we made a plan with the others to meet up in Utah at the Canyonlands.

I glance over at Ryke. He has his hard eyes set on the road ahead, but his hand has been on my thigh most of the drive. Now that we're alone, truly, it seems like more of our restrictions are disappearing. I love the freedom, and I want to make it last past this trip.

"Stop, Dais," he tells me. "That's fucking annoying."

I realize I've opened and closed the dashboard about fifty times.

"Play with the fucking window."

"I have," I say. "It's revolted against me and no longer rolls down."

He keeps one hand on the wheel and glances at me. "You have problems."

"What a true, true statement," I say with a smile. "Say another."

He flips me off and then messes my hair.

I laugh. "I can't help my fidgetiness. It's boring in a car." *And I've downed five Lightning Bolts! to battle my exhaustion. Thank you, insomnia.* I've already untied my sneakers and braided the shoelaces into bracelets. Now I'm considering playing Cat's Cradle with the strings.

Ryke's eyes flit to me, and then he reaches up and presses a button by the ceiling light. The sunroof groans open.

I beam, happy to have air and the wind. I unclip my seat belt and kiss his cheek quickly before standing on the middle console. A gust blows into me first, and I take a giant breath, filling my lungs. The road has very few cars. We're on flat land with no traffic lights and few cops in sight.

I raise my arms and shut my eyes.

I'm flying.

In this moment, I'm really, really happy.

Ryke is holding one of my ankles, but his hand runs up and down my leg. The friction and mystery of what he's going to do races my heart. But he won't...

His gentle movements turn rough, and his fingers urgently find the button to my jeans, and he yanks them down, all with one hand.

Holy shit.

He forces them to my feet, and I clutch onto the roof to keep my balance

He doesn't swerve the car.

Not even as he pushes aside my panties and plunges his fingers into me, filling me instantly. *Oh God. This can't be happening.* I'm standing up. Half suspended out of the freaking sunroof.

He pumps his fingers into me, and my body awakens with delight and exhilaration. I reach one arm down, back into the car, and I put my hand on his, feeling how big his fingers are compared to mine.

He hits the most sensitive place, finding it with ease, and I cry out, my voice lost in the wind. After I catch my breath, he starts building me to a higher peak. I grip his wrist, never wanting him to leave this place between my legs. *Dear God, send me Ryke Meadows morning, noon and night.*

Then a honk blares. I can barely turn my head, so dazed with these feelings. My lips are parted, unable to close. But I notice a family van behind us. Uh-oh.

I'm about to crawl into the car, but as soon as I duck my head in, Ryke says, "Stay." He must not be concerned about them filming us on their phones—but it's not like they can see much. The windows *are* tinted. Ryke puts his knee on the wheel to steer and he sticks his other hand out the window, flipping them off.

Why is that so sexy?

His fingers move faster inside of me, driving deeper, up and down. *Ahhh!* I clutch harder to the roof.

Mind officially blown.

His fingers aren't sweet. They're rough and hard, and my knees almost buckle with the brilliant force. I'm moaning, hunched over the roof, my eyes watering from the wind.

The van lays on the horn again. And then it switches lanes and speeds to our side. A father rolls down the passenger window where his wife sits. He shouts, "There are kids on this road!"

Ryke yells back, "They're going to fucking learn about it sooner or later. Might as well learn how to do it the best way."

AHHH!

I disintegrate. I can't even support my body any longer. Ryke takes his fingers out, and I drop down onto my seat and breathe heavily. I rest my forehead on his shoulders, my mouth agape. When I look through his window that he's ignored, I notice that the wife is flushed, the husband enraged.

I don't care.

That was awesome.

They honk again.

Ryke slams on the gas and takes off, leaving them far behind us. His fingers glisten, and he wipes them on the inside of his shirt before passing me my jeans.

When I finally breathe normally, I slip my pants back on. "Have you done that before?" I wonder. It seemed like he knew what he was doing.

"First time," he says, trying not to smile. The sudden glimmer in his eyes gives him away though. He liked it too. Maybe not as much as me. But he definitely enjoyed that.

"Your turn," I say, sitting up on my knees, ready to give him head.

"Later," he tells me. He turns the car off the exit. "We're here."

Wherever *here* is.

< 43 >

Ryke Meadows

We can't drive in a car all the way to the Canyonlands. She's too hyperactive and ADD—which is an actual fucking problem right now, even if we joke about it. No matter if I'd love to finger fuck her all the way there…and with half her body out of that fucking sunroof. *Fuck.* My cock despises me right now. I should have let her suck me off in the parking lot before I went into the store.

She gives amazing head.

But that didn't feel right. And I usually don't jump into things when my gut says *no*.

I shake hands with the sales person, and I step back out into the parking lot. Sunglasses on, shielding the bright afternoon light from my eyes. The wind picks up and I pull my leather jacket tighter. It's getting fucking cold. But what do you expect from October?

Daisy walks out of the gas station next to the dealership. She eats a Little Debbie brownie, a shopping bag hung over her right arm while wearing bright blue, flower-shaped sunglasses that I've never seen. They look like cheap plastic, but they're really fucking cute on her.

She waves when she sees me and starts walking over.

"Miss me?" she asks.

"I was fucking devastated."

"You look it." She nods, and I hook a finger on her plastic bag and peer into it. Hair dye. Lots of it. I spot pink and purple. I glance up at her, and she looks a little worried. Maybe she thinks I won't be into her if she dyes her hair. But I don't fucking care about shit like that.

Hair color. Skin color. Big. Small.

I like *her*. Not the body she comes in.

"Are you indecisive?" I wonder. "It looks like you have the rainbow in there."

"Precisely." She smiles, licking the chocolate off her fingers. "Unicorns love rainbows. I love unicorns. Therefore thy hair must be a rainbow."

"Interesting fucking theory." I start walking further down the parking lot and she follows me.

"One of my best?" She catches up to my side.

"No it's fucking stupid."

"It can't be interesting *and* stupid. Those are exclusive."

"You sound like Rose." As soon as I say the words, she brightens. I know she looks up to her sisters, and in a way she reminds me a little bit of both of them. The rest of her is just Daisy. Just wild.

We stop by a black sportbike that I just bought from the dealership. Like I said, we can't ride in a car anymore. I have the means to buy a motorcycle to appease Daisy's restless state, so I'm going to fucking do it.

"We're riding together?" she asks me with a smile.

"Yeah." I take her plastic bag and shove it into my backpack. "You okay with that, sweetheart?"

"Will you let me drive some?"

"I'd let you do whatever you want, as long as you pay attention so we don't fucking highside." Last thing I need is for her to fly off the fucking bike.

"What about lowside?" She's already done that once before: slid off the back of the motorcycle while it raced off without her.

"How about we don't ever fucking crash?"

"But if I crash," she says, slinging her leg over the seat. "I'd rather crash with you."

My brows rise and she smiles bigger, brighter, pulling her scar. "You tell that to all the guys you've hooked up with?" I ask her.

"No," she says, "because you're the only one I've dated who rides motorcycles."

I shake my head. "Your list of pickup lines, sweetheart, is insane. And I fucking swear you've used most of them on me."

"I have?" she says, eyeing my muscles with a little more desire than before. I can tell she's remembering the tent, when we had sex for the first time. "Looks like they worked." Her eyes flicker to mine. "I have you."

Her bedroom eyes are going to fuck me over like they never have before. I toss her a white helmet, not alleviating the moment. With us, the tension will probably stick around for seven whole days.

Everyone is taking their time driving to Canyonlands, so yeah, we have a week.

A week alone with Daisy.

For the first time, we're going to see how we are as a couple. No restraint. Very little boundaries.

I sense the excitement.

But I also see the trouble.

< 44 >

Daisy Calloway

I don't mind when I ride behind Ryke, on the same seat, not the one steering or revving the throttle. He speeds as much as I would on a two-lane highway with very little traffic and no hills in sight. The farm lands we pass remind me that we're in the Midwest, heading towards Utah at a leisurely pace.

If he's tired from sleeping even less than me, he doesn't show it. I wrap my arms around his waist, still entranced by him even though we're together. I'm drawn to Ryke the way penguins waddle in a group, one following the other, rarely all alone. He's masculine and tough and someone who chooses to feed my needs first and his second. I thought he'd want a twenty-nine-year-old, big breasted girl with lots of makeup and a tight bandaged dress.

Not eighteen, flat-chested, no makeup and ratty jeans and a loose fitting tee.

He keeps a lot in his head, and that's partly the reason I like him. The mystery of his actions. The danger he wears in his dark eyes.

The motorcycle suddenly slows down to the side of the highway. I scan the area, just rows and rows of cornstalks, way taller than me. I take my helmet off at the same time as him. He climbs off the bike, not saying a word, but I watch him with pure intrigue, my curiosity peaking.

"Why'd we stop?" I ask.

I think I might know why. This week is already crazy for us. Our first unrestrained time together, and like I had always fantasized, we're making up for the years we wasted on waiting.

He turns off the ignition and kicks out the stand while I'm still on the bike. And then his eyes meet mine, and they start a slow descent down my body, his chest rising in a deep, lustful inhale.

I smile. "You want to fuck me?"

With that darkness, he says, "I want to fuck you."

Ohhhh. The spot between my leg pulses. I climb off the bike and start to walk backwards while he follows me.

The cornstalks brushing my face as I enter the field. I want him to chase me. "Do you think you can catch me?" I ask in a silky breath.

He almost smiles. "I'll give you a head start."

I grin and then I spin around and take off, my blood pumping, my heart racing, my hands whipping through the stalks as I pass.

It's beautiful. The sun is hoisted in the perfectly blue sky, clouds rolling over to cool the heat. A gentle breeze. This is a moment that you'd find in your dreams—a place that you'd never think you'd be.

And Ryke took me here.

I don't know how far I go, but it's not long before he finds me, scooping me up in his arms and kissing me with aggressive, thirsty passion. I kiss back with the same vigor, a cry escaping as his body melds with mine. I lift off his shirt and unbutton his pants with excitement, and then he starts to slow down. When his lips part from mine, I sense that he's stuck inside his head.

"What?" I ask, using the extra time to give much needed oxygen to my lungs.

"It's just something I've been thinking about…"

This doesn't sound good. "It's not about the… period stuff, is it?" *Shut up, Daisy.* "I'm on birth control. Everything's fine now, you know that."

"Dais, it's not that." He draws me to his chest and whispers in my ear, "Have you let a guy go down on you before?"

I don't want him to think I'm inexperienced or too young to love. But I also don't want to lie, so I try to brush this one off. "Have you let a guy go down on you?" I ask him the same question with a playful smile.

"No," he says. He tilts my chin up so I'm looking at him. I didn't even realize I was avoiding his gaze. "It's okay if you haven't."

"It's not that I haven't wanted to," I explain, courage building to tell him the truth. "It's just that no guy has offered before."

His jaw hardens in a severe line, really sexy even if he's half pissed at these phantom guys that exist in my past. He ends up unbuttoning my shorts, staring down at me with a new determination. "Did someone offer to backdoor you?"

Ack…this answer, I don't like it either. "Number six," I say. "I tried it once, and honestly I don't ever want to try it again." It hurt like hell. I think I cried it was so painful. Like actual tears.

"I wasn't going to fucking suggest it," he says. "I'm just irritated that number *six* would do that before even going down on you." He slides my panties to my ankles. I don't know what he plans on doing with me; he won't say.

He's in his black boxer-briefs, and I pull my shirt over my head, stripping completely. It's different being in the daylight doing this with him. It feels real, not heightened by nighttime hormones or our closeness as we sleep. It's just us. On an adventure. Together. Trying to fully figure each other out, no barriers this time.

He steps out of his underwear, and my gaze drops to his package almost immediately. *I can't believe that was inside of me* is my first gut reaction. My second: *I hope it happens again. Soon.*

I close some of the distance between us and run my hands up his abs, across his tattoo and chest. He looks at me the same way he did when he climbed off the motorcycle. *Want* glimmering in his eyes. His hands settle on my hips, his touch quickening my heart. And like I weigh nothing, he lifts me up on his *shoulders*. Not his waist.

I smile wide, my legs dangling against his back, and he skillfully kisses the spot between my legs, his hand on my ass, his tongue doing things to a place that loves this new sensation. My head peeks through the cornstalks, able to see the cars whizz by on the street that we abandoned.

I tense and my mouth falls as he licks a sensitive spot. I grip his hair, my hands on his head for support. "Ryke," I cry. "What..." I want to say *what the hell? Have you done this like* this *before?* I've never seen this happen. On his shoulders. Legs open. His mouth right there. Not even in R-rated movies.

That's because this is reserved for the NC-17 stuff. Duh.

Heat gathers on my neck. "Fuck," I cry.

I can feel him smiling. Yeah, I guess he is a bad influence on me sometimes. But I know the opposite is true too.

I prefer being on his shoulders to the way he went down on the girl in his bedroom. This is better. Sexier. More fun.

He squeezes my ass, and his tongue—

Ahhhh! I moan, which turns into another cry, gasping repeatedly with that sound. All thoughts are deserted. All that's left is need for something fuller between my legs. Something hard.

My noises get to Ryke because he ends up sliding me down from his shoulders to his waist. I hold onto the back of his neck with both of my hands, still a mess from that.

"Whoa," I say with a tight voice, breathing heavy. His eyes consume my whole being, and he uses one hand to brace me to his body, the other to push his erection deep, deep inside of me.

There's a slight pinch when he fills me entirely, but the pain dissipates when he's all in. Another high-pitched sound escapes.

"*Fuck*," he curses, the word so sexual and heady off his tongue.

He begins to fuck me standing up, his body and strength doing most of the work, thrusting into me while I meet him with my hips a couple times. But really, I can't keep up with Ryke in this position. He's stronger and has an easy time forcing me upright and pounding hard against me.

I clutch him so tightly, my body bouncing on his cock, my head dizzy. The pressure so freakin' wonderful. The sensations too powerful to describe. I am floating. Rising. Towards the bright blue sky.

"Ryke," I start again, and my sharp gasps return, piercing cries attached that come in succession. "*Ahhh…ahhhh…*" Oh God. Oh God.

"Dais," he groans, one of his hands on the back of my head. "*Fuck*."

Fuck is right.

Fuck.

Fuck.

Fuuuuckkk. Oh my God. He jerks forward, coming inside of me, and I tighten around his cock, clenching over and over, riding a wave to the shore. He holds me as I slow down, as I gather my breath, and he rubs the back of my head, gentle with me, even after a pretty rough and deep moment.

I don't want to disentangle from him. I don't even want to go back to the motorcycle anytime soon. He appeases my silent command by setting me on his bike jacket, flattening some of the cornstalks. He kisses me from above, though he does pull out. His lips and tongue move with more affection and care, and I rest my hand on his bare bottom, spreading my legs on either side of him.

I'm not sure how long we kiss. All I know is that I could do this forever with Ryke.

He skims his thumb across my bottom lip, and his eyes rake over my features with fondness, a look that I've never seen from him before.

"What are you thinking?" I whisper. We're alone in the middle of a cornfield, but it seems too peaceful to talk loudly.

"I love this," he breathes, kissing my cheek, the one with the scar, as though it's perfect just the way it is.

My chest rises. "The sex?"

He shakes his head. "No, *this*. Right now." He kisses me again and then says, "But I do fucking love the sex."

I smile. "You're not too bad at it."

His brows pinch together like *yeah?* "Not too bad? Do we have a recording of your fucking voice?"

"You mean this voice?" I arch my back a little and cry, gasping with the same unraveling pleasure, though there is a slight difference in my fake orgasm and the real one. My voice cuts off shorter every time Ryke takes me hard, and here it's more drawn out. "Ryke, *ahhh…*" My chest rises and falls heavily, like I struggle to breathe.

He sits on his knees, watching me, and then he hardens, turned on. The fakeness in my body starts to switch into real, dramatic feelings. *Ahhh…*I moan a desperate moan.

Thankfully he doesn't make me beg for it or admit my sarcasm. He just drives his erection between my legs, filling me again. He pumps with a melodic rhythm, his forearm resting a little bit above my head, staring down at me as my noises tickle my throat.

It's way too much. Every single nerve is lit up. "I can't…" I moan.

He slows, and his cheek brushes mine as he whispers in my ear, "Yes, you can…you're going to feel it."

Not long after his words leave, my eyes roll back, and the most intense, mind-numbing sensation washes over me, heart-stopping feelings that transport me somewhere else. I can't even scream. It's so insane that my mouth opens and the sound is stripped from my throat.

When I come down, exhausted, he lifts me in his arms and sets me on his lap. I don't have the energy to do that again, but I know he does. I glance down. Oh. He climaxed with me, and I hadn't even noticed. He just holds me in his arms, wiping the sweaty hair off my face.

"I don't understand how I can go from never having an orgasm to *that*," I whisper. He must be a god. A sex god. And he's been sent to me from the heavens.

He has a more logical answer. "Generally when you're not attracted to the person you're with, Dais, you're not going to get off."

I turn my head and look up at him. "You know what this means?"

His brows harden, and I can tell he's expecting a joke and my normal theatrics. "What?"

I smile with sincerity. "I am very, very attracted to you."

The corner of his lips rise. "Funny, I'm also attracted to you. What are we going to do about that?"

"Make love and make babies."

His brows shoot up. "You already want to make babies with me, Calloway?"

"I want to do lots of things with you." I use a very diplomatic response, walking on a thin rope with this subject. I have no idea where his head lies. His thoughts could match his brother's. Lo doesn't want children because alcoholism is hereditary. Lily told me his stance on the matter. Well, really she told Rose and I was in the same room, and I kind of, sort of, inserted myself into the conversation. I realize that sounds annoying, but I just want to be close to them before they move away and start families.

He kisses my lips, his tongue easily slipping into my mouth and sliding against mine, and then he breaks apart and says, "Me too." He stands, setting me on my feet. And he grabs his underwear and jeans, beginning to dress. I gather my clothes and watch him with curiosity. I didn't think I would care this much about his feelings on children, but I am dying to find out.

"You know I was joking about the babies," I say, slipping my panties on. He hands me my shirt, and the tension of this conversation constricts my lungs. He doesn't let much through his dark gaze, which makes this hard. "But I'm curious…"

"You're always curious," he says, messing my hair with a rough hand.

"I'm *really, really* curious." I smile. "Are you hoping to get married and have kids one day?"

He pulls his T-shirt over his head and grabs his bike jacket off the ground, shaking the dirt off it. And then he runs a hand through his hair, a giveaway that my question makes him a tad bit anxious. "I'm not like my little brother, if that's what you're wondering," he says, putting his jacket on. "I do think alcohol may be an issue for whatever fucking kid I have, but this disease isn't going to take anything away from me. I won't let it."

The answer almost makes me smile. I wish Lo felt the same way, but I think it's different for him. He's been battling his addiction for much longer and he had a much bumpier road than Ryke.

He fixes his hair, trying to comb through the disheveled strands with his fingers. "Look," he suddenly says, his thoughts collected to form a whole response. "I can't do to my kids what my parents did to me. The separation, the divorce, the fucking fighting. I want to be in a serious, committed relationship before I have a child."

"You mean marriage," I say.

"When you're married, you can still get divorced. I don't take that much stock in the word. I just need the emotional fucking commitment." He motions with his head towards the path we came from. "Let's start walking."

I follow him, keeping up with his lengthy stride.

His eyes flicker to me a couple times while I stay silent and digest this information. "What do you want?"

I smile. "Look who's curious now."

He brushes a cornstalk out of my way. "Yeah, well when you joke around I have to read between the lines, and I don't always read you right. It's easier asking you."

I'm glad he asked. It definitely means he cares. "I want to be fully committed to someone, to be married, probably earlier rather than later. And I do want babies. Maybe like three. I also want to travel and visit the great seven wonders and scuba dive and stand beneath a waterfall in Costa Rica, kissing you."

He reaches out and holds my hand.

My heart swells.

"Not in that order," he tells me.

My lips pull high because he didn't discount a single one of my wants. In fact—I can see it in his eyes.

He wants all of it too.

< 45 >

Ryke Meadows

" Just take your time," Connor tells me over the phone. "We stopped in Roswell because Lily and Lo wanted to see the aliens. They spent four hours in the museum—excuse me, I mean the propaganda shit hole."

I hear Lo in the background. "And you made us spend three hours at a graveyard. Between us, who's the super freaky one, love?"

"It was a war cemetery," Connor tells me. "And Rose and I were searching for our ancestors."

"I won," Rose speaks up. "I have three more dead relatives than Connor."

I shake my head. "You all are fucked up."

I can hear his smile in his voice. "So we'll meet in Utah in about four days. We've lost most of the paparazzi, but there's a couple who always catch up to us."

"We haven't seen any paparazzi since we split up."

"Good. By the way, Greg has been trying to reach Daisy to make sure she's safe. Has she checked her phone?"

"I don't know," I say honestly. "But we've been getting shitty signal. I'll make sure she calls him today."

"Perfect." We say our goodbyes and hang up. I return to a parking lot where Daisy sits on the curb. Our motorcycle is parked by our campsite, which isn't hidden in thick woods like the Smoky Mountains. We made a detour to Wyoming, mostly grassy terrain, but a massive rock juts up behind us, trees surrounding it. Devils Tower. It's shaped like a thimble, the peak flat.

I debated taking her to Yellowstone since she's never been, but when I told her that I free-soloed Devils Tower—almost breaking the record for the fastest climb—she insisted we stop so she could see it. Now we're going to hike around the base…and apparently color her fucking hair at the same time.

Boxes of dye lie open around her on the cement, and she has aluminum foil wrapped in different sections of her hair. Why I assumed she'd do it the normal way—with a mirror and a sink—I have no idea. She does things her crazy fucking way.

She rises to her feet, wrapping a yellow scarf around her foiled head and slipping on her plastic sunglasses. She wears a shirt that says *wanderlust*. I've never seen her smile so much than this past week.

I lower my dark green baseball cap and slide my backpack on. "Have you called your dad recently?" I ask her. "He's been trying to get ahold of you."

She tosses the plastic bag with hair dye into a trashcan on our way to the trail. "Yeah, I texted him back. It must not have sent. He likes when I check in."

I adjust the strap on my backpack, that one statement putting pressure on my chest. Connor has told me numerous fucking times that Greg is protective of his youngest daughter, and it's starting to get real for me. I'm with her, and some day, I may need his approval. I'm just not sure what I need to do in order to get it. But I'm realizing that for Daisy, I have to make a bigger fucking effort. She's close to her parents. She loves them.

I would *never* fucking ask her to choose them over me. Severing a relationship with someone who undeniably cares for you—it untethers something in your soul. I think about my mom, and it's a loss that I can't quantify or calculate in words or fucking numbers. It's just there, eating at me. I hate and love myself for it. But I hate and love her.

I don't know how to go back to a woman who bulldozed all of my friends, my brother and *me*. How do I even begin to forgive her?

Daisy gasps. "Are those climbers?" She hops onto a gray boulder and peers up at the rock. From here, the harnessed climbers look like specs, barely visible. But they're all over Devils Tower, ascending in pairs.

"It's a popular climb," I tell her. "If the weather's good, there'll always be people here."

"How long did it take you to reach the top?" she asks, hopping down and joining me back on the path.

"Twenty fucking minutes." *Almost 900 feet of ascension.* Two minutes shy of the record. I debated on trying it again, but I'd rather focus on the rocks at Yosemite.

"You say it so blasé," she tells me. "Aren't you proud?"

"Shouting about it won't change anything." I'm not Connor Cobalt. After I left for college, every achievement has been an internal one, where I remember the road I took to get there. The labor, the time, the practice. My records don't tell that story. They're just numbers.

We walk past a couple of intense hikers in their Adidas running shoes, capris and reflecting sunglasses. I only now realize how fast my pace is, and Daisy hasn't complained. But I can tell she's struggling to keep up, her breathing heavier than when we started. A streak of purple dye starts to run down her forehead.

"Well if you're not going to boast, then I'll do it for you," she says, reminding me of Sully. She darts to another large boulder, the hike littered with them, and she climbs on it, using her knees to hoist her body on top. Then she throws up her arms. "I have an announcement to make! Birds, people, trees, please listen up!"

I cross my arms. The more I watch, the more my lips rise.

Some people glance over, but most just keep on walking. The birds actually seem more interested in Daisy, squawking and flying above us as she speaks.

I just shake my head but I can't ignore the fucking feeling in my chest. It's pride. But not for climbing Devils Tower. I'm so fucking proud that I have *her* in my life.

"My boyfriend right there." She points at me. "He climbed that mountain." She jabs her finger behind her. "And hey, he did it in twenty fucking minutes. Not just twenty minutes. Twenty *fucking* minutes! Rejoice!" She throws up both her arms, and I catch a couple park rangers walking up the path.

I motion for her. "K, celebration fucking over."

She jumps off the boulder and places her hands on her hips, panting for a second. "How'd I do?"

"The birds enjoyed it." I wipe the trail of hair dye off her forehead, staining my finger and smearing purple onto her skin. "You're about to turn into a fucking purple dinosaur."

"Aww," she says with a smile. "Barney. And Littlefoot! Is Littlefoot purple?"

I shake my head at her. "I have no fucking clue what you're talking about."

She gasps. "You don't know who Barney is? How did you cope as a child?"

I roll my eyes. "I fucking know who Barney is. Not the other one, Calloway."

She smiles. "*The Land Before Time.*"

We walk towards a secluded part of the woods, off the path and behind large rocks and trees. She unpacks her water bottles from her backpack and sets them along a boulder.

"Lean over," I tell her after she removes the foils from her hair. I uncap the water bottle, put a hand over her eyes, and then douse her head. I try to run my fingers through the strands, but they're knotted from being twisted in the foil. "You pack a brush, Dais?"

"Nope." She smiles deviously, turning her face towards me. "It's okay. I'll just finger it."

I force her head back down. "You finger yourself a lot?" I ask, pouring a second bottle onto her hair.

"Not as much as you finger me."

Fuck. My cock stirs. That turned very literal. My fucking fault. I don't feel as guilty as I would have before we were together. I just draw her ass back towards me while I finish washing her hair. She tries to look at me again, a full-blown smile lighting up her face.

"Stay fucking still," I say. "Or dye is going to get in your eyes." She complies, and when I finish, I take off my shirt and she dries her hair, splotching the white fabric with purple, green and pink. Then she runs her hands through it and watches my reaction since she doesn't have a mirror.

She has bigger pink highlights, a couple green ones, and a few purple scattered around her head. Still mostly blonde, but the color reflects her erratic personality. I know she'll love it when she sees it, which is why I begin to smile.

"That ugly, huh?" she jokes.

"So fucking ugly," I say, wrapping my arm around her shoulder.

We finish the rest of the hike, and her silence starts to concern me. This is about the time she'd be bubbling with happiness. She just dyed her hair, something she's wanted to do for a while.

"What's wrong?" I ask.

"When we get to Utah, is this going to end? You and me, together out in the open. For the first time, I feel like a real couple, like we're moving forward somewhere, and I don't want that feeling to just fly away, you know?"

Yeah, I fucking do. I don't want to hide any part of my life. I did that for so long, and starting it all over again feels like a regression. "So we tell them in Utah," I say, holding the strap of my backpack. "Big fucking deal." I want to be able to handle the backlash. And the closer we are to each other, the more I believe our relationship can withstand the criticism. But I wonder if I'm just fucking fooling myself. Maybe that's just fear talking though. The fear of losing her… and my brother.

"You sure?" she frowns. "Because Lo—"

"He'll get over it." I have to believe this or else I'll never take the fucking leap. I stop in the middle of the path and hold her face, my fingers stained different colors already. "I want to be with you, Dais. No more hiding."

I lean down and kiss her, cementing my decision.

< 46 >

Daisy Calloway

The woods have been replaced by desert. Red rock and endless roads with no one around. Much different than the congested streets in Wyoming, where cars slow at the sight of a deer, snapping pictures as though it's the most fascinating creature in the wild.

That would be the buffalo.

Or the black bears.

Ooh, and the wolves. I saw two gray ones, out grazing or maybe playing by the antelopes, but Ryke didn't believe me.

The closer to Utah, the closer we are to California, a destination that I haven't forgotten. Ryke will ascend El Capitan and two other rock faces in Yosemite, the summit much higher than Devils Tower. I love that I have the opportunity to watch him at his best, but I've Googled the statistics before.

A good majority of people who free-solo die while climbing.

I mean, there is a *tab* at the top of Rock Climbing Nation Information's website with the word DEATHS. They catalogue all of the climbers who fall and meet their end. I've always tried not to think about the risk, even when I tagged along with him to Yosemite while he practiced with a harness and rope.

I saw the rock.

I saw his climb.

I just didn't let myself believe that he could fall. With no harness, no support, no gears, just himself—it's a huge possibility.

But I would never tell him not to do something he loves.

I'm just going to pray that no freak accidents happen, no bad weather rolls in—that he goes up and comes back down without problem.

I wrap my arms tighter around his back, loving the feeling of the wind whipping around us on the motorcycle. I try to shelve my concern for Ryke. He doesn't need my worry while he's halfway up El Capitan. He just needs his strength and confidence.

All of this talk has clenched my stomach, and I make an impulsive, rash decision. Albeit one that's not even remotely safe. One that's probably dangerous like free-soloing, but definitely not *as* dangerous. One of my feet already lifts and rests on the seat cushion. I hold onto Ryke's back as I lift the other, crouching while he hunches over the bike, speeding down a flat road.

I can't see his expression behind his black helmet. He sits up, causing my hands to rise to his shoulders, and I stand up fully. *Oh… wow.* I am standing on the back of the motorcycle. Behind him. He taps my leg three times, which is our signal to "sit the fuck down."

I tap his shoulder twice, which doesn't mean anything. But we've never come up with a gesture for: *I want to fly.*

He squeezes my leg. *Hold on*, he's telling me.

I'm not going to let go of him.

He puts his hand on the brake, and the motorcycle begins to slow. I tap his arm once. *Faster.*

He looks back at me a few times, hesitating. I drape one arm over his shoulder, on his chest to show him that I'm not going anywhere.

And he holds onto that hand while he switches gears, pumping his foot, and then we're off. Returning to a high speed.

The force almost propels me back, but he clutches so tightly that I stay upright. And my legs have solidified to stone, not going anywhere. I laugh, the noise only in my helmet, but it exists.

I am flying.

Second star to the right and straight on 'til morning.

It lasts for a glorious five minutes. And then the bike decelerates again, and it rumbles to the emergency lane. I sit back on the seat as Ryke goes off-roading towards a looming red rock with more rocks stacked on top. Rocks on top of rocks. It's really cool even if it sounds lame. We've seen rams—like with giant horns—along with mountain lions on our way here, so I wonder if he's spotted an animal.

That doesn't sound right though.

Ryke wouldn't drive towards wild animals on the side of the road.

That's too crazy for him.

That's something I'd do.

The moment the bike stops, I take off my helmet. "Are you mad?" I ask. Maybe I misread his signals. I mean, he definitely said "sit the fuck down." But "hold on" could have been something else entirely.

He turns off the engine and kicks out the stand. The sportbike has a slight lean, but not bad. I don't climb off yet, even as he does.

"Turn around," he demands after removing his helmet. He runs his hand through his hair, his eyes narrowed at me. But he's not angry exactly.

"What do you mean?" I barely register what he said, too busy trying to make sense of his emotions.

"*Turn around.*" He motions to the front of the bike. He…he wants me to… I smile. He wants me to ride backwards like I tried to practice in the garage.

I excitedly switch legs over the seat, my back facing the handlebars as I lean against the gas can. I remember the first day he taught me how to ride a motorcycle. After heading to a grocery store parking lot, I killed the engine and rolled to a stop with a big smile. Only, I was dragging my boots the whole way, messing around.

He told me, "Pick up your fucking feet, Calloway, unless you want to lose them." He wanted to teach me the right way first, and then months later, the next time I killed the engine and dragged my feet, he just shook his head. He trusted me enough not to scold me. He didn't think the bike would fall on me or I'd run over my foot by that time.

But I haven't really earned any trust to ride backwards yet. So I doubt those are his true intentions. The mystery intrigues me more and more, and I study his features to solve it. He straddles the bike, facing me, tossing his helmet aside.

Don't need those. Okay. I toss mine too, my heart beating wildly before my mind catches up with me. My body knows what's about to happen. I swallow hard, and when his eyes meet mine, my heart thuds a few times. He wears a carnal look. Like he's ready to devour me whole.

Oh God.

My lips part, desperate for air like I'm crawling up a mountain.

We're on a motorcycle.

Together.

And.

And.

I can't think it. I just feel it.

I can't believe this is about to happen.

< 47 >

Ryke Meadows

I've never been this fucking aroused in my life. With her standing on the back of the motorcycle, I went from fear to desire in a minute flat. After I was certain she was safe, I kept picturing her behind me. I kept picturing what she looked like, holding onto my shoulders, one of my hands gripping hers. And then my mind rerouted and I pictured her legs spread open and my entire cock filling her.

I want this, right here, with her. My fucking body aches for it, and my mind is through hesitating. I remember how many times we've been on a bike together, and how restrained we've been. It all fucking flies out the window.

My mouth meets hers, and we consume each other with each fucking kiss, more natural, more animalistic than anything I've felt before. My core screams for her, as though she's mine and only mine, and I've finally returned home.

I don't want to spend an extra ten minutes stripping, so I reach into my boot and grab my knife. Her eyes widen, glimmering with that beautiful curiosity. She goes rigid, careful not to fidget while I unhook the button on her jeans and cut the fabric to the pocket. I sheath my knife in my boot and rip the jeans even more with one forceful movement. Her yellow panties are exposed, and I easily tear those off her body. She's already dripping and ready for me.

My cock fucking screams for release.

"Ryke," she breathes, her mouth open. I kiss her, holding the back of her head, and she practically whimpers underneath me.

Fuck. I suck her neck while my fingers fill her. She's wetter than I've ever felt, and it's not long before her body bucks up into mine, her cry piercing the open air. We're shielded from the road, private for the most part, but it's still new. It's still a place I've never fucked, and what we're about to do, I've never done.

On a motorcycle.

With a girl I fucking love.

I would smile if my body wasn't so pent up, ready to drive into her and fuck her hard and sweet. I unzip my pants, lowering them below my ass along with my boxer-briefs. And then I grab her legs and spread them wider before I guide myself inside her, slowly. I watch her reaction, making sure I don't hurt her.

She clutches my neck and starts rocking her hips before I'm even halfway in. So I go all the way. She cries and stops pushing forward, her noise seriously fucking messing with my head. It's high-pitched and full of unbridled pleasure, full of torrid lust.

I burn when I watch her, when I hear her, my senses blistering into ash.

"Dais," I say forcefully, reaching above her to grip the handlebar. It allows me to push deeper. Once. Twice. My erection fitting perfectly inside of Daisy.

She cries, her eyelids fluttering.

I lift her leg higher around my waist, and she breathes like she's having a panic attack.

"I can't…" She shakes her head from side to side.

I kiss her lips and slow down for a second. "You can, Dais." *I know. It's fucking intense.* These feelings are blinding.

And we're on a bike, straddling it together. I drop her leg and pull her closer to my chest so she's in a sitting position. Instinctively her feet rest on the seat behind me, her legs tucked around my waist.

She tightens around my cock as I thrust against her. I put my hand on her lower back, a grunt scratching my throat. *Fuck.*

"This is—" she starts and then she cries out, her sudden climax forcing her body to me, I hold onto her and only have to thrust two more times before I release, my mind breaking into a million fucking shards. As she pulses, descending off that cliff, she begins to laugh with so much happiness.

It's a full-bellied, world-altering laugh. Even as she takes a moment to engrain this image in her head, the two of us, as intimate and close as you can be, on this sportbike, she still smiles like it's the best picture in the world.

She meets my gaze. "This was the best ride you've taken me on so far."

I kiss her strongly and then say, "Want to go again?"

She answers by wrapping her arms around my neck and scooting closer, her grin brightening the universe.

The red dust whips around us. I don't give a fuck. I make love to her like it's the most primal experience in the world.

Like it's what our bodies are created to do.

< 48 >

Ryke Meadows

I ride through the night. Daisy sleeps in my arms for some of it, straddled backwards and facing me. I think she averages about four hours of sleep a day, which is better than what she had been doing off Ambien. But I wish I could hold her in my arms through the night, with no restlessness, no moment where she wakes and struggles to return to that peace. I just want what she had—before the media, before the mental trauma.

She is making more progress. We stayed at a hotel one night, and I didn't have to do our routine, showing her that I locked every single door and checking the shower. She could sleep for a couple hours without that knowledge and feel safe.

I kiss the top of her head and drive on.

The sunrise breaks across the horizon, oranges and reds spilling together. Out west, the quiet atmosphere tranquilizes me, clearing my head. I thought I could show this to my brother. I thought that we could share it, but circumstances or fate or whatever split us apart.

To have this time with Daisy means just as much, but I do recognize that each moment spent with her is a moment away from Lo during his recovery. A part of me is glad to be in Utah, meeting up with him, so I can be there if he needs me.

The other half selfishly wants to go back to the fantasy I had with Daisy—to hide for just a few hours longer before reality comes crashing into us.

I turn a corner and the bike rattles on a gravel road, stirring Daisy from her sleep. I park by a lookout point and remove her helmet before I take off mine.

She rubs her eyes and squints against the sunlight. "What time is it?" she asks with a yawn.

"Morning."

"Very…" she yawns again. "…accurate." She turns her head to catch the sunrise, the warm glow bathing her face in color. "It's gorgeous…"

It has nothing on her.

My phone buzzes in my pocket, and she wraps her arms around my waist while I check it with one hand.

We're in the Canyonlands. I'll send you a pin. You can meet us there. — Connor

I receive the pin and check the map. "We're ten minutes away," I tell Daisy. "They're already there. You ready to see your sisters?"

She nods, but I can see the slight apprehension in her eyes. Outing our relationship to them is the first step before she has to tell her mom. A woman who fucking despises my guts, and I worry once she sees Daisy's face, she'll hate me even more.

We put our helmets back on, and she changes positions, sitting behind me. I take off, heading in the right direction.

Seven minutes later, I roll up somewhere by the Green River, not very much traffic around. Mammoth canyons and red rock structures landscape the area. I recognize the black SUV parked by the start of a hiking trail, but I don't see any of them around.

I check the pin again and realize they've hiked towards one of the arches, made from the same red rock. They're popular formations, so I'm not surprised they're beside it. I'm just surprised Rose would walk in her five-inch fucking heels to go there.

It takes us about five minutes trekking across the red dirt to find them underneath the large rock that juts to the sky. As the hot sun begins to rise, larger shadows disappear, increasing the temperature.

"Hey guys!" Daisy waves to them, and they all spin around, but none come to meet us halfway. They all just stare.

And it's at this moment that I know something is very fucking wrong.

My gut knots with every step, and I can't tear my eyes off my brother's. His cheekbones are sharpened, his eyes cold and pissed. He can't still be angry at me for the paparazzi? I thought Connor would have talked him down from that. But Lo likes to harbor a lot of fucking resentment towards me. Yeah, I fucked up. The paparazzi found our campsite in Tennessee and destroyed my promises to him. His fury though, it looks like it's on another level.

Deeper.

Rawer.

From years and years of pain.

"Love the hair, Dais," Lily says as we get closer, but her voice breaks, like she knows something bad is about to happen.

And my brother—he breathes heavily, pure malice coating his amber eyes. His nose flares, and then he starts walking towards me.

I stop in my place. "Daisy," I tell her. "Go to your sisters."

"Ryke—"

"Fucking *go*," I growl.

She backs away from me, not joining her sisters. But she gives me enough space as my brother approaches with a frosty glare.

I don't know what this is about.

Maybe our father.

Maybe Daisy.

Maybe something else.

Maybe all of the above.

I have a laundry list of bad fucking deeds with good intentions.

"Lo." I hold out my hands in defense, surrender, mercy. I'm raising a white flag. I don't want to hit him. I can't hit him. "What's wrong? Let's talk about this." He's only ten feet away now.

"You wanna talk about it?" His voice is full of pain. "I gave you a million fucking chances to *talk* about it," he sneers. "I'm so done talking to you." His fist flies and hits my jaw hard. I go down when his knee drives into my stomach.

I cough roughly.

"Lo, stop!" Daisy screams.

I turn my head, and my heart pitches to my throat. She's running towards us, but Connor is faster and stronger. He picks her up while she thrashes in his arms.

My eyes soften in thanks. I barely produce that look of gratitude before Lo punches my face again. I turn my head and spit blood onto the dirt.

I hear Lily in the background, trying to tell Lo to calm down. I hear Connor, telling all of the girls to let us work this out.

He knows this fight was going to happen sooner or later.

It's finally arrived, and the agony tears at my chest. Not physical pain. Even as his third swing connects with my jaw—I can take those hits.

It's the torment in my little brother's eyes. It's the way he's looking at me—like I betrayed him. Like I ruined his life. Like I ripped up his fucking soul. I didn't want to hurt anyone. I didn't mean to cause him more misery. *You should have left him alone.*

But he would have been drunk! He would still be fucking drinking if I didn't walk into his life. I shook him as hard as I could back then.

I brought him to rehab. I talked to him nearly every night during his ninety day recovery, and afterwards, I looked after him.

Yeah? Look at him now.

Fuck! I want to punch something—I'm silently screaming for this internal battle to finally end.

"Hit me," he sneers.

I shake my head, my fingers digging into the red dirt, trying to form fists. *Stop, Ryke.* I could so easily stand up and beat the hell out of him. And he'll let me. It's what he wants. He's asking for that pain. It's like at that Halloween party when I first saw him three years ago.

He's begging to feel something more than these emotions, suffocating with this torment. He's asking for me to replace this fucking torture. And right now, I can't feed into that illness. *I can't.*

"Come on," he sneers, his eyes reddening with rage and sorrow. Tears welling. "I've seen you beat the shit out of guys twice the size of me. I know you want to punch me." He steps towards me. "Fight back!"

I pick myself off the ground, staggering unsteadily. "I won't."

He shoves me in the chest.

I raise my hands. "Lo—"

He punches me again. I stumble backwards but keep my balance this time.

Daisy wails in the background. "STOP IT!" She's crying.

Lily is crying.

I even think Rose may be crying. But she dusts off her tears quickly and sniffs.

Lo points at me. "You're a goddamn coward."

Now he's starting to sound like our father. I just keep my mouth shut.

Through gritted teeth he says, "You're so fucking scared to talk to our dad. You're so scared to talk to your own mom." He takes a few steps forward. I take a few steps back. I'm the prey, the thing he's about to skin alive.

"What do you want me to say?" I growl. "I'm fucking scared?" I point at my chest. "I'm *fucking* scared, Lo!" My eyes burn with this horrible fucking pain. *Fucking hell.* "I'm so fucking scared they're going to manipulate me into loving them when all I want to do is forget!"

"What'd they fucking do to you?!" Lo screams. "I lived with *our* dad. You sat in your pearly white fucking mansion with a mom who loved you!"

I shake my head. This isn't going to solve anything. My chest rises and falls.

"Tell me!" Lo yells. "Tell me how you had it so fucking bad, Ryke. What'd he do to you? Did he smack the back of your head when you got a C on a math test? Did he scream in your face when you were benched for a little league game?" He nears me, his eyes narrowed, his cheeks wet. "What'd he fucking do?"

I shake my head again. I'm not the victim like Lo. There'll be no good in explaining myself. It'll just be more shit on top of shit.

Lo pushes me in the chest again and this time something snaps and I respond, pushing back. He stumbles, but the force doesn't knock him to the dirt.

"I'm not fucking fighting you!" I scream. But he doesn't listen. He charges again, and when he tries to push me over, I shove him down to the ground.

I'm stronger than him.

I'm older than him.

I'm the best and worst thing that ever came into his life. I know this.

I pin him down on his back, my hands on his wrists and my knee digging into his ribs. "I don't want to fight you, Lo," I choke.

His eyes redden further. "You spend so much of your fucking time trying to save me," he says, "and you don't even realize you're killing me." A tear slides down his cheek. He takes shallow breaths and then he lets it out. "The news isn't just in Philly, you know. It's everywhere we fucking go. All the way to a gas station in Utah." His eyes are flooded with sadness. "They think he molested me. The whole goddamn nation. People think my own father touched me, and you won't do a thing about it." His broken gaze stabs me repeatedly. "Why do you believe them and not me?"

"I believe you," I whisper, no hesitation this time. I believe him. I think I may always have. Something more stops me from defending Jonathan Hale, something so raw that it hurts to touch. I'm forced to confront these emotions again because I returned to this life. I could have left it all behind like I planned to. If I had done nothing three years ago, if I had left Lo at that Halloween party, I would have never revisited this hate. I'd never meet these feelings that I had shelved away.

Lo must read the look I wear because he asks, "What the fuck did he do to make you hate him so much?"

He's asked me this once before, and I gave him a half-assed answer. The whole truth is going to seem vane and selfish. So fucking stupid compared to my brother who's had twenty-three years with him. But I owe Lo the truth. I've lied to him enough.

"He chose you," I say. "He chose his bastard kid over me and my mom, and I fucking lied for him my entire life. I hid my identity for him. I had no mom in public because I was Meadows and she was Sara Hale. I had no fucking dad to show for. I saved his reputation, and he buried me six feet in the fucking ground every single day he chose you over me, every day he paraded you around and shoved me aside. I couldn't breathe I was so fucking angry."

His nose flares again, holding back more emotion. "I thought you knew about me when you were fifteen."

"I told you that I met him at a country club every week. I knew his name. I knew he was my father. He was a fucking socialite, so I was smart enough to figure out that his son was my brother. They just didn't tell me until I was fifteen." I shake with this rage that throttles my bones. It's not at Lo. It's at the past, at everything that happened.

I wish I could reverse time and just wipe it all away. But it's here, and it fucking sucks. I lift my body off of his, but I can't stand. Too emotionally exhausted, I sink to my knees, drained and weak. My face throbs, positive that he's given me more than a couple of bruises.

He doesn't even sit up, his eyes burning into the sky.

"I hold grudges," I confess. "But I think you do too, Lo." I look at him and his jaw clenches tightly. He's never let me off the hook, never forgiven me for hating our dad and not seeking him out sooner.

"I just wish you could love me more than you hate him," Lo tells me. It's the most honest thing he's ever said. He turns his head and looks at me, eyes filled with tears. "Is that even fucking possible?"

My whole body aches. I've spent so many years regretting every evil thought I had towards Lo, every curse I fucking wished upon him, every piece of hate that darkened my soul. I know where he comes from now. A house where a mother never loved him. Where a father pushed him too hard. No support to pick him up after he fucking fell.

By not coming forward about the molestation rumors, I'm choosing to hate Jonathan over defending my brother. I never thought that was the case. I always thought that keeping quiet meant that I finally, *finally* stopped protecting a monster, stopped helping him cover his tracks.

I'm just like my mother.

I'm turning into her, trying to hurt Jonathan every way I can, and in the end, the people I care about are hit in the crossfire.

All this fucking time...Samantha Calloway had been right. She accused me of the same thing, back in Daisy's room. And I refused to hear her out. To believe her. I'm becoming someone I don't want to be, and I thought I was running far away from that person.

I exhale, my chest tight. "I love you, you know that," I tell him, patting his leg.

"You didn't answer my question."

"I don't know, Lo," I say. "I want to. I want to so *fucking* badly, but it's not as easy as wishing for that kind of peace. I hate him for things he did to me, for the things he does to you."

Lo shakes his head and sits up. He wipes his face with his shirt and his eyes turn cold again. "Jesus Christ," he laughs a bitter fucking laugh. "You don't get it. I deserved every word he said to me. You didn't know me in prep school, Ryke. I was a fucking shit. I was *terrible*."

I glower. "Don't ever fucking tell me that you *deserved* it. No one deserves to be beat down every fucking day."

He takes deep breaths, his muscles starting to relax. He looks up at me and says, "He's never touched me."

He knows that's not what this is about. I don't want to do this with him. We argue about this all the time. But I have to get it through his thick fucking skull. I lean forward and grab his face between both my hands. "*Stop* defending him. Not to me, okay?"

There are some things we will never agree on. No matter how hard he fucking tries to convince me. No matter how many times we end up on the ground.

He pulls away and I pull back, tension breaking between us. Silence thickens for a moment, and I think maybe he's waiting for me to apologize or maybe trying to work himself up to it. But then he points to my face.

"That bruise right there, that's for fucking my girlfriend's little sister by the way."

My stomach churns. *What?*

< 49 >

Ryke Meadows

L o's face sharpens again, but he flashes a half-smile. "Tabloids caught you making out just outside of Devils Tower." He grabs his phone out of his pocket and scrolls through it. Then he chucks the cell at me. "The photograph is on every gossip site." I avoid the tabloids, so I'm not surprised that I missed it. Just that it exists at all.

I stare at the picture with hard eyes.

Daisy is on my shoulders. We were putting a hammock up in the trees, and she tightened the straps on the last trunk. But the picture froze us in time: Her head dipped down, her lips against mine, my hand on her neck, my fingers stained with purple and pink dye. Her hair still wet.

She's smiling as she kisses me, which pulls her long, deep reddened scar.

Her fucking scar—it's all over the news. Her parents are going to find out about her face from a fucking tabloid. *Dammit!* My jaw locks and I throw the phone back to Lo with more aggression than I intended.

"Pissed you got caught?"

I don't say word. I can't speak without yelling.

"Please talk to me," Lo snaps, "because I need to understand what's going on or I may just punch you again."

I shake my head, my voice deep and low. "It just happened."

"It just happened?" Lo shakes his head, as though I always use that excuse. I'm sure I have before. "That's a really shitty thing to tell me." The red dirt coats our bodies and has turned Lo's hair a shade lighter. "You fuck Lily's little sister, and you say, *oh it just fucking happened?* What'd you fall on her? Did you add her to your tally of girls? Is it a one-night stand kind of thing?"

"That's not what I fucking meant." I grimace at all of those. I try to calm down about the photograph and about the truth reaching her parents before we could tell them. What'd we think, we could live in a fantasy forever? We should have told them about the riot before we left Paris.

"Then what did you mean?" he asks.

I meet his eyes. "It's serious."

"So serious that you shared it with everyone."

"Because I knew you were going to jump down my fucking throat!" Anger catapults me to my fucking feet. He stands with me, both of us breathing heavily again.

Round fucking two.

"If you cared about her," he says, pointing a finger at me, "then you wouldn't be sneaking around like you're doing something wrong!"

"Fuck you!" I shout. "You've made this *impossible*, Lo!"

"She's EIGHTEEN!" Lo yells. He takes two hostile steps towards me, and even though my body screams to run *at* him with a fist flying, I have to take two steps back again. "She's like my little sister. It *wasn't* supposed to be possible! But you didn't care. You still *banged* her."

I'm so fucking screwed. The betrayal flashes in his eyes all over again.

I force down this emotion that threatens to rise and overtake me.

Lo glares. "Your cock finally got the best of you, didn't it?" He's the worst devil on my fucking shoulder. And I love him. "She turned eighteen and you could *finally* stick it in—"

"No," I growl. "It wasn't fucking like that!"

"I should leave you alone in this desert," Lo sneers. "I am kicking myself right now, for every time I let you near her, for every time I let you be alone with her—"

"You don't know what you're fucking talking about." I think about all the times she was alone and afraid and hurt, and I was the one who was fucking there. No one else was around. He had his own shit to deal with, so why the fuck do I get vilified and then praised whenever it's convenient for him?

"I don't know what I'm talking about?" He rubs his lips and grimaces. "How long, Ryke? Tell me that, how fucking long have you liked her more than just a friend, and let's see if it's all in my head?"

"I don't know." I do though. I always have. I just can't stomach admitting it.

"I'm going to ask you again," Lo says, his voice rattling with anger. "How long—"

"Stop," I say forcefully.

He takes one step closer. "No, *how long*—"

"FOR YEARS!" I scream, veins protruding in my arms, my face reddening, unleashing this thing held captive inside of me. I step towards him. "Is that what you want to hear?! Years, Lo."

He clenches his teeth so hard. "You're lying?" He didn't want to believe it. He wanted to be wrong.

"I'm not," I say, hot tears burning my fucking eyes. "I have been so fucking attracted to that girl. And I *never* planned on doing a fucking thing about it. I never was going to try. And I tried..." I point at him. "I tried so fucking hard not thinking about her like that. It was wrong. I knew it was fucking wrong. I suppressed everything as much as I could." But when she was fifteen, sixteen, seventeen—I was drawn to her in immeasurable fucking ways. The guilt was always there. I chose to ignore it.

"Then why not stay away from her?" Lo retorts. "Why not put a hundred fucking feet between you and Daisy? You flirted with her every day, Ryke. You became her *friend*."

"I convinced myself that nothing would ever happen, so I thought it was okay to push further."

"You're a fucking idiot!" Lo yells at me.

I know.

"She was so hot that you couldn't say no after she became legal—"

"No," I cut him off before he continues. "It wasn't like that."

"Then what was it fucking like?!" Lo shouts.

And I explode. "I FUCKING LOVE HER!" I scream, my heart thrashing in my ribs.

His mouth falls, his brows furrowing in confusion the longer he scrutinizes my features. I feel like he's clawing at my insides for answers.

Here they are. "I fell in fucking love with her. It hurt to be away from Daisy. It hurt to watch her with other guys. Everything *fucking* hurt, and I didn't want to live with that pain anymore. I fucking couldn't." I inhale deeply. "I can't tell you when it became unbearable, but it did." Somewhere between Daisy eating a pomegranate in her kitchen and now.

He stares at me for a really long time, processing. "I know, more than anyone, how painful it is watching someone you love be with other people. But you can't really love her—"

"I've known her for over two years," I tell him. "I've spent so much fucking time with her, Lo. We've been through a lot together, so yes, I fell in love with her."

Lo glances back at Daisy, and I follow his gaze. She's crying in Lily's shoulder while she hugs her close. My heart tears open again, and I have to restrain myself from walking over there and consoling her.

When I force my attention back to my brother, I realize he's been studying me watching her. He doesn't say anything, but I will.

"You can leave me here," I say, "but I'll find a way back. I can't leave her, and I won't leave you, no matter how hard you fucking push me out." He needs me. He knows he needs me. And I want to be a part of his life. I don't want to return to the lonely one I had built, with relationships as surface level as you can get, with people who meant nothing, with friends who'd sell me out.

"How much did it hurt?" he suddenly asks.

"Did what hurt?"

"Watching her with other guys."

I choke at the flood of memories. "It felt like someone was drowning me in fucking salt water and lighting me on fire."

His lips almost rise in a fraction of a fucking smile. "Same." He takes a few deep breaths before he adds, "I need some time. But I'm not going to hit you again. So revel in that."

"Thanks," I say.

He nods a couple times and then says, "I wish you fell in love with another fucking girl."

At times like this, so do I. "I'm sorry. I really fucking am. For lying."

He shrugs. "You didn't want to get hit."

"No." I shake my head. "I didn't want to hurt you."

He nods again. "I'll get over it. Just…give me fucking time." He heads towards the girls, and I stay rooted to this place, so emotionally spent.

And then he pauses. Turns around and waits for me to join him.

It's a peace offering.

I see it in his face, the way a shred of guilt flickers in his eyes, still accompanied by a swirling rage. It's enough for me. I walk forward and join him. He starts moving again when I'm by his side.

Just like that.

The past and the present were spread bare in the dirt.

Now maybe we can move forward.

< 50 >

Daisy Calloway

October 31st.

We were supposed to make it to Yosemite by the end of the month, but a storm rolled in. The rain thrashes against the tin roof of a hole-in-the-wall Mexican restaurant somewhere in Nevada. Our cell service has sucked in the desert, so I haven't had the chance to talk to my parents about my relationship or the permanent damage done to my face.

I've been taking the days as they come. Kind of awkward.

No, mostly awkward.

I glance at Ryke next to me, faint bruises on his cheek and jaw. It looks much better than it did a few days ago. We've all kept to ourselves since the fight, and this is really the first time we've sat down as a group.

We're all seated in a round booth, our clothes wet and hair damp from being caught in the flash storm. And tension pulls from each couple. Lily and Lo huddled on one end. Rose and Connor in the middle. Ryke and I—we're across from his brother and my sister, in direct line of Lo's sharpened cheekbones and narrowed eyes.

He hasn't been malicious, so that's nice. I can tell he's trying to accept my relationship with his brother—but that doesn't mean he won't make comments.

Our six person dynamic has definitely changed.

Ryke's arm is around my waist, and we're so close that our legs meld together beneath the table.

"This is awkward," Lo states the obvious after the waitress takes our drink orders. His eyes flicker to Ryke and then away every so often.

Rose squeezes her hair, water dripping off the brunette strands. "Then maybe you shouldn't have punched your brother, Loren."

Lo twirls a knife in his hand and points at the cardboard coffin hanging on the ceiling, part of the Halloween decorations. "Go back to bed."

She opens her mouth, and Connor covers her lips with his hand. "It's his birthday," he reminds her. "Be nice."

Her eyes flash cold. Connor drops his hand, and she stays quiet. For seven seconds. "Get over it, Loren. They're fucking. His dick is going in her—" Connor is fast, his hand flying back over her mouth.

"Rose!" Lily says with wide eyes, her face red.

I ping-pong from wanting to laugh to wanting to stay quiet. I end up focusing on the napkin in front of me, trying and kind of failing to make a pumpkin shape.

Connor says to his wife, "I think we all understand the human anatomy involved with sex."

I smile. "I don't know," I quip. "I'm lost on that last part." I look up at Ryke. "Where does the guy's dick go?"

He stares down at me with raised brows and dark eyes. I swear he smiles, or *almost* smiles. I'll take it.

Lo groans and motions to the waitress. "We need some tequila shots."

Ryke goes rigid, his attention off me and his arms suddenly on the table. "Lo, you can't—"

"It's my birthday—"

"I don't give a fuck," Ryke says like his brother got struck by lightning, frying his brain when we weren't looking.

Lo cocks his head. "Let me finish." The waitress comes back with a tray of shots before anyone can say anything more. She also brings out a plate of chicken tacos that Lo ordered in advance—his favorite. The tequila shots sit beside the basket of chips like a bomb. I look to Lily and Rose, wondering what we should do, but Lily is sunk in her seat, still red, and Rose is glaring at her husband for some reason.

This is weird.

Now it's weird *and* awkward.

The waitress leaves, and Ryke says, "Explain."

Lo motions to Rose, Lily, Connor, and me. "These four can still drink. Just because I'm sober doesn't mean that I can't handle the sight of alcohol. I know I've screwed up recently, but I don't want to be reminded of it today. I want to prove to myself that I can be surrounded by *this*." He gestures to the shots with his knife. "Now drink—not you." He points his knife at Ryke. "But everyone else, take the shots. Celebrate my twenty-fourth year in this world. I'm sure I've impacted so many people for the better." He flashes a dry smile.

Ryke processes this for a second before he nods. "Okay."

"Love the speech," I tell Lo, reaching out for the first shot to cut the tension. It does a little bit, but Lily and Rose stay put.

Rose and Connor are having some sort of staring contest.

"Stop reading each other's minds," Lo says. "It's creepy."

I lick the side of my hand. "It is Halloween."

Ryke passes me the salt shaker, and I cross my legs underneath my butt, sitting up a little higher at the table. I put some salt on the wet part of my skin.

"Lil," Lo says, about to drag the tray of shots towards her.

She shakes her head. "I don't feel like drinking."

He frowns. "Are you sure?" His voice is softer with her. "Would you rather have a beer?"

"No, I think I'll stick with water."

She's not much of a drinker, so I'm not surprised she's rejected the offer. During family events, she'll go for the non-alcoholic options while Rose will drink mimosas, white wine, and dirty martinis.

Connor breaks his gaze off his wife's and collects two shots for them. Then he says something in French that I can't understand.

I wish Ryke could translate for me, but we're too close to everyone else. It'd be obvious that he understands the language. He acts like he's not eavesdropping, eating a chicken taco at the same time as Lo. No wonder he's been able to hide his fluency in French.

I can barely tell he's listening at all.

< 51 >

Ryke Meadows

I put more salsa in my taco while Rose glares at Connor, and he stares back in challenge. They're usually strange, but they're being *really, really* fucking strange right now.

He says, "Buvez avec moi." *Drink with me.*

Her nose flares as her eyes drop to the tequila. She snatches the shot glass, not backing down, and she raises it towards her mouth.

I bite my taco, and when I glance at them, I notice that Connor's jaw has tightened, his gaze darkened. I feel like they're playing a risky game of chicken. Like when I was at the bar with Lo, back in Paris. I sense the similarities in that and this, but my mind barely has time to add these facts together.

Rose puts the rim of the shot to her lips. Connor grabs her wrist and forces her hand down, the shot splashing as the glass meets the table.

Lo's brows furrow, holding his chicken taco. "What the fuck?"

Daisy freezes, a lime in her hand.

Connor stares harshly at Rose. "Vous êtes allée assez loin." *You've taken this far enough.*

Her eyes pierce him.

Connor shakes his head. "Dites-le tout simplement." *Just say it.*

She inhales sharply. "Ne faites pas ça." *Don't.*

Connor edges closer to her, and she surprisingly doesn't pull away. He cups her face, his thumb stroking her cheek as he says, "Vous n'avez rien à craindre." *You have nothing to fear.*

She tries to glance at us, but he forces her head straight at him, making her come face-to-face with whatever she's been hiding.

Rose has trouble surrendering and letting him win this long, drawn out game. Her eyes glance down at the spilt tequila, and he puts his hand over the top, telling her *no.* I finish my taco and grab my water, taking a large swig.

Connor pinches her chin between his fingers, and he says, "Vous êtes enceinte." *You're pregnant.*

I spit out my water.

Just like that. One word. Enceinte. And my cover is blown.

Fucking fuck.

They both turn their heads to look at me. For fuck's sake—my brother gapes like I've grown horns, and Lily might as well be catching flies with her mouth.

Connor's eyes continue to darken, his expression so rare that my neck starts to heat uncomfortably.

"Why are you fucking looking at me like that?" I ask defensively, backtracking. My efforts are useless. It's Connor Cobalt. If my brother figured out that I understood their conversation, then he definitely has.

"Vous savez pourquoi." *You know why.* He keeps shaking his head like he can't believe this. Maybe he's upset that he got something wrong. That he misread me. That I've been fucking overhearing his dialogs for years. All of the above, once again.

My muscles harden, and Daisy puts her hand on my leg underneath the table in comfort. I lace her fingers with mine and then nod at Connor. "You should be less focused on me and more fucking concerned about your pregnant wife, who almost drank a tequila shot to fucking one-up you."

"What?" Lo says. He leans back like a hurricane just knocked into him.

Rose glowers at *me*. "Go choke on your water again." That is an insult usually reserved for Lo.

I flip her off and she does the same thing in return, which is an awful fucking rebuttal to the middle finger. It's not like I'm asking her if she knows how to do it too.

I'd love to remove myself from this whole awkward situation, but we're stuck at the same table together, forced to deal with serious issues that we've kept from each other.

Lo has his hands on his head, his eyes darting between me and Rose. "You both take birthday surprises to a new fucked up dimension."

Rose blinks back tears. No wonder she's been emotional this whole trip. I've rarely ever seen her cry, and she's shed probably more tears in the past two weeks than she has in the past five years.

"Christ," Lo says, realizing this too. He cringes, looking a little guilty. She's been hormonal, obviously going through something, and he's picked on her a lot. I mean, she didn't even fucking tell Connor. She made him figure it out.

But their relationship—that's just how they do things, I guess. I wouldn't know unless I was in their heads. I'd rather a girl scream at the top of her lungs and throw things at me, telling me she's pregnant than spend months solving a mystery.

Connor rotates a fraction to look back at Rose. "You're five weeks along." He just states it, not as a question.

She holds her breath. "No."

He frowns. "Seven?"

She shakes her head once.

He looks fucking pissed. He rubs his lips to hide the emotion, but I see the hurt and anger pulsing in his eyes. "Eight weeks?"

She glares. "Ne me regardez pas comme ça." *Don't look at me like that.*

They glance at me with agitation, realizing I understand them now. Rose sighs heavily, reaching for her water.

"What'd they say?" Lily asks.

"I'm not getting into it," I tell her.

Rose says, "You're mad, Richard, that you were off on your numbers. I'm sorry you weren't right—"

"No, darling," Connor tells her with conviction. "I'm upset because it took you this long to talk about it. I thought you would have conceded a month in."

"How long have you known?" she asks quietly.

"When you had a flat tire, I was almost positive. Your GPS was set to the gynecologist, and you purposefully had a fight with me the next day so I'd sleep on the couch. I figured the doctors confirmed what you already knew, and you were too stubborn and afraid to tell me."

Lo frowns and looks at Lily. "You knew?" She had been in the car with Rose.

She nods, her shoulders turned into her body. "Moral support."

Connor glances at Lily cautiously before setting his gaze back on his wife.

Rose sits stiffly, and her chin trembles. "This wasn't the plan. I'm not thirty-five yet."

The waitress returns, cutting into possibly the most bizarre way a pregnancy can be announced. At a Mexican restaurant. With a tequila shot standoff. In French.

"Ready to order?" she asks.

"We need like ten minutes," Daisy tells her.

She nods, her eyes lingering on Daisy's scar before she disappears. I can't tell if the waitress recognizes us or not, but Daisy ends up resting her head against my arm. I comb my fingers through her hair.

"You're not aborting the baby," Connor tells Rose.

"I know," she retorts, fire coming back to her eyes. "You want a lineage. Eight kids, I remember."

"We're married," he says. "We have *billions* of dollars. We may be young, but we can be the best parents. You just have to trust that you'll be a great mother."

I've seen Rose around kids. She's about as maternal as a fucking brick wall, her nose curling in disdain when a baby cries or acts out. But I do know one thing—when she loves someone, she invests her whole fucking heart and time into them.

After a long stretch of silence, Rose says softly, "I thought about getting rid of the baby."

Connor's face stays unreadable. "I know."

She swallows hard. "Lily talked me out of it."

Lo kisses Lily's temple. I think we're all glad Rose didn't choose that option, even if she thought about it.

And I would feel worse for Connor if he didn't already know everything beforehand.

"I just..." Rose lets out a deep breath. "I figured that I had a couple of months before my body started to really change. Two months to ignore the fact that my world is going to flip upside down and a creature is going to grow inside of me. Give me that."

He smiles. "I did, darling."

"So," Lo says, holding his water, "how exactly do two geniuses *accidentally* get pregnant?" He sips his drink in amusement.

Rose starts putting her frizzy, wet hair in a sleek pony. "Why don't you answer this one, Richard? You're friends with Satan's spawn."

Lo laughs. "I think you've mistaken me for the 'creature' growing inside you."

Connor raises his hand to quiet them. Rose looks ready to pelt my brother with the contents of her purse. There's probably a canister of pepper spray in there.

"We have unprotected sex," Connor announces.

Rose points at me at this. *Fuck.* "You better be wearing a condom with her."

My face hardens. I already told her I'd be safe with Daisy. They all need to chill the fuck out. "That's none of your fucking business, Rose."

Daisy ends up saying it anyway, just to appease her sister. "I'm on birth control."

"So was I," Rose snaps. "And I *never* missed a day." She prides herself on this fact.

"Then what the fuck happened?" I ask, extending my arm in confusion.

"Birth control is only ninety-nine percent effective," Connor says. "We're, of course, in the one-percent."

Rose smacks him on the arm for that comment, and he grabs her wrist and kisses her deeply. She melts. I stop fucking watching.

And then I meet eyes with my brother, with Lo. He has his arm wrapped around Lily, and even with the news, he looks more at peace now, in this moment, than he did three days ago.

"So you know French," he says to me.

"Yeah, I know French."

Connor holds Rose's hand on the table, and he nods to me. "Where'd you learn?"

"Tutors as a kid, like you and Rose."

"I taught myself, actually," Connor says with a million-dollar grin.

Lo claps slowly. "Congratulations, love."

Connor only smiles wider, and I share it as well, surprisingly.

Lily perks up. "I've learned some French too." She clears her throat. I think we're all laughing internally, not at her, just fucking with her.

She's goofy as hell. In a more American accent, she says, "Comment allez-vous?" *How are you?*

Connor replies with a genuine smile, "Je ne pourrais pas être plus heureux." *I couldn't be happier.*

Rose relaxes into Connor's body. And Lily looks really fucking confused. He's already lost her.

Daisy slides her misshapen pumpkin napkin over to me. I squeeze her hand beneath the table. And for a brief second, I think about after California, after my climb. Back in Philly. Her parents... it doesn't seem like they should be a big roadblock. I'm twenty-five. But your family doesn't just leave when you become an adult. They're a part of you forever.

I add to the whole table, "Je serais génial, mais je sais ce qui me fait toujours obstacle." *I would be great, but I know what still stands in my way.*

Lo claps again. "Color me impressed," he tells me. He turns to Lily. "You're almost fluent, love."

She punches him in the chest, and he mock winces, acting like it hurt. They're both smiling.

My eyes flicker up to Connor, who stares at me with understanding and more compassion.

He says, "Tout ira bien, mon ami." *Everything will be fine, my friend.*

Connor has said that he doesn't believe in magic, but his words hold a possession all on their own, filling me with serenity, a temporary calmness, that I am grateful to have before my climb.

Everything will be fine, my friend.

I nod a couple times.

Everything will be fine.

< 52 >

Daisy Calloway

California.

We've made it. The national park is beautiful, and I'd revel in the atmosphere of Yosemite on any other day, but it's hard when we're in the brush, a giant rock looming one hundred feet in front of us. El Capitan is larger than Devils Tower. More ominous. But it does have a kinder name.

The sun isn't even out yet. It's 5 a.m. and Ryke plans to start climbing in the dark with a headlamp. He wants to climb three routes in under twenty-four hours. It's going to take endurance, strength and a dose of luck. It's that luck part that I'm worried about. Everything else—I know he'll ace.

Ryke talks to a park ranger at the base of El Capitan, nodding a few times. He ties his bag of chalk around his waist.

I pluck yellow weedy flowers by my feet in the brush, twisting the stems to make a crown. Every time I look up at Ryke, my heart thuds. I've never been this anxious for someone else before.

Rose slaps her arm and curses out the mosquitos. She sits on a wooden bench behind me.

"I told you not to wear perfume, darling," Connor says casually, sitting beside her.

Rose gives him a look. "I'm not going to sacrifice smelling good for stupid flies." She swats another away.

"You smell good without it."

She narrows her eyes. "It's Chanel. If I don't wear it, I feel like half of myself is missing."

Lo sits on top of a picnic table beside the bench, Lily's head on his lap as she sleeps. "That's because you mask your bitch scent," he says. "And your soul leaves when it realizes it's inhabited the wrong host."

"And I'm sure your brain cells fried coming up with that insult," she refutes.

Before Lo can retort, other voices shout over him. "Daisy, are you and Ryke together?!"

"Daisy, just one question!"

"Are you scared about Ryke's climb?!"

"Hey," Lo snaps at the seven or eight reporters congregated about twenty feet behind us, camera crews in place, lenses pointed at us and Ryke. "Calm down. We have twenty-four hours and I personally don't want to go deaf by the end of this."

I stand in front of the wooden benches and picnic tables, so I turn my head to see Lily awakening from all the commotion.

"Did he fall?" she asks in alarm, her eyes snapping open.

"No, love. He's okay."

She exhales loudly. "Okay, good."

A lump lodges in my throat. I'm not the only one concerned today.

The cameramen start flashing pictures at me, catching my face. When we left Nevada, word circulated about Ryke's solo climb. Apparently he had to register with the state parks, and those documents leaked to the press.

I think Ryke would be more nervous about the media being so close to us today if it wasn't for our team of security drawing a line between the cameras and our benches. So at least we can pretend to ignore them. Mikey is here, shaking his head at a couple of the guys who shout questions out to me.

It's still early in the morning, so we expect a lot more people to show up, probably some fans too.

My father also sent a note with Mikey:

We need to talk about Ryke.
Love, Dad

Having my parents find out about the relationship from a tabloid was not ideal, but it was the risk we both chose to take.

And I only received one text from my mom, not even a phone call.

I'm interviewing the best plastic surgeons in the city. You'll be okay. — Mom

I asked Connor to send out a tweet (he's the only one with a Twitter account) to tell people what happened. The rumors from the leaked photograph were horrendous. They ranged from a knife fight to rape. And then both.

Connor's tweet set everyone straight.

@ConnorCobalt: Daisy is fine. Her scar is from the Paris Rugby riot. Thanks for all the well wishes.

And of course he had to add a second tweet.

@ConnorCobalt: Apparently, I need to clarify for some of you. No. She was not raped afterwards.

He told me that the second tweet was for the media sites that love to stir stories out of nothing. I appreciated it, especially since it meant that I didn't have to go on any talk shows or phone into a radio to explain the situation.

When the park ranger leaves, Ryke glances back at us, and he actually walks over. My heart rises to my throat, but his eyes meet mine for a brief second or two before they pin on everyone behind me. And then he just treks right on past.

Okay...

"You realize how stupid this is, right?" Lo asks him, forearms on his knees, hands clasped. He has his feet on the picnic table bench like Lily.

Ryke just smiles. "I love you too."

And then surprisingly Lo rises off the table and hops down. He hugs Ryke and pats his back. "Don't die on me, okay?"

"I don't plan on it," Ryke says.

That one fight in Utah—with the red rock and dirt swirling—has cleared the air between them. Whatever bad blood they had between each other was left in that state, and I hope it won't ever return.

They split apart, and Ryke faces Lily now. She jumps off the picnic table quickly and flings her arms around him. Then she pulls away and presses a sticker on his shirt. "It's Spider-Man. For good luck."

"Thanks, Lily." I can't see his smile this time, just his back. But I'm sure he's smiling because Lily's eyes are flooded with emotion.

I shift my weight from one foot to the other, just watching him go down the line.

Rose and Connor stay seated. My sister has on designer sunglasses even though the sun has yet to rise, and Connor is wearing an expensive suit. They do not fit in. But they don't care much.

Ryke holds out his hands. "Please, don't stand up for me."

"I'll hug you when you come back down," Rose tells him in her clipped voice. "It'll give you something to look forward to." She swats another invisible fly out of her face.

Ryke nods and looks to Connor. "And you?"

"You don't need my luck." His words are velvety smooth, like he's telling Ryke he has all the confidence in the world in him.

Ryke nods again. "Thanks guys. For being here. See you on the other side." He starts walking back, and I think he's going to stop in front of me, for a private moment. But he just keeps on hiking towards the rock face.

I don't think twice. I sprint after him, taking off. No one calls me back to the tables.

No one reprimands me for following a boy much older than me.

No one says to stop.

I go with freedom in my chest, freedom in my heart. And I block his path with my body, holding my hands out.

Ryke's dark features brighten as soon as he sees me. His lips rise far beyond an almost-smile. He notices the flower crown still in my clutch, and he steals it from my hand. I watch as he sets it atop my blonde locks, some strands painted with color.

"I was waiting for the sun to chase me," he breathes, drawing me to his chest. In one swift movement, my lips are on his. The world is spinning. He kisses me like this is the moment he's envisioned all his life. Like this is heaven on Earth.

For me, it is. A blissful moment before something that could be the end. The rush before the fear. He whispers, "I fucking love you."

I smile, my lips tingling. "Guess what?"

"What?"

"I love you more than chocolate cake."

He kisses my head, and his mouth returns to mine, his tongue sliding sensually, lasting and perfect. Then he flips off the cameras, the *click click click* in the background like buzzing insects.

When our lips break away, he just stares at me, his eyes grazing over my face, spending an extra moment on my hair and the crown of flowers. I can tell he's engraining this image in his head. In case he falls.

"Don't miss me too much, Calloway," he says. And then he starts to drift back towards the rock, his hand leaving mine.

This is it.

I watch Ryke Meadows climb.

< 53 >

Ryke Meadows

Connor may hate Confucius but there's something he said that I never challenge. "It does not matter how slowly you go as long as you do not stop."

El Capitan looms before me. All those fears loom behind.

It's just me and the ascent.

Years of hard work and labor coming full circle to this one day. And I'm fucking ready.

I take a deep breath, blink one last time.

And I ascend towards the summit.

< 54 >

Ryke Meadows

"Man, I wish I could've been there," Sully says, my cell pressed to my ear while I walk into the private airport with my brother, Lily, Connor, Rose, and of course Daisy. "The pictures online are insane. Those photographers caught some awesome shots of you on the Northwest Face of Half Dome."

"I haven't seen them yet," I admit.

"Not like you need to. You lived it, man," Sully says.

I lived it. I didn't beat any fucking records. I just set my own, and I completed a challenge that seemed impossible in my teens. I can't adequately express what this feels like. When I dropped on the ground, I was so fucking exhausted but so fucking overwhelmed with joy.

I did it. I free-solo climbed the Yosemite Triple Crown. 19 hours. A goal for me. Not for anyone else.

"How's Venezuela?" I ask him.

"Hot and humid," he says. "But the routes on Mount Roraima are incredible, and the whole place feels spiritual—hard to explain in words. You'd love it here though. I'd ask you to come join me, but… you know." I hear him smiling on the other end.

"Sorry, Sul. Can't read your fucking mind." But I have a feeling he's talking about Daisy. I hold her hand as we walk through the quiet airport, heading to our gate where our private plane is supposed to be waiting to fly us to Philly.

"You're probably sore as hell."

I am. My muscles fucking scream even as I keep stride with Lily and Lo's leisurely pace. "That's not what you were about to fucking say."

"Please, *please* invite me to the wedding." I picture his smile reaching the ends of his scraggily red hair.

I roll my eyes. "Don't get ahead of yourself."

"I just want you to know that I called it. I'm like a relationship whisperer." He laughs at his own joke, which makes me fucking smile. "Anyway, that picture of you two outside of Devils Tower is seriously becoming iconic. It's everywhere. Even in a Venezuelan newspaper."

"Yeah, someone else told me the picture is pretty popular." A friend from college texted me the photo, which landed on the cover of *Time* magazine. It's famous because they're pairing it with the Paris riot, even though it was taken a while after that. But after the press learned that's how she got hurt, Daisy's scar has become a symbol of what happened that night. People like to hold onto the good in the wake of the bad. And in the photo, she's on my shoulders, kissing me, smiling, my fingers stained with colors. It looks like a fairytale, something setup. But it was completely candid—captured by a hiker's cellphone who recognized us.

I care less about being an international icon and more that the coverage may help Daisy accept this new, jarring change in her features. She has barely looked in any mirrors since the hospital, and I think confronting the permanent reality of what's happened may be hard on her. She's been avoiding those feelings like she usually does.

"Is she around?" Sul asks. "Let me talk to the girl. She probably misses me."

"She's right here." I pass the phone to Daisy. "Sully wants to talk your fucking ear off."

She brightens, taking my cell.

"Fucking cut him off if he starts any story with *when we were twelve*." He loves to talk about how I streaked at night during summer camp and did a backflip into the lake off a rock. I don't find the story as entertaining because I snuck in a flask of cheap vodka that year. I was wasted. And a fucking idiot.

But I'd still do all of that stuff now, minus the booze.

Daisy puts the phone to her ear. "Hey, Sully." She smiles wider. "I did massage his ass, thanks for asking."

I snatch the phone back from her, and Sully is cracking up laughing on the other end. "Please have children," he tells me, not able to stop cackling. "I have to see if they'd be as fun as her or as moody as you."

"Fuck off," I tell him lightly.

"Hugs and kisses from Venezuela. See you in a few months? Keep in touch."

"Yeah," I say. We hang up at the same time, and I watch Lo carry Lily on his back. It's early this morning, so I'm not surprised, but she has been more tired recently. She presses her head on his shoulder, sleeping.

"What happened when you were twelve?" Daisy asks, lacing her fingers with mine.

Rose and Connor lead the pack with a flight attendant, opening the door to our gate. They walk down the stairs to the runway, where the private plane waits for us. Daisy and I let Lo catch up so we'll be last out.

"I fucking streaked around my summer camp at night," I tell her.

She laughs. "No way. I did the same thing when I was fourteen." She gasps. "It's like we were always meant to be."

I run my hand through her hair and then kiss her forehead. If we are supposed to be together, then why does going home seem like returning to a black fucking storm?

Lo passes us and whispers, so as not to wake Lily, "Hey, you two, your PDA is scaring the little children."

"You mean you?" I retort, following him close behind as he heads down the stairs to outside.

"I mean anyone who was once a child," Lo says like a smartass. He smiles bitterly, and then I almost bump into Connor's back who's standing still on the cement.

"What's the fucking hold up?" I ask. The plane is here, but it's not Connor's private jet parked ahead of us, a thick layer of smog clouding the sky.

My face falls.

I recognize the massive white Boeing 787, ostentatious, in your fucking face.

Just like my father.

He emerges down the stairs of the plane, buttoning his black suit jacket, his dark brown hair starting to gray on the sides.

The flight attendant says, "Mr. Hale's plane arrived an hour ago. Once the gas tanks are filled, we'll be off."

Rose is texting like crazy, and Connor has his hand on the small of her back. He gives the flight attendant a genial smile. "Will Mr. Hale be flying to Philadelphia with us then?"

She nods. "They came to pick you up."

They?

And right behind Jonathan, another man descends the stairs, tall and confident and entitled. It's my father's best friend, his hair lighter brown, in his fifties, a less hard and severe face than my dad's.

It's Daisy's father. My stomach sinks. *Fuck me.* I've never seen Greg Calloway do anything other than smile and shake hands, but worry blankets his face, looking more paternal and more protective than I've known him to be. It's the look that Connor says he wears frequently. I just haven't been around him long enough to see it.

Greg's gaze lands on Daisy immediately, but he stays beside the plane, waiting for us to approach like my dad.

I didn't think it could get worse, but one more fucking person appears through the doorway, heading down the stairs in heels, a strand of pearls around her neck, her brown hair in a bun.

Samantha Calloway.

Her eyes are tight with concern like Greg's, and her gaze fixes to her youngest daughter. Samantha places one palm to her chest, as though swept up in emotion upon seeing Daisy. Knowing she's safe. But then her eyes focus on me.

And she glares.

"Shit," Lo says under his breath.

We're about to be stuck on a plane for five hours with our father and the girls' parents.

With no way to escape.

This is going to be a fucking nightmare.

< 55 >

Daisy Calloway

My mom holds my hands while I sit with her on the long cream couch that spans the back cabin, another leather couch on the other wall, a glass coffee table in between. It's like we're in a compact presidential living room, not flying above the clouds.

"You should have called me the *moment* you woke up in the hospital," she says, throttling my hands for the fourth time with worry. And then her eyes pin to Rose on the other couch, who looks irritable. "And don't get me started on you."

"Mother, I—"

"You knew Daisy was in the riot, and you didn't tell me."

"There was a lot going on," Rose says. She hasn't announced the pregnancy to our parents yet, and I know Connor wants to do it soon. "She was in good hands."

"I'm *her* mother. When you have kids, you'll realize what it feels like—hearing that one of your children is hurt *weeks* after it happens…" She shakes her head.

Rose purses her lips. "That must be why you were so concerned about Lily when you heard she was sick."

Our mom inhales, and I think she's going to say: *Lily brought that upon herself. An addiction isn't a disease.* But instead she goes with, "Let's not get into that, Rose."

Lily is sleeping in one of the bedrooms. I think she's hiding from our mom, who likes to ignore Lily when she's in close vicinity. Lo is with her, so it's not like she's all alone in there.

I glance back at the door to the front cabin. It's the cigar club area with chairs and a flat-screen television. I smelled the cigar smoke the moment I walked into the plane, embedded in the cream leather.

Ryke is in there.

Right through those doors.

With my father. And his father. And Connor. Though I'm not sure Connor can be much of a peacemaker in that situation.

It sounds fairly awkward and uncomfortable. I want to go save him from my dad, but something tells me that he'd find a way to talk to Ryke no matter what.

My mom rotates back to me, and her eyes fall to my graphic T-shirt that says: *Sorry, I only date boys with tattoos.* I'm *not* sorry about the shirt. I like it. And so I'm wearing it, regardless if she finds it distasteful or not.

Her fingers circle her pearls unconsciously, but she doesn't ask me about Ryke. "I've scheduled a doctor's appointment for you when we arrive home. The plastic surgeon is going to take a look at your cheek." Her fingers fall from her pearls, and she rubs my hand again. "What pain medication are you on?"

I shake my head. "I'm out."

"We'll get you more."

"No, it doesn't hurt. It's fine." If I touch my cheek, I can feel the raised wound, slightly puffy, descending from my temple, across my cheek, to my jaw. Everyone sees it but me. So it's hard to confront the issue head-on when I'm not staring at it.

"You were so lucky," my mom says. "You could have lost your eye. It could have cut through your lip." She shakes her head at those brutal images. "The doctor will smooth out the scar, and then I'll talk to your agency—"

"What?" I cut her off. I was willing to go to a doctor and get the scar looked at, but I can't stomach going back to modeling. No one will hire me anyway.

"You're beautiful, Daisy," she says, squeezing my hands. "They'll take you back."

"No they won't, Mom." I need her to accept this failure and move on, so I can too.

"How is this any different than having a uni-brow or gap-teeth?"

"It just is. I already told you. I don't want to model, and it has nothing to do with my face." I tried to explain my decision on the phone, right after I left the hospital. And she hung up on me. Now she has no phone to cut me off with. She has nowhere to go.

I am so resolute and adamant about my choices. I'm no longer scared to express myself. She can't stifle my voice or take my opinions away. I matter.

My mom just keeps shaking her head. "We'll talk about this later. You've been through a lot." She pats my leg.

"I've thought about it for *years*," I tell her.

She actually stays quiet and just listens.

I let out a breath. "I've only ever wanted to make you happy, but in doing so, I've become so, so depressed, Mom." I shake my head as tears brim. "I've spent so long pleasing you that I haven't even found my own dreams."

My mom swallows hard and says, "Why haven't you told me this sooner? We could have found something else for you to do."

"I tried a couple times," I say. "You wouldn't listen."

My mom processes this. She doesn't handle change well, but these facts glass her eyes. "I guess it makes this easier." Her gaze lands on my scar. "You need to start looking at colleges then. You'll be a semester behind…"

"I'm not going to college," I say, adamant. "I have a lot of money saved from modeling, and I know this is going to hurt you…" I take another deep breath. "…but I don't need your input on what I should do in the future. I have to discover that myself."

My mom looks *pissed.* "You're only eighteen, Daisy."

"Mom," I say. "You have to let me go. I promise, I'll be okay."

"I don't understand. I let you get your own apartment. You're off on your own—"

"I'm not saying goodbye to you," I cut her off like she's done to me so many times in my life. As shitty as it seems—it feels damn good. "I just need to be the one to decide the direction of my life. That's all." I don't know what I want to do, but I do know that I have years to figure it out. And that freedom builds my confidence and gives me the wings that I use to fly right on out of this nest.

She inhales. "And you won't go to college?"

"No."

She stares at me for a while and says, "You've always been the most scatterbrained of the girls. I guess I shouldn't be surprised." Her eyes narrow a little though. I guess that's the best I'm going to get. It's good enough for me.

And then she scrutinizes my hair, combing her fingers through the shorter, badly hacked strands with a crinkled nose. "We can get you some extensions and take out this color… Did you cut this yourself? It's god-awful." She takes out her phone and makes a note to call the salon. Just like that, she acts like I didn't make a pledge, but I won't ever back away from it. Even if she chooses to forget or feign confusion. I'll remind her.

"I love it," I say.

"Funny," she says, typing on her phone.

"No, I do," I tell her seriously. "I love that it's not perfect, and I like the highlights. I'm not changing it." I glance at Rose, and she wears a proud smile.

"You can't like this," she says. "It's ugly."

Rose butts in. "It's her taste."

"Well she has bad taste," she snaps. "And I'm trying to help her see that."

Rose groans. "Mother, why do you have to be so—"

"Because I want what's best for my girls," she retorts. Her eyes land on me. "I don't know what's gotten into you. You always liked your hair before."

"I never did," I say.

She glares. "It's Ryke, isn't it? You're changing because of a boy."

"Ryke never told me how to cut my hair or what color to make it. He's only ever told me to think for myself."

I catch her eyes flickering to the door of the front cabin, where Ryke lies. She glares at it like it accosted her somehow. She blames him for my thoughts and feelings and probably my sudden career change.

"Is he telling you to push me out of your life?" she asks.

"Mom, *no*. He's never been like that."

"He doesn't like me," she says. "I wouldn't be surprised if he's telling you all of these things—"

"Listen to me," I plead. "He's *not* saying a word about you. I love you, Mom, and he respects that."

She shakes her head, disbelieving. She doesn't even need to add the next line for me to sense it, but she does anyway. "You would have never gotten hurt if Ryke didn't follow you to Paris." She shakes her head again and again.

The sad thing, there is some truth to that.

I would have never gone to the pub to retrieve Lo if Ryke didn't show up.

We would have never been stuck in that riot.

But without that violent wake-up call, I would have never realized how much I needed to voice my opinions. Even if it hurt my mom. Even if it pissed her off. All of this had to be said.

For me.

No one else.

You are your own anchor. Do you want to keep burning or are you going to let yourself rise?

No more dragging myself down.

I'm finally ready to rise.

< 56 >

Ryke Meadows

I'm in a room alone with my fucking father, my girlfriend's dad and Connor. Right when I stepped onto the plane, Greg put his hand on my shoulder and said, "We need to talk."

I thought he was reserving that talk with Daisy, but I'm sure he'll have another one with her later, just to confirm that I didn't sleep with her when she was fifteen.

He steered me into the front cabin and pushed me onto a cream leather recliner.

My sore muscles tense the longer I'm in a room with the fucking devil and his sidekick. That devil, by the way, has already poured his second glass of whiskey: straight, one ice cube. By the window, he takes big sips, sitting on a chair next to Connor, watching Greg face me in his own seat.

"I don't even know where to start," Greg admits, his green eyes zeroed in on me like a fucking target.

I rub the back of my neck and say, "You can ask me anything." I can't look at my father, only ten feet away, right fucking there. I haven't been this close to him in years.

"I can think of a hundred places to start," my dad pipes in, swishing his glass of whiskey. Instead of meeting my father's eyes, I look at Connor beside him, his expression unreadable, drinking red wine. He easily fits among these men who are twice his age, and Connor exudes far more fucking confidence than either of them.

I'm no longer outdoors. I'm no longer in my element. I've entered Connor's fucking realm, and I wonder if he's mentally snapshotting this picture of me, here. Like I did to him back in Tennessee.

Greg's eyes never leave mine. "I have this, Jonathan." His jaw clenches once, and he says, "I let you chaperone my daughter on her sweet sixteen trip." His voice shakes, seething. "I put my trust in you, and you spat at me."

I don't interrupt him. I breathe through my nose, trying not to get defensive.

"I want to know," Greg says, clutching his knees, "if you've been avoiding me for the past two and a half years because you knew what you were doing was wrong."

"No," I say, my chest inflating with these raw emotions.

"Speak up, Ryke," my father says from the window. "And he deserves more than a half-hearted *no* from you."

I run my hand through my hair. That movement stretches my sore deltoids and biceps, and I stifle a fucking grimace. I wonder if it looks like I'm pissed at Greg.

I know I'm hard to read. I know the only thing people see is this fucking black expression.

Truth is, I care what he thinks of me. Maybe a year ago I'd say *believe what you want. I don't give a fuck.* But I don't want Daisy to have to choose between me and her parents. I don't want this fucking headache for her. I'm trying to do what's right.

"I never thought being her friend was fucking wrong," I start. "So no, I never intentionally avoided you because of Daisy." *I avoided you because you were friends with my father, who I never wanted to see.*

I can tell Greg is fuming inside. He breathes heavily. "Let's cut the bullshit. You were more than just her friend."

I'm too exhausted to lean forward and start shouting. Which may be a fucking good thing. "No, I wasn't. I never kissed her until Paris," I tell him the truth.

Greg is still on the offensive. "Help me to believe you, Ryke. I work eighty hours a week. I don't have time to hover over my daughter, but I have been very aware of how much time she's spent with you. And I've been very aware of how much she's fallen for you."

"Then why not tell her to get the fuck away from me?" I ask, extending my arms. "If you thought I was such a bad influence, then why let her hang around me for so fucking long?"

He lets out a tight breath. "Samantha didn't care for you, but I remembered you as a young boy. You were tough and strong, and you didn't take shit from anyone, not even Jonathan."

My dad smiles at that and raises his drink. His eyes meet mine, and I see a glimmer of fucking pride. That I'm strong like him.

My stomach roils.

"Out of my four daughters, Daisy is the most reckless. She never sits still. Even as a child, she always found a way outside when her mother or nannies weren't looking. And you came into her life around the same time that our family became a public spectacle."

I read into the rest. "You liked that I could keep up with her," I realize. "You wanted me to be her fucking bodyguard, and you never thought I would be stupid enough to cross that line." No matter how hard Daisy flirted, no matter how much she teased me, he believed I would never take her shit. I'd shut her down every time.

I didn't.

I couldn't.

Because I fell in love with her.

He nods once. "All this time I'd been worried that you'd lead her on and she'd be crushed from the rejection, but I never actually thought you'd get with her." He lets out a short breath. "It was naïve of me."

I shake my head. How do I change how he sees me? *I don't know. I don't fucking know.* I comb my hand through my hair again, a weight on my chest. "I'm not like her ex-boyfriends," I say. "I'm not in it for…" *Fuck.* I can't end that thought.

Greg looks just as uncomfortable.

"The sex," my father finishes for me. "No need to beat around the proverbial bush."

Greg rolls his eyes. "You don't have any daughters, Jonathan."

"Thank God for that."

Connor looks amused by the whole conversation. He leans back and sips his wine.

Greg has simmered down some, but his shoulders still stay locked and rigid.

"Let me help you out, Greg," my dad says. "It'll be easier for me to ask the harder questions." *No. Fuck no.* Still, I don't shoot to my feet. I stayed glued to this fucking chair, my eyes flickering to an ash tray on the glass end table. Avoiding my dad's gaze for another moment. The plane shakes as we fly through a cloud.

My dad rises and holds onto the back of Greg's chair, the turbulence rough. "Did you ever think about Daisy sexually when she was fifteen?" my father starts.

My chest inflates with anger again. "Fuck off."

"I'll take that exceedingly rude and annoying answer as a yes," my dad says, sipping his whiskey.

I glare. "*No.* I had no intention of…" I trail off and glance at Greg.

"Act like her father isn't in the room," my dad says.

That's fucking impossible. He's four feet away from me. "Look," I say, "Daisy is gorgeous, but I tried not to think of her like that."

"Tried? Did you fail?" he asks.

"Why are you prosecuting me like a fucking lawyer, Dad?" I retort.

His eyebrows rise in genuine shock. "So you still consider me your father? That's funny *considering* you've returned only one of my calls in a year." Before I tell him to fuck off again, he asks, "Did you masturbate to her image or likeness?"

"No," I growl. *A few times. Once recently. She was eighteen already.* A part of me will always feel guilty for it.

"That's enough, Jonathan," Greg says. His eyes actually soften on me, noticing how worked up I'm getting. I've balled one of my hands into a fist, and a bitter, nasty taste rises in my mouth.

Greg asks, "What's your longest relationship, Ryke?"

"A few months, maybe four."

Greg sighs. "Okay, here's where I stand. I believe that you weren't with my daughter until Paris, but that doesn't mean I approve of you with her. You're still twenty-five, and maybe in ten years the age difference won't seem as significant, but what you've just said makes me think you'll last three months. You say you're not in it for the sex, but I'm not *that* naïve." He pauses and adds, "She's given you her heart, and if you're going to give her anything less than that, then you need to end this right now. Understand?"

I nod a couple times. I can't just leave it like this. I dig inside my soul, trying to produce something more. "I hope," I say, meeting Greg's gaze, "that one day you'll be able to see how much I love your daughter."

"If you stay with her long enough, I just might."

It's definitely better than where we started. He reaches out to shake my hand.

It's a kind offer, one that I won't fucking reject.

I'm going to build a relationship with her father, even if it means having to get closer to mine. It's a sacrifice I am willing to make a thousand times over.

I'd fucking call that love.

< 57 >

Daisy Calloway

How I ended up in the back cabin with all the couches, alone with Lo and his father, I have no idea. We have two hours left of the flight, and my mom wanted to go talk to my dad, and everyone kind of shuffled around. I think Rose is announcing her pregnancy to our parents.

Jonathan pours a glass of whiskey and sits back next to Lo while I sprawl out on the other couch, a monogrammed burgundy blanket covering my legs. *HALE* in black lettering. I braid my hair for the twentieth time, bored and anxious.

I learned that my dad wants to "get to know" Ryke. Jonathan mentioned that, so my dad made him stay up front with everyone else.

I'd join them, but my mom is in there.

So here I remain.

Jonathan looks to his son. "You need to send me your sales report for Halway Comics by next weekend. I need to know if you're driving the fucking thing into the ground."

"It's been slow," Lo says. "I took a month off for the road trip."

"That's your goddamn fault," he refutes. "You're running a business now. You can't afford to take month-long vacations."

"Connor took the same time off," Lo defends.

"And he's running a multi-billion dollar company with a staff of thousands. You don't even have an assistant. Christ, you don't even have an *annoying* assistant, the kind that screws up coffee orders and likes to share personal life stories that you don't give a fuck about."

This is why Lo doesn't come to Sunday family luncheons with Lily. He gets berated and my sister either gets ignored or scolded. I don't blame them for skipping.

"It's called *initiative*," Jonathan says after he takes a pretty giant swig of whiskey, without grimacing. And then his eyes fix on me, realizing that I've been watching. He stands. "Daisy—I think you and I should have a talk." He sits on the couch next to me. "Loren, can you give us a minute?"

Lo frowns deeply. "Why do you need to talk to her?"

I've never had a conversation alone with Jonathan Hale. I don't think I ever needed to.

"She's dating my son."

Lo doesn't move. He's twenty-four and wears anger like a weapon. It almost makes me shrink back, but he's on my side of things. If anything, I should be recoiling from Jonathan, right?

"I'd like to talk to her alone," Jonathan repeats.

I'm confused. I don't know what to do because my boyfriend doesn't talk to his father, so even entertaining the idea of listening to Jonathan kind of feels like a betrayal. Should I cold-shoulder Jonathan too? In solidarity? I don't know how this works.

These are deep waters that I actually need help swimming in.

"I'm not leaving her alone with you," Lo snaps.

"Stop being a little—"

"If Ryke found out that you talked to her in private, he'd kill you. So think of it as me doing you a favor." Lo crosses his arms.

Jonathan rolls his eyes and then focuses his attention back on me. I sit up and tuck my legs to my chest. His eyes fall to the saying on my shirt, and his lips rise in amusement. "How long have you and Ryke been dating?"

"A little over a month."

I have to remind myself that I've known Jonathan since I was a little girl. He's even Poppy's godfather.

Jonathan tilts his head at me. "Your father is warming up to that timeframe, but your mother seems to think you've had a relationship long before that."

I'm not surprised that she believes that. The tabloids have been throwing out those rumors for a while. "She's wrong. Ryke wouldn't ever be with someone underage." Even me.

"I know," Jonathan says, surprising me. "Ryke's a lot of things: stubborn, hardheaded, foul-mouthed." He stares at his glass. "But he's made it clear that he'll never follow in my footsteps." He washes back the liquor.

Lo tenses on the couch, and his eyes briefly flicker to me. I know the truth, what Jonathan is talking about, like the rest of my family, but it's different airing it out like this.

Twenty-four years ago, Jonathan had an affair with an underage girl. Lo's mom.

The press doesn't even know the identity of Lo's mother. It's what's kept Jonathan out of jail.

"Is that all you wanted to ask?" I wonder. "Whether or not Ryke was with me before I turned eighteen?"

"That and I wanted to know if you could talk to Ryke for me. I'd like to have dinner with him next weekend, catch up. You're welcome to come too. The more the merrier." He almost takes another sip of his drink, but he realizes his glass is empty. But he doesn't stand to refill it again.

I glance at Lo. I don't know what to say.

Lo suddenly rises from the other couch. "Dad, I'd like to talk to you alone."

"Well we all can't have what we want, can we? I said I'd like to talk to Daisy alone, and you mouthed off to me. So I will kindly do the same to you. Cheers." He raises his empty glass.

My heart thuds. I've never, in my life, been in a room alone with the two of them. And from what I've heard, it can get nasty.

Lo turns his head, his eyes hitting mine. "Give us a minute, Daisy."

I stand to leave, but Jonathan destroys my chance to escape. "Don't be ridiculous, stay. My son doesn't dictate when I speak to people."

I freeze.

Lo glowers. "I know what you're doing. And it's not going to work, so just stop."

Jonathan raises his brows and leans back against the couch, his arms outstretching over the top. He waves him on. "Please, Loren, tell me what I'm doing. *Enlighten* me, since you think I'm so dimwitted."

Lo grinds his teeth.

Jonathan just smiles and says, "I'm waiting."

"You can't use her to get to him," Lo retorts. "Just leave her alone."

"Is that it?" Jonathan asks.

Lo stays quiet.

His dad straightens up on the seat. "Let me educate you, Loren," he says, "when there are paths to be taken to achieve a goal, real men don't stare at them with their cock in their hands. They take the goddamn path whether it fucking works or not." He points at him with his finger. "And I will do *everything* I possibly can to get my son back, just as I would do for you."

The first half of that speech makes me cringe, and the second makes me reevaluate the first half. Now I can see why it's confusing having him as a father. I don't know whether to run away or stay and hear him out.

Lo looks at me again. "Go, Daisy."

"*Stay,*" Jonathan snaps, his voice harsher after all the booze. His gaze heats on Lo. "You're a goddamn terrible listener."

"You know what, so are you," Lo sneers. "Because if you'd listen to anything I've been telling you or what Ryke has said, you'd know that he'll hate you if you bring her into this shit. You can't be forgiven for that. So I'm helping *you*. Open your goddamn ears." He turns around and grabs my wrist, tugging me into one of the plane's bedrooms.

"Loren!" Jonathan yells, but Lo just shuts the door and locks it—truly closing his father out.

It makes me nervous that he'd switch the lock—that somewhere, he'd fear his dad rushing in and doing what? Cold blows through me, and I shiver.

Lo stares down at me and says, "This is about the hundredth reason why I don't want you dating my older brother."

"I'll be able to handle it," I say. "It's not like my parents make Ryke feel warm and welcome."

Lo shakes his head. "Greg's third-degree and my father's are not even comparable, so don't try."

I realize this is the first moment I've been alone with Lo since he learned about my relationship with Ryke. "I love him, you know? I've been with a lot of awful guys, and he's the only one that's ever made me happy."

Lo stares at me for a long moment and then a knock on the door makes me flinch back. The knob jiggles. We both stiffen, and then a rough voice calls through the wood, "Fucking let me in, Lo."

I relax as Lo unlocks the door, and Ryke scans his brother's features quickly before turning to me. I hear the door shut, and Ryke hugs me to his chest immediately, his hand on the top of my head.

"Was she left alone with him?" Ryke asks Lo.

"No, I was there."

"Just you two?"

"Yeah, it was fine," Lo says. "Nothing happened."

"Then why the fuck did I hear Dad scream your name at the top of his lungs?"

I look up and Ryke's dark gaze focuses on his brother, but he keeps holding me like if he lets go something bad may happen.

"We had a disagreement," Lo says, sitting on the edge of the bed. He rubs his eyes like he's just tired from everything.

"About Daisy?" Ryke frowns. "Or about me?"

"Both."

Ryke's eyes flash murderously. "He needs to leave her out of our family shit."

"You need to talk to him or else he's going to bring her in it."

"*Fuck*," Ryke curses. He lets out a deep breath and then he looks down at me. "You okay?"

I nod. "Yeah." I give him a smile. "I get all of you, right? This is just another part."

"This isn't a fucking part I wanted to give you, ever."

"Something we agree on," Lo chimes in with a half-smile. And then all of a sudden, a body stirs underneath a mass of pillows and blankets. Lo turns his head and pats what I guess are feet.

Lily sits up like she rose from the dead, rubbing her eyes and stretching. The way Lo is watching her—it's like he's witnessing daylight for the first time. It makes me smile because their love is so transparent, and it immediately slices through any awkward tension that clung to the air.

She sees us and smiles shyly. "Oh hey. What'd I miss?"

"I talked to Ryke's dad," I tell her.

Her eyes bug out. "Whaaa…"

"It was interesting," I say with a small shrug.

"What a weird day," Lily says. I think that defines the whole situation very nicely. She whispers in Lo's ear, and he nods, whispering back, and then they both turn to look at me, their expressions morphing into something serious and real. Lo nods and says, "Welcome to the family."

The words hit me straight in the heart. For so long I considered Lo a part of *my* family; even though he had his dad, even though he's a Hale, he always felt like an extension of Lily. A Calloway.

Now I'm starting to think that maybe all this time it's been the other way around, and I've just been too narrow-sighted to see it. Lily's always been a part of *his* family.

The Hales.

They're kind of fucked up.

< 58 >

Ryke Meadows

We survived the fucking plane ride. It's another accomplishment that I can tack on with my climb—even if Samantha Calloway can't look me in the eyes.

Behind me, Daisy playfully bites my shoulder, climbing down the plane's stairs, straight onto the private runway. We're the last off.

I glance back at her, and she's smiling so fucking bright that it's hard not to share it.

"You look happy," I say.

"I'm not just happy," she tells me. "I'm *fucking* happy."

I kiss the top of her head and step onto the cement. The overcast sky darkens the airport. We follow our parents and our friends towards two parked black Escalades and one limo. Nola, the Calloway's driver, opens the Escalade's door.

"Congratulations again, Rose," Samantha says, kissing her daughter's cheeks. "If Connor's too busy to go to any of your doctor's appointments, you call me. I'll be there."

Rose gives her a tight smile, which is polite for Rose's fucking standards. And then her mom disappears inside the Escalade.

Greg gives Connor a hug before he climbs into the car behind Samantha. They leave first, and Connor says to Rose, "I'm not missing your doctor's appointments."

"Thank God." She lets out a breath.

"Thank *me*, darling."

She glares at him, and he stares at her like he'd enjoy taking her in his limo and fucking her hard.

I just shake my head and then turn to my brother. "Daisy and I are going to call a cab."

"Nonsense," my dad says, still here apparently. He walks over to me and then gestures to Anderson, his driver that has opened the backdoor of the second Escalade. "I'm headed to Philly. I can drop you both off at your apartment complex."

Daisy watches my expression, and I shake my head at my dad.

"It'll save gas," he says dryly. He flashes a half-smile, one that reminds me of Lo.

My brother, Lily, Connor and Rose just stay and witness the disagreement, waiting for me to make a fucking decision.

I don't think long about it. "Thanks for the offer, but I'm going to call a fucking cab."

But I have no real time to even take out my cellphone. At that same moment, another car drives up on the runway. As soon as I get a good look at it, my face hardens, my shoulders lock, and my heart fucking drops.

"What…" Daisy's voice pitches with fear.

The vehicle rolls to a stop beside the Escalade, blue lights flashing silently on the roof. A police officer emerges, his eyes locked on me, confirming my gut feeling.

I'm about to go to jail.

"What's going on?" Lo asks, looking to our father for answers.

My dad's brows furrow, and I see the confusion all over his face. He didn't know about this. The officer approaches me with a stern gait, and Daisy holds tightly onto my hand, refusing to let go.

"Daisy," Rose calls, stepping towards her, but Connor forces his wife back with an outstretched arm.

"Lily, keep Rose here," he orders.

"Richard—" Rose refutes.

"Let me handle it," Connor says calmly. Rose backs down, and Lily does as she's told, grabbing Rose's hand and keeping her by her side, away from whatever the fuck is about to happen.

"What's going on?" my brother asks the officer again.

He answers by stopping right in front of me. "Ryke Meadows?"

"Yeah." I don't know why he fucking asks whether it's me. He knows it is.

Then the officer takes out handcuffs, and I hear a car door shut. I look up, and a second police officer is coming as back up.

I immediately shake off Daisy's hand. "You need to go with Connor," I tell her. He's already walking towards Daisy to take her home.

"No." Daisy shakes her head repeatedly, and I think we both know what this is about and where this is headed.

"Yes," I growl. "This isn't up for fucking discussion. You're going home with them. I'll see you later."

"You did nothing wrong," she tells me, tears welling. Connor puts a hand on her shoulder and starts guiding her backwards towards his limo. "You did *nothing* wrong!"

Doesn't fucking matter.

"Ryke Meadows," the first officer says, ignoring Daisy, "you're under arrest for statutory rape—"

Daisy bursts into tears. "No!" she cries like someone stabbed her heart. My face contorts in pain as I watch her, knowing she's blaming herself for putting me here. But it's not her fucking fault.

"You have the right to remain silent…." I can't hear anything else. My ears buzz. All the happiness that I saw in Daisy just completely snuffs out in a fucking instant. She tries to rush over to me, but Connor grabs her around the waist, forcing her back. She sobs, and I can't do a fucking thing. I just have to stand here and watch.

I clench my teeth so hard that my jaw fucking aches. The officer comes behind me and aggressively pulls my arms to my lower back. My strained muscles burn as he cuffs one of my wrists and then the other.

I'm fairly certain I know who called the cops on me. The woman who couldn't meet my eyes for the last half of the flight. The woman who threatened me with this very fucking thing in Daisy's bedroom.

"…in a court of law. You have the right to an attorney—"

"He didn't fucking do anything!"

That's not Daisy.

That's my brother. He's defending me. My stomach twists, filled with too much emotion to speak, to move just yet.

"If you cannot afford an attorney, one will be provided for you—"

The officer doesn't stop, not even for Lo. The second one comes forward to steer me to the police car.

"HEY!" Lo shouts, about to fucking lose it. "Did you not fucking hear me?!" He steps between the second officer, blocking him from the cop car.

"Lo," I cut in, my heart hammering. I'm more fucking scared for him even though I'm the one cuffed right now. My brother doesn't need to be thrown in a jail cell with me.

The second officer glares at Lo. "You need to step out of the way or we're going to have to take you in too."

"He's a good person!"

My father is still here. "Loren, don't be an idiot." He motions for Lo to join him by the Escalade.

"Off of what evidence are you taking him in?" Lo sneers at the officer.

"You need to step out of the way, sir," the second officer repeats.

"Lo," I say, instinctively trying to walk over to him, to reach him, to pull him in the right fucking direction. Which would be very far away from me. I jerk to a stop, being held by the first officer, his hands on the cuffs that detain me.

"I guess you're just going to have to take me in then," Lo says, his eyes pulsing with rage. "Because I'm not fucking moving."

Fucking hell. I rip out of the first officer's hold. "Lo, fucking stop!" I shout. Our dad reaches him before I do. He takes Lo by the arm and tugs him to the side, out of the way.

And then the first officer forces me to the fucking ground, my face hitting the pavement hard. Pain shoots through my body.

"Resisting arrest," the first officer says.

"Don't be so stupid!" our dad yells at my brother.

I grit my teeth, and the police officer puts his knee on my back. He says something to me about settling down, but I'm not even fucking moving anymore. Loose gravel embeds in my cheek, and I look out and see Daisy on her knees, Connor crouched behind her, whispering in her ear.

She's crying like this is the end of us. Her grief is like a thousand knives inside my stomach. The police officer jerks me to my feet with unkind force, and he pushes me towards the car. I pass my father and my brother.

Lo takes a step forward to intervene again.

I shake my head at him.

"You didn't do anything," he says, his eyes reddened, his cheekbones sharpened like fucking ice.

I nod at him, forced to keep walking to the white and blue vehicle. I can't speak. I can't say a fucking word.

Not until I climb into the backseat of the car, not until the door slams and the tires roll down the road—do I scream.

All the emotion I restrained for my brother, for Daisy, comes pouring out of me. I could kick the door. I could punch something if I had use of my hands. But instead, I just scream, releasing the anguish that rips apart my insides.

I just completed the Yosemite Triple Crown.

I just accomplished a lifelong dream.

I had Daisy.

I was fucking happy.

And now I'm here.

Cuffed.

Arrested.

Going to jail.

I'm going to jail.

< 59 >

Ryke Meadows

They haven't booked me yet. I sit alone in a holding cell, my nerves jumping every time a cop walks by, expecting them to usher me out for a mug shot and fingerprints.

Statutory rape.

Rape.

It's something that makes me physically ill. I'd rather be falsely convicted of murder. My throat burns, and I rest the back of my head against the cement wall, silent and trying to be numb. I don't know what happens from here. I don't know how much evidence Samantha could try to use against me. What witnesses can she pay to lie for her? I'll be tried criminally. It's not like I can settle this fucking case by paying someone off. I'm looking at fucking jail time.

I remember all the cameras flashing as I climbed out of the cop car, all the questions yelled at me.

"Ryke?! Are you innocent?!"

"Ryke?! Are you guilty?!"

"What kind of evidence do they have against you?!"

And then I entered the police station, cuffed. I fucking hate that 'rape' is going to be beside my face on headlines of magazines. Nausea barrels through me, but I already puked once. I shut my eyes and take a deep fucking breath.

Everything will be fine, my friend.

Not even Connor's magic fucking words can unknot the ball of pain inside my chest.

"Ryke Meadows?"

My eyes open. An officer stops by my cell, cutting into my thoughts. My stomach still flips. I don't move off the bench, but he unhooks a set of keys on his belt and sticks one into the lock. They've come to officially book me.

He swings the cell door open. I'm about to stand, but he says, "There's someone here to see you."

I stay fixed to the bench, my limbs solidifying into stone as soon as the person saunters down the hallway, buttoning his suit jacket. My father stands there.

My fucking father.

With a hard gaze like mine.

With a severe jaw and dark brown hair and my fucking eyes.

I look more like him than my brother. But Lo would say it's better to fucking look like Jonathan than to be him, to act like him, which Lo wades into on occasion.

But if Lo was here, he'd want me to make nice. He'd want me to bury the resentment. Back in Utah, he asked if I could do that. I told him the truth. *I don't know.* A part of me wants to try. The other part just wants to push Jonathan so fucking far away.

One side is stronger.

"You can close the fucking door," I tell the officer.

My father cocks his head. "Don't be a little shit. You're sitting in a cell right now."

"I never asked you to fucking be here," I retort.

"But I'm here, Ryke. And I'm not going anywhere. Whether you want me to or not, you don't have much of a choice." And then my dad steps into the jail cell. "Can you give us a few minutes?" my dad asks the officer.

"I'll have to lock you in."

I expect my father to pull out a wad of cash, to threaten or bribe, but instead he just nods and says, "That's fine."

I frown, watching as the cop shuts me in a cell with my father, and my dad doesn't balk, not fucking ashamed to be here. He just stands opposite me, hands in his black slacks.

After the loud *bang* of the door shutting, the cop disappears down the dark hall.

Why are you fucking here? I should ask him. But I'm back at that country club, quiet, seventeen and hateful, no matter how much I just want to let it all go.

"I have my team of lawyers sorting through this mess," he says. "It's being taken care of. You should be out of here in fifteen minutes."

I open my mouth to tell him that I don't want his help, but he cuts me off.

"You are *my* son. I don't know how many times I have to fucking remind you of that—it's like Sara fucking burned my name out of your head."

My jaw locks tight. I don't want to reignite all of those issues. I don't want to hear him call her a bitch or shout about how she's brainwashed me. I just want to sit here in fucking peace and deal with the charges myself.

"Ryke," he says my name like it means something to him. "What do you want from me?" He extends his arms, his palms flat like he's opening himself to me, like he's trying so fucking hard. "Or am I just swinging at an invisible ball, here? That's it, right? There's nothing I can fucking do. You've made up your mind that you don't want to have a father anymore."

Something snaps inside of me. "Stop acting like this is your noble way of getting your son back," I growl, rising to my feet in hot anger. I point at him. "This has *never* been about just wanting me in your life."

He frowns with clear confusion, not contrived. "Then what has it been about? Please, fucking tell me."

My stomach hurts. I don't want to have this conversation. I don't even want to look at him. "Just get out of my *fucking* life!" I run a hand through my hair, pulling at the strands. "Fucking leave!"

He doesn't even flinch. "You're angry at me. I understand that."

"Oh, do you?!" I just keep shaking my head, my neck aching. "You shit on me for years. You shit on Lo. And *now* you want to be my father? How fucking convenient. My mom blows your cover, the world knows my fucking name and my relations to you, and *now*, now you want to say, *that's my son, right there. Look at him. He's mine.*" I point. "Fuck *you!*"

"I've always wanted to be a father to you—"

"LIAR!" I scream at the top of my lungs, my throat burning. "You *fucking* liar! If you wanted me as a son, then why the fuck did you choose to protect yourself over me?! You chose to hide me so you could save your fucking reputation! So tell me, Dad, how the fuck am I supposed to feel *anything* but hatred towards you?"

He looks away, and that empowers me.

"And now," I continue, opening my arms. "You'll do anything to have me back in your good graces. You want me to come forward to the media, to tell them how you could *never* molest my little brother. How that evil deed isn't in your fucking nature." I'm boiling alive, my blood coursing through my fucking veins. "Ten years later, Dad, and you want me to protect you again. That's all I am to you. Someone you can use when it becomes fucking necessary."

He just watches with a hard gaze, not recoiling, but there's something deep in his eyes, something foreign. Something sad.

I take a step towards him, pointing at my chest. "You can't fucking use me anymore. I won't be the son by your side, making you look like a fucking hero when you're the worst fucking villain." I breathe hard, trying to catch the air in my lungs.

I don't remove my searing glare off of him.

"Are you done?" he asks roughly. He takes my silence as an answer. "Maybe you should remember, Ryke, but I never once asked you to say anything about me to the media. That's *never* what this has been about, and if you continue to think that, then it's your own delusion guiding you to that goddamn place. Not me." He shifts on his feet, but he doesn't break my gaze. "I can live with these allegations. What I can't live with is losing you, losing Loren. I would die protecting the two of you, and if you can't see that then I don't know what more I can do to show you."

He doesn't say *I'm sorry for putting you through hell. I'm sorry for kicking you aside and yelling at your brother like he was a piece of shit loser day in and day out.* "Why can't you just fucking apologize?" I ask. "Why can't you admit that you fucked up?"

"Because I didn't," he tells me, burning a hole through my chest. "I made a tough decision back then, and if I was put in the same position, I'd make it again. If I didn't lie about you, Ryke, then the alternative would be to admit to something that would send me to the place you're standing in right now." He motions to the cell. "And then where would Loren be?"

My stomach drops as I think of my brother, conceived from statutory rape. My father would have gone to jail and my brother… born from a mom who didn't want him. Would he have landed in foster care? Or would Jonathan have given him to Greg Calloway to raise? Were they even fucking friends back then?

"I love you," he tells me. "I've always loved you. Whether you can believe it or not is up to you. I'm not here under false pretenses. I don't want your fucking statement to the media. I don't want your forgiveness. I just want you in my life. I want my son. If that means having to listen to your insults every goddamn dinner we have, fine.

But I'd rather have that than nothing at all." He spreads his arms wide. "Your decision, Ryke."

I run my hand through my hair. I want to believe him. In the core of my soul, I want this all to end, and I want the fucking father that he claims to be. But beneath this unconditionally, fucked up love—there is years and years of pain. How does that ever go away? "How am I supposed to accept you?" I ask, my voice low.

"Ask me anything. I don't have a problem being honest, even if you don't like my fucking answers."

I don't know why I realize it now of all fucking moments—but I curse just like him, just as frequently, just as badly. What does that mean? He rubbed off on me? He was around enough that he could influence me somehow. That even if he lied about me—he was there, trying to be a part of my life.

I take in my surroundings, the metal toilet, the sink, the bars behind my father, the grimy cement wall behind me. My father is giving me an out. I've only ever seen black and white when it comes to my family. But maybe this is too gray—maybe there's no right and wrong choice. There are just decisions that will hurt my brother and decisions that'll hurt me.

"Why am I even here?" I ask, needing someone to verify my suspicions.

He scrapes his finger against the pole, irritation pooling through his eyes. "That would be Samantha Calloway's fault. She apparently emailed her friend mid-flight to call the cops on you. She went a little fucking overboard on her anger." He looks at me. "Her daughters are all a bit nuts, so you know exactly where they get it from."

"She called the fucking cops on me," I retort. "That's not nuts that's—"

"It's nuts," he rebuts.

"It's fucked up."

"That too," he says. "But what do you expect when you stick your dick around a fifteen-year-old girl when you're twenty-two."

I glare. "I didn't—"

"I know," he says. "Like Greg, I believe you, son. But Daisy is their youngest daughter, the last to leave. You're encroaching on Samantha's fucking territory." He checks his watch. "Like I said, you'll be out of here shortly. She has a few fake statements that'll hold you in here for another ten minutes."

"They're going to book me soon."

He nods. "They're backed up in there. I'm sure they'll want to fingerprint you in a half hour." I do the math easily. He's saying I'll be out of here before they can even fucking charge me. He smiles at me, knowing I understand.

"I resisted arrest—"

"I talked to the officer. They're dropping it."

I breathe through my nose, my heart beating quickly. I don't know why all of a sudden I feel so fucking overwhelmed. I realize that I'm thankful that he's here. And the sad thing—I don't want to feel that way. I'd rather stay angry. Why do I have to hate all the good parts of a person? My mom—I think she fucking taught me that. Every time I thought about my brother in a good light, she'd crush that vision, she'd focus on the bad, and so I did too.

I can't do it anymore.

I rub the back of my neck. "What about Lo?" I ask my father, not willing to dodge this topic.

"What about him?"

"You're fucking terrible to him," I say in a deep breath. "What you say to him—it makes me sick. You beat him down, and then he returns to you like a wounded dog. I can't be around you when you treat him like that." I'd rather Lo not be around him either, but we've tried that way, and look where we are now. Lo loves our father, and he's going to keep going back, even if it kills him.

My dad absentmindedly unclips and clips his Rolex watch on his wrist. "He's not you, Ryke. He dropped out of college. He can't even fill a resume. He shit his life away, and if that means I'm a little tougher on him, fine. But I'm not going to fucking watch him continue to throw his potential down the drain."

"So tell him like a normal human being!" I scream. "Stop saying things like he *shit his life away*."

"This isn't about Loren. This is about you and me," he refutes, cutting off that topic. As if there's no room to even discuss it.

Fuck him. "If you love him, like you say you do, you'd support his sobriety and you'd stop tearing him down every chance you get."

He glares. "If I didn't motivate him, he wouldn't be where he is. *That's* love. You'll understand when you have your own children."

No fucking way will I ever raise my kids like him. Fuck that.

I stare at my father for a long moment. He will never change. He is so fucking rooted in his beliefs. It's either I accept him like this or do what I've been doing—try to forget he even exists.

He opens the door further for me. "Are you ready to put this bullshit behind us, or do you still want to hold onto the fucking past?"

I'm frozen again. Stuck to the middle of the floor. There's no nasty retort on my tongue. It's those words that get to me the most.

Do you still want to hold onto the fucking past?

I'm living back there. Where my dad leaves my mom. Where I'm lying for years and years about who I am. Where I feel lost of an identity to call my own.

But I have all of that *now*. Fuck, I have more than I ever dreamed of.

I have a girl I love.

I have a brother.

I have a mom who loves me, even if she fucks up.

I have a dad who wants to be there for me…I look up at him. Who *is* here for me.

And I'm Ryke Meadows. I'm a free-solo climber. I'm a celebrity. I'm a fucking sober coach. I have an identity that's *mine*. No one took it from me.

I glance over at my dad again, and I want to see the villain, but I think, maybe, all this time the villain was me. For not moving past this, for not realizing that he's free to make mistakes too. I don't know if I'm willing to forgive him right now, but he's not asking for that.

He's letting me take all the fucking time I need.

I inhale strongly, and I say, "I may never see eye to eye with you."

He nods. "I'd rather fight with you at every Sunday dinner than never talk to you again." He shrugs. "That's the goddamn truth."

"You love me that much?"

There are fucking tears in his eyes. "More than you can possibly understand, son."

A pressure bears down on me, and I ask him something that I've never fucking asked him in my entire life. I just always thought I knew the answer. Now I'm not so sure. "Would you be willing to stop drinking for Lo and for me?"

After a heavy silence, a single tear rolls down his cheek. I see now that he's fighting an internal battle probably just as powerful and just as rebellious as the one Lo has, as the one I have.

What he does will change everything.

<　60　>

Ryke Meadows

"I still can't believe it," my brother says while I drive to our father's house with Lily and Daisy in the backseat, my Infinity speeding along the roads until I get stopped by another red light. The girls are quiet, both looking out their windows.

"Me either," I say. "Seems fucking surreal."

"He threw out thousands and thousands of dollars' worth of booze." Lo shakes his head. "He had a rare two-hundred-year-old scotch he was planning on giving me as a wedding present, you know that?"

My eyes flicker to him. "He wanted to give you booze when you're sober?" Lo has visited our dad almost every day since he started this long journey. It's been one week since his proclamation in the jail cell, and he hasn't backed out.

In my father's words, *He's no fucking pussy.*

"No, he told me that he was planning to drink it at my wedding himself. He'd have an extra glass for me." Lo stares off for a second and then he smiles. "We ended up watering the plants with the scotch."

He laughs and says, "You know that son of a bitch has three sober coaches to keep him in line?"

I hear the happiness in my brother's voice, and it lifts me to a new place. I'm proud of my father, for finally going to this length for us. It's not an easy decision. It's not an easy road. It's one that Lo knows better than me, and he can say, firsthand, how much pain there is in giving up a crutch rather than relying on it.

But we're both going to be here for him.

"I expected a fucking army," I tell Lo. "If he's not going to rehab, he'll bring rehab to him." I glance in the rearview at Daisy, who is abnormally still on her seat. Her faraway gaze clenches my stomach. She's been ignoring her mom after I got arrested. It's not something I ever wanted for Daisy.

I drive through a gated community right in the suburbs of Philly, and I park in my father's driveway. I snap off my seatbelt, and both Lily and Daisy climb out of the car and shut the doors before Lo and I get out. I turn to my brother, a gnawing question surfacing while we're here.

"I meant to ask you something," I say under my breath.

He removes his gaze off Lily who nervously bites her nails. She's been more anxious than usual, and I haven't really talked to my brother about it. But her health is not really my main concern right now. "Yeah?" he asks.

"Does Lily have many conversations alone with Jonathan?"

I've asked her this once. When I first met her. She told me that she tries to avoid the Hale household—which I took to mean Jonathan, seeing as she was always over the actual house.

"Is this about the rumors?" Lo wonders with a frown.

The molestation rumors. They're still there, growing…festering. Lily's name is being thrown around, but she's publicly denied the allegations that Jonathan had any influence on her addiction.

Add in my "almost" charge for statutory rape, plus our father's sudden moment to seek addiction counseling, and our family seems like a perfect soap opera.

"It's about Daisy," I say. "I want to make sure I know how much shit she's going to endure now that she's dating me. He's still an asshole, even sober."

Lo lets out a short laugh. "Yeah, he told one of his sober coaches to lose twenty pounds and then come back to him."

"In those words?"

"No way. I think he made a forty-year-old man cry." Lo nods to me. "Don't worry about Daisy. He won't talk to her unless it's about you." I just don't want her to be torn down by his harsh comments. He absentmindedly checks his phone, as if something's been on his mind too. "So I have a list of ten comic manuscripts that I have to narrow down to three. I'm having some trouble deciding. I thought maybe you could help me."

I don't hide my surprise. "Lily and Connor weren't available?" I know I'm his third fucking choice. I always am.

"I didn't ask." He pauses, an insecurity bubbling up suddenly. "But if you don't have time or don't want to, I can have Lily read them. It's not a big deal." He goes to check his phone again, but I'm pretty sure there's no new text.

"No," I say quickly. "I want to help."

It's his turn to look surprised. "You sure?"

Something swells in me. I actually feel like his brother—not just a fucking sober coach he pushes away. "Yeah," I say with nod. "But I can't promise that you won't hate my fucking opinions."

"I can definitely promise that." Lo smiles, not a half-one, not dry or filled with resentment for not being here sooner. It's a real fucking smile. "But that's the point. I need someone to look at them a lot differently than me."

And I've always seen everything different than Lo. Life. Love. Family. It's like our lives are reflected in a mirror, upside down and flipped. It's nice to finally meet in the middle, somewhere that makes sense for both of us.

< 61 >

Daisy Calloway

I lie on my stomach beneath Ryke's sheet, naked. In his apartment. I have my head buried underneath the pillow and my hand shielding the blue glow of my phone, trying not to wake him.

3:14 a.m. blinks on the top of my cell, reminding me that not even a night of wild sex—from his kitchen counter to the floor to the bed—puts me to sleep for long. I average a solid four hours, which sucks.

I open a series of missed texts from my older sister.

I need out of this house. We're considering moving to an apartment, but Lily says I would hate it. What do you think?
— Rose

We've been on the East coast for a whole week, which has given our publicists enough time to make a press release: ROSE COBALT IS EXPECTING A BABY! Gossip sites are going crazy speculating the baby's name and the gender. Lily said the paparazzi tried to climb the hedges the other day, wanting a photo of Rose's belly. She's not even showing yet. I heard Connor strengthened the security around their Princeton house, but Rose must have called it quits.

I send back: You'd absolutely hate it. Not enough closet space.

And then I open another missed text. We're looking for places in Philly or around the area. — Rose

I smile. *I'm* in Philly. Ryke is in Philly. But there are other reasons they'd choose this location too. Calloway Couture *and* Cobalt Inc. are located here. Nothing is tying them to Princeton, New Jersey. Their commute already sucks, and Lily finishes her final college class in December. She'll be an official graduate, free to move wherever she likes.

If they decide to keep living together, that is.

No one has talked about the separation of Lily and Lo / Connor and Rose yet. They've been rooming in the same house for so long that it'd be kinda weird for them to split up. But Rose is pregnant now. Maybe everyone's just going to move on with their own lives.

My smile fades. If that's the case, then I barely got any time with my sisters before they started their own families.

Being the youngest blows.

I click into another text.

I'd really love to talk to you. Please, Daisy. — Mom

I delete it almost immediately. I don't even want to think about what she did. I don't want to let those emotions in, so I push them away like I've seen Ryke do so many times before.

Last unread message:

Ugh. I need a fucking drink. Pregnancy is making me empathize with Loren. I already hate it. — Rose

And then my pillow is flung off my head. I'm caught red-handed. Ryke edges closer to me, fully naked, and his leg brushes against mine as he grabs my phone. He checks the time, and his eyes harden. "You slept for a fucking hour, Calloway."

"I know. I feel badly about that," I say. "You can go back to sleep. I won't disturb you anymore." I'm about to slide off the bed, but he spreads his strong arm across my back, keeping me on my stomach, right here on *his* mattress.

The place between my legs clenches. *Oh God.* Again? I am so insanely attracted to Ryke Meadows that my body doesn't know how to handle it.

He shifts on top of me, and his lips brush against my ear. "That's not how this works, sweetheart," he breathes. "I want you in our bed, all fucking night." *Our bed.* I smile, being reminded that we're moving in together. We haven't told anyone, and we've been bouncing back from his apartment to mine, not sure which one we should pick.

It feels normal though.

And I guess, in a way, we've been doing this since I graduated, just without the sex.

He pushes the covers off of me, exposing my bare back and bottom underneath him. He kisses my shoulders, his tongue stroking my skin with each deep, sensual kiss. It's torture—his kisses. They're the best because they heighten every sensation, but they also make me crave for something hard between my legs.

I turn my head to watch his broad muscles flex, the lines of his abs sharpening. He is so effing hot. I blink, just to make sure that this isn't a dream—that I'm truly with the brooding, rough, sexy guy that I've known for years.

His lips descend to my ass, holding my bottom as he kisses my smooth flesh. *Ahhh...* I feel wet just by the way he's staring at my body. We share the same expression, the same attraction.

He flips me over, and I pant heavily. He's kneeling, towering above me, and my eyes trace his sculpted, lean muscles, the darkness in his eyes. I feel small beneath him. Not because of my age. Just feminine. A girl to his man.

I *need* him inside of me. "I think...I think I'm addicted to sex," I say, not able to catch my breath and I'm just lying here, looking at him.

He almost smiles. "You love sex. That doesn't mean you're addicted to it."

"How do you know?" I breathe shallowly.

"Because you'd be insatiable. You would've been looking at porn on your fucking cellphone right then, even after I came inside of you tonight."

My lips rise. "Twice."

"About to be three times, Calloway."

I bunch the sheets in my hands around me and turn my face into the mattress. "You aren't real," I say dramatically with a big smile.

And then he suddenly steps off the bed and yanks my ankle so I reach him. Oxygen rushes out of my lungs. I look at his cock that's a lot harder than before. There's not as much pain when he fits inside of me, but if I'm not wet enough for him, he'll grab lube. He's really aware of how easily he can hurt me, and his attention to this only makes me love him more.

But he doesn't fill me yet.

He bends my knees, and his head drops between my legs. I gasp before his mouth even touches the tender, aching place that begs for his skill. Ryke excels in many areas, but this has to be on a whole other level.

I grip his hair as his tongue and lips work on me in sync. I like that he's the only guy who's every gone down on me before, who's ever kissed that intimate spot. He locks my legs from moving, his arms around them as he holds my waist with two strong hands.

I alternate from clenching his hair or placing my hand on his. "Ryke," I gasp, my breath quickening. "Oh God…I can't…" My back starts to buck, and I clutch his head.

His mouth is right there.

His head is between your legs.

He's kissing you.

He has your body in his grasp.

He's naked.

I'm about to freak out.

I cry, my mouth opening and my fingers scrunching his thick brown hair. *Oh my God.* I barely catch my breath as I watch him stand up and then place one knee on the mattress. I've seen him do this move so many times before—the one knee on the bed to get a little closer to my body. But never without clothes. Never with an erection and me lying naked below.

He pulls my leg up to his waist, and as he grips his shaft, he slowly slides his hard cock inside of me. I think I just whimpered.

Normally I'd sit up to meet him, but my limbs have jellified. I let him pound against me just like this. And I watch him absorb the way our bodies meet, his hardness rocking into me with a pulsing rhythm. I feel so full—I can't even describe. There's no room for anything else but him.

A nerve electrifies, and I moan. The sensations never die down. His gaze focuses on me. He looks intoxicated by my reactions and body's responses. His lips part at one point, and he ends up putting his hand on the mattress, lowering closer to me, and his erection goes deeper. Still one foot on the ground.

"Ryke!" I cry, the pleasure too much. I cover my face with my hands. I'm done. Blown away. A million pieces. But that's not true. I'm still climbing this freakin' mountain. It's so intense that I just want to reach the top already. I suffocate for breath, but my lungs won't cooperate.

He tears my hands away from my face, and I rest them against his neck as he kisses me strongly. He helps me breathe with the embrace, forcing oxygen to my lungs, and then he lifts my leg a little higher, and my head tilts back.

He drives into me without stopping. His pace picks up, and his eyes flicker between his dick hammering into me and my mouth that refuses to close, cries breaching my lips.

He groans. "Fuck." He moves faster and faster. So hard. So crazy. So fucking insane. "Dais…"

"Ryke…" My hands find his, one on the backside of my thigh, raising my leg, the other on the bed beside my hair. I hold both, and with one more thrust, he's true to his word.

He releases, and I feel my body clenching around him. I shut my eyes and breathe. I just ran around the world in thirty-five minutes.

He stays inside of me while he crawls onto the bed and pulls me into his arms. We kiss for probably another five minutes. And then as we both relax against each other, he says, "This wasn't to help you fall asleep."

He's mentioned on numerous occasions that he would never medicate me with sex. "It was a *just because* fuck?" I ask with a smile.

"No," he whispers, "it was an *I love you* fuck."

I brighten. "No wonder it was my favorite."

He combs my hair, my breathing beginning to match his steady rhythm. "Do you need me to check the doors?" he asks.

"I'm okay." I'm not as paranoid as I was before we were together. I don't think starting a relationship necessarily fixed my problems. But knowing Ryke will be here for me one-hundred percent—it's a security that I didn't have before. It squashes most of my irrational fear.

I rest my cheek against his chest. I don't fall back to sleep right away. And he stays awake with me for however long it takes. Just holding my bare, tired body until slumber finally calls me to a peaceful place.

I drift to sleep in his arms, where I know I'll be safe.

< 62 >

Ryke Meadows

Movie night at Rose's Princeton house has already turned into a fucking fight. *Gravity* stays paused on the flat screen with Sandra Bullock suspended in space. Besides the furniture, the TV is the only thing left standing in the living room. All the books are packed away and the pictures on the walls have been taken down and rolled in bubble wrap.

Lo and Rose have been fighting for the past ten minutes, and unfortunately Lo's go-to move is to throw popcorn at her. She swats away another flying kernel.

"I'm trying to talk to you *civilly*," Rose combats. "Stop pelting me with your popcorn."

"I will when you start fucking listening to me." He throws another kernel at her, and it lands on her lap.

Connor has to grab Rose around the waist, since she looks ready to spring off the couch.

"Careful, Rose, you're pregnant. You're not going to be able to take out your claws for seven more months," Lo tells her in his edged voice.

"Don't be an ass," I cut in. I hold Daisy on my lap as we sit in the big chair facing the TV. She stays quiet, always the spectator of fights, never really in them. It's not a coincidence. She hates this shit and tries to avoid inserting herself into these situations. I'm not as nice.

Lo and Rose continue to bicker, and I drift out of the argument as I watch Daisy delete a text message from her mom. My stomach caves.

"Hey," I whisper, and her big green eyes meet mine. "Don't make my fucking mistakes, okay?" I tuck a strand of pink hair behind her ear. I'm the cynical one who holds grudges. She's the lighthearted girl who forgives and opens her arms to strangers. I don't want her to change because of this.

"She called the cops on you, Ryke," she murmurs. "It's not okay."

"I'm already fucking over it," I say. My publicists have been blasting the media, denying the allegation, and reminding people that Greg Calloway confirmed to *People* that our relationship started after Daisy turned eighteen. It was his way of apologizing for his wife's rash, emotional decision.

But the pictures of me going to jail—the headlines that circulated through every major magazine—those won't ever disappear. Not even with a public statement. The backlash—I felt it, even if I don't read tabloids. The nasty stares at the gym, the glares at the fucking grocery store. *Time* magazine pulled that issue of us off the racks.

There is a whole lot of fucking hate towards me. And a lot towards Daisy too, for sticking by my side. I don't care what anyone thinks except the people in this room and our families. But the more people attack "Raisy"—as the press has called us—the more she blames her mom.

The more her hate stirs.

"How?" she asks. "I watch you get handcuffed, all because of her."

"It was her way of protecting you and saying *fuck you* to me. That's it, Dais. She loves you, you know that." I pause. "And you love her."

Daisy stares at her cellphone with a watery gaze. I hug her close and kiss her head. Our mother problems have always been similar; mine are just a few more years down the road from hers. I took a wrong turn, and I don't want her to follow me this time.

I tilt her chin up, and she says, "I'll think about what you said."

"Okay," I nod. My voice lowers even more. "Are you going to talk to your sisters about your sleeping issues?"

Her face falls. "After this?" This past week, she's been more open to the idea of sharing all the details of what happened in the past, even the most painful one.

"Yeah." I give her a look, to make sure she knows what I mean.

Her shoulders slacken a little and she nods. "Okay, after this."

Lo opens his mouth to speak again, but Connor interrupts, "We're offering a solution. It's nothing to be upset about."

Lo presses his hands to his chest. "I'm not going to live with you. You've been a great roommate for these past two years, but you're having a baby, man." He shakes his head. "You don't need to be dealing with our shit on top of that."

"You're not ready," Rose butts in like she did before. "You relapsed only a few months ago—"

"I'm never going to be ready, Rose!" Lo yells. "If you're waiting for me to be cured, then you might as well give up now. This is going to last forever. Not a month. Not a few years. I'm an addict. I could very well stay sober for ten years and relapse again. You gotta accept that."

Her lips draw into a thin line. "And what about Lily?"

"I can take care of her like I always have," Lo snaps.

"Oh, you mean when you spent years letting her have sex with different men every night," Rose refutes. For fuck's sake—she has less of a filter now that she's pregnant. She just says whatever's on her fucking mind.

Lo scowls, so coldly that I'm surprised Rose doesn't shrivel back. I'm ready for him to tear her apart with something completely nasty. But then he says, "That's your pregnancy pass for the fucking night. Whoever is growing in your belly is a demon. Straight up making you evil."

Rose narrows her eyes, ignoring the slight to get back to the topic at hand. "I don't care about the baby. I want Lily to live with us, and if she wants to, then you shouldn't be fighting me on it."

"She doesn't."

"Have you asked her?"

"Yes!"

I look to the couch beside Lo, where Lily used to sit. But she went to the bathroom...

I turn my attention to Connor.

He's checking his watch. The same thought must be crossing his mind. "How long has she been gone?" My voice cuts Lo and Rose's fight, silencing them.

Lo rotates and notices the bare cushion to his left. "Shit," he curses and stands up, his eyes wide with worry.

"Twenty minutes. Maybe fifteen," Connor says, following my movement as I rise to my feet.

Lo doesn't even hesitate.

He just runs.

< 63 >

Ryke Meadows

"Kitchen bathroom!" Rose calls out before Lo sprints up the staircase.

I'm right behind him, my hand on his back as he rushes through the house. Connor follows close behind, and I just think…*please fucking God be okay.* Please let everyone be overreacting. It wouldn't be the first time someone barged in on Lily taking an extra-long piss, reading her magazines. She lost Lo's trust a long time ago. I think when he realized her recovery is a lot fucking bumpier than smooth.

The shower pipes groan through the walls.

Fuck.

Lo picks up his speed, and when he reaches the door, he slams his fist against the wood, trying the locked knob.

"LILY!" he screams, his voice full of unadulterated fear. He told me yesterday that he tried to kiss her, and she turned away. For Lily, rejecting a kiss isn't a small thing. Her reasoning was that she didn't feel good, and he let her go back to sleep.

She's been doing that a lot too—sleeping.

Lo keeps jiggling the knob. "LILY!"

"Move," I tell him.

He does, and I slam my shoulder into the wood. It takes two hard rams before it swings open. I run ahead of Lo, and I whip the shower curtain aside.

Lily is fully clothed, sitting in the tub as shower water sprays down on her. She shivers, her arms clinging around her legs, and her knees pressed to her chest. Her black long-sleeve shirt is wet and suctions to her thin body.

As I shut off the faucet, the shower pours on my arm, the water *freezing* cold. It almost jolts me backwards.

What is Lily's fucking obsession with having meltdowns in tubs?

Lo jumps in, soaking his pants, and he holds Lily's colorless cheeks steadily. "Lil, talk to me." His voice is choked, pained beyond belief. Before the shower cuts off, it douses him, his light brown hair wet, and beads of water rolling down his razor-sharp cheeks.

She looks fragile in his clutch, but my brother seems just as broken, just as dark and pained. My heart pounds as I watch her hurt exchange between them. Without the water gushing, her sobs echo in the high-ceilinged bathroom. Heavy sobs that morph into cries.

"Lil, shhh," Lo says. "You're okay."

I step into the bathtub behind her and feel around with my foot, the ice cold soaking through my jeans. Then I squat and use my hands, searching for anything: razors, sex toys, all of the fucking above. I find the closed drain and lift it up so water begins pouring out.

"I'm...sorrrry..." Her teeth chatter and she buries her face into his shoulder.

"Sorry for what, Lil?" he whispers, rubbing her back to warm her body.

Rose is pacing by the sink, her phone at the ready, one minute from speed dialing either an ambulance or a psychiatrist.

I climb out of the tub, and Connor nods to me. "Anything?" he asks.

I shake my head and stand beside him on Lily's purple bath rug.

"I meant to tell you…" Lily says under her breath, her tears still dripping, but they're silent, accompanied by deep fucking sorrow. "Yesterday, I was going to… I got scared…" Her entire body quakes from being soaked with ice cold water, most likely done to combat her cravings. I've seen her do it before, but not like this. She usually jokes about it, making an ice bath, jumping in for two seconds before shrieking and running away. "Sexual urges be gone!" she'd say with a smile.

This is fucking different. This is way more intense.

Connor hands Lo a towel, and he wraps the soft purple cotton around her trembling frame.

"Lily…you can tell me anything," Lo says.

"Not this." She shakes her head, tears pooling down her cheeks. "Not *this*."

She fucking cheated on him? I set my hands on my head at that gut prediction. *She fucking cheated on him.*

But then Lo takes her hand in his, lacing their fingers slowly, as if each one is more important than the next. His eyes stay focused on their hands, as if he can't bear to look anywhere else. And I wonder if he thinks the same thing as me.

"You have to tell me, Lil," he murmurs. "I can't guess." His voice turns into a choked whisper. "Please don't make me guess."

She nods repeatedly as if working herself up to it. No one speaks, too frightened that she might crumble into nothing at someone else's interjection. She opens her mouth and then something must click because her expression flips from realization to complete devastation. "Do you think…you think I cheated?"

Lo looks heartbroken. "I don't know, Lil," he whispers. "You've been acting distant, and you didn't come with me to Paris, so you had all that time alone… I just, I don't…I don't know."

"I *didn't* cheat," she says with so much fucking conviction. "You have to believe me." She searches his eyes for it.

I let out a breath. My brother exhales a fucking bigger one than me.

"I do, Lil." He touches her cheek. "But you have to fucking tell me what's going on."

"I was upset…overwhelmed. And I wanted to do things and I just thought…this would help." Her eyes flicker to the showerhead and back to her kneecaps, closing up again.

"Just spit it out," Lo urges. "Whatever it is. Just get it off your chest right now, love."

It's her turn to stare at their hands. "I didn't know how to tell you…I thought while you were in Paris, I'd figure out a good way to say it, but I don't…I don't think there's a good way. And I just kept putting it off, thinking *tomorrow will be the day*." She wipes her eyes quickly and with a deep breath, she says, "I'm eight weeks pregnant." She barely looks at him.

My hands drop off my head. *What?* I wrack my brain for signs, but I can't think of much other than Lily being anxious—like she normally is. Maybe her boobs were bigger? She's so unassuming and comes across shy and introverted unless you really, really talk to her that it's hard to notice these things.

Now I realize how she kept a sex addiction secret for so long.

Lo is stunned to silence. We all are…except. I look at Rose and Connor, and they carry a content expression. They've known. Fuck them.

"You can't be…" Lo finally says. He lifts up her sopping shirt, and I zoom in on her belly. I think we all thought she was just gaining a healthier amount of weight, but now with this answer, I can tell the fucking pudge isn't from eating more.

This is very fucking real.

Lo turns his head and finds Rose. "*You're* pregnant."

"We both are," Rose says softly.

"That's not possible."

"The probability is slim but it's not impossible," Connor answers, his hands in his slacks. "Their cycles had synced up after living together. I don't use protection with Rose, and I'm sure you didn't with Lily."

"I forgot to take my birth control a few days," Lily breathes. "I didn't realize it…" She trails off and keeps staring at her fucking hands. I can understand why she's kept this information to herself. My brother has been getting better since the road trip, but he was at a horrible place. And he's been so adamant about *not* having kids.

I don't want to believe it, but I think this knowledge could have sent him over—caused him to jump off the fucking deep end. No one could know for sure, but it's clearly not a gamble Lily was willing to take. I'm not sure I would have either.

"You could have told me sooner," Lo says quietly, but his brows furrow, trying to think back to that time. Probably realizing the same thing as me.

"I know you don't want kids, and I didn't want to stress you out with this…I'm sorry." She sniffs louder, trying hard not to cry.

"Shhh." Lo holds her tighter. "It's okay, Lil."

"It's not," Lily says, wiping her tears even faster, an attempt to control them. She pushes him back a little so she can stare up into his amber eyes. "You don't want a baby."

"That doesn't matter anymore." He lets out a long breath and touches his chest. "We're addicts. You and me." He motions between them like they share the same favorite color. "Maybe we shouldn't have kids, but we have the means to raise him or her well."

"And you have us," Rose says. She glances at me.

And I nod at my brother. "You have us, Lo. We're here for both of you." Rose, Connor and I have this kind of confidence that Lo severely lacks, and we'll support him one-hundred fucking percent. I won't let my brother fall.

Both Lo and Lily look overwhelmed. My brother nods back at me like *thanks*. And then he whispers to Lily, "We did this together. It's not your fault, love. We'll figure it out."

"I've fucked up," she says.

"I think I've beat you these past few months," he murmurs. "You've been there for me, and I've been fucking stupid."

"No," she says with tear-filled eyes. "You've been really strong." And then they hug at the same time. Both magnetically drawn to each other, arms wrapped in such soul-deep comfort that I can't fucking watch.

We give them privacy, but Rose purposefully leaves the door open, so maybe not that much privacy. And my head whirls as we go into the kitchen. "How did she not get pregnant when she was screwing different guys every day?" I ask in disbelief.

"She said she was much more careful. It was her only worry back then," Rose tells me.

Now that we know Lily didn't slit her wrists or anything, Rose leans against the kitchen counter like it's Sunday afternoon.

"So you knew about her pregnancy the whole fucking time," I assume. "You didn't think to tell Lo?"

"It wasn't my place, Ryke," Rose says.

I look at Connor. "And you? You've never been known to butt out of other people's business."

"I think you're confusing me with you," he says casually, "and if you want my honest answer, no, I didn't want to tell Lo. I didn't think he could handle it. Be glad you didn't have to make that decision because it was a fucking hard one."

I'm known to lie to my brother's face if I don't think he can handle certain things. Like my own fucking identity when I first met him.

I don't envy the knowledge they had. I wouldn't have wanted it.

I scan the kitchen, the granite counters, expecting an easily excitable girl to be sitting there, swinging her legs against the cabinet. She's not around, so I walk through the archway to the nearly empty living room, searching for Daisy, but she's not here either.

I stop in place, realizing something...she was going to tell her sisters about what happened months ago. She was going to finally spill these harrowing details that have fucked her over for weeks.

And of course, Lily's issues came out today, pushing Daisy to the side. I can imagine how she feels—like her problems aren't significant, like they don't matter in the grand scheme of things. She's going to shut down again, to crawl back into her hole where she hides her feelings and covers it with jokes and sarcasm.

My heart lodges in my fucking throat. "Daisy!" I call out, my nerves escalating. Why the fuck was I helping Lily? I don't ever, ever want to choose Lily over Daisy. Just because Lily cries harder. Just because Lily screams louder. It doesn't mean that Daisy's pain isn't more.

I run back through the kitchen, and Connor and Rose ask me what's wrong. I shake my head and check the guest bathroom.

I have the worst kind of feeling in my gut.

I sprint to the garage while I take out my phone and call the security at the front of the gate. I grab my bike keys out of my pocket. "Did Daisy leave?" I ask, but I find my answer. My black Ducati sits lonely—without its red match.

"Fifteen minutes ago," he says.

Fuck. I hang up.

"RYKE!" Rose screams at the top of her lungs to get my attention. "What's going on?" She stomps into the garage that's already halfway open, the doors groaning as they rise.

"I'm taking care of it," I tell her, fitting my helmet over my head. I start the fucking bike, changing gears, and then I ride the hell out of there before she can say another word.

I'm so fucking angry at myself.

But most of all, I just hope she's okay.

I hope I find her before she does something completely fucking insane.

< 64 >

Daisy Calloway

I need air. The kind that bursts your lungs. The kind of jolt that sends your entire body reverberating with energy and electricity.

I want to wake up.

I'm tired of being in a half-sleep. Of seeing the world through a foggy lens.

I park my Ducati on a bridge that overlooks a murky lake. The night air whips around me, reminding me that it's almost December. The chill awakens my bones, and I peel off my green cargo jacket. Just a thin tank top and jeans left. I easily hoist my body on the old brick ledge, welcoming the cold from up high.

I had to leave the house. When Lily relapses or has some sort of emotional event, I feel in the way. Like a piece of furniture blocking everyone's path. It's best just to be gone. And there's nowhere I'd rather be than here.

On a bridge.

Outstretching my arms, the air seems to pinch me, wake me up, fill me with something *more*.

I love escaping to the roofs of buildings and shouting at the top of my lungs, but my voice dries in my throat tonight, pushed too deeply to retrieve. I just want to fly through the air. I just want to soar.

I peer down at the waters, nearly black in the darkness, the crescent moon casting an eerie glow over the rippling surface. I've jumped off this bridge before. It's not too high, but the tree banks are shallow and muddy tonight, and the water line looks low. Too low? I don't know.

I can't explain these feelings.

A pressure on my chest threatens to combust.

Just wake up, Daisy.

Jump.

I look around to make sure I'm alone. No lurking cameramen who followed me here. But headlights beam from the left.

I focus back on the water, bumps dotting my arms as the cold sweeps me in a sharp embrace. Half of my feet stick off the ledge. I brace myself.

"CALLOWAY!"

< 65 >

Ryke Meadows

She looks over her shoulder, startled by my voice, her face illuminated by the moon. She never anticipated on being found. Drawing attention—that's not her fucking ploy. Every time she runs off, she does it alone, and I've always feared the one time where she won't return, floating dead on the surface of a lake, an ocean, a river.

Not tonight.

Not fucking ever.

I climb off my bike, anger darkening my features and tensing my muscles. Her father has been paranoid since we arrived back in Philly. He put a GPS locator in her bike. One call to him, and I found out she decided to ride to Carnegie Lake.

"Hey," she says like she's window shopping at a mall. She smiles and spins around so her back faces the lake, but she dangerously sticks more of her heels off the ledge. "The question is: backflip or frontflip?" She wags her eyebrows.

"Neither," I snap. "Get the fuck down." I rarely tell her no, but I remember when I chaperoned her sixteenth birthday. That cliff in Acapulco. I screamed at her, veins popping in my fucking neck, telling her to stop.

There are some things so dangerous that death looks more probable than life. That's when I'll grab her. That's when I'll try to force her down.

"I've jumped from this before," she says with a shrug. "It's okay."

"It's not," I tell her. "The water levels are fucking low." The only reason I know this is Connor Cobalt—a throwaway comment a few days ago about the Princeton row competition being canceled because of shallow waters.

"The danger," she says theatrically, her mouth curving upward.

I climb onto the fucking ledge next to her, and she stiffens at my presence, some of the humor exiting her face.

"What?" I snap. "You jump, I jump. That's how this works, Dais. So you want to break your leg, split open your head, you're going to do the same to me. Can you fucking handle that?"

Her eyes flicker from the water to me. And her voice turns into a whisper, no more games, no more jokes, she says, "Just let me go."

My body runs cold. "Do you want to die?" I question. I've asked her this once before, after Acapulco. She never answered me, but I knew it anyway. This light inside of her dims if you watch closely enough, and she's searching and searching for something to ignite her spirit, a power to keep her alive.

She stares into my hard gaze, where I never go easy on her, and tears well in her eyes.

"You know what you fucking are?" I ask, edging closer, my hand dropping to her waist.

She shakes her head, and our boots knock together, but we both maintain balance.

I reach out, and I hold her cheek with the scar. "You're a hothouse flower," I tell her. "You can't grow under natural conditions. You need adventure. And security and *love* in order to stay alive."

Her shoulders tense and her collarbones jut out from the thin straps of her tank top, barely breathing. She is suffocating. And she's looking for a way to relieve that pressure. An adrenaline rush is a temporary fix. She needs something more.

"Explode," I tell her, still cupping her face.

She frowns at me. "What?"

"Let it out," I say. "*Scream.*"

She shakes her head like that's impossible, like *what will that help?* "I just want…" She blows out a breath from her lips. I can see that pressure bearing down on her, trapping her. She wants to fucking jump so badly. My hand tightens on her waist.

"I can't fucking hear you," I growl.

Anger flickers in her eyes. *Good.*

"Get fucking angry, Daisy. Be something. YELL!"

She opens her mouth but no sound comes out.

I push her harder by saying, "You can't talk to your sisters because you're so fucking afraid of causing a scene, but there's something inside of you that wants to get out." I point at her heart. "There's something in there, and if you don't burst, it's going to fucking tear you apart."

She breathes heavily. "Stop."

"It fucking hurts, doesn't it?!" I shout at her.

She cringes, and her eyes start to redden.

"Why are you holding back? No one's fucking here but you and me!" My hand slides to the small of her back. "Stop pretending to be fine when all you really want to do is fucking scream?!"

Her chest collapses. I almost have her there.

"Do it!" I shout, my blood pumping. I'm in her face, not letting her dodge this, not letting her give up on herself. "Finally, for the first time in your fucking life, let go!"

And then she grabs onto my shoulders, and I feel her body before I hear her voice. How she has to clutch onto me, how she has to brace herself to something fucking sturdy. Her scream pierces my ears, the most powerful fucking thing in the universe. The pain and ache rip through her yell.

She jostles me, shaking me like she's shaking the entire fucking world. And I support both of us on the ledge, careful and attentive so we don't fall.

For another full minute, she releases everything she's buried inside, and then she crumbles into my arms. I hold her upright, brushing the hair off her face. And her green eyes meet mine, drained but light. So fucking light.

I don't say anything.

I just kiss her, breathing more life into her body. On a ledge. A shallow lake below. She responds by clutching the back of my head, her fingers tightening in my hair. Her body curves towards mine, and I inhale, wrapped in the heat of her skin and the beat of her heart, pounding against my chest.

We're not there for long before a car rolls to a stop in front of us. A concerned stranger opens his door, but I keep kissing her. And her lips rise into a smile, not breaking apart just yet.

"Hey," the man yells, "the water is too shallow!" He squints and gets a good look at us. "Are you two crazy?" He shakes his head and climbs back in his car.

Daisy's lips leave mine, and a gorgeous fucking smile overtakes her face. Her light restored. Powered up and fucking charged.

My hothouse flower that I will always keep alive.

"We are pretty crazy," she whispers to me.

I mess her hair with a rough hand, the blonde strands tangled wildly, and I remember what Sully said awhile back about her being fun and me being fucking moody. "Yeah? Maybe our kids will be crazy like us."

She gasps playfully. "You want to make babies with me?"

I answer by kissing her with a strong force, and she runs her hands through my thick hair. I lift her in my arms and bring her off the ledge, to safety. And back home.

< 66 >

Ryke Meadows

C onnor pours coffee into a Styrofoam cup since all the mugs are packed in boxes. I sit on a bar stool next to Lo while the girls talk alone in the living room, an archway from us. Some months ago, there was a drooping banner hanging over it, saying *Bon Voyage, Daisy.* Now this place is empty, bare, a house full of so many fucking memories that we're all going to leave behind.

I can't see the couch from here or Daisy seated on the cushion. I'm nervous *for* her, but I'm also relieved that she's finally going to get this shit off her chest. Before we left the bridge, she said, "I don't want to drag myself down anymore."

There is no good time to release news that hurts people.

Lily said something like that tonight, and I think Daisy has finally learned that too.

"Is she okay?" Connor asks me.

"She's better. She just needed to scream," I say, twirling a fucking salt shaker on the counter.

"That's not surprising." Connor hands me a cup of coffee. "I have to force Rose to scream every now and then. Must be a product of being raised by Samantha."

Lo shakes his head. "Lily doesn't have that problem."

We both look at him. He doodles fucking circles and squares on a paper napkin, and his pen stops at our silence.

Connor tells him, flat out, "That would be because Samantha didn't raise Lily." Lo's best friend, his girlfriend, his fiancée—she was pretty much the undesirable daughter, I've come to realize over the years. She was the one Samantha let run off to the Hale residence, the ugly fucking duckling, even though she is beautiful, just too shy for Samantha to understand.

Lo doesn't deny the claim, but he doesn't say anything either.

"You can't control the past, Lo," Connor adds. "And I raised myself too. It's not such a shameful thing."

He resumes drawing on the napkin. I nudge Lo's shoulder. "How you holding up?"

"Ask me again when it fucking sinks in," he says.

"That you're going to have a kid?"

"Yeah," he nods. "And I already feel fucking awful for the thing."

"He may not have addiction problems, Lo," I say.

"No, it's not that." Lo looks up from his napkin and points the pen at Connor. "Our kid is going to have to compete with *theirs*. It's already fucked and it's not even born yet."

I can't help it, I smile. Connor tries hard not to, hiding his grin into the rim of his cup. "Connor's kid is also going to be a snot, so you can rest assured that yours won't be totally fucked," I say.

Connor opens his mouth, about to retort, but sudden sobs come from the living room. I straighten up. Hell, we all do.

"Should we go in there?" Lo asks, gripping the edge of the counter, ready to jump.

Connor's the only one who seems at ease. "Five more minutes."

I hope I can wait that long.

< 67 >

Daisy Calloway

L ily has started to cry and I've barely begun. I sit on the hardwood
floor while they're bunched together on the couch. They offered
me room on the cushion, but I decided to face them directly, head-on.
No more breaks.

Rose gestures to me. "Keep going. She's hormonal."

"I am," Lily nods and accepts the tissues that Rose throws on her
lap. "I'm sorry, Daisy. I just think I know where this is going. But yeah,
keep going. Please." She nods again and lets out a slow breath.

First I explain how my sleep has been terrible for almost a year.
How I've had to see a therapist, and how all the doctors and sleep
studies concluded that I'm an insomniac. How I was prescribed
Ambien with night terrors attached. I skip over the *whys* and save those
for last. They're the most difficult to even admit.

Rose is quick to fill the silence when words escape me. "You've
been going through this alone, this whole time?" Her expression
transforms into regret and guilt. I try not to focus on the pain in her

eyes, or in Lily's. I've only ever wanted to make people smile, not cry. But there's no avoiding this.

"I had Ryke," I say. "He's been there for me."

"But you didn't have us, your family," Rose says, clasping the box of tissues with an iron grip. "You know you can come to us with anything, Daisy, right? We love you."

Lily nods in agreement. "Whatever it is, we're here."

I believe it, but they haven't heard the *whys* yet. They just have part of the story, but I know I have to paint a clearer picture. I describe the easiest moments first. The ones that I've recounted to my therapist and Ryke a million times over.

The cameraman who broke into my bedroom.

The pissed off pedestrian that attacked my motorcycle and then attacked me.

But the story that hurts the most is after all of those. It's the one begging to be released, pleading to be shared and let go. It's just a matter of starting.

Beginnings are the hardest because they're the parts that pull people in, that make them want the ends. And endings are the most painful, the parts that can leave you bleeding out.

I don't have any more time. I just have to begin.

I stare at my hands, unable to look them in the face. "I was sixteen when your sex addiction became public, Lily." I pause and take a deep breath before continuing. "I remember the day I went back to school. My friends asked all these questions." At first I hesitate on repeating them, but I look up and Lily actually nods at me, encouraging me to continuing.

She says, "It's okay."

My sister's strength floods into me, and it propels me to continue, like a gust of wind blowing me in the right direction.

Even if it hurts, I say it.

"My friends would ask: *Does your sister just sit in a room and fuck all day? Does she bang girls?*" I cringe as I remember more. "*How bad does she want it? Would she fuck me? Would she fuck a homeless man?*" I swallow. "And I didn't have any answers for them. And I didn't know if it was true, but I defended you anyway." I'd still defend her today. I'd do it all over again. I can't ever regret that. "The questions started to change though."

"To what?" Rose asks with a frown.

I shrug. "They started asking me things. Like, *do you do it all the time too? Do you like it in the ass, Daisy? Would you fuck me? Would you blow me?*"

"God," Rose says, whipping out her cellphone. "Who are they?"

Lily reaches for Rose's hands and whispers in a small voice, "Let her finish, Rose."

My fiercest sister reluctantly turns off her phone and waits for me to continue.

I rub my eyes and keep my gaze on the hardwood as the seriously deranged part takes ahold of me. *Please say it, Daisy. Please don't be a coward.* I breathe deeply. "The entire time…I thought my friends, Cleo and Harper, were still my friends. I mean…" I let out a weak, tearful laugh. "I grew up with them. I knew Cleo since she was six, and I thought childhood friends were the ones that last…like you and Lo," I say to Lily. My eyes drop to my fingers. I scrape the yellow paint off of my nail.

I see the rest play out in my head. I see the scene like it was yesterday. A flash bulb, a memory that surfaces to haunt me and to release me from this hell.

Cleo and Harper had called me to go shopping with them, but their breath stunk of booze. They'd been at a "brunch" party with a handful of other kids from school. Hunch punch was served apparently. And they said that I was talked about a lot, but they never said what. They just giggled and laughed, in a drunken stupor.

I should have left, but I was worried they'd do something stupid, like shoplift. So I stayed with them, and I rode with them up the elevator to Cleo's penthouse apartment—where she lived with her parents and this pretty black cat named Shadow.

And then Cleo, with her silky blonde hair and coveted Birkin bag on her arm, did something…she pressed the emergency stop.

I smiled at her devious grin, thinking they wanted to pull a prank on maintenance. "What are we doing?" I asked.

"Seeing if it fits," Cleo said, and she shared a furtive glance with Harper. They both giggled again. Cleo wobbled in her heels, and Harper dug her hand in a shopping bag, revealing a pink dildo.

My smile vanished. "What's going on?" I asked.

"Some of the guys wanted to know," Cleo said, "how many inches fit inside you. We told them we'd find out."

I tried to laugh it off, charm her. She was drunk. Harper was buzzed. They didn't know what they were doing, right? "Very funny," I said. "Come on, let's go up to your place." I tried to hit the buttons, but Cleo blocked me while Harper stood off to the side, the sex toy in her hand.

The hairs on my neck stuck up in alarm. "Cleo, come on." My voice was no longer joking. I wasn't playing around. "It's not funny."

Harper waved the dildo at me. "You've probably had ones like this in you *all* the time."

"Yeah," Cleo said. "You'll love it. *Whore* runs in your family." And then Harper grabbed my arms.

"Stop!" I screamed. I jerked out of her hold and instinctively backed into the wall. I was frozen with this horrifying shock and fear, and then Cleo made it even worse.

She said, "If you don't do this, we'll make your life a living hell until graduation. Every day in the hall, every day in class." I learned that the guy who prodded Cleo to do this to me in the elevator was Houston Boggs, a senior that she had a crush on.

She had to follow through, and if she didn't she'd look bad in front of him, all talk, a tease. And she wanted to show him that she could play in the big leagues. She wanted to fuck me over, and I just wanted to be left alone.

"Stop," I said. "*Please.*"

The waterworks came the moment Harper gripped my wrist and yanked me to my knees.

"Do it, slut!" Cleo yelled—as though I wasn't even her friend. She laughed, and Harper smiled. And I cried.

I started unbuttoning my shorts because I thought—*I can't be tormented for the rest of prep school.* I had six months left. Half a year. That was six months too many.

What was one moment compared to weeks and weeks?

But I cried.

I cried as I slipped off my shorts. I cried as I was forced to make a decision that had no good end. The longer I hesitated, the more Cleo threatened me—the more I feared. She said they'd break into my bedroom. She said they'd watch me while I was sleeping. She said that the whole grade would get behind her, rallying against me and my slut sister.

She said all of this with a slur, the alcohol glazing her eyes. And then I thought—*I'll get away. They won't remember this in the morning.*

So in my panties with the sex toy by my knee, I made a decision that would haunt me for six more months and counting.

I stood up and cried, "No." I shook my head, my hair tangling at my waist. I stepped back into my shorts, zipping them with trembling hands.

And I pushed the girls out of my way. They were screaming behind me, tugging my hair, but I got the elevator moving, and when the doors burst open, I sprinted.

I sprinted, took the staircase back down, and I kept looking back—terrified, haunted.

The next day at school, my locker was filled with condoms.

The next day after that, two guys cornered me in the hallway and tried to give me a titty twister in jest and cruelty.

I always looked over my shoulder. I always locked the door. And I prayed for the end.

Graduation may have come. But my fear always, always stayed.

I wish I could go back and choose the other option. I've told that to Ryke before, and he said it probably wouldn't have made a difference. Maybe he's right.

"Daisy," Rose says, her voice breaking.

I realize that I'm crying so hard. And both Lily and Rose are kneeling on the hardwood beside me with tears of their own. My throat burns, and it takes me a moment to recognize that everything swirling in my head came right out of my mouth.

That story—they heard every little detail. All the bits and pieces and the pain.

"It's over," Rose says, rubbing my back. "They can't hurt you anymore. We won't let them."

I nod, believing her words. I haven't been confronted by someone in months. Ryke's made sure of that.

"Daisy." Lily speaks, her voice surprisingly steady. She's the one that holds my hand tight. I finally look up, staring into her bloodshot eyes that flood with tears. "I'm really sorry this happened to you. And I know...I know it's hard sharing this stuff, but thank you for telling us."

My chest swells, and I nod a couple times.

Rose wipes some of my tears for me with the brush of her fingers to my cheek, and she asks, "Have you told your therapist?"

"Parts," I whisper.

Rose shakes her head. "Daisy, you have post-traumatic stress. It's probably why you aren't sleeping."

My tears just keep coming, silently.

"You need to tell your therapist the rest, okay?" Rose adds, sniffing. She dabs a tissue under her eyes, careful not to smudge her mascara.

"I told Ryke all of it," I murmur.

"And I told Lo about my problems," Lily replies sweetly. "It's not enough."

I stare at Lily's hand in mine. Her nails unpainted and bitten to the beds, but she has a beautifully strong grip, one that makes me feel okay and safe.

"Boys are like pillars," Rose tells me. "Ryke is something to lean on. But they don't make you move. You have to do that for yourself."

"I want to be stronger," I whisper. "I just don't know how."

"One step at a time," Lily says.

"And you've already taken the biggest one." Rose kisses me on the head and Lily tackles me with her hug. I smile into these tears, this sadness that is ready to leave.

I don't think I've ever cried so much.

But it feels good.

I feel light. Airy. Like I can breathe.

< 68 >

Ryke Meadows

We don't rush the living room. I walk back and forth in the kitchen a couple times, and then I see Daisy curled on the couch and Rose tucking a flannel blanket around her. Her black dress rises to her thighs as she sits beside Daisy, stroking her hair. Normally Rose would pull down the hem of her dress, but she's too concentrated on her sister to notice. She whispers to Daisy, who tries to sleep.

Lily pads into the kitchen first, dried tear marks all the way down her cheeks. Lo pulls her into his chest, leaning against the cabinets while she wipes her face.

I've spent the last ten minutes explaining what happened with Daisy's friends to both Lo and Connor. She asked me to do that part, so it would be less awkward. I would have told everyone months ago, but it wasn't my place. That story is too fucked up and personal and she needed to talk about it with other people. I couldn't do that for her.

When Rose's heels clap into the kitchen, the tension breaks. Her blazing yellow-green eyes are on me, and my back straightens, on the fucking defensive. "I've tried to get her to talk—"

"Thank you," she cuts me off. Surprise coats my face. I can't hide it, but she continues anyway. "You were there for her, and if you weren't, I don't think she could have managed... So thank you."

My throat squeezes, and I nod in reply.

Connor sidles behind his wife, and his arms slip around her waist. I notice how his palm rests on her stomach for a brief moment or two. His head lowers, and he whispers in her ear.

The silence strings through the kitchen, and there's this unspoken feeling of regret, of wishing we could have been there to fucking stop it from happening. The most I could do was protect her afterwards, but it was hard while she was still living with her parents. She had to walk down the hallways and find an inner-strength that I couldn't give her. I don't think anyone could.

Rose is the first to disrupt the quiet. "I can't believe it was her own friends."

Friends aren't forever. Daisy used to tell me that a lot. One of her fucking theories. I wish I could disprove it, but we've all had shit luck with friends since the fame. Small price to pay, most people would claim.

"I never fucking liked her friends," I say, stuffing my hands in my leather bike jacket. "They were fake."

"I'm not surprised," Connor adds. "Teenagers can be crueler than most. They feel above the law, especially the ones who come from our kind of lifestyle."

Lo nods like he understands that. In prep school, he was known to be a fucking bully and be bullied. But he was also verbally abused as a kid—not an excuse, just a fucking fact.

Lo stares down at Lily as she starts drifting off into space. "You okay, love?" he asks.

"I wish that had been me," she says softly.

He kisses her temple and holds her closer. The room blankets in a velvet silence. No one saying much of anything. But I think everyone's heads are at the same place. The kitchen is barren, with boxes and boxes piled high. We're all moving, separating, but it seems like we're not at the place we should be.

Any of us.

Splitting apart—it feels fucking weird, not right.

"Does your offer still stand?" Lo asks, his eyes on Connor.

"Which offer?"

"The one where we move in with you guys," Lo says. "I was thinking that we could buy a house with a lot of security. More than this place. And Daisy could live with all of us. I think she might feel safer than living alone with Ryke. And then when the babies are born, we'll just… we'll figure it out then."

It's probably the most selfless suggestion my brother has ever made. Because I know how much he hates to be moving back in with Connor and Rose. How much he feels like a little kid on a leash, even though it's probably saved his ass on numerous occasions. But I also know how much Daisy will love this.

How much it will help her.

It's why no one says anything else about it.

It's just understood.

< 69 >

Ryke Meadows

My phone vibrates in my pocket as I walk down the carpeted staircase. I simultaneously check my text and follow Lo out of the heavy double doors. Our new house sits in this rich neighborhood in Philly, not the same one our parents live in—but fucking close. At least it's gated.

At least we can fucking run down the street without fearing a swarm of paparazzi.

I open my phone.

I love you. Maybe we can meet up, if that's alright. Anywhere you want. — Mom

I stop on the stone steps outside, the birds singing. 6 a.m. My favorite time of day. The sun hasn't risen, but the sky is lighter and the air is fucking cooler.

My mom.

She hurt me more than my father ever could have. Because I loved her unconditionally. Because I sided with her against Jonathan out of blind loyalty. Because she destroyed Lily and her family, and there's no going back from that.

But she's still my mom.

She's still the same woman who went to my track meets, hugged me tight Christmas morning and signed me up for any hobby that I asked, for any sport that caught my eye. She gave me the fucking world—I was just a little fucking lost inside of it.

I'll always have those good memories. I just need to hold onto them.

"You coming?!" Lo calls, already at our mailbox, stretching his legs.

"Yeah! Hang on." My fingers move quickly across the screen.

I'd like that.

I press send and slip the phone back in my pocket. It's the first text in two years that I've replied to, the first hand I've extended. Time to start over.

I walk to Lo, and I stretch beside him in the yard, not saying anything at first. But then he speaks up. "So…I watched the interview."

I don't look at him. I just sit on the fucking grass and reach out to my shoe, my muscles pulling in taut strands. "Yeah?"

"Was it hard?" he asks.

I stare off, my gaze on the dewy blades of grass, the ground cold in the December morning. A couple weeks ago, I sat down with a reporter.

I tell Lo the honest truth, no lies. "It was one of the hardest days of my fucking life."

It had been more difficult than climbing three rock faces back to back. More difficult than sitting in a jail cell. More difficult than having a civil lunch with my father.

"You didn't stutter or anything during it," Lo says. "Connor was worried you were going to forget your name."

I laugh lightly. "Yeah…" It's all I can really say. The reporter, a woman in a sleek gray suit, a microphone attached to her blouse, asked me pointblank what the nation has always wanted to know.

"Did Jonathan Hale ever inappropriately touch Loren?"

I denied every allegation, every claim that painted my dad in a bad light and caused my brother pain.

Lo's Nike sole knocks into mine as he stretches on the ground too. "You said the hardest things are usually the right things, right?" His brows furrow. I think he's worried that I'll regret making a statement to the press.

I don't.

Not all. The allegations weren't true. There was no reason to keep quiet other than to punish my father, and I needed to unhook that fucking chain from my ankles. "It was definitely the fucking right thing," I say with all my confidence.

His shoulders relax. "Thanks," he says. "I mean it. Not just for this but for taking care of Daisy, for being here for me during these rough months. I take you for granted sometimes, but I never fucking forget that you're the reason I'm sober."

I actually smile. I think my face says it all. Sometimes it's hard to tell that he cares, and when moments like this come, the tough parts don't seem so fucking bad. It's worth everything.

We stand at the same time and head to the mailbox again, letting go of the heavy shit before we run.

"Five miles," Lo says jumping up and down to warm his blood. "You're not beating me this time, big brother. Watch yourself."

I stumble on his use of "big brother"—said with endearment. Somewhere along the way, I've earned the title. *That* feels fucking good.

"Hey you, staring off into space, did you hear me?" Lo asks, waving his palm at me.

I smack his hand away. "You have a lacrosse stick lying around? I like my fucking legs, so don't break them."

Lo spreads his arms out. "No cheating. Fair race. I expect a fucking trophy when I beat your ass at your own sport."

"Fat fucking chance."

And then we both look at each other, no countdown. We just take off at the same time.

Our paces are mimicked. Stride for stride. Leg for leg. Step for fucking step. He runs right beside me, our rhythm exactly the same. He pumps faster, and I push harder. Matched.

My breathing steadies and my head feels light. When I look beside me, for the first time, I don't see that weight on my brother's chest. I don't see anything tugging him backwards.

He's fucking smiling.

The sun streams through the trees, our distance shortening with each step. Pride, for him, consumes me.

And it's at four miles in—when he leaves my side and takes five lengthy strides ahead—that I know.

He's going to outrun me.

< 70 >

Daisy Calloway

"Oh my God, it's cold," Lily complains, hugging one of Rose's white fur coats tighter around her tiny frame. Along with her Wampa cap, she looks like a little furry creature. Totally huggable. Which is why I have an arm around her shoulders, taller than my older sis.

Our breath smokes the air, standing in two feet of snow that blew in yesterday. We hide behind a fir tree in the front lawn. Or as Lily likes to call it: *the big ass Christmas tree.*

"I agree," Rose says, so cold that her bones have frozen her into a rigid stance.

"I offered you my sweats," I remind her. She's in black tights and a maxi dress that soaks in the snow. Her booties are completely sunken in the white powder. My outfit isn't better. I slipped on the shoes by the door in my haste to pull my sisters outside quickly.

They were flip-flops.

Let's just say the chill is most definitely creeping in, and my numb toes scream for a warm bath.

Rose gives me a look at my comment, and I think she would put her palm to my face like *don't even*. But she's too cold to stretch her arms past her sides.

"I promise this is going to be worth the pain," I say with a big smile. I reach out and shake both of their arms playfully. I love that I have more time left with them, and Lily shares my smile like it's contagious.

Rose rolls her eyes. But I swear the corner of her lips lift. She takes out her cell, and Lily reaches over me to grab it, but she's too far away. Rose easily clutches the phone to her chest.

"This is a stealth mission, Rose," Lily whispers.

I snatch the phone out of Rose's hand and pass it to Lily, who starts checking her texts.

Rose sets her hand on her hip. "Why are you whispering?" she snaps. "There's no one here but us."

Lily gapes at the screen. I lean over her shoulder and see a series of texts back and forth between her and Connor. "You couldn't leave his texts unanswered for an hour?" she asks.

"He was annoying me," she retorts. "My voice had to be heard."

My own phone buzzes in my jeans, and I check it quickly.

Will you be coming to the luncheon on Sunday? — Mom

A pit forms in my stomach. I text back: Yeah, but Ryke is coming with me.

I wait a couple seconds since she usually replies quickly, but my phone stays silent. Every time I stop by the house, she refuses to acknowledge Ryke. I think she's partly embarrassed by what she did with the cops, and she's too proud to admit fault.

So she's sticking to her guns.

But I can't be fake to her. I can't be friendly when she's being rude. And I've told her numerous times that if she doesn't apologize to

Ryke, then I won't be the warm, cheerful daughter around her. I'll be a little colder.

I'm willing to meet my mom halfway. My dad told me that she loves me too much to be stubborn for so long. To just give her time. I hope he's right.

"Shhh," Lily whispers, her eyes bugging. As the silence descends, I hear the sound of Rose's Escalade rolling into the driveway.

"One…" I whisper, listening to a couple car doors popping open.

Lo's edged voice resounds across the yard. "Christ, we need to get someone out here to plow the driveway again."

"Two," I count to my sisters.

"I can do it later," Ryke tells him.

I smile wide. "Three." We run out of our hiding places, or really, I run with frozen feet and they walk. Snowballs lie in their gloved hands (mine gloveless).

I focus on the guy in the leather jacket, carrying a case of Fizz Life and a carton of eggnog. And I pelt him with a snowball, square in the chest, the snow bursting open and soaking his gray shirt.

I grin. And his eyes darken on me while his brows rise. "Really, Calloway?"

"Really, really," I say, already scooping up more snow for my second attack.

Lily shrieks, and I glance over, realizing that Lo's hair is wet and he's started chasing her around the snowy yard. She abandons her pre-made snowballs and runs away with a silly smile, her hands on her head like her Wampa cap may blow off.

"Nice hit, Lily!" I call.

She gives me a thumbs up.

And then cold blasts my bare skin. Right in the face. Waking me in an instant. I smile and look at Ryke who has ditched the soda and eggnog. He bends down to make his second snowball.

Game on.

I dodge his next shot and land another one at his shoulder. I try to take a step towards him, but my flip-flop gets stuck underneath the snow. I outstretch my arms for balance, but my weight tilts me backwards and I fall, the white powder catching me like an icy pillow. My hair and my long-sleeve tee is soaked through and through.

A six-foot-three guy suddenly hovers above me, blocking the sliver of sun, undisturbed by clouds. His dark eyes swirl with protectiveness and lust. He grabs my ankles out of the snow and inspects my footwear. His face hardens. "You're fucking insane." He removes my flip-flops and rubs one of my reddened feet.

I tilt my head back and almost moan. "That feels so good."

And then his eyes pin on my chest.

I glance down. My nipples are totally hard, and the thin white shirt is see-through. The words printed right below say: *Taken.*

He shrugs off his leather jacket, his intense gaze still pinned on my boobs, and my chest rises and falls heavier than before.

"Didn't you hear?" I ask, watching him watch me. "I'm taken."

"I heard," Ryke says, scooping me in his arms and wrapping the jacket around my shoulders. His eyes meet mine. "I also heard that he's the only one who can keep up with you." And then he lifts me in his arms, the breath blowing out of my lungs.

With his hands underneath my back and legs, he carries me towards the driveway. I realize that we're outside, alone, and the other two couples have retreated to the warm indoors. I don't even think Rose participated, but at least she withstood the cold in camaraderie.

I reach up and run my fingers through the hair by the back of his neck. And his hard muscles tighten, his eyes descending down my body once more. Then he kisses me, his tongue effortlessly sliding against mine, heating every inch of my skin.

I'm in his arms.

No longer just the sister of his brother's girlfriend.

Or the sister of a friend.

Not even just a friend.

I am his.

And as he carries me into the house, the kiss turning more and more urgent and fiery, I realize something, deep in my heart.

We are free.

No matter if the public hates us. No matter if my mom never accepts him. We've done all that we can for now.

I smile into the next kiss, my hand rising in his thick hair.

"I can't narrow it down to ten," Rose tells Connor, cutting into our moment. We both break apart and turn our heads.

Rose has her legs tucked beside her on the cream suede couch while Connor passes her a mug of coffee. His hand is draped over her thighs, keeping her close to his body.

"You need to unless you want to have fifty kids, darling," he tells her.

Rose looks over to Lily and Lo, the latter of which is watching me in Ryke's arms. Even though Lo is still getting used to seeing us like this, he doesn't scold or reprimand Ryke. He just lets us be.

"How many names do you have picked out?" Rose asks Lily. "Connor thinks it's ridiculous that I have *options*." This must have been the subject of their text war.

Connor says, "You can have one or two options, anymore becomes superfluous."

"Why am I married to you?" she retorts.

He replies in French, and I'm fairly certain he says: *Because you love me. And I love you.*

Ryke must have his fill of them because he starts carrying me to the staircase. But I see the look on my sister's face, something pure and magical and beautiful.

Definitely love.

"We only have two names, one if it's a boy and one if it's a girl," Lily tells Rose.

Her mouth drops and Connor gives her an *I told you so* expression. They all break out in discussion, Lo starting to bicker with Rose.

I was worried that they'd all change now that they're having kids—that they'd desert their twenties for the mini-van and every time-suck that seems to come with children. Maybe they will eventually, but right now, I revel in the impromptu snowball fights, the game nights and the dinners we cook together. We're rooming as though we're living on a college campus, saving rent, but we're also living as sisters.

It reminds me every day that I'm only eighteen. They're only twenty-three and twenty-five.

We have years to grow up and split apart.

That time doesn't have to come yet.

Halfway up the stairs, Ryke sets me on my feet, his eyes grazing me from head to toe with powerful want. I want him too. I walk backwards and he follows in close pursuit.

"You know what would make me closer to my sisters?" I joke. And then I rub my belly.

His eyes darken. "You know that handstand you did this morning?"

"Yeah."

"And that cartwheel?"

"Uh-huh."

"And how you tried to do a fucking backflip off the trampoline?"

I smile at the fresh memory. "That was really fun." Snow blew up at my face with each bounce. I take a couple more steps backwards, ascending the staircase. He matches me.

"Imagine not being able to do all of that for nine fucking months, Calloway."

I stop on one of the stairs, my smile fading. That sounds…not fun.

He reaches me and holds the back of my head, his lips brushing my ear, "No restraints. One-hundred-and-fifty miles per hour. You and me, sweetheart."

My smile returns. *That sounds much better.*

< 71 >

Ryke Meadows

There are so many things left that I want to do before I settle down and have a family.

And I want to do all of them with Daisy.

Every time I imagine myself in another country after a climb, traveling, living—she's by my side. I know we'll make it a reality. I know that wherever she goes, I'll go. Wherever I go, she'll go.

We're no longer the out-of-place fifth wheels.

This is fucking real. And I'm determined to make it last.

I peel off her sopping wet shirt, no bra, but she turns her back to me before I catch sight of her breasts. She accidentally steps on a skateboard, hidden below wrinkled clothes, and it rolls underneath her feet. She trips, and I grab her by the waist.

"What was that?" she asks, her breath knocked out of her chest.

"Your skateboard."

She scans our room. It's fucking dirty. Clothes littered everywhere, the bed unmade, the sheets tangled and the blinds crooked. I almost smile as I remember smashing her back into the window last night, rough and slow sex, but fun sex. Standing up.

It didn't help her sleep. I never expect it to. She gets about five hours now, and I just hope the more she opens up about the fucking past, the more she'll stop waking in the middle of the night.

She's definitely not as scared though.

It's a start.

She wrings out her wet hair from the snowball fight and then belly-flops on the mattress. Staring at her bare back causes my breathing to heavy more than usual. Her jeans are fucking soaked, but I want them off for many fucking reasons. I yank them down her thighs and off her ankles urgently, my eyes trailing the tattoo between her shoulder blades as I do so. I was with her the day she got it.

She's smiling, her head turned as she catches my reaction.

I wear desire pretty easily now. But beneath that there's something else. Something I haven't shared with anyone but her.

The best fucking *love*.

I climb onto the bed, and my fingers outline her tattoo before my mouth and tongue follow. The ink on her skin forms a dream catcher, with three feathers.

But along the frame is a small design of a wolf, protecting all of her restless and wild fucking dreams from the bad.

I love the tattoo. I love her. I love *this*—being able to kiss her without fear. There is judgment still, but it's nothing I can't handle.

She rolls over on her back, and I press my hands on either side of her head, caging her beneath my body while I stare down.

"Costa Rica," I tell her, staring into her bold green eyes. "That's where I want to take you next."

She smiles. "Will we be kissing underneath waterfalls?"

"There will be more than just kissing."

Her face brightens to the hundredth degree. And I skim the scar that pulls her cheek, rising from her jaw to her temple.

She watches as my gaze dances over the old wound. "Am I the beast to your beauty now?" she asks, her eyes glimmering.

I shake my head. "No, sweetheart, we're both fucking beasts." *I'll show you in a second.* I'm about to kiss her, but her smile slowly vanishes, lost in her head for a moment.

I frown. "What's wrong?" She told me something yesterday that's stayed with me. She said that she's not used to making people so uncomfortable, and when strangers look at her face, that's what happens.

"Does it remind you of that night?" she asks. "I've always wondered...if those bad memories return when you see the scar."

I can feel my features darkening, my face turning to stone. "No."

"You don't have to lie. It's okay." She flushes, hot with anxiety.

"I'm not." I don't have any fucking flashes of that night when I look at her cheek.

"Then what does it remind you of?"

I comb her hair off her forehead, and I turn her head towards me so I can see her scar fully. And my lips start to rise as the answer hits me. "It reminds me of all the reasons why I fucking love you." I trace the edge by her temple. "You're wild and daring and so fucking crazy." It fits her feral nature—as odd as that fucking seems. I lean down and whisper in her ear, "I am proud to have you, Dais. Just like *this*."

My lips meet hers roughly, my body driving forward against Daisy's with every deep kiss.

When I part once, I run my fingers through her chopped blonde hair, and I breathe against her ear, "I want to hear you fucking roar, Calloway."

Her smile overtakes her face. And I stare right into her green eyes, ones that I will look into for so many more fucking years.

Acknowledgements

To our family—you're all crazy in your own right, and we love you for it. Thanks for being the best rock to lean on.

Thanks to our daring older brother, who inspired one of the biggest events in this book. You are beyond fearless, and we admire your courage more than you know.

Big thanks to two of the sweetest fans, who've been a tremendous force behind the series: Jenn and Ate Lanie. You girls—your love for our work means so much to us. No words can thank you for the support. And thank you, Sue! You've been reading our books from nearly the very start. We can't think of someone who loves Ryke & Daisy more, and we constantly thought of you while writing this one.

Thanks to Nieku, for more kickass French translations and being there on such short notice. You're an amazing friend!

And lastly but most importantly, we want to thank all of our fans. Even saying we have any has been a dream. But if it wasn't for all of you, this book would have never been written. These characters would have never come to life. And these stories would have never been told. Not to this extent.

Your love for this series is what keeps it going.

Stay wild.